To preserve life . . .

Timmons followed Latham out of the operating area into the locker room, where they were left alone.

"George . . . the kid *died*," Timmons said.

Latham looked at him with hard eyes. "I don't need you to tell me that."

"It's an omen, George. We should stop this right now."

Latham suddenly grabbed Timmons by the arms and shoved him against the lockers. "It is *not* an omen! It's a chance occurrence. It won't happen again."

"But there'll be an inquiry . . ."

Slowly, Latham let Timmons go, and a sudden calm passed over the surgeon's face.

". . . which will find absolutely nothing," he said, and turned to change his clothes.

Do No Harm

DO NO HARM

Don Donaldson

JOVE BOOKS, NEW YORK

DO NO HARM

A Jove Book / published by arrangement with
the author

PRINTING HISTORY
Jove edition / October 1999

The Penguin Putnam Inc. World Wide Web site address is http://www.penguinputnam.com

ISBN: 0-515-12650-0

A JOVE BOOK®
Jove Books are published by The Berkley Publishing Group, a division of Penguin Putnam Inc., 375 Hudson Street, New York, New York 10014. JOVE and the "J" design are trademarks belonging to Penguin Putnam Inc.

PRINTED IN THE UNITED STATES OF AMERICA

10 9 8 7 6 5 4 3 2 1

Acknowledgments

It's often said that writing is a lonely business. But it can also be a stimulus to interact with wonderful, interesting people. That was certainly true for me as I gathered background information for this book. At the top of that list is Dr. Deborah Nelson, who patiently and with good humor spent hours teaching me enough pediatric medicine to portray Sarchi Seminoux in a convincing fashion. Whatever success I've achieved with that must also be credited to Dr. Ginger Coreil, who was a third-year resident in peds when I was following her around the hospital and generally making a nuisance of myself.

I've also drawn unmercifully on my colleagues in the department of Anatomy and Neurobiology for help. Dr. Eldon Geisert provided some extremely important plot suggestions as well as guidance on the needed molecular biology. Neuroanatomical and background information on Hunting's disease came from Dr. Tony Reiner. Dr. Dennis Steindler, who actually coined the term "brain marrow," kindly allowed me to attribute that to one of my characters. Everything Sarchi and I know about caving we learned from Dr. Mel Park and the terrific book he let me borrow. Sarchi's view of single-engine planes and the other tidbits of the private aviation subculture came from conversations with Dr. Jim Evans and a short flight over Memphis with Jim at the controls.

I was mesmerized and greatly helped by watching Dr. Michael Muhlbauer remove an arachnoid cyst from the brain of a young girl. Medicine truly at its best. For answering all my pages as promptly as if I were a patient in trouble, for explaining some of the mysteries of neurosurgery, and for sharing the tribulations of a resident in that specialty, I'm indebted to Dr. Brannon Thomas.

A hearty thanks also to Brenda Canady, Sally Discenza, Maggie Aiken, and Pat Speck at the Memphis Sexual Assault Resource Center for taking me through the victim examination process and helping me understand what a sexual assault or the belief that one might have occurred does to a victim psychologically.

Important contributions were also made by Dr. Walter Manning, Dr. Kevin Merigian, Dr. Joan Chesney, Dr. Allen Wyler, Dr. Malinda Fitzgerald, Dr. Eldridge Johnson, Glenda and Elliot Henderson, Evalie Hill, Sara Hull, Lynn Browder, and Detective Paul Sheffield.

For the many years of our marriage, my wife, June, has supported me spiritually in everything I've done. She's also turned out to be a pretty good editor. This time, in addition to making me rewrite the usual number of scenes, she provided two suggestions that were absolutely first rate. (And now that I've said so in print, she'll have something to show me when, as she predicts, I eventually come to believe they were *my* ideas.)

Sincere apologies to anyone who should have been mentioned here and wasn't. Any errors in this book are, of course, my fault.

Prologue

Dr. George Latham pulled the inner core of the biopsy probe from the outer sleeve and handed it to the scrub nurse, his eyes fixed on the small amount of blood welling out of the sleeve's opening.

This didn't happen often, but when it did it always stopped. And today, it *had* to, because as deep as he was in this child's brain, if it didn't, there was nothing he could do.

To Latham's left, Dr. Christopher Timmons, present for the inaugural operation that signaled the final phase of everything they'd worked for, sensed something was wrong. He leaned over and whispered through his mask. "Does it always bleed like that?"

Latham gave him such a sharp look, Timmons took a step back. Now he knew for sure . . . the bleeding was unexpected.

Ten seconds later, as blood continued to issue from the sleeve, the beep of the pulse oximeter slowed, and its tone dropped. Both Latham and Frank Michaels, the anesthesiologist, looked at the heart monitor, where the beat was still steady.

"George, do we have a problem?" Michaels asked.

Before Latham could answer, the child's pulse fell below

the warning setting on the oximeter and the beep became a continuous buzz.

"Talk to me George," Michaels pleaded. "Can you handle this?"

Latham turned to his scrub nurse. "Get me a 10-cc syringe, filled with saline."

Latham's voice was calm, and he seemed under control, but Timmons was finding it hard to breathe, and there was a metallic taste in his mouth.

The nurse brought the syringe, and Latham discharged a small amount of saline into the biopsy sleeve, hoping to wash out the blood clot he knew was forming in the child's brain. Blood diluted with saline kept coming, but no clot.

As the child's blood pressure continued to fall, Michaels thumbed the IV lines to full open and poured fluids in, trying to compensate. "Is it a big bleeder?" he asked. "Is that the problem?"

"You just concentrate on keeping this kid alive," Latham said. "I'll handle the surgery."

Timmons glanced at the heart monitor. Although he was the laboratory arm of their enterprise and wasn't accustomed to reading heart rhythms, even he could see that the tracing was becoming abnormal. Then, to his horror, the tracing suddenly flatlined, setting off the EKG alarm.

With the patient crashing, Michaels assumed control, shouting orders. "George . . . get on her chest. . . ." Then, to the circulating nurse standing out of the sterile field, "Doris, call Doctor McCloud and get some more hands in here."

In seconds, help flooded the room. Being untrained and useless, Timmons took up a position against the wall and out of everyone's way, the stink of fear pouring from his skin.

For the next thirty minutes the team that had formed so quickly fought off the child's impending death with the same ferocity they'd have shown defending their own lives. Finally, after failing to get a single heartbeat in all that time, Latham looked into the child's eyes and announced what no one wanted to hear. "Pupils fixed and dilated."

The action stopped in freeze-frame. In a flat monotone, Latham made it official. "Let's call it." He yanked his mask down and looked at his scrub nurse. "Lee-Ann, finish up here will you?" Stripping off his gloves, he turned and headed for the door, throwing the gloves against the wall as he left.

Timmons followed Latham to the locker room. Once he was sure no one else was there, he stood beside Latham, who was already taking off his scrubs.

"George . . . the kid *died*," Timmons said.

Latham looked at him with hard eyes. "I don't need *you* to tell me that."

"It's an omen George. We should stop now."

Latham suddenly grabbed Timmons by the arms and shoved him against the lockers. "It is *not* an omen. This was just a chance occurrence. It won't happen again."

"But there'll be an inquiry . . ."

Latham let Timmons go and returned to changing his clothes. "Which will find nothing."

THREE YEARS LATER

1

If anything, the spot where George Latham had touched Lee-Ann on the shoulder had become even warmer and more tingly by the time she reached home. Moreover, it had been augmented by the most delicious prickly sensation between her thighs.

What a fool she'd been. He *did* care. Those hours she'd spent hating him for his indifference . . . the *days*. All without reason.

Her imagination frequently got her into trouble. But even knowing that, it was hard to avoid the trap. Often, she didn't see it until it was too late. That's the way it is with your imagination.

Trying to ignore the other feeling, the unpleasant gnawing anticipation higher up in the pit of her stomach, prompted by what she must do in less than two hours, Lee-Ann carried the tissue retractor she'd stolen into the bedroom. At the dresser, she opened the bottom drawer, which was filled with bagged and dated instruments from each of the operations in which she'd assisted since joining Latham's team, minus of course any from those that had taken place during the times when she hated him.

She dated the new plastic bag with a marker from the top

of the dresser then added the bag to the others and stood for a moment admiring her collection. It was like owning a part of him.

She wanted to linger and spread all the bags out on the bed in chronological order, reminisce about each case and picture him working, but there was no time.

It was now time to think.

She went to the bed, sat on the edge, and closed her eyes, trying to see the physical layout of the eight-story parking garage adjacent to the restaurant where she was to meet Greta Dunn. Dunn would almost certainly never find a place for her car on the street and, if she did, the maximum time on those meters was only fifteen minutes. That meant she would surely choose the garage. So that was the scenario Lee-Ann thought about.

In short order, the same imagination that had gotten her into this spot showed her a way out. It wasn't a perfect plan, but given the circumstances, it seemed to offer the best possibilities.

She would need paper for signs. But how many?

She thought there were only two elevators, but there could be three. Better to overplan than be caught short. Did she even have any paper?

A frantic search turned up something better—three old jumbo Christmas cards, which, along with a roll of adhesive tape, she took to the bedroom. There, she ripped the front halves off the cards and with the Magic Marker she'd used to date the bag containing the stolen retractor, jotted the same three words on the back of each card.

She put the cards and the tape in her handbag.

One more item and she'd be ready to leave. But what item?

She went to the kitchen and pulled out the drawer containing the tableware. While considering the choices laid out before her, she remembered her late father's old toolbox in the basement, which contained just the trick. But she'd have to change handbags. Go with the straw beach bag.

But it was fall, and straw was out of season. In the end, deciding that being in fashion was the least of her worries at this point, Lee-Ann packed everything in the straw bag.

Was that it? Did she have everything? Latham had put her in charge of supplies, and it was her job to make sure they always had plenty of everything on hand, which she was very good at. But this was different. And she found her mind clouded and disorganized.

Gloves . . . of course.

She added a pair of thin tan gloves to her bag, then leaned into the mirror and fussed with her hair.

Lee-Ann hated her appearance, those fat cheeks that resisted every diet she'd ever tried. She could get almost anorectic and those cheeks would never change. When most women smiled, they looked more attractive. But not her. Oh, no, not Lee-Ann. She looked like a demented chipmunk.

It was genes. Some people get good ones and others, like her, get the pot scrapings. That was why she'd sprayed all the mirrors in the house with hair spray, leaving only a few small clean spots where she could do her hair or lipstick without being reminded of the total obnoxious picture.

And there were only two people responsible. There were times when she missed her parents and times when she worried about how arsenic could be found in tissues many years after death. But mostly, she felt nothing toward them and barely remembered what they'd looked like.

Lee-Ann arrived at the garage twenty-five minutes before her meeting with Greta Dunn, who was driving into New Orleans from Baton Rouge. She took her ticket from the automated dispenser and started looking for a parking place.

The restaurant where they'd agreed to meet was one floor below street level in a ten-story medical arts building so busy that only rarely could a space be found on the garage's lower levels. Today was no exception, and Lee-Ann had to go up to level E before locating a spot.

She didn't know what kind of car Dunn owned, but even if she did, she wouldn't have been able to stand on level E and watch the street out front for it because the woman might

find a slot on a lower floor. There'd be nothing she could do
then.

Her heart tripping, Lee-Ann hurried to the elevators,
which she noted were two in number, just as she had remembered. She took the right member of the pair down to
ground level, got off, and positioned herself beside a white
van where she could see the driver of every entering car as it
passed, but she would not be visible unless the driver looked
to the left.

Lee-Ann had listened through the door when Dunn had
her preoperative discussion with Latham. And she'd seen her
at her son's bedside before leaving him in Latham's care. In
both instances, the woman had been composed and in control
of herself. Next to beauty, Lee-Ann admired toughness more
than any other trait, and Greta Dunn seemed to have that in
spades. That was why when Lee-Ann was wondering who
could create the most trouble for Latham, she'd thought of
her.

It was raining hard now and gusts of wind were blowing
in through the open front of the garage, soaking the entry
ramp. Behind Lee-Ann, a burgeoning waterfall seeped copi-
ously from a supporting beam overhead, splattering the cement retaining wall behind her.

A car passed into view from the entry, and Lee-Ann was
pleased that she had no trouble seeing the driver clearly even
though he'd put his window up after taking his ticket. To get
a feel for how things would go when Dunn arrived, she
moved down the van to where she was still concealed from
anyone entering and watched the car that had just come in.

When it turned at the end of the garage and started back up
the ramp behind her, Lee-Ann realized that her plan was in
major trouble. If Dunn didn't find a slot on the ramp behind
her and had to go up several floors, it was going to be hell
keeping up with her.

Lee-Ann studied the wet retaining wall behind her. She'd
have to scale that wall. Then . . .

Hearing another car coming in, Lee-Ann turned to get a
look at the driver, praying it wasn't Dunn. It was too soon.
Her plan needed shaping.

The sharp clang of a ticket issuing from the dispenser rang through the garage. A pause was followed by the simultaneous sounds of a power window closing and the car's engine revving.

The sound came closer, and the front wheels rolled into view. The hood . . .

Good God.

It *was* her.

The first car that had come in had gone up to a higher level, so Lee-Ann knew there was no slot on the ramp behind her. Springing into action, she threw her straw bag up to that ramp, stepped onto the van's bumper, and grabbed the horizontal steel cable that bisected the opening above. Receiving a healthy spattering from the indoor waterfall, she pulled herself onto the cement wall and dropped to the floor between a pickup and a convertible as Greta Dunn's car passed, heading toward the elevators.

Lee-Ann scraped her knee going over the wall but was barely aware of it as she snatched up her bag and hurried after Dunn's car, her mind focusing on the fact that if Dunn found a parking spot on this floor, there'd be no way to get to the elevators before she did. And that would be disastrous.

But the floor was fully occupied, so when Dunn reached the elevators, she turned left and went up to the next level. Afraid she would lose her, Lee-Ann broke into a run.

By the time she reached a point where the sloping floor on the next level was low enough so she could climb over *that* retaining wall, Dunn's car was turning onto level C. Lee-Ann gave chase, her throat already raw from all the air she'd taken in through her mouth.

Going over the next wall, the metal cable snagged her coat. Now Dunn's car was once again between Lee-Ann and the elevators. But once more, the floor was full.

Doubting she could keep this up much longer, Lee-Ann chased Dunn's car up to the next ramp, where, as before, every spot was taken. Soon they'd be on the floor where Lee-Ann had parked. She should have just waited up *there*.

She wasn't sure she could climb another wall. But the

thought that she was protecting her man propelled her forward.

Miraculously, a few steps later, looking through the gap where she could see up to the next ramp, Lee-Ann saw an empty slot at the far end of the garage. She waited just long enough to be sure Dunn wasn't going to do something crazy like pass it up, then she turned and bolted for the elevators behind her.

There was so little time . . .

The elevators she was heading for were one level *below* the ramp where Dunn was parking. And Lee-Ann needed to be on the *same* level. Elevators or stairs—which would get her there the quickest?

Sometimes you could wait forever for an elevator . . . and she didn't want Dunn to see her get off one. So she took the stairs, her footsteps and ragged breathing echoing in the closed space.

Twenty seconds later she burst into the lobby a floor above, just as an old man in a green John Deere cap stepped off one of the elevators.

Damn. Had Dunn seen that the elevators were working?

Lee-Ann looked through the glass enclosing the lobby and saw Dunn on her way, the slight incline causing the woman's head to tilt slightly down, so her gaze was more on the floor than straight ahead. There was a chance . . .

The OUT OF ORDER signs she'd made from the jumbo Christmas cards were now useless. There was no time . . .

Lee-Ann dropped into one of the blue plastic chairs beside the elevators, put her bag in her lap, and let her chin fall to her coat, trying to slow her thudding heart and gain control of her breathing.

If only no one else gets off the elevator . . .

Ten seconds later Greta Dunn stepped into the lobby, walked to the elevators, and pushed the down button.

"They're out of order," Lee-Ann said without looking up. "You'll have to use the stairs."

Lee-Ann watched Dunn's feet to see what she'd do.

For a moment, Dunn didn't move. Then she headed for the

stairs. As soon as Lee-Ann heard the stairwell door close, she jumped out of her chair and followed.

When Lee-Ann entered the stairwell, Dunn was halfway down to the first landing. She didn't look up.

From that point on, everything Lee-Ann did was instinctual. No weighing of alternatives or consequences, just raw response. The door behind her was still closing as Lee-Ann's hand closed around the ice pick in her bag. A heartbeat later, her feet thudding on the stairs, she closed in.

Hearing the urgency in Lee-Ann's approach, Greta Dunn turned and looked up. Without hesitating, Lee-Ann brought the ice pick down in a looping overhand stroke, burying the pick to the handle in the top of Greta Dunn's head.

Eyes wide with surprise, her mouth open, Dunn stared into Lee-Ann's face.

Fearing that the pick might not have done enough damage, Lee-Ann rocked the handle from side to side, horribly scrambling Greta Dunn's brain. She then raised her foot and kicked the woman down the stairs.

When the body came to rest at the door to the next level, Lee-Ann could tell from the odd angle of the head that Greta Dunn's neck was broken.

Lee-Ann's training told her to make sure, to check for a pulse. But she'd already pressed her luck too far. Afraid that at any moment someone might find them, she fled.

Later, driving home through the rain, Lee-Ann felt so close to Latham. Even through he didn't know it, they now shared something very special. The only blemish on the moment was that she'd had to carry a straw bag out of season.

2

Jackie Tellico pulled into the Immaculate Heart Academy parking lot in midtown Memphis and found a slot that provided a good view of the playground as well as Alicia's car a half block away.

Tellico was the name on Jackie's birth certificate, but he had fifty other names, each with a driver's license, credit cards, and a passport. Fifty names and fifty faces. Whenever he worked this operation, he was Jake Drum. For some jobs it was best to look gentle and good-natured. In others, you had to let people know you wouldn't take any shit. For Jake Drum, he'd chosen a lean face with high cheekbones, a combination of Jack Palance and Danny Lucchesi, the guy who'd turned stoolie on John Masserano. It was better not to look too much like Lucchesi or he might get whacked by mistake. He removed the last apple from the plastic sack on the seat next to him, took a bite, and waited for events to unfold.

In the car down the street, Alicia looked at the clock on the dash. "They should be out in about ten minutes," she said to the child sitting beside her.

"I told you we'd make it," the boy said, shrugging out of his jacket.

The woman looked at him pointedly. "And God knows,

you're never wrong." She reached back between the seats for her bag and opened it in her lap. She removed a small plastic case from the bag, flipped down the visor mirror, and slipped a pair of contact lenses from the little case into her eyes, changing their color from green to brown. Eye color was something most people never noticed, but it was better to be extra careful. At least that was Jake Drum's opinion. She then added a mouth appliance that much more drastically changed her appearance, another trick she'd learned from Drum.

While Alicia was doing all this, the boy put his jacket in his lap, pushed his left sleeve up as high as he could, and folded the cuff under. Satisfied that the sleeve wouldn't slip, he opened the glove compartment and removed a small Styrofoam box. Inside the box, nestled in formed depressions that held them snugly, were a rubber-stoppered bottle filled with a clear liquid and two clear plastic boxes, one containing a half dozen disposable 1-cc syringes, the other, the same number of 27 gauge needles.

The boy opened the box with the syringes, removed one, and stripped off its paper wrapping. He did the same with a needle and fitted it to the syringe. He then drew six tenths of a cc of liquid from the bottle and looked at the woman, who always found this part so distasteful she couldn't do it herself.

"Well, come on," the boy chided.

She had already unbuttoned her coat. Now, reluctantly, she pulled up her dress, revealing a smooth shapely leg that parched the boy's mouth to look at it. The dress went higher . . . to her thigh. And it was almost more than he could bear.

She looked straight ahead, out the windshield. "All right. Just do it."

It *was* more than he could take. He put the syringe carefully on the open glove compartment door, leaned over, and thrust his hand along her thigh under her dress. He'd barely felt her panties when her fingers bear-trapped his arm. She yanked his hand from under her dress.

"You little fuck," she said, her eyes ripping him. "You want to lose that hand, just keep it up."

"You think because I'm small I couldn't satisfy you?"

"You want to satisfy me, do your job. Otherwise, stay the hell away from me."

"You're a narrow-minded bitch, you know that?"

"We're running out of time, pissant."

Victor, the midget dressed as a child, picked up the filled syringe, leaned over, and plunged the needle into Alicia's thigh. As he emptied the contents into her, he emitted an orgasmic sigh.

"Pig," she said, looking out the windshield.

Victor returned the syringe to the Styrofoam box and assembled another, which he used to inject himself with two-tenths of a cc, a smaller dose due to his smaller size.

They arranged their clothing and waited for the drug to find its way into their blood.

"They're out," Alicia said, a few minutes later, looking through the windshield.

"Not yet," Victor replied, as if she didn't know the drill.

When it was time, Victor reached into the glove compartment for the water pistol they carried safely contained in two zip-top plastic bags and they both got out of the car. Victor slipped the bags into his jacket, and they walked toward the playground where twenty children from the Immaculate Heart kindergarten were making use of the brightly colored outdoor equipment.

Seeing his team move into position, Jackie sat straighter in his seat. There hadn't been a slip-up in months. But that didn't mean it couldn't happen.

A few moments later, Alicia and Victor entered the playground. Alicia headed for the playground supervisor. Victor wandered toward the children, looking for the boy they'd seen a few hours earlier leaving home with his mother, a woman so beautiful she'd made Victor's heart ache.

As Alicia walked toward the children's supervisor, she noted that the woman didn't look particularly intelligent.

"Good morning. My son and I are new to the neighborhood, and I was wondering if your kindergarten has any openings?"

The supervisor leaned to her left and looked at Victor. "Isn't he too old for kindergarten?"

"He'll be five in March," Alicia said, sliding a step sideways so she blocked the other woman's view.

"I don't handle admissions," the supervisor said. "You'll have to talk to Mrs. Wilson. She's probably in her office. It's . . ."

Victor spotted the boy over by the slide and walked toward him, his hand reaching into his jacket for the water pistol. "Hey, Drew, want to play?"

The target turned, wearing a curious expression.

Victor pulled out the pistol and pumped the trigger, aiming for the boy's eyes. The incubation medium from the gun drenched Drew's face, and he took a surprised breath. Then he began to howl.

Alicia and the supervisor hurried over.

"Shame on you," Alicia said, smacking Victor a couple of times on the rear. "You go onto the sidewalk and wait for me."

Keeping his face turned from the supervisor, Victor left the playground. Alicia remained behind and apologized profusely while the supervisor dried Drew's face with a tissue.

"I am *so* embarrassed. I couldn't blame the school at all if they wouldn't even talk to us about my son coming here. Please, don't think he's always this badly behaved. Under the circumstances, I just can't face Mrs. Wilson now. I'll come back another time. I'm *so* sorry."

From the parking lot, Jackie saw his team come out onto the sidewalk. As he had been too far away to see exactly what had taken place in the playground, he watched Alicia anxiously for the sign. She brushed an imaginary piece of lint from her shoulder.

Jackie relaxed.

The pair walked to their car and got in. A few minutes after they pulled out of their spot, Jackie left the parking lot and drove to the quiet, tree-lined street a quarter mile away where they were waiting.

He pulled in behind them and they got out and walked to

his car. Knowing that Victor hated the rear seat and not wanting to argue about it, Alicia got in the back without comment.

Jackie took two envelopes from his jacket pocket and gave one to each member of his team. "We work again a week from today."

Alicia put her envelope in her purse without looking inside. Victor opened his and pawed through the contents. He counted his money and looked at the destination on his plane ticket.

"Why the hell didn't we do this one while we were in Albany?"

"That's none of your business," Jackie said.

Victor clenched his jaw. "I'm really gettin' tired of you talkin' to me like that."

Jackie glanced up and down the street. Satisfied that no one was watching, he slipped his left hand into the molded pocket in his door and grabbed the plastic sack that had held his apples. Moving with animal quickness, he pulled the sack over Victor's head. Before Victor could react, Jackie pulled him across the seat and turned him so he was facing the passenger door. In that position, it was easy to reach across Victor's chest and grab his right arm, a move that also pinned his left. With his free hand, Jackie wrapped the mouth of the sack around Victor's neck.

Behind them, Alicia leaned forward to object, then, thinking better of it, sat back and kept her mouth shut.

Victor kicked and squirmed in Jackie's grip like a hooked trout. Jackie was a good judge of these things and could soon tell by the diminishing strength of the midget's movements that his brain was close to shutting down. He held on for a few seconds more, then, at the very last moment, pulled the bag off Victor's head and pushed him back in his seat.

Victor reclaimed his life without dignity, gasping and sucking air so obnoxiously that Jackie felt like slapping him. When the blood had risen in his death pallor and Jackie was sure he could hear, Jackie said, "Tell me what that was about."

"My big mouth," Victor replied, his voice strained.

"Exactly."

Jackie had two rules about murder: never kill anyone in front of a witness and never kill someone you still need. Victor had gotten his reprieve on both counts.

"I believe we're through here," Jackie said. "I'll see you in a week."

Alicia and Victor got out and went back to their car. When they were gone, Jackie drove to the target child's house where, seeing a woman letting her black Scottish terrier sniff the home's shrubbery, he kept going.

Returning a few minutes later and finding the area deserted, Jackie pulled to the curb, got out, and went up the walk. He stepped onto the porch, added a stamped manila envelope to the other mail the postman had left at the house, and went back to the car.

3

The hospital . . . It seemed there had always been the hospital. She could remember little of her life before she'd passed through its doors. Even her first two years of medical school, the basic sciences, seemed a blur. The hospital had become her father, mother, lover . . . and master.

As she took the elevator to the neuro ward, Sarchi Seminoux shook her head at this melodramatic train of thought. Jesus, if she was in this state of mind only twelve hours into her thirty-six hour shift, what lay ahead?

The problem was actually Gilbert Klyce, the one patient on her service she dreaded having to deal with. When she had checked on the boy a few hours before, he had been doing fine, or at least his pneumonia seemed well on the run. Beyond that, Gilbert would never be fine because his brain had been largely destroyed by what was presumed to be viral encephalitis four years ago. Now, as long as he lived, he would be in a vegetative state. The best doctor in the world could do nothing for him but send him back to the Brunswick Developmental Center with clear lungs, still blind, still deaf, still out of touch with the world. It wasn't fair and it wasn't right and it hurt to have that thrust in her face.

When she arrived at Gilbert's bedside a minute later, the

nurse who'd paged her, a large, raw-boned woman with small, gentle hands, was waiting. So was Gilbert, his little body permanently contracted into a fetal position, his perpetual smile belying his terrible condition. At times, Sarchi almost believed the smile meant that Gilbert lived in a state of continuous, if misguided, bliss. But then her training would always ruin the illusion, reminding her that it was only some sort of brainstem reflex.

Sarchi's eyes left Gilbert and looked at the nurse. "What have we got?"

"His oxygen alarm went off a few minutes ago and I had to increase the mix to 35 percent. He's also running a 102 temperature."

Sarchi bent over Gilbert and put her stethoscope to his chest. At the bases of both lungs, where the pneumonia had settled, she heard sounds like crunching snow, so-called crackles and rales, noises not found in normal lungs. But Gilbert's abnormal sounds were slight and no different from those of the day before, when he had no fever. He was also still on the antibiotics that had beaten back his pneumonia, so those bugs were out of the picture.

"It's criminal if you ask me," a voice said from the doorway.

Sarchi turned and saw one of the other floor nurses. "What's criminal?"

"The resources being squandered on him. What's the point? He doesn't know where he is, or who he is, and never will. And who's paying for his care? We are. Money I could use for my own kids is being taken from me and given to him. It's absurd."

Sarchi's anger flared at this reminder that her best efforts would have no impact on Gilbert's quality of life. "How about getting out of here and letting us do our jobs," she snapped.

"Well pardon me for having an opinion," the nurse said, leaving them.

Eyes blazing, Sarchi removed the oxygen tube from the tracheostomy they'd installed when pharyngitis had closed Gilbert's throat and she directed the beam from her penlight into his trachea. What she saw wasn't good. "I don't like the looks of his tracheal secretions. Would you send a sample down to the lab for a culture?"

"Sure."

"And let me know if anything changes."

Sarchi stopped by the nursing station and jotted a few notes in Gilbert's chart. She turned the dial on the spine to red—indicating she'd entered lab orders—and was just putting the chart back in the rack when her pager went off.

The number displayed indicated a call from outside the hospital. She picked up the phone behind her and discovered it was Marge Harrison.

"Sarchi, it's Drew," Marge said, her voice filled with dread. "He's on his way there in an ambulance."

"What happened?"

"I don't know. It was weird. One minute he was fine and the next . . . Sarchi, I'm so scared. Can you meet me in the emergency room and make sure he gets seen right away?"

"Of course. I'll go down there now."

Before she could quiz Marge any further on what had taken place, Marge said, "I'll be there in a few minutes myself," and hung up.

Sarchi hurried to the elevator, praying that Drew's situation merely appeared serious. Riding down to the ER, a telephone call she'd never forget came flooding back.

"It's for you."

Sarchi looked up from her pathophysiology notes. "Who is it?"

"Your father."

Sarchi threw her notes on the sofa and went to the phone. "Dad? Is anything wrong?"

He didn't answer. "Dad?" Sarchi's heart was fluttering. Something was terribly wrong. She could feel it. "Dad, is it Carolyn?"

He began to sob and she knew her older sister was dead. "Dad, tell me what happened."

Sobbing and choking he put it into words. "Carolyn and Bill . . . they're gone . . . car accident . . ."

Sarchi's tidy academic world was ripped to pieces. Tears

flowing, she choked out another question. "Was Drew in the car?"

"He was with a neighbor."

Sarchi was the senior resident on call. That also made her the hospital's admitting physician, so Marge's request that she watch out for Drew had actually not been necessary as she would have been notified of his arrival by the ER as a matter of procedure.

There was no discernible rhythm to patient traffic in the ER. Sometimes, in an entire night only a handful of kids would come in. Other nights, when the moon or something else was out of kilter, the place would be a madhouse, and they'd have to open another ward to house all of the patients. So far tonight, it had been quiet . . . a six-year-old asthmatic around five o'clock and an hour later, an eleven-year-old diabetic whose blood sugar was off the meter. So as Sarchi walked up to the ER nurse's station, Bernie Kornberg, the physician in charge, was sitting down, hands folded behind his head, talking to a nurse about University of Memphis football.

"Five games, four losses—three of those by just three points each. They've got talent, they just don't know how to win. I may have to go out there and take over."

In the chair opposite him, the nurse was making no effort to hide her lack of interest. Seeing Sarchi and recognizing escape when she saw it, her eyes brightened. "Doctor Seminoux, we're always glad to see you, but at the moment, we don't have any patients."

"You will any minute," Sarchi said.

"A psychic pediatric resident," Kornberg said, amused. "Do you have a hot line?"

They heard the distant sound of an ambulance.

"That's probably him now," Sarchi said.

In short order, an ambulance pulled up outside.

"Oh, I get it," Kornberg said, standing. "Somebody called you. Too bad. I could use some advice on my investments."

The ambulance attendants wheeled in a gurney bearing five-year-old Drew Harrison, straps across his blue *Star Trek* pajamas securing him to a spinal board, his head between padded blocks, a C collar stabilizing his neck. With her own eyes nearly as fear-filled as Drew's, Sarchi rushed to his side and cupped his cheeks in her hands. "Baby, it's Aunt Sarchi. Everything's going to be fine. Don't be scared. I'll take care of you."

"His vitals are basically fine," one of the ambulance attendants said. "He's just limp. Can't stand or move his major muscle groups. His airway is clear and, as you can see, he can breathe on his own. And he can swallow okay."

Sarchi raised Drew's limp arm a few inches and let go. It flopped back onto the gurney. Probing his arms with her fingers, she found the flesh abnormally compliant, indicating he had lost muscle tone as well as voluntary motion. She slipped her finger into Drew's hand and curled his fingers around it. "Drew, baby, try to squeeze my finger."

Nothing happened.

"Can you hear me Drew?"

His eyes appeared to respond, but he made no attempt to speak. "If you can hear me, Drew, blink your eyes twice."

Drew's lids closed and opened twice in rapid succession.

"Squeeze my finger, Drew."

Nothing.

She felt his legs and noted the same loss of tone there. An inventory of his reflexes with her tapping hammer produced no response. She lifted his right leg and stroked the sole of his foot with the edge of a tongue depressor. Again, there was no reaction.

"Let's get him out of the hallway," Kornberg said, grabbing hold of the gurney.

They wheeled Drew into an examining room where, as soon as the gurney stopped moving, Sarchi reached for an ophthalmoscope and looked into his eyes. Thankfully, his pupils were of equal diameter and reactive to light. There was also no papilledema—protrusion of the optic nerve into the eye—which would have indicated a buildup of cranial pressure.

Although Drew appeared to be paralyzed over a large part of his body, Sarchi had seen him move his eyes. She now tested the extent of that ability by asking him to track her finger as she moved it from side to side, then from corner to corner.

All those movements were intact.

From the moment she'd received Marge's call, Sarchi's heart had been hammering in her ears. Now, because of the obvious severity of Drew's condition, she was fighting panic. Kornberg was great at stabilizing patients who were crashing, but he wasn't someone to turn to in a situation like this. For now, it was all on her shoulders.

And the burden was huge, not just because Drew was her nephew and she loved him fiercely, but because she hadn't taken him when Carolyn died. With Bill's parent's too infirm physically to care for a child and her father's mental state deteriorating, Sarchi had been the logical choice. But she'd procrastinated over the decision, stalled by being a medical student, with no time for herself let alone a child. And there was the matter of money. Carolyn and Bill were just getting started and had left more debts than assets. So there was no money for Drew from their estate. How could someone existing on student loans and already tens of thousands in debt for her education take on the additional financial responsibility of raising a little boy?

Then Marge, Carolyn's best friend, had stepped forward, taking the pressure off Sarchi. For a while Drew's new parents seemed the ideal solution but then, with Marge's divorce, she became a single mother struggling with her own finances. The whole episode had left Sarchi with a smoldering sense of guilt. Now she held Drew's life in her hands. She just *couldn't* fail him again.

Stay calm, she thought. *Use your training.*

"Drew honey, can you talk?"

Once again he just looked at her without speaking.

"If you can't talk, blink your eyes twice."

Still, he just stared back.

Sarchi turned to Marge. "Has he said anything since it happened?"

"He hasn't made a sound."

"Drew, say your name for me."

No response.

"I'm trying to make you better, Drew. You can help me by saying your name. Will you do that?"

He still seemed to be making no attempt to speak.

Giving up for now on that point, she continued her exam. First, she rechecked Drew's vital signs and verified that, allowing for the fear he was experiencing, they were all within normal limits, just as the ambulance attendant had said. Over the next few minutes, she determined that his heart rhythm and sounds were normal—no murmurs, gallops, or rubs. The lungs were clear, and the liver and spleen were normal in size. There was no guarding of the abdomen and no tenderness.

"What is it, Sarchi?" Marge said, from the other side of the bed. "What's wrong with him?"

She had obviously been crying, and her eyes were red and swollen. Normally, Marge was beautiful even without makeup. In its absence now, her skin was blotchy and raw.

"It's too soon to say," Sarchi replied.

"Doctor Kornberg, we've got an asthmatic infant out here who's in a desperate state," a second nurse said from the doorway.

"I've got to go," Kornberg said to Sarchi. He touched Marge's shoulder lightly. "Your son is in excellent hands with Doctor Seminoux."

Sarchi could not remember when Marge wasn't in total command of whatever situation arose around her. But tonight, she looked frail and lost.

Speaking to the nurse who'd accompanied the gurney into the room, Sarchi said, "Sallie, let's get him on the monitors, but turn the sound off so we can talk." When she'd cupped Drew's cheeks in her hands, he hadn't felt hot, but she still added, "And get his temperature."

Turning to Marge, she gestured toward a couple of nearby chairs. "Come over here and tell me exactly what happened." Marge took a long look at Drew then went with Sarchi and sat down.

"I was just reading to him . . . he was next to me on the sofa, alert and interested. Then his chin dropped to his chest and he got limp. I thought he was asleep. But when I picked him up, I saw his eyes were open. But he couldn't move. What the hell is it?"

"In the last few days, has he fallen and hit his head?"

"Not unless it was at school. But I'm sure they would have told me if something like that happened."

"Has he been sick . . . fever . . . cough?"

"No."

"Has he had any blisters lately around his mouth or anywhere else?"

"I haven't seen any."

"Any recent immunizations?"

Marge shook her head.

"Vomiting or a rash?"

"No."

What did he have for dinner tonight?"

"I made him his favorite . . . spaghetti."

"How was his appetite?"

"He ate like a little horse."

"Did you have the same thing?"

"Yes."

"You haven't seen any evidence he's been into the medicine cabinet or any cleaning chemicals?"

"He knows to stay away from those places."

"Has he been around any animals?" Thinking of cat scratch fever, Sarchi added, "kittens in particular."

"Not that I know of. But I suppose some stray cat could have wandered into the backyard. And there are a lot of raccoons in midtown."

"He's never out alone after dark?"

"No."

"Raccoons are nocturnal. It's not likely he'd encounter one during the day. And I don't see any fresh scratches on him. I wonder if any of his classmates are sick?"

"I can try to contact his teacher."

"She could tell us who missed school today, but I'd also like to know if any became ill tonight."

"That'll be tougher to find out, but I'll try."

"If you do reach his teacher, ask her if Drew hit his head

anytime in the last day or two. There's a phone at the nurse's station you can use."

Marge got up to leave but paused and took a long look at her son. Lips trembling, she looked at Sarchi. "He'll get better, won't he?"

This part was hard. Without knowing what was wrong, it was impossible to venture a prognosis. But right now, Marge needed support and encouragement, not accuracy. So Sarchi lied.

"I'm sure we'll get to the bottom of this and he'll be home in no time, whole and happy."

Before showing Marge to the phone, Sarchi wrote orders for a battery of blood tests and gave them to the nurse.

The paramedics who'd brought Drew in had correctly treated him as though he might have a broken neck. Fractured vertebrae do not always shift and damage the spinal cord at the time of the bony injury but may do so later. This meant that even though Drew's paralysis had begun when he was merely listening to a story, a broken neck was certainly a possible, albeit terrible, explanation for his condition. So when Sarchi saw one of the radiology techs at the nurse's station as she took Marge to the phone, she asked him to move the mobile X-ray unit to Drew's room and get some neck films.

Then, as difficult as it was to concentrate on another case, she shifted her attention to the asthmatic that had come in. By the time that child was stabilized and Sarchi had written up the admitting orders allowing him to be sent to the ICU, Drew's X-rays were waiting for her in his room, where she clipped them to the viewing screen and began her inspection.

Finding every vertebra intact, she went to Drew and gently removed his C collar, hoping to make him more comfortable. His neck wasn't broken, but Sarchi's heart still felt as heavy as a deck plate on the *Titanic*. Among the many possible diagnoses remaining was some kind of acute encephalopathy, an abnormality in his brain. As hard as she fought it, the image of Gilbert Klyce kept bulling into her mind.

No . . .

That was not going to happen to Drew. She would find the problem and make him better.

She had to.

She just had to.

4

"You took his collar off," Marge said.

"His neck is fine, so we don't need it," Sarchi replied. "What did you find out?"

"I got hold of the woman who runs Drew's kindergarten, and she gave me the phone numbers of his teacher and the parents of his classmates. His teacher says she has no knowledge of Drew hitting his head. One of the other kids has a sore throat, but her mother says she gets that every couple of months. None of the others are sick. Where does *that* leave us?"

Where indeed, Sarchi thought, a dozen possibilities tumbling in her head: Guillain-Barré syndrome, a tumor, cat scratch fever, bacterial or viral meningitis. But the onset was so sudden and there was no fever. He could have had a stroke, or maybe it was multiple sclerosis. But how often do you see those in a five-year-old? If he'd had an immunization recently, she'd have suspected the disease he was being inoculated against. God knows that's not unheard of. But he'd had no shots. Possibly some kind of electrolyte imbalance?

"Sarchi, where does that leave us?" Marge repeated.

"We'll know better when we get the labs."

"When will that be?"

Sarchi checked the time. "Twenty minutes, maybe."

"Isn't there anything we can do now?"

An idea popped into Sarchi's head. "As a matter of fact, there is. There's a disease called tick paralysis that lasts as long as the tick is attached and clears up within minutes after its removal."

Marge's face lit up. "Do you think that's what it is?"

Actually, the chances were so remote, Sarchi was sorry she'd given Marge that hope. But it was something to do while waiting for the labs.

"Let's check," Sarchi said, heading back to Drew's room.

Sarchi spent the next fifteen minutes searching every inch of Drew's body for ticks, most of that time prowling through his hair. As expected, she found nothing.

Marge was obviously disappointed.

"You stay here with Drew," Sarchi said, trying to hide the continuing sense of dread she felt. "I'm going to see if any of the lab results are back."

There was only so much you could learn from a physical exam. Sometimes it pointed you in the right direction, but often it didn't. In either case, without the lab, medicine was just a lot of guesswork. So, as she walked to the chart room, Sarchi hoped at least some of the tests were done.

In the chart room, Sarchi sat at one of the computers and logged in her password and Drew's name. After a short pause, the screen filled with data.

Her eyes hurried down the chem 20 results, looking for aberrant values, but everything was within usual limits. That neither Marge nor any of the other kids in Drew's school were ill made botulism an unlikely possibility. Even so, she'd ordered a test to determine if the toxin was present in Drew's blood. It wasn't.

Moving on to the hematology data, she found Drew's hematocrit normal. His distribution of white cells, the so-called diff count, was also what you'd expect in a normal, active five-year-old. If he'd had an elevated neutrophil count, it would have suggested a possible bacterial infection. More lymphocytes than normal would have turned her thoughts to a virus. But there was no support for either of those diagnoses. Although the full panel wouldn't be complete until tomorrow, the preliminary results of the drug screen she'd ordered were negative.

She returned to Drew's room and relayed what she'd learned to Marge. "All his blood work is normal." Despite her irritation and disappointment at finding no clue to Drew's illness in his lab work, she tried to spin it for Marge's benefit. "So that's good news."

Marge's brow furrowed. "In what way?"

"It narrows the possibilities."

"To what?"

With Gilbert Klyce constantly hovering on the edge of her thoughts, Sarchi was even more concerned now that Drew's problem was in his brain. Of all the prognoses a parent might hear from a doctor treating their child, brain damage is one of the most feared. Wanting to spare Marge from the torture that possibility was wreaking in her own head, Sarchi parried the question. "The list is still too long for us to discuss right now." Seeing from the look on Marge's face that she didn't like this answer, Sarchi said, "Instead of talking about a lot of potential explanations, wouldn't you rather we keep working to find the correct one?"

Unable to fault this logic, Marge nodded. "You're right."

"I'm going to have someone else look at Drew," Sarchi said. "I'll set it up and come back."

Sarchi went to the nurse's station, where Kornberg inquired about Drew's status.

"So far I'm sucking wind," Sarchi said. "I need a neurology consult and then I'm sure we'll be wanting a CT scan."

Kornberg reached for the phone. "I'll take care of it."

At that moment, Sarchi's own pager went off. The number displayed was 7 West, the surgical ward. She picked up the other phone and checked in.

As the senior resident on call, she was responsible not just for her own patients, but for every kid in the hospital. Had the call concerned one of hers she might have been able to handle it without going upstairs. But it was an ulcerative colitis patient from someone else's service, running a fever. Being unfamiliar with the case, she needed to look over his chart. "I've got to go to 7 West. If I'm not back by the time the neurology res gets here . . ."

Kornberg waved her away. "Leave him to me."

When things would heat up and she barely had a moment to think between patients, Sarchi had often pictured herself as Lucille Ball working the runaway chocolate line. Though tonight was relatively slow, her wish to concentrate fully on Drew's case sent chocolates speeding through her head as she headed up to 7 West.

Upon her return to the ER, she was surprised to find that the neurology resident had yet to show. He finally walked in five minutes later.

Charles Lanehart was old for a resident and overweight, with multiple chins. Rumor was he'd given up a successful law practice for medicine, which seemed to Sarchi an odd decision. "I was just about to page you again," she said sharply.

Lanehart looked at her with an expression of incredulity. "I'm covering two hospitals tonight. I wasn't even here when I got the page."

"Sorry. I'm just particularly worried about this one. It's my nephew. He's in here."

Sarchi led Lanehart to Drew's room, where he looked at the neck X-rays and conducted pretty much the same exam- ination she had. When he was finished, Sarchi gave Marge a reassuring squeeze of the hand and went into the hall with Lanehart to hear his views on the case.

"I don't know if he can't talk or just won't, but assuming it's the former, it looks like locked-in syndrome to me."

"What's that?"

"Destruction of the major motor pathways in the basilar pons."

"From what cause?"

"Hard to say, a bleed maybe. We need a CT scan. I'll make the arrangements."

"I told Kornberg we'd be wanting one, so the tech should be waiting." Sarchi went back to Drew's room to find Marge pacing. "We're going to give Drew a CT scan."

"Why?"

Seeing what was coming, Sarchi tried to avoid it by a judicious use of words. "So we can get a direct look inside his head."

"You think something's wrong with Drew's *brain*?" Marge asked with terror in her voice.

So there it was, out in the open. She should have known earlier she'd have to admit this possibility eventually.

Sarchi put her hands gently on Marge's shoulder and looked her in the eye. "It's just a possibility at this point. And even if it is the source of his problem, that's no reason to become pessimistic about the outcome. We're going to stay positive. We're not even going to *think* anything but complete recovery."

Eyes swimming, Marge didn't respond.

A few minutes later, the ER's two nurses entered Drew's room with a gurney. Sarchi went to Drew's bed and stroked his hair.

"Drew honey, we need to get a better look at you so we can find out what's wrong. So we're going to put you in a *Star Wars* machine. It's like a big doughnut with some pretty lights. We'll strap you in just like you were flying a spaceship, only you'll be lying down. Your mother will be there with you, and I'll be in the control room monitoring the flight, which will be so gentle you won't even know the machine is working."

Drew's eyes seemed less fearful. Hoping that this wasn't just her imagination, Sarchi signaled for the nurses to put Drew on the gurney. When he was safely transferred, they wheeled him to the scan room.

The CT tech was a young man with a soft friendly face. He continued the spaceship analogy.

"Yessir, Captain. We've been waiting for you. Engineering says the ship is ready for flight."

The scanner was a huge putty-colored square that practically filled one end of the small room. In its center was a round hole for the patient's body. Were it not for a narrow beam of intense ruby light that ran in three directions across the face of the machine from the doughnut hole, it would have appeared inert.

Drew was placed on the scanner table on his back with his head pointing at the doughnut hole. Even though he couldn't move, his head was put in a holder and surrounded by foam padding. A chin strap locked it firmly in place. The tech then covered Drew's torso with a lead-lined blanket.

"Is that for me?" Marge said, gesturing to the rocking chair nearby.

"If you'd like to stay," the tech said.

"I would."

The tech pointed at a protective apron hanging on a peg behind her. "Just put that on."

The tech looked back at Drew. "All right, Captain. If you're ready, we'll get under way. As I understand Star Fleet's orders, we'll be maintaining a speed of warp eight for the entire trip. At that speed we'll reach our target very quickly." He saluted and Sarchi followed him into the scanner control room, where Lanehart was waiting. The tech took a seat in front of the CT control panel with its two monitors and began pushing buttons and flipping switches.

Pleased at how gentle he'd been with Drew, Sarchi said, "You're a big ham, you know that?"

"Runs in the family, my dear," the tech said, doing an imitation of W. C. Fields that proved her point. His fingers scurried over the keyboard, choosing functions that were then displayed on the left monitor. They watched as Drew's head entered the doughnut.

An X-ray image of Drew's skull and vertebrae of the upper neck appeared on the right monitor. The tech superimposed a series of parallel green lines on Drew's skull to indicate the different levels where the scanner would X-ray Drew's brain, and the first in a string of images simultaneously appeared on the screen.

It was an absolute marvel . . . instant pictures of an entire brain at a dose of X-rays far less than you used to get in a chest film. And when all the images were collected, if you wished, the computer could take you on a boat ride down the reconstructed interior of any vessel you chose.

As the ghostly images appeared on the screen, Sarchi bent closer, trying to read them. There were structures at each level she couldn't name but she had a pretty good working knowledge of the major landmarks.

There . . . the first appearance of the lateral ventricles, a division of the bizarrely shaped interconnecting cavities deep in every brain.

A little deeper was the internal capsule, the narrow boomerang-shaped collection of major fiber bundles surrounded by neuron accumulations known as the striatum.

As the machine probed deeper and deeper, Sarchi focused hard, looking for any telltale density where the image should be pale, but also alert for the opposite situation. A density could be a tumor, a pale zone, an area of degeneration, or a bleed.

But when the last image had been added to the collection, Sarchi had seen nothing abnormal. Apparently, Lanehart hadn't either.

"Could I see them all again," he said, "full size?"

The tech ran through each of the pictures again, changing them only when Lanehart asked. To Sarchi, everything still looked normal.

Finally, Lanehart turned to her and said, "I see nothing here to support a diagnosis of damage to the pons or anywhere else for that matter. It's a little difficult though on a CT scan to see through the bone around the pons, so we should probably do an MRI in the morning."

"If we *are* dealing with locked-in syndrome, what's the treatment?"

"If it's caused by a big bleed, you're basically hosed. There's always so much damage and so little hope for any recovery that no one even bothers removing the clot."

"Even without the MRI, we know that's not the case here."

"Right. Which leaves trauma or ischemia-induced damage. In those cases, you still can't do anything, but you can hope there'll be some return of function after the acute phase passes."

"That's it?"

Lanehart shrugged.

With no effective treatment available, Sarchi wanted very much to believe Drew wasn't suffering from locked-in syndrome. "If you can't see any pontine damage on a CT, how likely is an MRI to show some?"

"Not very."

"But there *is* a possibility?"

"I suppose."

Wanting pontine damage completely off the list of differential diagnoses, Sarchi said, "It's ridiculous that we don't have an MRI tech on call."

"That *has* been pointed out to Koesler," Lanehart said. "But he said it's a matter of money. The hospital can't afford it."

"Which is no excuse," Sarchi snapped. "Whoever discussed it with him shouldn't have accepted that."

"So you would have pressed the point?"

"Of course."

"Well, here comes your chance." Lanehart gestured over her shoulder with his chin.

Turning, Sarchi saw Irwin Koesler, the hospital's medical director coming their way, apparently touring the ER on one of his surprise visits. He stepped into the control room and curtly acknowledged all present by their last names.

Koesler was the best-groomed man Sarchi had ever seen, his silver hair perfectly coifed, his white coat and the shirt under it of blinding purity and wrinkle free, the knot of his tie expertly crafted. In addition to being the hospital's medical director, he was also a board-certified pediatric nephrologist, designations he carried like a jeweled scepter. Around the corridors and wards, he was widely known as the "immaculate misconception." It was said the only people he viewed as worth his time were his reflection and God, in that order. He looked through the window at Drew. "What's the case?"

Lanehart let Sarchi handle it. "The boy is paralyzed from the neck down."

"Have you pinpointed the cause?"

"Not yet. We're trying to rule out pontine damage but to do that completely we need an MRI."

"How are his vitals?"

"He's stable."

"So he's in no immediate danger."

"If you mean in no danger of dying, that's true."

"Of course that's what I meant. So, you'll get the MRI first thing in the morning."

Sarchi could feel Lanehart and the CT tech's interest in the conversation sharpen. Here was her opportunity to tell Koesler how unacceptable that was. But as much as she believed he was wrong on this position, she couldn't tell him to his face. "Yes," she muttered. "In the morning."

Then, to her horror, Lanehart said, "Actually, Doctor Seminoux thinks it's ridiculous not to have an MRI tech on call at night."

Koesler's eyes cooled. "Is that right?" he said, looking at Sarchi.

"No . . . not ridiculous," she said. "It's just . . . sometimes . . . it'd be convenient to . . . in this case, for example. I'd like to know for sure we're not dealing with damage to the pons. That way we could concentrate on other diagnoses."

"We can't afford the extra staff," Koesler said.

"I understand. I just . . . It'd be useful. That's all I meant."

"Anything else?"

"No. Nothing."

"Good."

He turned and left the room. When he was out of earshot, Sarchi turned to Lanehart. "What's the matter with you?"

"Hey, I was only helping you express yourself." He squinted at her. "What's that?" He reached out, aiming a finger at her nose. "You've got something brown right on the tip . . ."

She pushed his hand away. "I didn't hear *you* stand up to him."

"I'm not the one who feels so strongly about needing an MRI tonight."

"Don't be so judgmental. He's not only the medical director and head of the pediatric residency program, he's one of the pediatric attendings. In three months, I'll be on his admitting team again. Surely you know how miserable he can make my life."

Lanehart threw up his hands. "If you can knuckle under like that and still respect yourself, I don't mind."

"It's easy for *you* to talk. Your residency program isn't even administered in this hospital." Her defense of her behavior rang hollow even to Sarchi. It wasn't the first time she'd taken a dive in the face of authority, and it wouldn't be the last. It had never been something she'd been proud of, it was just who she was.

Getting her mind back where it belonged, she asked Lanehart to stick around for another few minutes, then stepped outside and told the nurses to take Drew back to his room.

"What did you find?" Marge asked.

"Nothing to worry us. I'm going to confer with Doctor Lanehart a bit. You go with Drew and I'll be there shortly."

While the CT tech straightened up the scan room, Sarchi briefed Lanehart on the lab findings. Nothing he said in response lit up the room.

Large brain tumors and conditions that cause the brain to swell increase intracranial pressure. In such cases, if a spinal tap is done, the sudden loss of pressure from below causes a downward displacement of certain regions of the brain into compartments too small for them. The resulting compression causes irreparable neural damage, if not death. While there was still some question whether Drew had any pontine damage, the CT scan clearly eliminated any concern about proceeding to a spinal tap. This next diagnostic step would bear upon a number of nasty illnesses, including meningitis, a disease that could easily turn a brain into a cauliflower. Sarchi saw now that she'd been wrong earlier to compare this night to a runaway chocolate line. It was a house of horrors with more stops yet to come.

5

Four hundred miles from Memphis, Lee-Ann stepped out of the elevator into the subacute neuro ward of the Metro East Hospital. It was the second time in twelve hours she'd been there. But this time she was wearing a newly purchased housekeeper's uniform. Her first visit had been a reconnoitering trip in which she'd learned that only six of the ward's ten beds were occupied. This meant that the night shift would likely consist of no more than two people. And that's exactly what she saw at the nurse's station. Noticing one of them looking her way, Lee-Ann reached into her bucket for her spray bottle of 409 and went after an imaginary heel mark on the beige tiled floor.

It was 2:30 A.M., a half hour after the two women on duty should have made their rounds and turned to their paperwork. When Lee-Ann adjusted her position a minute later so she could surreptitiously check on them, that's what they were doing.

So far, so good.

The unit consisted of the nurse's station backed by a chart room where the attendings could work when they rounded, and ten rooms arranged in a U on the perimeter. The room Lee-Ann was most interested in was in the worst possible location, directly opposite the nurse's station. As hard as she'd thought about it, she'd been unable to come up with a flawless plan to get in there unseen. So, as she pursued another phantom mark on a tile that took her deeper into the unit, she stayed alert for the right moment.

For the next ten minutes, Lee-Ann made sure she stayed within earshot of the two women on duty. Then, very close to when she thought it might happen, one of them said, "I'm going to take my break before we have to round again."

"You're staying on the floor?" the other asked.

"Yeah. Call me if you need help."

The one dressed like a nurse's assistant left the station and went to a windowless room tucked into a small alcove next to the elevators.

Lee-Ann picked up her bucket, hurried down the hall, and went around the corner of the U. Hidden from view by the chart room behind the nurse's station, she pushed open the door to a patient's room and peeked inside. Seeing that the occupant was awake, she tried the next room.

Better. Much better. For this patient, heavily bandaged about the face, didn't stir when she looked in. Believing someone so badly hurt was likely in a drugged sleep, Lee-Ann went inside and approached the foot of the bed.

"Are you awake?"

No response.

She reached out and grasped the patient's leg through the sheet and rocked it, repeating her question.

Still no reaction.

In the dim light, she moved toward the head of the bed and picked up the patient's IV line, which she kinked and tucked under him.

Back in the hall she resumed her housekeeping act. In short order, the patient's IVAC alarm went off.

When the nurse left her station to see what was wrong, Lee-Ann darted into Greta Dunn's room, where, just as she had been told at the desk, the woman was still in a coma. It was unlikely Dunn would ever be able to identify her or anyone else again, but Lee-Ann wanted to be absolutely certain. She reached into the pocket of her smock for the preloaded syringe she'd brought and unsheathed the needle. Forcing her hands to perform without shaking, she slid the needle into the injection port on Dunn's IV and delivered a bolus of potassium chloride into her blood.

Knowing she had only seconds to make her escape, Lee-Ann grabbed her bucket, threw the syringe inside, and darted from the room. She bolted for the stairwell, then paused on the other side of the closed door to listen. She'd taken perhaps three ragged breaths when Greta Dunn's heart monitor began to squeal.

6

Drew's MRI scan the next morning was completely normal. Likewise, the laboratory analysis of his spinal fluid provided no clues to the cause of his condition. The final results of the drug screen came back negative, and his new blood work produced values no different than those from the previous night.

"And so far, his blood and urine cultures haven't grown anything," Sarchi said to Kate McDaniels, her attending.

"Of course, it's early yet on those. So what should we do now?" Kate asked.

"I'd like to try a Tensilon test."

Kate was by far the most fashionable attending in the hospital. Somehow she always looked elegant, even in scrubs and a lab coat. In part it was her hair, slate gray without apology and always carefully arranged in a French twist. But mostly it was the way she carried herself, as if her ancestors had owned a country. She was an excellent teacher, leading you to knowledge instead of stuffing it into you. She was also patient, allowing her residents time to form their own ideas about the cases they worked. She did not, however, have a poker face. When she was pleased, you knew it, when she wasn't, you knew that as well. Sarchi now saw that Kate had been thinking of a Tensilon test herself.

"What's a Tensilon test?" Marge asked, joining them in the hall.

"A way to determine if Drew has a condition known as myasthenia gravis," Sarchi replied. "It's an autoimmune disorder in which for some unknown reason, antibodies are made against the proteins in muscle cells that receive messages from nerves. The test involves the administration of a drug that prevents the breakdown of the normal chemical messenger between nerve and muscle so that the antibodies blocking communication can be overcome. It's a quick test and very dramatic. If this is the cause of Drew's paralysis, we'll know just a few minutes after the test is done."

"So the problem isn't in his brain?"

"We still can't rule that out entirely."

"But the CT and MRI scans . . ."

"They simply eliminated some obvious things."

"And *now* you think the problem is in his muscles?"

It was hard enough to deal with Drew being paralyzed. Having to justify her every thought to Marge was draining what energy Sarchi had left after being up all night. Still, she could appreciate Marge's position and because of that took no offense at the critical tone of her last question.

"There are many potential explanations for Drew's condition," Sarchi said patiently, trying to keep her own anxiety out of her voice. "When we pursue a particular possibility, it doesn't necessarily mean we believe that's the cause. It's detective work. We gather the clues and eventually they'll point to the culprit." She took Marge gently by the shoulders and looked into her eyes. "Okay?"

Marge took a deep breath and nodded.

Ten minutes later a runner brought a vial of Tensilon up from the pharmacy. While Kate loaded a syringe, Sarchi went to Drew and closed his right hand around her finger.

"Drew honey, I want you to do something for me. I want you to squeeze my finger as hard as you can."

Though she obviously had Drew's attention, she felt no response.

"Are you trying? Blink twice if you are."

His lids flicked twice.

"Okay, you can rest now. But soon I'll want you to try again."

Sarchi watched as Kate delivered .2 cc of the drug into the injection port of Drew's IV. When Sarchi's Mickey Mouse watch had counted off thirty seconds, she snugged Drew's hand around her finger and asked him again to squeeze.

Once more, she felt nothing. While Marge and Kate watched solemnly, she waited another thirty seconds and asked again.

Drew's poor muscles still could not mount a response.

If the drug has an effect, it only lasts two or three minutes. So after Drew failed to show any improvement in three more tries, Kate gave him another dose, doubling the amount.

This also had no effect.

They repeated the procedure one more time as the test protocols recommended, emptying the vial. No one in the room was surprised when Drew remained as helpless as before.

"Where does this leave us?" Marge said.

"We've got a lot of tests going," Sarchi replied. "The clue we're looking for will likely be in those results."

"How long before everything is back?"

"That's a problem. Cultures can take a while, a day or two for bacteria, longer for viruses.

"We're in a period now when data will be coming in slowly," Kate said. "You might want to take advantage of this time by going home and getting some rest."

An expression of incredulity crossed Marge's face. "Rest? How can I rest when my child is . . . like this?"

"I understand," Kate said, touching Marge's shoulder. "But I'm sure a shower and a change of clothes would lift your spirits."

This seemed to make sense to Marge. "I need to tell my partner at the agency I won't be in today. And I could get some of Drew's books and read to him."

"There you go," Kate said kindly.

"I won't be gone long." Marge looked at Sarchi. "Should

anything change before I'm back, you'll call me right away?"

"Count on it."

When Marge was gone and Sarchi and Kate were out of Drew's hearing, Sarchi said, "I love that woman, but having her as an audience while I flounder around playing doctor is wearing me out."

"You're not *playing* at anything," Kate said sharply. "All you've done for Drew has been correct. You're not God, and you never will be."

Sarchi smiled wearily. "I don't know about that. I could become a nephrologist."

"I'm glad you still have your sense of humor."

Sensing that Kate was leading up to something, Sarchi's eyes narrowed with suspicion.

"I guess you haven't checked the results of Gilbert Klyce's cultures this morning," Kate said.

"What's he got?"

"Four plus MRSA."

"Oh, shit." Methicillin-resistant *Staphylococcus aureus* was among the worst bugs Gilbert could have acquired. "So now he goes on vancomycin."

"It's all we can do."

Vancomycin was an antibiotic sledgehammer. "I hope his kidney's are strong enough to handle it."

"You'll write the orders?"

"I'll go up there next. Getting back to Drew . . . You think he might have Guillain-Barré?" She was referring to another autoimmune disease that, unlike myasthenia, causes degeneration of the fatty covering of nerve fibers.

"The loss of deep tendon reflexes fits, but there was no protein increase in his spinal fluid."

"Isn't the protein initially normal in some cases?"

"True, but there's also the fact that his condition came on so suddenly."

"Acute onset . . . That's the harpoon in any diagnosis I can think of, except maybe a bleed. But there's no evidence of that on the scans. What do you think?"

"That I've got ten more kids to see this morning. We'll talk about this later, when we've got more data."

Sarchi went to the nurse's station to get Drew's chart, but it wasn't in the carousel. She asked the floor supervisor where it was.

"Your friend Harry Bright has it. He's in the chart room."

Harry Bright. Sarchi's blood pressure rose to dangerous levels, and she stalked to the chart room, where she found Bright reading Drew's growing hospital record.

"What is it with you lower life-forms?" Sarçhi said. "Do you have some kind of primitive sense organ that draws you to other people's misfortunes?"

Bright looked up. "Matter of fact, we do." He reached for his zipper. "Want to see it?"

"Sorry, I didn't bring my magnifying glass."

Bright didn't look like a smart-ass. With his well-trimmed mustache and goatee, sad eyes and thin lips, a sensitive ex-patriate Russian poet seemed a better fit . . . until you talked to him for a few minutes. Then it was smart-ass all the way. He was the local rep for North American Medical, an HMO that paid the bills for about twenty percent of all the hospital's patient's who weren't on Tenn Care, the state program for indigents.

Bright tapped Drew's chart. "What do you think's wrong with him?"

"It's too early to say."

"Hope you figure it out quick. You're really running up a tab."

"That's not my concern."

"See, that's why people like me and my company exist. For too long, you doctors have thought you were the dog and the rest of us were the tail. Well doc, I'm here to tell you things have changed. And you're just gonna have to get used to it."

"I never knew the other way. But I know this is wrong."

"If it was wrong, it wouldn't exist."

"Change can work both ways," Sarchi said. "Remember the Edsel."

"You just cling to that hope if it makes you feel better.

Meanwhile, let's talk about Michael Green. Isn't he well enough to be moved out of the ICU?"

Sarchi feigned a confused expression. "Tell me again where you obtained your MD."

"I'll stake my five years of nursing experience at Mass General in Boston against your training any day of the week."

"That's the problem."

"Then you won't be moving Green?"

"When we feel he's ready. *Could* be today."

"There now, cooperation isn't so hard."

"I need that chart."

Bright handed her Drew's chart, and she took it to an empty chair. He watched over her shoulder while she entered the Tensilon results.

"So it's not myasthenia gravis," he said before she'd written her conclusion.

"Don't you need to be somewhere?"

"Actually, I do."

But he didn't leave.

"What's the matter, forget the location of your next feeding station?"

"I hear you're quite a racquetball player."

"Who said so?"

"You get around, you hear things."

The thought that Bright was inquiring about her was infuriating. "I'd prefer you not discuss me with people."

"The urge to gossip is such a fundamental human trait it ought to be in the constitution."

"I believe you were leaving."

"Play *me*."

"What?"

"Racquetball. You think I'm such an asshole, you could put me in my place."

"I've got better things to do with my time."

"Yeah, that's true . . . you might lose. And how would that look—a nurse beating a *doctor*."

Tired of this conversation, Sarchi got up and took Drew's chart to the nurse's station. Bright followed.

"Play me."

Ignoring him, Sarchi put the chart in the carousel and walked to the elevator, Bright close behind.

When the elevator arrived, she was relieved that he didn't get on with her. As the door closed, she heard him say, "Michael Green . . . don't forget."

Going up to the neuro ward, Sarchi tried to tell herself Bright was merely a horsefly on the flank of the medical profession. But she knew better. Bright and his company and the others like them were greatly influencing the way medicine was practiced, substituting their judgment for the physician's. And as much as she didn't want to admit it, it could be a long time before things got better.

In the neuro ward, Gilbert Klyce was still running a fever. Sarchi wrote the orders to start him on vancomycin and also ordered a blood culture to see if the Staph had invaded his bloodstream. She alerted the floor nurse to what she'd done and left for the asthma ward.

Around thirty minutes later, her pager buzzed. When she looked at the number she groaned. Practically before the sound died in her throat, she had the neuro ward on the line, where a voice said, "Gilbert Klyce is not breathing."

7

As Gilbert was wheeled away to the ICU to be put on a ventilator, Sarchi suddenly felt like hitting something. It hadn't been a reaction to the vancomycin that had made him go into respiratory arrest. More likely some kind of autonomic vagal reflex kicked off while his trachea was being suctioned.

There was no perversity to Gilbert's respiratory vacation, no conspiracy to coax her back to the neuro ward, where, if Drew's condition worsened, he too might end up. But it sure felt like it.

She still had four hours to go on her thirty-six hour shift. Normally, by quitting time on such a haul, all she wanted was to sleep. But Harry Bright had planted a seed that took root. She reached for the phone, hoping Carl Lanza's schedule was flexible.

The call rang four times then rolled over to his lab.

"Carl, this is Sarchi. I know it's short notice, but would you be interested in a little racquetball today?"

"Actually it's the big racquetballs I like."

"Very funny. You must be having a better day than I am."

"So far it's been one to hang on the wall. I got a phone call an hour ago inviting me to give a talk at the international brain conference in Lucerne this summer."

"That's wonderful." Carl was a molecular biologist who studied gene expression in nerve cells. His wife, Gail, was a resident in orthopedics at Campbell Clinic. Feeling sorry for Sarchi's impoverished social life, they often invited her over to dinner.

"Am I being insensitive to crow like this when you're having a bad day?" Carl asked.

"Just say you're free at 4:45 to play and I'll overlook it."

"The way I feel I'll be tough to handle."

"We'll see. Think we can get a court?"

"The medical students are all getting antsy about their upcoming exams, so a court shouldn't be a problem. I'll check. If it is, I'll call you. Otherwise, we're on."

After a few hours on a ventilator, Gilbert began to breathe on his own again—a human zucchini back on automatic pilot, hardly a reason to become giddy. And there was Drew, still undiagnosed, with her waiting for the results from a lot of cultures that couldn't possibly point to a disease that fit the profile they'd developed. *What was wrong with him?*

By 4:30, Sarchi's desire to hit something was so strong it overwhelmed the guilt she felt at leaving the hospital before Drew was diagnosed.

Fall and winter in Memphis are schizophrenic; gorgeous life-affirming days alternate with gloomy, cold, wet ones that arrive from the Arkansas rice fields across the Mississippi with a gale that turns umbrellas inside out. Such a wind had blown in the night before but had now departed, leaving the sky a pewter color that did nothing to buoy Sarchi's spirits as she stepped outside the hospital.

It took her a little over five minutes to walk the few blocks to the University of Tennessee fitness center. She was such a regular there that the guy sitting at the check-in waved her through without asking for her member's card. Luckily, she had clean shorts, an athletic bra, and a fresh pullover in the locker with her racquet.

Carl was warming up when she ducked through the small

door off the hall and entered the court. He'd just slammed one off the front wall so hard it hit the rear wall near her head. He caught it on the rebound.

"I should warn you," he said. "I'm feeling merciless today."

"So I see."

Carl had clean-cut good looks but nasty hairy legs that were thick at the ankles. Gail always said that from the waist up he was *Homo sapiens*. Below, he was a troglodyte.

"Everything get straightened out at the hospital?" he asked.

"I sort of came here to forget all that. Do you mind?"

"Not at all. I was just being polite when I asked anyway." He grinned at his lie.

"How's Gail getting on with the orthopods?"

"Every once in a while one gives her a break."

Sarchi groaned. "That's really bad."

"It's not my joke, it's Gail's. Blame her. I suppose you'd like to warm up before I teach you the game." He tossed her the ball.

It was good to be out of the hospital, and for a time Carl's repartee and the physical involvement of stroking and following the ball provided a respite from those concerns. But it didn't last.

Usually, their games were close. Her workouts three days a week in the fitness center's weight room had lent a surprising power to Sarchi's swing. Carl, though, had more. But she was better at predicting where the ball could best be intercepted. Normally, she could resist the temptation to hit it at the peak of its first bounce and wait until she could stroke it low, sending it into the front wall so close to the floor that it was nearly impossible to return. But today, the faces of Gilbert Klyce, Drew Harrison, and Harry Bright continuously looped through her thoughts, destroying her concentration to the point that she invariably stroked the ball at the top of its bounce, caring more for the fury of her swing than its accuracy.

Predictably, the first game went to Carl by a comfortable margin. She fared no better in the second.

"If you'll forgive the observation," Carl said, "your game today is out to lunch."

Flushed and enjoying the feel of the ball against the strings of her racquet and the satisfying *splat* when she drove it into the front wall, Sarchi wiped the sweat from her brow with the back of her hand and dropped into a receiving stance. "You gonna talk or play, Lanza?"

Carl proceeded to whip her a third time.

"You can't want any more of this," he said.

Suddenly, the anger boiling inside her was gone, replaced by numbing exhaustion. "You're right. I'm through. You're just a monster today."

"You didn't exactly make it difficult."

"Guess I could have used a phone call like the one you got this morning. Say hi to Gail for me and don't tell her how badly I played."

Sarchi took a long shower, dressed, and headed for the parking garage across from the hospital, thinking of her warm bed and a night uninterrupted by her pager.

At the entrance to the garage she paused. Then, as much as she didn't want to see the place again today, she crossed the street and entered the hospital.

Marge was in Drew's room reading to him. Sarchi slipped in unnoticed and stood by the doorway listening to the story, which was about a rabbit family with irresponsible kids who got into all kinds of trouble by not listening to safety rules from their parents. It was advice that would be of no use to a paralyzed boy, and the optimism in the choice of books pulled at Sarchi's heart.

Marge was a good woman, and she obviously loved Drew as much as if he'd been her biological son. Looking at them together, the old guilt lifted its head and whispered in Sarchi's ear. *"It should have been you who took the boy when Carolyn and Bill were killed. You both have Seminoux blood. Whatever the cost, it should have been you."*

Then the voice added a new twist: *"If you had taken him, he might not be sick now."*

At the end of the story, Marge let the little song engineered into the book play for a bit, then put the book down.

"Are you going to stay the night?" Sarchi said, moving to Marge's side.

"Oh, hi. I didn't hear you come in. There's nothing at home for me."

Her answer felt like a rebuke. To walk away from Drew now seemed so wrong. But if she didn't get some rest, she'd be worthless to Drew and the rest of her patients tomorrow. She was so tired, she'd have trouble spelling her name. Maybe if she hadn't played racquetball she'd have the stamina to remain.

"I want to stay, too. I really do. But . . ."

"You don't owe me an apology," Marge said, kindly. "We don't need a symbolic gesture from you. We want you as sharp and alert as you can be. So get out of here."

"Call me at home if there's the slightest change."

"Seems like I was saying the same thing to you a few hours ago. I'll call. Now go."

Sarchi kissed Marge on the cheek, did the same to Drew, and set out once more for her car.

Driving home, she dwelt on her inability to figure out what was wrong with Drew. She then recalled her conversation in the scan room with Koesler. He'd been standing right in front of her, and she didn't press the issue about the MRI. She'd firmly believed it was in Drew's best interests to get one that night, but she'd let Koesler walk away without taking a stand. Right now, she didn't like herself very much.

Sarchi lived barely two miles from the hospital in a newly remodeled forties-era bungalow on a street lined with huge oaks. The clincher in her decision to purchase it was its location across from an estate so heavily wooded, the turn of the century Victorian mansion in its bosom wasn't visible even in winter.

Turning the corner, she realized the Dumpster that had been a neighborhood eyesore for the last three months in the yard of the empty house next door was gone, replaced by fresh sod and a FOR SALE sign. But now the damned thing was in the yard on the *other* side of her house. No rest for the weary.

To swing the purchase of the bungalow on a resident's

salary, she had taken Linda Grainger, another third year resident, in on the deal as a partner and housemate. Linda usually hit Huey's for happy hour and dinner after work, but tonight, her red MR2 was already home.

Getting out of her car, Sarchi smelled the faint odor of Old Spice wafting in from the drum reclamation plant in the field behind the house. The realtor had pointed out that the plant made absolutely no noise, and with the rows of pines along the property line, couldn't even be seen. So they hadn't let its existence affect the deal. But shortly after moving in, they'd found that sometimes you could smell the contents of the containers the plant was reclaiming. In her troubled state, Sarchi saw this as just one more situation she'd mishandled.

Linda was in the kitchen watering Sarchi's miniature rose on the shelf over the sink. Most of the plant's leaves were in the pot, dried and curled.

"Thanks for the effort," Sarchi said, "but I'm afraid even life support wouldn't save it now."

"That's why I don't have plants," Linda said. "They always die. I hate that. I think just before they put them in stores, they change the soil so they'll croak. Guess you saw we're in for another three months of mud and noise on the *opposite* side of us."

"At least they don't work at night."

Linda was about Sarchi's height, also with dark hair that she, too, kept short. But that's where the resemblance ended. Opting for low upkeep, Sarchi wore hers in a boyish cut, swept back on one side, carried gently down to her eyebrow on the other. Feeling that a man's early impression of a woman was influenced at least as much by her hair as her breasts, Linda's hair was always a carefully staged event. And she was a master at makeup, which she wore so skillfully she reminded Sarchi of a television commercial in which the sponsor's product was in color and the rest of the world was in black and white. In short, where Sarchi was viewed by most as merely homespun cute, Linda was generally thought to be a sloe-eyed flamboyant beauty. Tonight, in a form-fitting black dress and heels, pearls at her throat and ears, she certainly looked the part.

"Where are *you* going?" Sarchi asked.

"The Memphis symphony ball." She threw her head back and primped her hair. "Please don't hate me because I'm popular."

Actually, Sarchi couldn't have handled being popular if it meant dressing like that. If L.L. Bean or Lands' End didn't sell it, Sarchi didn't own it. Although she possessed legs that would make even a bishop want to sneak a look, she usually covered them with jeans, twills, or chinos. The rest of her closet was taken up by sweaters, knit pullovers, and simple oxford shirts. Any occasion requiring more than that was probably one that wouldn't interest her. And pearls? Come on . . .

"Who's the guy tonight?" she asked.

Linda wagged a finger at her. "Ah-ah . . . no prying."

"I don't know how you do it."

"You live too closed a life. You have to get out, go places. You can't catch fish in a toilet."

"You think the hospital's a toilet?"

"It's a metaphor, hon. It means to find a man, you have to move among them. Whatever happened to the guy you met last year on that caving trip? He should have been a natural for you. But you haven't mentioned him in months."

"On the trip he seemed fine, but later, his e-mails were so drenched in testosterone, I lost interest."

"That doesn't sound so bad."

"Just because I love caves doesn't mean I'm looking for a caveman."

"There's your problem. Your standards are too high. Are these pearls enough? Maybe a pin of some sort . . ."

"You look great."

". . . or a scarf instead of the necklace . . ."

While Linda went off to her room to fidget, Sarchi threw the rose in the wastebasket. She considered hanging around to get a look at Linda's catch of the day but decided instead to head for the bathroom to wash her hair.

Sarchi's father lived alone in the family home in Johnson City, a small town in the northeast corner of the state. The death of her mother six years ago had affected his mind, so he had embarked on a grand plan to revisit every place in the world the two of them had ever been together, starting with Sarchi, Costa Rica, their first destination outside the United States and where they thought Sarchi had been conceived. His quest covered so much territory he still hadn't completed the circuit. When Carolyn died barely a year after her mother, he began to spend much of his time between trips writing down, in minute detail, every memory he had of his two lost angels; what they wore on this occasion, what they said, and how they said it. It was practically all he talked about and except for his trips, all he thought about. Whenever he found his memory about a particular point fuzzy, he turned to Sarchi for help. To facilitate that, he had provided her with a monster computer with far more capacity than she needed to answer his frequent e-mail messages.

Initially believing he would be her only e-mail contact, she soon discovered it was a fine way to keep in touch with former classmates as well as the friends she'd made in the Cave Research Foundation.

After washing her hair, she checked to see if anything had come in during the last thirty-six hours. As expected, she found a caver's digest and a note from her father. There was also a message from a former medical school classmate, announcing her engagement. A month earlier Sarchi had accepted an offer to join a team being put together to explore some new leads in Kentucky's Flint Ridge Cave System the following February. Her regular workouts in the weight room were partly to ensure that she'd be physically up to the task. The last e-mail message was from the leader of that expedition asking if she had any suggestions for replacing someone who had dropped out.

Too tired to deal with any of this, she turned off the computer, changed into her pajamas, and climbed into bed with a pediatric medicine text to see if she could get any new ideas about Drew's condition. She read about six lines then fell asleep, still sitting up with the book in her lap.

The next two days were awful. Twelve hours after Gilbert Klyce completed the regimen of antibiotics he was being given for the pneumonia that had initially brought him to the hospital, he spiked a fever. The cause couldn't be his Staph infection kicking up because he was still receiving vancomycin. While waiting for results from the blood and urine cultures, his neutrophil count tripled. Then they got the bad news: his cultures came back positive for yeast. Now he had a damn *Candida* infection, which probably meant six more weeks in the hospital while he was treated for *that*.

Drew didn't get any worse, but the blood and spinal fluid cultures grew nothing, and no botulism organisms were found in a stool sample. His blood chemistry and differential leucocyte count remained normal, and a series of nerve conduction studies indicated that his peripheral nerves were functioning properly.

On the fourth day after Drew's admittance, Mel Pierce, the reining neurology guru on staff discovered that Drew had developed a bilateral Babinski sign, a splaying and elevation of the toes when the sole of the foot is stroked. This classic indicator of a lesion in the major motor pathways of the central nervous system prompted Pierce, in part, to schedule a PET scan, an additional noninvasive way of looking at the brain. Because it can show by different colors which parts of the brain are metabolically abnormal, everyone hoped this scan would finally provide the clue that had so far eluded them.

It didn't. Nor did Pierce contribute anything to justify his reputation. The case quickly became a cause célèbre in the hospital, and a steady procession of residents and attendings made their way past Drew's bed. But no one had a decent explanation for Drew's condition.

In her years of caving, sitting hundreds of feet underground in huge limestone chambers with her carbide lamp creating ghostly shadows on the alien landscape, Sarchi had often felt her mind expand. More then once in such surroundings she had seen the answer to some perplexing personal problem. Unable to figure out what was wrong with Drew, she had even tried sitting in her darkened bedroom with only a small lamp illuminating her huge poster of the candelabra room in Lechugilla, the fabulously beautiful cave in New Mexico. But nothing came of it.

Late on the seventh day, when Sarchi returned to Drew's room after an hour spent on the asthma ward, Marge stood and said, "I heard from my insurance company today. They won't pay to keep Drew here any longer. He has to go to a clinic in New Orleans that's had a lot of success with cases like this."

Sarchi was embarrassed at her performance on the case and was relieved that the spotlight was about to shift off her, especially if it meant Drew would get help.

"I wonder if . . ." Marge faltered.

"What?"

"I know it's a lot to ask, but would you . . . Could you go to New Orleans with me . . . to the clinic and be there while I talk to the doctors? I'd feel much more comfortable with you there."

Considering how badly she'd let Drew and Marge down, there was only one answer Sarchi could give. "Of course I'll go."

8

"The doctor is available now," the nurse said.

Sarchi followed Marge through the door off the waiting room, down a hall, and into a well-furnished office where a white-coated man with coarse features stood as they entered.

Drew had left Memphis for the clinic in New Orleans by medical transport the previous day. Marge had wanted to follow in her car, but Sarchi had convinced her to fly the next day, pointing out that it would take at least eight hours for Drew to reach the clinic, and he would have to be evaluated before there could be any discussion about his treatment. As an inducement to this rational course of action, Sarchi had offered Marge one of the frequent flyer tickets she'd accumulated from her father, who sent them regularly in hopes she'd use one to come home for a visit. To get free, Sarchi had convinced another resident to cover for her.

"I'm Doctor Latham," the man behind the desk said, offering his hand.

Marge shook it and introduced herself. "And this is Doctor Seminoux, she's Drew's aunt and was also his physician in Memphis."

"A pleasure, Doctor," Latham said, taking Sarchi's hand.

He tried to make his face match the cordial tone of his greeting, but Sarchi sensed that he was not pleased to have her there. That wasn't surprising. Considering all the big egos in medicine, he probably believed she was angry at having Drew's case taken from her. Boy, was he mistaken.

Latham waited until they were seated before returning to his chair. "Mrs. Harrison, I'll get right to the point. We've evaluated your son's condition and I'm pleased to say I think we can help him."

Relief spread across Marge's face. Her pent-up anxiety came out in a long sigh, and she lowered her face into her hands. "Thank God." She looked up. "What's wrong with him?"

Latham leaned back in his chair and brought his hands together, steepling his fingers. "It's a condition caused by the malfunction of a small cluster of neurons deep in his brain. They are sending erroneous messages to their many relays, ultimately affecting the motor cortex, the cells where voluntary movement originates."

"What causes it?" Marge asked.

"We don't know."

"How is it treated?"

"We send a small instrument into the brain and sever the outflow fibers from those cells."

Sarchi stiffened in her seat, reminded of the ill-conceived notion popular years ago that prefrontal lobotomies were an acceptable way of treating certain personality disorders. In those, too, they'd simply cut fibers, often producing effects worse than the original condition. But Latham's work had obviously passed scrutiny by the bean counters at Marge's HMO. He must be getting patients back on their feet in a functional state. But, of course, a lot of the people working for HMOs were morons.

"Sever . . . you'll be cutting on my son's brain?"

"In a very precise way and in only a tiny area."

"Is this a complete cure?"

Latham leaned forward and folded his hands on the desk. "The odds for significant improvement are very high. Some of the cases we've treated have shown complete recovery within weeks after treatment. Others show some residual deficits that improve over time, often resolving completely. In a small percentage, minor deficits persist."

"Is there any way to predict what will happen with Drew?" Marge asked.

"Unfortunately, no."

Sarchi had planned to keep quiet during this session, but she now found it impossible. Latham was treating a disease no one at her home hospital could even diagnose. This was something she needed to know more about. "Forgive me for interrupting, Doctor, but to further my own education, could you tell me exactly what cells are malfunctioning?"

That look again—veiled and brief, but unmistakable. He didn't welcome the question.

"Doctor Seminoux . . . is it?"

Sarchi nodded.

"You seem young to be a practicing pediatrician."

"I'm a third-year resident."

Latham smiled. "I see, still in the fold."

Sarchi felt he was stalling. She half expected him to ignore her question, but then he said, "The cells in question are those that form the ansa lenticularis."

It was a term she vaguely remembered hearing in neuroanatomy a lifetime ago, but she couldn't recall any of the details. And this certainly wasn't the time or place to admit that. Instead, she took a different course. "I'd love to read more about this. Have you written up any of your work?"

"No. There are several papers in draft form, but I've just been too busy to get them out. Now, if you'll pardon me for saying this, we're not here to fill the gaps in your education. We're here to make a little boy better."

Sarchi felt her face flush.

Latham turned his attention to Marge. "The way we work is this: you leave Drew with us for five days, during which we allow no visitation— "

"I couldn't do that," Marge said. "Can't I stay with him?"

"I'm sorry, no. Children are very good at picking up on the anxiety their condition creates in their parents. They do much better emotionally when left entirely in our care. Of course, you may call whenever you like and check on the boy. I'll give you the number. If you leave Drew here today, he'll go home next Wednesday, in all probability very much like he was before this difficulty arose."

He reached in a drawer and brought out a sheet of paper. "We'll need your signature on this surgical release form. There is a clause in there I should call to your attention. By signing, you wave your right to any litigation that might arise from our treatment of your son."

"You mean I could never sue for malpractice?"

"It's an ugly subject to bring up at this point, but we are such a litigious society, we have to protect ourselves. As Doctor Seminoux pointed out by her question, this is a relatively new treatment, and for us to be able to offer it requires the immunity that clause provides.

"In any event, you need time to think. But I already have a great many obligations scheduled in the next few months, so if you do decide to proceed, I must have your decision before the end of the day. Now, why don't you and Doctor Seminoux discuss this and let me know. I don't mean in the next few minutes. In fact . . ." He looked at his watch.

"I have a meeting coming up that will occupy the better part of the next three hours. If it's agreeable with you, let's get together again right here at four-thirty and see where we are. Don't stay in the hospital. It's such a fine day, you should get out to talk."

Before they met with Latham, Sarchi and Marge had visited with Drew in his room at the clinic to reassure him about what was happening. They stopped by his room again briefly, then took Latham's advice and headed for the front entrance.

"What do you think?" Marge asked, stepping off the elevator on the first floor, unaware that someone from Latham's office was now tagging along close enough to overhear Sarchi's answer.

"Do we really have any choice? Latham's is the only treatment your insurance company will pay for. He has to know that, which means, this time he gave us to discuss it is an empty gesture."

"Forget the insurance. If we had complete freedom to choose, would you put Drew in Latham's care?"

"I sure don't like the guy."

"Because of the remark he made about your education?"

"Not just that. This three hours to talk is manipulative."

"Does liking him really matter?"

"No."

"What else?"

"There's nothing to read about his treatment."

"He explained that."

"But only in a very sketchy way. Where are the case re-ports?"

"You heard what he said. He's been too busy to write them up. Isn't that possible?"

"Absolutely."

"Well?"

"I've never heard of this disease and neither has anyone at my hospital, so his treatment of it has to be experimental. Even long-accepted protocols sometimes turn out to have problems. Take Thorotrast, for instance. For years, doctors gave people Thorotrast to increase the detail that could be seen in X-rays. Completely harmless, they said. Now, we know a lot of it ends up in the liver where it remains for the rest of your life and is a factor in liver cancer."

"But this isn't like that. He's not giving Drew any chemicals, and he's done enough of these cases to know what the results are."

"How many *has* he done? We don't know. And how *long* has he been treating these cases? I'll bet he only knows the short-term results. What about ten to fifteen years from now?"

They reached the front entrance and went outside, leaving the eavesdropper behind.

"You haven't answered my first question," Marge said. "If the decision were yours and the insurance wasn't a consider-ation, would you do it?"

There were actually two issues here. One was money, and the other was getting Drew well. It was theoretically possible that somewhere in the world there were other doctors who understood Drew's condition and had a safe and effective treatment that wasn't so experimental. But who were they? Pierce hadn't suggested a name, so he didn't know of any. And he read *everything*. If they didn't go with Latham, Drew would remain paralyzed while they followed other leads and took him to other clinics for evaluation, all of which would eat up money neither Marge nor Sarchi had. More important, the longer Drew remained the way he was, the greater the risk to his life. If only they could feel more secure about Latham. Then, Sarchi had an idea.

"Look, we've got a couple of hours before we meet again with Latham. I've got a friend doing a residency at Charity Hospital here. Why don't we call her and see if she's heard anything about him or knows anyone who has."

This wasn't the only reason Sarchi wanted to make the call. Before leaving Memphis, she'd sent Sharon McKinney, her best friend from med school, an e-mail message saying she'd be in town today and, if there was time, she'd try to contact her.

"There are probably some public phones in the hospital," Marge said. "You go on, I'll wait in the car."

Sarchi went back inside and found the phones. The most direct access to any doctor is through their pager. Fortunately, Sharon had given Sarchi the number of hers by return e-mail.

Sarchi punched in the pager number, waited for instructions, then added the number of the phone she was using. In two minutes, it rang back.

"Sharon, this is Sarchi."

"Obviously, you're in town."

"Across the river in Gretna . . . at the Westbank Medical Center."

"How long will you be here?"

"I'm not sure, maybe just today."

"Can you get free for a bit?"

"Possibly, but listen, do you know anything about a neurosurgeon over here named Latham?"

"I don't, but there are a couple of people here with ties to Westbank. I could ask them."

"I'd appreciate that. We're under a time constraint, so could you do it quickly?"

"Sure. Give me an hour, and then how about we meet at Cafe Dumond?"

"Sounds perfect. See you there."

The weather in New Orleans was much better than what they'd left in Memphis. The sky was cloudless, and the temperature was in the high sixties, minimizing the smell of the carriage horses that lined Decatur along Jackson Square. As usual, the area was barely contained pandemonium.

In the few blocks from the parking lot beside the Jax Building to Cafe Dumond, Marge and Sarchi encountered three little kids keeping the art of tap dance alive, a living statue dressed like a 1920s flapper, and a talented musician playing *My Way* on a sax.

Being the signature stop on most tourist's visit, Cafe Dumond was hopping. They were fifteen minutes early, but Sarchi still scanned the throng looking for Sharon. Not finding her, she and Marge grabbed a table in back, just as the previous occupants were leaving.

"You'll like Sharon," Sarchi said. "She's a lot like you— tough, assertive, which didn't always play well in med school. She's real petite, and her fingers are short. So one day a group of us, including Sharon, are learning how to do proctology exams on a plastic model. But Sharon's fingers couldn't reach far enough into the model's rectum to even touch the prostate. Well, the guy who was supervising this exercise, an evolutionary throwback about six-foot-six and thirty pounds overweight, who didn't think women belonged in medicine, starts ridiculing her about it. I'll never forget her reaction. She didn't cry or get mad, she just looked this guy square in the eye and said, 'Doctor, surely you have observed before this that, like assholes, fingers come in a variety of sizes.'

"It was clear to all of us what she meant, but I don't think he fully got it. Oh, he picked up on the tone, but to this day, I don't believe he knows what she did. He put something in her file about being disrespectful, but she was so good at her work it didn't matter. She finished third in a class of 170. Had an uncanny ability to predict what the exams would stress."

"Didn't you finish second?"

"Well, yeah, but only with Sharon's help."

"I doubt that."

A busboy came and cleaned away the debris from the previous occupants. He was followed by a waiter who was put on hold until Sharon arrived, which she did a few minutes later.

Sarchi and Sharon hugged, then Sarchi introduced her two friends.

Sharon was indeed a small women. She had long red hair with bangs and skin as smooth as Drew's when he was an infant. Her eyes were large and expressive. A strong chin, however, upset the balance.

"I've just been hearing of your exploits during the proctology exercise," Marge said.

Sharon rolled her eyes. "Sarchi always makes more of that than it deserves."

Marge was surprised at Sharon's husky voice.

Noticing that the remaining member of the party had arrived, the waiter returned, and they all ordered the traditional beignets and coffee.

"Sarchi told me a little about why you're here," Sharon said to Marge. "I'm so sorry for your trouble."

Marge acknowledged Sharon's expression of sympathy with a wan smile.

"I guess Latham is your son's doctor?"

"Not quite yet," Sarchi said. "We're supposed to say 'yes' or 'no' in about two hours."

"I talked to the people I told you about," Sharon said. "And I can tell you he's Westbank's prize pony. His service generates about twenty-five percent of the hospital's billables."

"But is he any good?" Sarchi asked.

"I wouldn't think he'd be pulling those numbers if he wasn't." She opened her handbag and reached into it. "I stopped at Tulane on my way here and looked him up in the specialty directory." She unfolded a sheet of paper and handed it across the table to Sarchi.

There were lots of bios on the page, but Sarchi was able to go right to Latham's because Sharon had circled it. "At least he's a board-certified neurosurgcon," Sarchi said, seeing that first. "Good training—a five year residency at Albert Einstein, fellow in neurosurgery at University Hospital in Zurich . . ." Her eyes dropped to the abbreviations of his society memberships. "What's AANS?"

"American Academy of Neurologic Surgery," Sharon said.

"And CNS?"

"Congress of Ncurologic Surgery."

The waiter came and distributed mugs of coffee and hot beignets dusted with powdered sugar to the three women.

"The smell in this place alone has doubled my triglyceride levels," Sharon said, looking at her plate. "Do I really need this?"

"You made that decision when you ordered," Sarchi said.

"Good point." Sharon sampled one of her beignets and washed it down with coffee. "One of life's simple pleasures," she sighed.

"Well, he looks good on paper," Sarchi said. "But did anybody at Charity comment directly on his skills?"

"No. That's the second time you've questioned his ability. Do you have reason to doubt him?"

"He rubs her the wrong way," Marge said.

"If they got rid of every testosterone-driven jerk at Charity, the place would be practically deserted. It's almost an axiom: if it's a man, the better the doctor, the bigger the jerk."

"You and Steve have had another fight?" Sarchi said.

"Am I that transparent?"

"Where's the Windex?"

"If you don't mind, I'd rather not occupy a single neuron thinking about him. Did anybody directly say Latham was skilled? No. Did anybody say he wasn't? Also no."

A certain look crossed Sharon's face.

"You've thought of something?" Sarchi asked.

"The guy who runs our clinical labs, who's actually kind of hunky, used to work in the lab at Westbank. He said

Latham was always ordering PCR reactions on tissue from his patients. But what Latham was looking for was never there. Not once."

"What's a PCR reaction?" Marge asked.

"It's a way to amplify tiny quantities of DNA," Sarchi said. "To the sample you want to test, you add two primers that will bind to different regions of the DNA you're looking for. You throw in the right enzymes and some raw materials and if the DNA in question is there, the piece between the two primers will be made over and over from the raw materials."

"Like stamping out a truckload of gaskets from one mold," Sharon said.

"With PCR you can detect as little as one copy in the original sample." Sarchi said. "The guy who invented the technique won the Nobel prize for it a few years ago."

"And revolutionized biological science," Sharon added.

"Did your friend say what they were trying to amplify?" Sarchi asked.

"He doesn't know. Latham just gave him the primers and told him the size of the product that would be detected if there was a hit. Considering what you've told me about the kinds of cases he handles, I'd guess it's probably a screen for encephalitis virus or something like that, to rule out an infection."

They chatted for a while longer, then Sharon got a page. She called in from the restaurant phone and returned to the table to say she had to get back to Charity.

As Sharon made her way out of the restaurant, Marge said, "Well, what do we tell Latham?"

"I guess we say yes."

"I don't want to leave Drew alone here. Maybe I'll stay at a motel near the hospital."

"I'm having the same feelings, but I've *got* to go home. And you might as well come, too. You didn't bring any clothes."

"I could buy a few things."

"Latham said we couldn't see Drew, so what's the point of staying? You'd have nothing to do but worry. At least if you were home, you'd have your work to think about. And it's really not such a long time."

"I suppose you're right."

"So you'll be coming back to Memphis with me?"

"I guess so."

"Then I need to see if there's a late plane we can take today."

Their waiter directed Sarchi to the phone, and she managed to get them on an eight o'clock flight. They spent the next hour distractedly hitting the antique shops on Royal Street, then returned to the Westbank Medical Center.

Latham took the surgical release form from Marge. "I realize being separated from your son will be difficult," he said. "But you can be sure he'll get the best care possible. And when you next see him, I think you'll be very happy." He pressed a button on his intercom. "Julia, will you come in here please?"

"If you'll go with Julia, she has a few more papers for you to sign."

A nurse who smelled heavily of lavender appeared in the doorway, and Latham gave her the surgical release form for Drew. Sarchi and Marge then followed her to another room.

Across the hall from Latham's office, where the billing was handled, the woman who had eavesdropped on Marge and Sarchi's discussion earlier on their way to the car, and who had overheard both conversations through the thin office door when they'd met with Latham, stepped into the hall and watched them leave. Both attractive women, she thought. Everywhere there were attractive women. But not her . . . oh no, not Lee-Ann.

9

Reaching home after the flight from New Orleans, Sarchi grabbed her neuroanatomy text and read about the ansa lenticularis, the fiber bundle Latham was going to sever to treat Drew. The neural connections involved were so diffuse and complex she didn't learn much.

She woke the next morning to the sound of hammers and the tearing of wood. Looking out the window, she saw a work crew attacking the house next door.

This poor start to the day continued. Upon arriving at work, she discovered that Gilbert Klyce's creatinine levels had gone from .3 to 1.2, meaning that the antifungal drug he was being given for his yeast infection, in combination with the vancomycin he was receiving to combat the MRSA, was damaging his kidneys.

Welcome home.

She responded by cutting the antifungal dose in half and ordering a new set of blood, urine, and tracheal cultures. At the first opportunity she located Mel Pierce, the neurologist Kate had called in on Drew's case, and questioned him about the ansa lenticularis. He patiently explained what it was then went on to say he didn't see how cutting those fibers could have any effect on Drew's condition. This made Sarchi even more apprehensive about Latham.

There had been no equivocation in Latham's statement that Drew's treatment would be complete in five days. So after making sure she could take the time off, Sarchi dipped again into her cache of frequent flyer tickets and scheduled Marge and herself on a flight back to New Orleans the following Wednesday. For the return, she put all her pessimism aside and reserved *three* seats.

By the next morning, Gilbert's creatinine had improved to .9, and his cultures, miraculously, were negative. Fortunately, this was his last day on vancomycin. Over the next three days, his creatinine inched back to normal, and repeat cultures stayed negative. The swelling in his pharynx also subsided to where they were able to remove his trach tube. After consulting with Kate, Sarchi substituted an oral antifungal for the one Gilbert had been receiving intravenously, and she shipped the boy back to Brunswick.

A win for the good guys—or at least a draw.

Marge contacted Latham's clinic daily to check on Drew, then called Sarchi. And every day the message was the same: "Drew is doing well, and everything is proceeding as expected." On Tuesday, the clinic reminded Marge to bring Drew some clothes when she came to pick him up.

The next day Sarchi and Marge left Memphis on an eleven o'clock flight and by one o'clock were walking through the Westbank Medical Center's main entrance.

"I am so scared, I'm shaking," Marge said.

"They've had plenty of opportunity to tell us if anything was wrong and have said nothing. So let's go get him."

Despite her expressed bravado, Sarchi's insides felt like cold dishwater. As instructed, they took the clothes to Latham's waiting room and gave them to Julia, the nurse who smelled of lavender. She smiled and told them it would be a few minutes before Latham could see them. She gave Drew's clothes to another minion in white, who went out the waiting room door carrying them.

Sarchi took a seat to wait, but Marge paced. After a few minutes of that she came over and sat as well.

Sarchi took Marge's hand in hers.

"My palms are sweating," Marge said.

"It's natural."

"Yours aren't."

"I'm a hardened professional."

As they waited, it struck Sarchi that there were no other patients in the room. Considering what Sharon had said about the money Latham was bringing in, the place should have been jammed. Maybe there was another waiting room. Or possibly Latham was making so much on each case, he didn't need volume.

After what seemed like an hour but was actually a much shorter time, the waiting room door opened and the woman who had taken Drew's clothes returned—*with Drew*.

And he was walking—no, *running*—toward his mother.

"Momma, I'm better."

Marge caught Drew in her arms and hugged him so tight he complained.

"I can't breathe."

Marge held him up and covered his face with kisses. Sarchi's eyes grew watery, and she fought to keep from crying openly. "Don't I get a hug?" she said.

Marge handed Drew to her and she kissed him on the cheek and then gently on the small scabs above each eyebrow. Drew pulled his head back and gave Sarchi a serious look. "That's enough kissing for now."

It was one of the most exciting days of Sarchi's life. Drew was cured. All Sarchi's reservations about Latham were gone, washed away in this stunning demonstration of his competence.

"Well, what do you think?" Latham said from the doorway leading to the back.

Latham walked over to Drew and gently rubbed his knuckles against the boy's shoulder. "Hello there, young man. Are you happy to be going home?"

"Are you coming too?" Drew asked.

"No. I have to stay here and work."

"Nuts. We could play with my trains."

Sarchi offered Latham her hand. "Doctor, I'm awed."

"Don't be," Latham said, taking her hand. "I'm sure you do as much for your patients. May I?" He held his arms out for Drew, and Sarchi handed him over.

Latham then turned to Marge. "Mrs. Harrison, these little scabs above each of Drew's eyebrows are where the device we used to guide our instrument into Drew's brain was screwed to his head. I know it sounds terrible, but it really isn't. Those scabs will quickly fall off. Up here. . . ," he gently touched a spot in Drew's hair, "there are two places with metal clips in the skin, where the incisions were made for entry of the instrument."

"There was more than one incision?" Marge asked.

"The brain is bilateral. There was one affected area on each side. Hence two incisions. Some surgeons shave the entire head, but the hair takes so long to grow back I thought you'd prefer this way. The clips should be removed in a week. I'm sure Doctor Seminoux would be happy to take them out. He hasn't been having any headaches, but that wouldn't be unusual. If he begins to have some," Latham reached in the pocket of his white coat and took out a prescription which he handed to Marge, "have this filled."

In Latham's arms, Drew's head suddenly turned to the side, and his mouth gaped open in a grotesque parody of a yawn.

"That's the other thing I need to mention," Latham said. "From time to time, he'll do that. It's a residual behavior related to his illness. It's not uncommon and will probably resolve itself in a few months." He put Drew on the floor. "So, if there are no further questions . . ."

Sarchi and Marge said nothing.

"Then I'll say good-bye."

Sarchi walked by the big Christmas tree that had been set up in the hospital lobby long before any other decorations had appeared in Memphis. As she passed, a woman in street clothes walking in the opposite direction glanced at it and commented to her friend. "I guess now they're gonna make Christmas a permanent holiday."

Abruptly, eyes and a big red mouth appeared out of the

voice-activated tree's branches. And it spoke. "Hello, there. I hope you're havin' a nice day, cause I sure am."

The two women nearly jumped out of their clothes in surprise.

"Would you like to hear a song?" the tree said.

"No, damn it, I wouldn't," the woman who'd activated the tree said.

Smiling, Sarchi headed for the cafeteria, where she picked up a Caesar salad and queued up at the cash register behind Mel Pierce, the neurologist she'd questioned about the ansa lenticularis.

"Doctor Pierce, haven't seen you in a while."

"I've been at a conference in France."

Pierce was in his mid-forties. He had a high forehead, small eyes, and thin lips, a cold face that made it difficult to picture him with a personal life. But then it was hard for Sarchi to imagine *herself* with one.

"How'd your nephew come out at that clinic in New Orleans?" he asked.

"He's cured—running, walking, talking. Except for one small residual tic and a couple of incisions where they made burr holes in his skull, you'd never know any of that happened."

Pierce paid the cashier and waited while Sarchi did the same.

"Could we talk more about this?" Pierce asked. "I know we spoke briefly about it a week ago, but I'd like to hear the details again of the diagnosis and treatment and more about the boy's present condition."

"I'd be happy to tell you what I can."

They found an empty table, and Sarchi related what had taken place over the past few weeks, finishing with a comment on Drew's yawning tic. Pierce was the most intense listener she'd ever encountered. When she finished, he said, "You say this apparent yawn is not held like a real yawn, but is cut short and there's a straining of the muscles?"

"Right. What do you think?"

"This treatment the boy had—has the surgeon written anything about it for publication?"

"Said he's been too busy."

Pierce lapsed into thought, the tines of his fork tapping at his fish. "How long has it been since the boy came home?"

"About a week. I'm taking the clips out of his incisions tomorrow."

"Is the tic changing in frequency?"

"It's about the same as it has been."

"Which is how often?"

"It's variable—maybe five or six times an hour, more if he's excited."

"I don't know if you were aware of it, but that tic is a stereotypical movement associated with Huntington's disease."

Sarchi had missed that but did know HD was a genetically inherited disorder involving degeneration of certain structures of the brain. It was characterized by slow involuntary movements that progressively become more pronounced until voluntary movement becomes impossible. Death inevitably occurs between fifteen and twenty years after onset.

"And I'm sure the boy didn't have HD," Pierce said. "That's one of my particular research interests."

"What are you saying?"

"I'd like to do another MRI on this boy and see what's going on now in his head."

Sarchi was curious enough about that same question to support this proposition when she broached it to Marge, which she did in a phone call to her agency right after lunch.

"Marge, it's Sarchi. When did you want to bring Drew in tomorrow for me to remove those clips?"

There was a pause, presumably while Marge checked her calendar. "How about four o'clock? That way it won't break up the whole day."

"Could we do it at three?"

"If that's better for you."

"I had a talk with Mel Pierce at lunch and he showed a lot of interest in Drew's yawning behavior."

"Interest? What does that mean?"

"He doesn't understand why it should be happening."

"He didn't understand *anything* when he examined Drew earlier."

"He'd like to do another series of scans."

"For what purpose?"

"It might explain why Drew has a tic."

"Do we really care? Doctor Latham said it was going to clear up on its own."

"This would also help Doctor Pierce with his work—make him a better neurologist."

"Forgive me for being so selfish, but I don't care about Doctor Pierce. In the last three weeks Drew has been through enough. Let's just leave him alone."

"Would you do it for me? We can schedule it for tomorrow when I take Drew's clips out."

"My insurance company is not going to pay for another scan."

"Pierce will cover the cost from his research grant."

There was another pause. "Just some scans, nothing more? No needles?"

"I promise."

"Where should I bring him?"

"The resident practice clinic across from the hospital, at three o'clock."

Mel Pierce pointed at the scan on the computer. "There's the explanation for Drew's HD symptoms."

On the screen, Sarchi saw a slightly dense track that marked the course Latham's instrument had followed through Drew's brain.

"He hit part of the caudate nucleus," Pierce said. "The caudate contains the medium spiny neurons primarily affected in HD."

"He hit it? As part of the treatment?" Sarchi asked.

"You said the treatment was to sever the fibers of the ansa lenticularis. I can't tell if the track reaches the ansa, but he definitely hit the caudate on both sides and left a fair-sized lesion."

"So he made a mistake."

Pierce hesitated, apparently weighing his answer. "It's

possible to reach the ansa without going through the caudate. In fact, it's preferable. It all depends on how you set the co-ordinates on your stereotaxic device."

"And he set his wrong?"

Pierce looked at her without speaking, then said, "In my opinion he made a mistake."

10

"Latham told us Drew might be left with some residual behavioral deficits and that they would probably disappear within a few months," Sarchi said. "But if Drew's problem was caused by a mistake, Latham's assurance means nothing."

"I agree," Pierce replied.

"Is Drew going to have this thing the rest of his life?"

"It's hard to say. The brain is very malleable in children. In time, it could fully resolve. But it's just as possible it won't. I wish I could say the odds were distinctly in Drew's favor, but I can't. We'll just have to wait and see."

The thought that Drew might go through his whole life maimed was horrifying to Sarchi. Kids were so cruel. He'd be taunted mercilessly about it. Drew the spaz. "Hey spaz, we're over here, why are you lookin' that way?" "Better close your mouth spazoid, or somethin' will fly into it."

He'd be the last one picked for baseball or basketball, *if* he could even play those games. What kind of work could he find? Would he be limited to occupations where no one could see him, like some subterranean animal? And could he ever find love? Or would he be so damaged emotionally by the re-actions of people to his problem that he would become inaccessible to affection . . . never giving a woman a chance to know him and to love him. The more she thought about it, the angrier she got.

She motioned for Marge to join her and Pierce in the control room, then looked at the scanner tech. "Will you entertain the boy for a few minutes while I speak with his mother?"

"I can do that."

Marge stepped into the room. "What did you see?"

"Latham screwed up. He damaged a part of Drew's brain that would never have been at risk if he'd done the operation properly."

"But Drew is cured."

"The yawning tic wouldn't be happening if he'd been more careful."

"Latham said it would go away." Marge looked at Pierce.

"The brain in children is very malleable," Pierce said. "Meaning that it can adjust much better to insult than the adult brain. There's no way to say for sure what will happen, but I agree that, in time, the tic could disappear."

"If it doesn't, you could have the basis for a malpractice suit," Sarchi said.

"This subject gives me the chills," Pierce said. "So I'm gonna leave you two alone to discuss it."

They let Pierce go, then Marge said, "Considering what Latham did for Drew, I hardly think he deserves a malpractice action. Besides, I signed a form waving the right to sue."

"I'm not sure that would hold up in court."

"You sound like you want me to sue."

"I just want what's best for you and Drew."

"Even Pierce agreed that the yawn would go away in time."

" '*Could* go away' is what he said." Not wanting to upset Marge, Sarchi decided not to resurrect the entire conversation she'd had with Pierce before Marge joined them.

"Then what's the rush?" Marge said. "Let's wait and see what happens."

In a Westbank mall parking lot, Latham pulled up beside a low-slung black sports car but didn't get out. He'd been acting uncharacteristically jovial all morning, and now from her own car Lee-Ann saw why.

The door of the sports car opened and a striking strawberry blonde wearing a shiny pewter raincoat over a creme colored turtleneck and slacks got out. She walked to the passenger side of Latham's Caddy and got in. Through the rear window of the Caddy, Lee-Ann saw them meet briefly in a kiss, then Latham put the car in gear and headed for the nearest exit to the street.

Trollop. Whore.

The woman was obviously low-bred and easy. She'd probably spread her legs for any man who'd buy her a meal.

But she was also beautiful. It was always the same, the beautiful women get everything. And there was nothing you could do about it if you had bad genes. She'd thought of plastic surgery but knew too many horror stories of operations that went sour, leaving the hopeful patient worse off.

What would it be like to walk past a man and be so attractive he would turn and watch you walk away? Well, don't worry about it, Lee-Ann, cause you ain't ever gonna have that experience.

What she'd just seen showed her that she'd been right all along. Latham was not worth her love. He was a whoremonger and needed to be punished. But she couldn't set it up like the last time.

After she'd arranged to meet Greta Dunn to expose him, she'd felt like a Judas. She'd still wanted him hurt, but the prospect of being so directly responsible had made her ache inside. There had to be a better way. A few minutes later, she thought of one.

She was caught up on all of Latham's billing, and his next operation wasn't until the day after tomorrow. Even so, she drove back to the office, where she found Julia on the phone with the father of an incoming patient.

When Julia was finished, Lee-Ann said, "Where are the admitting records for Drew Harrison? I need to check something in them."

Julia went to a bank of file cabinets and found the records, which like those for most of Latham's kids was quite an armful.

"Is he back from lunch yet?" Lee-Ann asked.

"He said not to expect him before three."

The image of Latham writhing and sweating on top of his whore flooded Lee-Ann's vision.

Julia noticed the hard set to her face. "What's wrong? Did you have an appointment with him?"

"Oh, do I need an appointment now to talk to him?" Lee-Ann snapped. She turned and stormed out. In her black mood, she decided she had never really liked Julia either.

Lee-Ann took Drew's records to her office and plunked them onto her desk. After a few minutes of staring hot rivets at Latham's closed office door, she began searching the records for a readable signature.

Finding one a few minutes later, she turned to her computer and logged onto the Internet, well aware that this could take all afternoon and even then might not produce anything.

She began by entering the URL four11.com, which would allow her access to 6.5 million e-mail addresses.

Forty-five minutes later, she emitted a small grunt of satisfaction as her search paid off. She jotted Sarchi's address on a scrap of paper, put it in her wallet, and left for the day.

"Anyone want to see a raging case of triple scabies?" Sarchi asked, coming into the hall of the outpatient clinic where all the residents worked half a day each week. "No takers? Where's your spirit of inquiry?"

"Ah heard those bugs can jump halfway 'cross a room," drawled Dave Grant, a second year resident from Houston.

"Well, sure," Sarchi replied. "I wouldn't show you the case unless you had quick reflexes." She turned to her attending, Kate McDaniels, who had just walked in. "Must be something in the air. I don't think we've had a single no-show today."

"I've picked up a bit of news that might interest you," Kate said.

"Really? What about?"

"The position of chief resident for next year. Koesler's made his first cut. It's between you and Rachel Moore."

"She'd make a good one."

"Don't be so damned agreeable to defeat," Kate said sharply. "There's nothing wrong with ambition."

"I just don't want to get too used to the idea when there's still doubt about the outcome."

"Hell, enjoy the prospect. Life isn't about arrival. It's about travel. And this is a scenic view out the window. What does it hurt to take a look? Besides, I also heard—and you didn't get this from me—that Koesler's leaning distinctly in your direction."

Without that last comment, Sarchi might not have taken Kate's advice. But having heard it, she worked the rest of the afternoon with a renewed sense of purpose and a warm glow of satisfaction in her belly.

Today had been Gail Lanza's day off from the Campbell Clinic, and she had spent part of it making her famous seven-layer lasagna. Sarchi was aware of this because Carl had invited her to come over at seven for dinner. Carl was allergic to the tannins in red wine, and Gail didn't like white. So on her way home Sarchi dropped by Buster's liquors and picked up a bottle of each.

The crew working on the house next door regularly showed up at first light. Thankfully, though, they were usually gone by the time Sarchi got home, as they were tonight. So far, the place looked worse for their efforts.

She paused on the porch to collect the mail and went inside. Sorting through what had come, she found nothing with her name on it but wastebasket fodder. Linda, however, had received an interesting Orvis catalog, which she briefly thumbed through before putting on Linda's pile.

The major order of business before heading to the Lanza's for dinner was a long, hot bath. Of less importance but still on the list was checking her e-mail. Accustomed to doing many things at the same time, she flicked on the computer so it could boot up while she started the water for her bath.

Returning to the computer a few minutes later, she turned

on the flashmail option and waited while the modem dialed her server. The connection was quickly made and the subject line of an e-mail message appeared in the flashmail box while the message itself was downloaded for later reading. Often she could tell just from the subject line who a message was from. This one was obviously a reply to a question she had asked the guy setting up the Flint Ridge cave expedition.

The next message was clearly from Dad. While it was being downloaded, the mail icon remained active, indicating there was at least one additional message in the pipeline.

A few seconds later, the subject line for that message rolled across the screen: "DREW HARRISON."

Sarchi's attention sharpened. How peculiar. Who would be sending her e-mail about Drew? It couldn't be Marge. She never communicated with Sarchi by computer.

The mail icon darkened, indicating there were no further messages. Eagerly, Sarchi waited for the server to disconnect. Following that, she opened the file folder containing the downloaded mail and double clicked on the "Drew Harrison" message. When the file opened, she was rocked by what she saw:

Things are not what they appear at the Latham Clinic. If you haven't asked yourself why Drew has a yawning tic, do so. To help you with the answer, visit Raymond and Regina Stanhill in Clinton Corners, New York, tel (914) 555-3810. Listen carefully to what they say and think about what you see and hear. Don't ignore the beginning of it all.

11

Sarchi sat dumfounded, wondering what this message could mean and who could have sent it. The return address bore no name, just six numbers and four letters that didn't spell anything. From the bathroom, the sound of running water made it hard to think. In a daze, she went to the tub and turned off the faucets.

Returning to the computer, she clicked on the *reply* box and typed, "Who are you? And who are . . ."

She brought the original e-mail message to the front and checked the names of the couple mentioned. Her memory freshened, she brought the "reply" box forward and typed, "Raymond and Regina Stanhill? "

After adding her own name at the bottom, she clicked the "send later" box, then called up "flash session" and sent the message on its way. As it departed, she wished she'd also asked how her mystery correspondent knew her e-mail address.

With her reply sent, Sarchi sat reflecting on the possibility that it could be hours or days before she heard back. Or, maybe, she'd *never* hear. If the author had wanted to be identified, they'd have signed the message.

Raymond and Regina Stanhill were names she'd never

heard before. She reopened the original message with the Stanhill's number and reached for the phone.

While it rang in Clinton Corners, she tried to figure out what she was going to say. As it turned out, she didn't have to worry about that, because she got only their answering machine.

If she hadn't been going out for the evening, and it wouldn't have required the Stanhills to make a long distance call, she would have left her name and number. Instead, she simply hung up.

Usually when she soaked in the tub, Sarchi made a point of allowing her mind to dwell on nothing but the sensation of soothing hot water against her skin. But tonight she might as well have been dressed and sitting at the kitchen table, because she couldn't stop thinking about that enigmatic message: "All is not as it appears . . ."

What could that mean? Did this person know Latham had accidentally hit Drew's caudate nucleus during his operation? Had he made the same mistake on the Stanhill's child? And what if he had? What would she do about it? What *could* she do about it? Why had this landed in *her* lap?

The questions just kept coming. At dinner she tried to hold up her end of the conversation, but the evening was punctuated by many awkward periods of silence.

The first thing she did when she got home was to head for the phone and try the Stanhills again. This time a man answered.

"Is this Raymond Stanhill?"

"Yes," he said, warily.

She still hadn't planned what she was going to say, so what came out was entirely extemporaneous. "I'm Doctor Seminoux, a pediatrician in Memphis. One of my patients is a boy who was treated for a paralytic disorder by Doctor Latham in New Orleans."

At this point, it seemed unwise to reveal her suspicions that Latham had botched Drew's operation. Instead, she said, "It was such a puzzling disorder and so new to me I'm trying to learn more about it."

"Doctor, you don't know how good it is to hear from

you," Stanhill said, his voice now friendly. "Our daughter, Stephanie, was treated by Doctor Latham a month ago, and what he did for her was absolutely incredible. When she went to him, she was almost totally paralyzed. Now, she's nearly back to normal."

Nearly back to normal. Had Latham inadvertently damaged their daughter's caudate nuclei too? "Are you saying your daughter has residual effects?"

"Yes. Latham said it would probably clear up eventually, but after a month there's been no improvement. Latham is a fine man and a great doctor, but frankly, we're becoming concerned about this and have been wanting to talk to other parents with children who have had the treatment to see what their experiences have been. We asked Latham for some names, but he said it would be a violation of doctor-patient confidentiality to give them to us. We asked him to pass our name along to some of the other parents with an invitation to contact us and he agreed. But so far, we haven't heard from anyone until now. Did *he* give you our name?"

"Not exactly." Afraid he might follow up on that point, Sarchi quickly changed the subject. "This residual effect—it makes Stephanie appear to be yawning?"

"No. It's an involuntary movement of her right shoulder, sort of like she's shrugging. It goes on fairly constantly. Then sometimes her whole arm will lash out."

Sarchi was shocked. Since Pierce had identified Drew's tic as a characteristic symptom of Huntington's disease, she had been reading up on the disease in any spare moment she could find. In that reading, she'd encountered a discussion of how HD tics differed from other movement disorders. One point that had stuck in her mind was how HD tics of the limbs generally involved the hands and fingers and the forearm. Stephanie's movements sounded more like those seen in a condition known as ballismus, a disorder not generally associated with damage to the caudate.

"Tell me about your daughter's symptoms when she was sick."

Though he was probably only a layman, Raymond provided her with a surprisingly detailed account of Stephanie's condition, even down to the absence of tendon reflexes below the neck. In all respects, her condition mirrored Drew's.

"The boy you mentioned," Stanhill said, "he came out of his operation with a yawning disorder?"

Without thinking, Sarchi blurted out, "Mr. Stanhill, I'd like very much to see your daughter."

"We'd like to talk to you as well. But how?"

Sarchi's mind grappled with the same question. How? Her day off was near. "I'll come to Clinton Corners the day after tomorrow. When would it be convenient for us all to get together?"

"Since you're the one who's traveling, we'll do it at your convenience."

"Let me check on flights and get back to you. But just exactly where is Clinton Corners?"

Stanhill told her they lived about two hours by car north of New York City. Sarchi called Northwest Airlines and made reservations for an early morning flight two days hence that would put her into Kennedy at 10:10. To be sure her day wouldn't be rushed, she booked the latest possible flight home. She then called Raymond Stanhill back and set up a one-thirty meeting. Afterward, she sat by the phone for a long time, worried about where this was headed.

The next day, she went to her attending's office to let her know she'd be gone. "Kate, I need to be away tomorrow. Jim Hartley will cover for me."

"Nothing wrong I hope."

Given that opening, Sarchi laid the story out for Kate. When she finished, Kate looked concerned. "Just what do you predict will be the outcome of all this?"

"I haven't thought that far ahead. But it looks like this guy Latham may be making a lot of mistakes during his operations. He certainly did with Drew and maybe with this girl in New York. That's probably what the anonymous e-mail I got was trying to tell me."

"What makes you think mistakes were made?"

"Pierce said he didn't have to go through the caudate to get to the site he was going to lesion."

"Maybe Latham didn't tell you everything. A caudate lesion might be part of the treatment."

"That's not what he said. And Stephanie, the girl in New York, has what sounds like a fundamentally different kind of tic than Drew has. If damage to the caudate is part of the treatment, why is her tic different?"

"Let's assume you're right and Latham *has* made mistakes. What would you do about it?"

"I don't know."

Kate looked hard at Sarchi. "You should think very carefully about this. You're a fine doctor, one of the best I've seen at this stage of your career. I'd hate to see you jeopardize your future.

"If you were to initiate an action against Latham, there are many in our profession who would view that as an act of treason. Don't misunderstand me, I'm not saying that's my opinion. It's merely something you need to consider. There was a time when you could practice medicine alone, but now, with the cost of malpractice insurance so high, a young person can't do it by themselves. You'll need a group behind you. And they'll all want a team player. It may not seem like it, but medicine is a small community. Cross the brotherhood and you're marked."

These were chilling words, but certainly nothing new to Sarchi. For years she'd avoided any confrontation with her superiors that would label her a troublemaker. As a medical student, she'd heard one particular resident make so many crude comments about his patients she couldn't count them, but she'd done nothing about it. And she'd ignored every personally demeaning insult that came her way, including that horrible day in her medicine clerkship.

She'd requested clarification on a question the attending had asked her on morning rounds, and he'd ridiculed her in front of everyone, wondering aloud if she'd gotten into medical school by sleeping with the admissions committee.

Burning with embarrassment and anger, she'd held her tongue, telling herself over and over: "Do not respond."

And she hadn't.

She'd believed she was simply being smart. But with all

that had happened recently, her behavior now just seemed like a character flaw.

"Team player . . ." Sarchi said in a small voice. "This isn't a football game. We're talking about people's lives."

"Suppose he did make a mistake. Who hasn't? In addition to what I've already said, consider the good Latham does. If it weren't for him, Drew would likely still be paralyzed, because we sure as hell didn't know what to do for him. And there's also the Stanhills' child and who knows how many others he's helped. Just think ahead before you react."

Sarchi left Kate's office unsure of what to do. Something was wrong at Latham's clinic. Could she ignore that and look the other way just to avoid personal risk?

It *was* true though, Latham had done a remarkable amount of good in treating Drew and Stephanie. And probably a lot of other kids. But was the problem just mistakes? That anonymous message had said all is not as it appears at the clinic. She hadn't mentioned it to Kate, but that sounded like more was involved than mistakes. In any event, her travel arrangements were made, and she'd already talked Hartley into covering for her. What harm could come from simply visiting the Stanhills?

She hadn't counted on snow. It had been falling heavily in New York since early morning, a heavy white cascade that reduced visibility to fifteen yards at best. And traffic was crawling, so the hour and twenty minutes she'd added to Raymond Stanhill's estimate of the time it would take to reach their home from the airport was quickly consumed.

Ahead on the right, through the driving snow, she saw a convenience store. Should she call and let them know she'd be late? Deciding she didn't want to waste the time and believing that when she didn't show, the Stanhill's would surely realize she'd been delayed by the weather, she stayed on the road.

A half mile farther on, the brake lights of the car immediately ahead of her flared, and its back wheels fishtailed. Sarchi tapped her brakes and came to a safe stop. Taken by surprise, the guy behind her hit his brakes hard and went into a slide. Through the back window she could see wide-eyed fear on his face and his hands spinning the steering wheel. She braced for a hit, but at the last minute he navigated to her right, sliding past on the shoulder. Five cars up the road, the one who'd had caused all this completed a left turn, and the procession once more got under way.

It took a lot of concentration to drive in this kind of weather. But a part of her mind still wandered, fancifully imagining that the snow was a plot to keep her from reaching the Stanhills. Despite the hallucinatory nature of this thought, the weather increased her determination to examine their daughter.

Fifteen minutes later, the snowfall lessened and she found herself in a region that hadn't been hit as heavily as the area around the city. The flow of traffic gradually picked up speed, and she began to make much better time. For all the difficulties she'd encountered, she arrived at the Stanhill's driveway only forty-five minutes late.

They lived in a wonderful two-story house of classic Georgian design with so many multipaned windows that if the mullions weren't snap-ins, they'd take a month to wash. Judging from all the fresh tire tracks in the driveway, the snow hadn't kept the Stanhill's from getting out. She pulled up behind a silver Lincoln Town Car, killed the engine, and stepped into air sharp as a knife's edge.

The industrial-strength snowstorm that had hindered her earlier had faded to a few drifting crystals glinting in the bright afternoon sun. Except for a well-trod path on the sidewalk leading to the porch, the yard was covered in an unblemished white quilt that made Sarchi think of Latham and how the good he did seemed to be covering something bad. When she stepped up on the porch, a man in a gray suit opened the door before she even rang the bell.

"Doctor Seminoux?"

"Sorry I'm so late . . ."

"Yes, yes, the weather. We heard it's been horrible south of here. Come in, come in."

Sarchi stepped inside.

"We never have snow this early," the man said, shutting the door behind her.

"It's been that kind of year in Memphis, too. Not snowy, but cold."

"My wife and Stephanie are in the back. May I take your coat?"

With his large glasses and pronounced chin, Raymond Stanhill reminded her of Garrison Keillor of *Prairie Home Companion* fame. While he put her coat in the hall closet, her attention wandered to a small oil painting of two rabbits chewing a lettuce leaf. Under it was a long table bearing dozens of flower pots holding the most realistic fake vegetable collection she'd ever seen—carrots and asparagus spears standing upright, a cauliflower, a big artichoke, snap beans, red peppers, all highly original. If Regina Stanhill was responsible for this whimsical scene, Sarchi liked her already.

"Come on back," Raymond said, leading the way.

She followed him down the hall and past a room in which she caught a glimpse of the mounted head of a buck deer with a shotgun displayed across its antlers. Hanging from the fireplace mantel like Christmas stockings were several stringers of carved fish. Had to be Raymond's study. He hadn't struck her at all as an outdoorsman, just another example of things not being what they seem.

They emerged from the hall into a large, high-ceilinged room where snow-reflected light pouring in from multiple sets of French doors and tall windows was warmed by rugs and walls of summer yellow. A woman in a yellow skirt and pale yellow blouse was standing with her hands on the shoulders of a beautiful little girl whose long blond hair was held back from her face with a barrette. The girl was wearing a purple polka-dot skirt and white blouse under a green sweater vest decorated with colorful lady's hats. The only discord in this harmonious scene was the girl's right shoulder, which was in constant motion.

The woman stepped toward Sarchi and offered her hand. "Doctor Seminoux, I'm Regina Stanhill. We're so glad you've arrived safely."

Tall and blond, Regina was a woman who by careful attention to her hair, makeup, and clothing maximized her assets.

"And this is Stephanie." Regina turned and held her hand out to the child, who eagerly came over and looked up at Sarchi. "I'm five. I'll be six in . . ." She looked at Regina.

"Three months," Regina said. "Doctor, can I get you anything? Coffee, tea? Are you hungry?"

"I ate at the airport."

"Let's sit down," Raymond suggested.

After Sarchi had taken a seat, Stephanie came over to her and perched on the edge of a small leather trunk that served as an end table.

"Where do *you* live?" Stephanie asked. She had lovely gray eyes and only the barest indication above her brows where the stereotaxic device had been screwed to her skull.

"I live in Memphis, Tennessee. Do you know where that is?"

Stephanie put her hands on her hips, leaned forward, and smiled, showing her little teeth. "No."

Sarchi held her palm up and pointed to the tip of her middle finger. "This is where you live. And I live way down here." She pointed at the end of her life line.

Stephanie looked into Sarchi's eyes, then postured again. "That's ridiculous. People can't live on other people's hands."

Stephanie's shoulder shrugged again, but this time her entire arm danced to the side.

"That's what I was telling you about on the phone," Raymond said. "It happens about once every twenty minutes."

"Do any of these movements occur while she's asleep?"

"I'm sure they don't," Regina said. "I know, because sometimes I just watch her sleep, wishing she was the way she . . ." Regina's eyes misted and she bit her lip.

"Stephanie, can you touch your nose with this hand?" Sarchi pointed to the child's affected arm.

"Anybody can do that," Stephanie said.

"Some can't."

Stephanie brought her hand up and touched her nose with ease. "I told you."

"Can you do it with your eyes closed?"

Stephanie repeated the maneuver, hitting the target with precision. This showed that she not only retained voluntary control over the affected limb, but the circuits for sensing position of the arm and hand in space were intact.

Sarchi reached out and gently stroked Stephanie's affected limb below the sleeve of her dress.

Stephanie giggled. "That tickles."

Sarchi stroked the girl's forearm near the wrist. "Can you feel it here, too?"

"Yes. Can I tickle you now?"

"If you like." Sarchi unbuttoned the sleeve of her blouse and pushed it up her arm. Grinning, Stephanie ran her little finger lightly down Sarchi's skin. Sarchi gave an exaggerated shiver. "Please, no more."

"Don't you want to see me do this?" Stephanie raised her affected hand and touched her thumb with each of the fingers on that hand, another standard neurological test.

"Where did you learn that?"

"From the doctors who made me better when I was sick. I couldn't move. It was terrible. They shaved some spots on my head while I was asleep. Want to see?"

"Could I?"

Stephanie removed her barrette, tilted her head toward Sarchi, and parted her hair. "Can you see the spots? They'll grow in eventually."

Sarchi did indeed see the two shaved areas, directly opposite each other, *and in a distinctly different place than they were on Drew's head.*

12

If two kids have the same disorder, and one can be cured by a lesion in the ansa lenticularis, it follows that the other would require a lesion in the same place. So why were Stephanie's scalp wounds farther back than Drew's were? Sarchi said nothing to the Stanhill's about this, mostly because she didn't know what it meant. Their location, however, reaffirmed a decision she'd made when she'd talked to Pierce about Stephanie before leaving Memphis.

"Doctor, do you need Stephanie anymore?" Raymond asked.

"Perhaps later."

"Stephie, go to your room now and play," Raymond said.

"Do I have to?"

"Stephanie . . ."

The tone in which he said her name sent her scurrying. When she was gone, Raymond said, "What do you think, Doctor? Will that odd movement in her arm ever go away?"

The arrival of this moment had posed a problem from the time Sarchi had told Raymond she was coming. He thought she'd bring answers, but all she carried were questions. It didn't feel good to be so deceitful, but the circumstances had left her with little choice. For now though, she didn't have to admit anything.

"It's too soon to say. I'd like to get her an MRI—it's something like an X-ray . . ."

"We know what it is," Raymond said. "God knows, she's had enough of them. Why do you want that?"

"Just to see what things look like in her brain now that some time has passed since the operation."

Thankfully, that answer seemed to satisfy him.

"We won't have to get permission from your insurance company. There's a neurologist in Memphis who has a large program to study movement disorders in children, and he's agreed to let us charge the study to his grant."

"So after you see the MRI results you'll know better what Stephanie's prognosis will be?" Regina asked.

"I hope so."

"We won't have to take her to Memphis, will we?" Raymond asked.

"We can do it here, at whatever hospital did them before. I'd also like copies of the scans that were done before she was treated. Would you release those to me?"

"Of course. When do you want to schedule the new ones?"

"I'd like to get them done today if possible. Otherwise, you'll have to send them to me. If you'll give me the phone number of the hospital, I'll set it up."

"It's in my study."

Raymond rose to get the number, but Sarchi stopped him.

"Before we do that, there are a couple of things I'd like to discuss." She certainly wasn't going to tell them about her anonymous e-mail message, but the last admonition on it— "Don't ignore the beginning of it all"—was on her mind. "I'd like to hear how Stephanie's paralysis began."

"It was a Wednesday," Regina said. "I remember because it was the last day I had to get out a marketing survey I was working on, and I was afraid I'd be late picking Stephie up at her day care. They're very strict about pick-up time. For every minute past five-thirty, they charge you ten dollars, and you have to pay right then. But I made it with about two minutes to spare."

"When you picked her up, did she seem normal?"

"Perfectly—talkative, energetic, just my usual Stephie. I stopped at our favorite bakery, picked up some French bread, and drove home. Ray got in about seven as usual—he works in New York City—and we had dinner."

"You all ate the same things?"

"Yes, fish and a spinach casserole. We had some wine, but of course Stephie didn't."

"And there were still no signs of weakness or difficulty standing?"

"She was completely normal. She even helped me set the table. After dinner, Ray and I watched TV awhile, and Stephie played with her dolls. Then, just before bedtime, I read her a story. I was sitting in the rocker in her room and she was in my lap." Regina's eyes misted again.

"She was pointing at the pictures in the book, and we were discussing the story. By the time I'd finished, she'd apparently nodded off, except she wasn't asleep, she was . . ."

Sarchi's brow furrowed. Regina's story was much like the one Marge told about Drew when *he* got sick—both kids normal all evening, both suddenly falling ill while being read to.

"Did anyone ask the day care if Stephanie had hit her head or fallen down or had anything unusual happen to her either the day before or during the day she became ill?"

"That same afternoon, a bratty kid visiting the playground with his mother squirted her in the face with a water gun," Regina said.

"Nothing else?"

"We questioned them pretty hard, but that's all we got."

"How do you think she acquired this thing?" Raymond asked.

"I'd love to know the answer, but I'm afraid it's still a mystery."

Then Raymond finally took the conversation in the direction Sarchi had been hoping to avoid.

"When you first called us, you mentioned that Dr. Latham had also treated a patient of yours . . . a boy, you said. How's he doing?"

"He has a residual problem too."

"But different from Stephie's . . ."

"Yes."

"Why is that?"

"At this point I'm not sure." At least that was the truth.

"Have you done a postoperative MRI on him?"

"We just completed it."

"What did it show?"

This was getting tough. Hoping she didn't look as nervous as she felt, Sarchi said, "We're still evaluating the results. Being able to compare his with Stephanie's will help us understand both sets better." Sarchi moved quickly to a remaining issue she needed to bring up about their daughter.

"In order for Stephanie's new MRI to be useful to the neurologist in Memphis, he asked me to bring him a videotape of her from which he can see for himself the nature of her disorder. Would that be all right? I've got a camera in my bag."

"As long as the tape is only used for medical purposes and Stephie's identity is withheld from everyone but the neurologist," Raymond said.

"I'm sure he'll agree," Sarchi said.

"Would you like to do it now?"

"If it's convenient."

Regina got out of her chair. "I'll get her."

The hospital couldn't do Stephanie's new MRI until the following day. Nor could Sarchi obtain the pre-Latham scans in the time available. She therefore, had to leave New York without either set. As it happened, Pierce was traveling the next day and wouldn't have been around to help read them anyway. All the scans arrived at Sarchi's hospital by Federal Express a little after 4 P.M. the day after her return. Hoping Pierce was back from wherever he'd been, she paged him on a house phone. He returned the call almost immediately, and they agreed to meet in ten minutes in the ER X-ray suite. Wanting to get a quick look at the films before Pierce did, Sarchi picked up the video she'd made of Stephanie and headed for the ER.

During the month since Stephanie's surgery, the tracks of

Latham's lesioning instrument had slowly faded, making the new scans more difficult to interpret than Drew's, so when Pierce showed up a few minutes into her attempts to read them, she was more than ready to turn the job over to him.

"How'd you like New York?" he asked.

"I could have done without the blizzard."

"Let's see what you've got."

"Here's the videotape you asked for, and those are the scans," she said, yielding her chair. "This set is before her treatment; those are after."

Setting the tape aside, Pierce sat down and began his study.

Sarchi found another chair, dropped into it, and waited breathlessly for his analysis. Even though he hadn't done so when he'd looked at Drew's scans, she hoped he'd comment on each one as he viewed it. But again, he worked silently, looking at one and moving to the next, occasionally going back to recheck some feature, his hand pulling at his earlobe.

Sitting there in the darkened room, watching him work at a maddeningly slow pace, the suspense was unbearable. In an attempt to pry some conversation out of him, Sarchi said, "There should be something of interest in those films because—" Pierce silenced her with a raised finger.

Finally, he turned and faced her. "The new films are bizarre. Admittedly, the tracks are fading, but I see no evidence of any attempt to lesion the ansa. Instead . . ." He turned and moved back two films. "See this light area and this one?" He pointed to a pair of spots Sarchi had also noticed when she'd first looked at the scans. "They aren't on the preoperative films."

"Meaning?"

"There's no doubt in my mind Latham damaged the substantia nigra on both sides."

This was bad news for Stephanie. The area Pierce was talking about was the one involved in Parkinson's disease, a disorder in which the afflicted have difficulty initiating voluntary movements and exhibit a characteristic "pill rolling" tremor in their hands. Because all the nigra's work can be done by as few as five percent of its cells, Parkinson's disease ordinarily shows up late in life, only after decades of cell death. Presently, Stephanie showed no such symptoms, probably because the damage there had left her with enough cells to function normally. But since nerve cells cannot replenish their numbers, she now had a much smaller safety margin.

"So the girl may have Parkinson's disease in her future?" Sarchi asked.

"It's not likely to be a problem anytime soon, but after she's grown, her risk will certainly be greater than normal."

"Is there any rationale for lesioning the substantia nigra to treat a paralytic disorder?"

"I can't think of any. In fact, as I mentioned once before, I don't see how lesioning the ansa lenticularis could have had any beneficial effect in these cases."

"I'm sure that's what he said he was doing."

"Makes no sense to me. But he is getting results."

"Aren't you curious about his treatment?"

"Immensely."

"Why not call him and discuss it?"

"Anecdotal conversations on the phone aren't useful. When he publishes, we'll see what he's got."

"Do those lesions explain Stephanie's tic?"

"Not as well as something else I found." He turned back to the films and pointed at another light spot Sarchi too had noticed before he'd arrived. "On this side he also hit the subthalamus. That's the area usually damaged when someone shows the kind of symptoms you said this girl exhibits."

"Ballismus," Sarchi said.

"Exactly."

"Then what's this?" Sarchi pointed to yet another light spot.

"A lesion in the ventrolateral nucleus of the thalamus."

"Christ, he was all over her brain."

"Interestingly, this last one is in an area sometimes intentionally lesioned to *alleviate* ballismus."

Pierce was leading up to something, but Sarchi couldn't see what. "I'm sorry, you'll have to help me."

"It looks to me like this guy intentionally went after the

substantia nigra, but on one side he accidentally hit the sub-thalamus. I don't know whether he knew it when he did it or found out later when the girl showed symptoms of ballismus, but I'll bet that lesion in the ventrolateral nucleus was an attempt at damage control."

"Why did he lesion the nigra?"

"I'm a neurologist, not a fortune-teller."

"He's dangerous isn't he, this guy?"

Pierce shrugged. "It appears he's not as careful as he could be."

"Shouldn't somebody do something about that?"

"There you go again, making me nervous."

"What's the prognosis for this girl's ballismus? Can you say with certainty it'll go away?"

"No."

"And she's now faced with an increased risk for Parkinson's. How can we ignore that?"

"It'll take a little willpower, but I believe I'm up to it. It helps to look at the balance sheet. A girl comes in paralyzed, no one else can do anything for her, and Latham sends her home walking and talking. Occasionally, to accomplish the greater good, surgeons have to cause damage. In removing a malignant tumor, it may be necessary to cause some degree of paralysis."

"But this isn't like that. The damage he did to cause the girl's problems wasn't necessary. Isn't that correct? And likewise, he didn't have to damage Drew Harrison's caudate. In my view, his knowledge about this paralytic disease would be better placed in more competent hands. He needs to let the world in on what he knows, then step back and let more careful surgeons handle things."

"That's not gonna happen."

"Not if we turn our heads."

"Instead, you'd rather we put them on the block."

"You're established. You can't be hurt."

"No? Say a close friend of Latham's is the primary reviewer of my next grant renewal. Latham drops a word in his shell-like ear and I get hammered at study section."

"One biased opinion could put your funding at risk?"

"The word is politics. Become familiar with it."

"What do I tell Stephanie's parents? They're expecting a report from me."

"There's nothing to be gained by telling them the truth. The girl may never develop Parkinson's, so why compound their problems by raising the issue?"

"Give me some estimate of the chances her ballismus will go away."

"She's young. Her brain may adapt and find pathways around the lesion."

"What are the odds?"

"Some people do much better than you expect, some do worse. I can't give you the odds."

Seeing no point in continuing the conversation, Sarchi left the hospital and took the long way home, wondering what she was going to say to the Stanhills. By the time she walked into her living room, she still hadn't decided. Finally, she accepted Pierce's position. As distasteful as it was, she'd be noncommittal and vague and get off the line quick.

She made the call at five-thirty, six-thirty New York time, hoping she'd get Regina.

"Hello."

Nuts . . . it was Raymond. She considered hanging up without answering, but that seemed so childish she decided to push on and get it over with. "This is Doctor Seminoux."

"Yes, Doctor. What news do you have for us?"

"I'm afraid the scans were inconclusive. I'm so sorry to have put you through all that for nothing."

There was silence on Raymond's end.

"Mr. Stanhill?"

"I don't believe you. I saw your face when you looked at the shaved spots on my daughter's head. You were surprised then, and I think you found something on those scans you're not telling me."

Sarchi was so surprised by his response she was caught speechless. "I . . . I'm . . ." And this was making it worse. Say *something*. "I'm sorry you feel that way. I wish you all the best and hope Stephanie's problem clears up soon." She hung up without giving Raymond the chance to reply.

Lying was bad, but being caught at it was worse. Her heart was thudding against her blouse, and her palms were slick with sweat. She took a couple of deep breaths to calm down, then went into the bathroom and splashed cold water on her face, which was on fire. Obviously, she didn't have the constitution to be a con woman.

There was a knock at the door. "Sarchi, you want to grab a bite to eat at that Vietnamese place?"

It was her housemate, Linda. She went to the door and opened it. "Sure, give me a minute."

Linda's almond-shaped eyes widened. "Jesus, are you trying a chemical peel or something? Your face is the color of my favorite lipstick."

"I just told a lie to someone on the phone."

"You need more practice."

"And I got caught."

"With you amateurs that's always a danger. I'll drive with the windows down so you can cool off."

On the way to the restaurant, Linda angled for details about the lie, but Sarchi didn't want to talk about it. The food at Min Chou's was ordinarily a delight, but tonight it could not compete with the bitter aftertaste of her conversation with Raymond Stanhill.

During dinner they chatted about hospital politics, Sarchi's chances of being named chief resident, and whether Linda should sleep with her latest boyfriend. After they ate, Linda talked Sarchi into doing some mall window-shopping. Despite all the distractions there, Sarchi's thoughts kept bouncing between the lie she'd told and what, if anything, she should do about the Latham clinic. Both Kate McDaniels and Mel Pierce had advised her to tread lightly. And they were senior staff. Maybe she *was* wrong to pursue this.

In the center of the mall, where the various wings met, was a large carousel that filled the place with calliope music. Sarchi stopped and watched it turn, the horses going up and down, the bright lights spinning past, kids laughing with delight. She turned to Linda. "Come on, let's ride."

"On that? You're kidding."

"I want to."

"You go ahead. I'll work the stores nearby and come back when you're finished."

It was only a minute or two before the carousel stopped to take on new passengers. Riding it was a thing Sarchi wouldn't normally have done, but something about the innocence of the whole picture had drawn her to it. She followed a mother and her little girl onto the ride and then had to choose between a conservative adult seat or one of the decorated circus horses. Deciding to go all the way, she climbed onto a white stallion with a red saddle and blue and red reins. The music started, and the carousel began to turn.

She'd hoped for a few minutes respite from events of the past few days, but even here, where her heart seemed to be pumping out circus music instead of blood, she felt a palpable premonition that this Latham difficulty was pulling her into something deep and dark, and the faster the carousel whirled, the closer it seemed to bring her to the brink of that pit.

It was one of the worst ear infections Sarchi had seen in the last six months, on a baby with possibly the best set of lungs in the state. So as she withdrew to the nurse's station to write up her physical exam, her head was ringing from the child's cries.

Kate McDaniels was waiting at the station. "Hard to believe all that can come from such a small body," she said.

"He's got an ear infection. Finally, something I can cure for a change, unless of course there's a residual hearing loss."

Kate had hoped to find Sarchi in a better frame of mind. She briefly thought about holding back the news she had, but then, realizing there would probably never be a good time for this, said, "Koesler has made his decision."

From the look on Kate's face, Sarchi knew the rest. "Rachel's the next chief resident."

"I'm afraid so."

Though she'd tried not to admit it even to herself, Sarchi had wanted that job far too much. And now that it wasn't to be, she realized she'd also been counting on it. "You heard this from Koesler himself?"

"Ten minutes ago."

"I thought I was the front-runner."

"So did I."

"Did he say why he chose Rachel?"

"Some hokum about her having the edge in organizational skills."

"You don't believe him?"

"Nobody in this hospital is better organized than you."

"This isn't making me feel any better."

"I'm sorry. If it had been me making the decision . . ."

"I know. Thanks anyway for telling me."

"It's actually not that great a job. You'd be spending more time in front of a computer than on rounds. A doctor needs to be with patients. You going to be all right?"

"This was always a possibility. I knew that. Guess I'll have to start checking the journals for jobs."

"There's a pediatric group in West Memphis looking for someone. If you like, I'll make a call."

West Memphis, Arkansas, the land of truck stops and flooded farmer's fields. "Thanks, but let me do a little hunting first."

For the next two hours, until her shift ended, Sarchi carried her disappointment on her back, her steps slowed by its weight. Later, soaking in the tub at home, she began to bounce back. Okay, plan one is out; proceed to plan two.

As she was drying off, the phone rang. Linda couldn't get it because she was out. Wrapping herself in a towel, Sarchi went into the bedroom and picked up.

"Doctor Seminoux?"

A man's voice—vaguely familiar and with the sound of anger in it.

"Yes, this is Doctor Seminoux."

"Who the hell do you think you are?" the voice said.

Sarchi stiffened in shock. It was Latham.

13

"I don't know how you got to the Stanhills," Latham said,
"but I'm warning you, stay away from my patients and
their families or you'll lose more than a chief residency."
The line went dead.

In a daze, Sarchi hung up and stood there in disbelief.
Latham was responsible for her losing out to Rachel Moore.
And he had *threatened her*.

Suddenly, she began to tremble. Irritated at this, she took
a deep breath and forced herself to stop. This was ridiculous.
For years, she'd regularly risked her life in underground passages that could flood if there was a sudden rain. And here
she was becoming unglued over a phone call? Dammit. She
shouldn't have visited the Stanhills. But by God, Latham had
no business interfering in her promotion, either. Could she
take this without giving any kind of response? After several
hours of debate with herself, she reached a shaky decision.

The next day, with her first spare moment, she tracked
down Pierce.

"I heard about the chief residency slot," he said. "Sorry
you didn't get it."

"It was Latham. He pulled some kind of strings so I'd be
passed over."

"How do you know that?"

"He called me last night and said so."

"Why would he want to interfere? He *called* you?"

"He knew I'd talked to the Stanhills. My guess is because of my visit to them, Stephanie's father, Raymond, called Latham to press him for more information on Stephanie's condition. Raymond must have mentioned my name during that call. Latham warned me to stay away from his patients."

"This is just the kind of situation I was afraid of."

"He shouldn't have called me, and he shouldn't have blocked my promotion."

"No argument there."

"His actions prove he's got a lot to hide."

"That may be overstating things a bit."

"I've tried, but I simply can't look the other way on this."

Pierce winced. "What are you going to do?"

"I don't have the time or the resources to gather any more information on his other patients, so I'm going to schedule a meeting with the administration of the hospital where his clinic is housed and lay everything I know on the table. To do that, I'll need copies of Drew's and Stephanie's videos and all the scans we have of them."

"I wish you wouldn't do this."

"Believe me, I'm not looking forward to it myself. But I'm convinced what we've learned about him is only a fraction of the harm he's done."

"Sarchi, I like you, and I hope you won't take what I'm about to say personally, but I can't allow you to use my name in conjunction with any of this when you go to New Orleans."

"Fair enough. But will you at least help by providing copies of all the materials I'll need?"

Pierce hesitated.

"Surely you're not going to deny me even that, when I'm willing to take the heat."

"I don't want to encourage you."

"Latham's phone call was encouragement enough. All I'm asking for are copies. It's a reasonable request, and you know it's the right thing to do."

Pierce groaned in resignation. "Okay, they're yours."
"When?"
He looked at his watch. "Come by my office between three and three-thirty. I'll have them then."

With that settled, Sarchi turned to her next task: setting up a meeting with the chief administrator of Westbank Medical. Not wanting to proceed without having a name to ask for and knowing something about the person, she called Sharon McKinney's pager at Charity Hospital.

Sharon returned the page promptly.

"I need a favor," Sarchi said. "Could you check with those people at Charity who worked at Westbank Medical and ask them the name of the chief administrator over there? If you could, also get me a thumbnail personality sketch."

"I'll try. What's up, if I'm not being too nosy."

"Long story, but I may be coming back to New Orleans in the next day or two. I'll fill you in then."

"How long will you be here?"

"Like last time, probably just for the day. I can't afford to take any more time than that."

"I'll check and get back to you."

"I'm at the hospital. You've got my pager number?"

"I have it."

They connected again twenty minutes later, and Sharon relayed the information that the man Sarchi wanted was Harold Pelligrino.

"They also said he was a pain in the ass," Sharon added.

"Maybe he's just misunderstood."

"I'm sure. Let me know when you're coming. I'm dying to hear what you want with this guy."

After getting the number of Westbank Medical from information, Sarchi's next call was to Pelligrino's office via the medical center's switchboard. A woman answered.

"This is Doctor Sarchi Seminoux in Memphis. May I speak with Doctor Pelligrino?"

"I'm sorry, but he's in a meeting." From her tone, she seemed to think Sarchi should have known this.

"Would you ask him to please call me at his earliest convenience? I'm afraid I'll have to give you my pager number."

"May I tell Doctor Pelligrino what this is about?"

Sarchi paused. This wasn't something she wanted brought to Pelligrino's attention by a secretary. "I'd prefer to talk to him directly."

"Very well." The woman's displeasure at being cut out of the loop was obvious in her voice.

Pelligrino returned her call a few minutes before she was to pick up the copies of Drew and Stephanie's data from Pierce. Fighting the temptation to forget the whole thing, she responded to the page and soon had him on the phone. She introduced herself, then got to the point. "Recently, a patient of mine was treated in your hospital by Doctor George Latham."

"Yes, one of our shining stars."

"I'm afraid that might not be altogether true."

"I don't understand," Pelligrino replied, his voice frosting over.

"It's not something that can be discussed over the phone. I'd like to arrange a meeting with you so that we can talk about this face to face, and I can show you some illustrative material."

"What kind of material?"

"Some videos and brainscans."

"Then this would be in the nature of some sort of criticism of Doctor Latham?"

"I'd prefer we not get any deeper into that until we meet."

"My schedule is quite full, but I suppose I could make room for you tomorrow. I assume you'd like to do this as soon as possible."

"I would."

"Tomorrow then. Two o'clock, in my office."

"I'm sure you understand the need for confidentiality regarding my visit."

"The concept is not unknown to me."

Several minutes after the call, Sarchi's nerves were still sizzling. It didn't help any to realize that the worst was yet to come.

Her luck with last-minute travel plans finally ran out along with her cache of frequent flyer tickets, for there was not a seat to be had on any flight to New Orleans the next day. Having made the first step in getting the Latham issue settled, she had no desire to prolong things by rescheduling her meeting. This left her with only one alternative. Distasteful as it was, she'd just have to drive.

Sarchi looked at the swamp bordering the elevated roadway. Only thirty miles to go. She'd covered the previous three hundred and seventy in a sort of trance, trying to ignore the monotony of the ride. But now, with her meeting less than an hour away, she became alert and more than a little nervous. Even though she knew they were still there, she glanced at the two videos and the jacketed brainscans on the seat next to her. Then, eyes back on the endless strip of pavement through the black, cypress-dotted wilds around her, she went over what she was going to say to Pelligrino.

She arrived at Westbank Medical with no time to spare. She'd cut it close on purpose to avoid the jitters that would accompany waiting around. Even so, she found herself on edge, partly because she was afraid she might run into Latham in the hospital corridors. To avoid that, she checked everyone coming her way long before they passed. Afraid Latham might get on the elevator with her, she took the stairs to the fourth floor, arriving at Pelligrino's office with her heart beating hard against the videos and brainscans clutched against her chest.

Pelligrino's outer office was opulent, with dark paneled walls, huge gilded mirrors, and muted Oriental carpets. The receptionist sat at a French desk with a lot of intricate wood inlay. Considering it had all been paid for by the misfortunes of the sick, Sarchi found this open display of affluence in poor taste. Suddenly, she no longer felt nervous. People like this were to be pitied, not feared.

The woman at the desk, a silver-haired, hounds-tooth-bedecked veteran of the receptionist wars, looked unfriendly.

"I'm Doctor Seminoux. I have a two o'clock appointment with Doctor Pelligrino."

The woman glanced at her watch, then looked at Sarchi.

"It's two minutes *after* two," she said. "Punctuality is a virtue you should cultivate."

Not wanting to get into a row with her, Sarchi let the impertinent comment pass. "I'll keep that in mind."

The woman lifted the phone and punched a button. "Doctor Pelligrino, Doctor Seminoux has *finally* arrived." She looked at Sarchi. "You may go in."

Sarchi took a deep breath and opened the office door.

Inside, across a vast expanse of more Oriental carpet, Pelligrino sat behind a desk big enough to land a plane on. He stood and beckoned. "Doctor Seminoux, did you have a good trip?"

Sarchi crossed the room, her feet sinking into the carpet. "It was your basic uneventful car ride." Pelligrino was tall and slim with a face that reminded her of an apple drying in the sun.

"That's a long drive. You must have wanted to see me very badly."

"I did."

"Please, have a seat."

Sarchi sat in one of the two upholstered armchairs in front of his desk. He returned to his own chair and leaned forward with his forearms on the desk and stared at her, his lips pursed. "How is your final year of residency going?"

The question set off an alarm in Sarchi's head. "How did you know I'm a resident?"

"You mentioned it during our brief conversation on the phone."

"Did I?"

"I'm sure you said so."

Sarchi was just as positive she hadn't. Her memory on the point was particularly clear because it was something she'd specifically decided to omit, fearing that if he knew she was still in a residency, he might not take her seriously. Obviously, he'd done some checking around—nothing wrong with that, but why didn't he simply admit it? And where was the equipment to view the videos and scans she'd brought? She had mentioned *those* on the phone. "Doctor Pelligrino, much of what I have to say will require that we look at the material I mentioned. But I don't see—"

Pelligrino stopped her with a raised hand. "I've asked someone else to be here for this. So if you don't mind, I'd like to wait until he arrives."

This was actually something Sarchi had expected. In fact, she anticipated he might want a neurologist present or maybe their legal counsel. She wondered if the receptionist would give the new arrival a lecture on punctuality.

It soon became apparent that Pelligrino had no intention of making small talk while they waited. Searching for some alternative to staring at him, Sarchi focused instead on the flames flickering over a realistic set of gas logs in a fireplace to her left. About the time her neck began to hurt from being turned so long in that direction, Pelligino's phone rang. He picked it up. "Send him in." He looked at Sarchi. "We can proceed in just a moment."

Hearing the door behind her open, Sarchi turned in her chair, but the back was too high to see over. She heard the soft rustle of footsteps on the carpet.

"I believe you two know each other," Pelligrino said.

Sarchi looked up into the grim countenance of George Latham.

14

Sarchi felt her face flush as she glanced at Pelligrino. "I thought my visit was to be confidential."

"I made no such agreement. In any event, having Doctor Latham here is the best arrangement. That way, he can respond directly to your concerns rather than have me relay them to him with the distortions that inevitably occur in serial verbal discourse." He looked at Latham. "How are you, George?"

"Busy," Latham said harshly. "And in no mood for this."

"I can understand that. But I think we owe Doctor Seminoux the right to be heard. So, if you'll just turn that chair to the right and make yourself comfortable . . ."

There must have been a button out of sight on the desk because there was a whirring sound, and the paneling above the wainscoting on the wall to Sarchi's right parted, revealing a bank of X-ray viewers. She heard the tinkling of fluorescent lights starting and the panels brightened. Beside them was a television and a VCR.

"There's a remote on the shelf by the VCR," Pelligrino said. "And a laser pointer."

Still reeling from the shock of having Latham there, Sarchi left her chair, and placed the videotapes of Drew and

Stephanie beside the VCR. Refusing to let them see her hands shake, she then hung the scans on the viewing panels. While she worked, Pelligrino came from behind his desk and pulled the other chair over beside Latham's. He whispered something to Latham, then sat and waited for Sarchi to begin.

Sarchi's hands were cold, and her face was hot. In the past, the old trick of imagining her audience in their underwear usually calmed her. But even when she mentally defrocked them, Pelligrino and Latham were still intimidating. Hoping her voice wouldn't quiver, she started talking.

"I first met Doctor Latham when I accompanied the mother of one of my patients, a paralyzed little boy named Drew, to this hospital to consult with him about the boy's condition." Sensing that her voice was a little thin, she pushed harder. "After examining Drew, Doctor Latham expressed his belief that he could cure the boy."

Much better.

"Drew was left in Doctor Latham's care the required five days. At the end of that period, his mother and I returned to the hospital to find Drew remarkably improved."

"Cured would be more accurate," Latham said.

"To me, cured implies a complete return to normal," Sarchi countered, feeling much more confident. "Drew was not normal. He was left with a behavioral tic." She pushed Drew's tape into the VCR and used the remote to advance the tape past the leader to the first title: *Drew Harrison: 7 days after his release from the hospital.*

The scene shifted to Drew sitting on the floor and playing with some toy trucks. In the lower corner, a counter rolled off the time. After thirty seconds of normal behavior, Drew twisted his neck and appeared to yawn. To save time, Sarchi hit fast-forward, stopping just before the tic struck again. "He exhibits this yawning behavior about every eight to twelve minutes," Sarchi said.

Latham interrupted. "Doctor Seminoux, did we not discuss the possibility there might be residual behavioral anomalies after treatment?"

"That's true."

"Then why are we here?"

"Because of this." Sarchi stopped the tape and moved to
the scans. "The boy's yawning tic is a classic symptom seen
in Huntington's disease, a disorder normally produced by
damage to the medium spiny neurons in the caudate nucleus.
When we scanned Drew's brain, we found lesions in both
caudate nuclei here and here."

Pelligrino got out of his chair and moved in for a closer
look.

"A comparison of the scans we made before Drew was
admitted to Doctor Latham's care show no such lesions."

Pelligrino studied the comparison scans. He turned to
Latham. "George?"

"Lesions in the caudate are part of the treatment," Latham
said in a disgusted tone.

Sarchi's pulse quickened. She had him. If damaging the
caudate was part of the treatment, Stephanie's scans should
show the same thing. But they didn't. He'd just hung himself.

"This is the first time Doctor Latham has ever mentioned
that the treatment involves lesioning the caudate," Sarchi
said. "When we conferred in his office before the operation,
he said only that he was planning to lesion the ansa lenticularis, which can be reached without damaging the caudate."

Pelligrino's brow furrowed. "So you're saying . . ."

"He mistakenly damaged the caudate by improper posi-
tioning of the coordinates on his stereotaxic device."

Pelligrino looked at Latham.

"The treatment for this boy involved lesions in both sites.
The primary benefit was derived from severing fibers of the
ansa. I simply didn't mention the caudate during our conversation, just as I didn't discuss a hundred other details associated with the treatment."

Pelligrino turned back to Sarchi. "Is that the extent of
your presentation?"

Sarchi bristled at the question. Of course it wasn't. Anyone could see she hadn't even referred to Stephanie's scans
or the other tape yet. Round one had obviously gone to
Latham.

"No sir, I'm not finished. This next tape is of a little girl Doctor Latham treated for the same disorder." Sarchi ran enough footage of Stephanie so Pelligrino could see the characteristics of her tic. "It's important to note that this girl was left with an entirely different type of disorder than the boy. Her tic is more typical of a disorder known as ballismus, which is commonly caused by damage to the subthalamus. When we scanned the girl's brain three weeks after she was returned to her parents, we found bilateral damage to the substantia nigra here and here—damage that, as you can see, is not present in these preoperative scans. Moreover, if you look closely here, you can see that Doctor Latham also caused damage to the girl's left subthalamus and here, to her left ventrolateral thalamic nucleus. We believe the lesion in the subthalamus was a mistake and the one in the ventrolateral nucleus was intentional, done to alleviate the symptoms the mistake caused."

Pelligrino looked down his nose at Sarchi. "You keep saying, 'we'. Is that an affectation that really means 'I' or did you develop these theories with help?"

His question caught Sarchi by surprise. She'd expected the burden of the proceedings to shift now to Latham. This delay would give him time to work on his reply. And how should she answer? Pierce had forbade her to use his name. Knowing she was on the edge of trouble, she said, "These conclusions are shared by one of this country's most eminent neurologists."

"Who?" Latham asked.

"I can't tell you."

"Then how do we know he really exists?" Latham said. "I don't think he does. No one of that standing would ever arrive at the conclusions you've presented with so little knowledge of the paralytic disorders I treat. In my opinion, this is solely a delusion of your own making, a distortion from the mind of a confused, ill-informed *trainee*."

"If there is such a person as this neurologist, I would certainly like to have the name," Pelligrino said. "If for no other reason than to satisfy Doctor Latham's right to know his accusers."

"I can't give it to you."

"As you wish." He turned to Latham. "George, my inclination is to stop at this point and let you go back to your work, but before we do that, could you just explain the girl's scans to Doctor Seminoux?"

"Of course." He looked at Sarchi. "There are several subtypes of the paralytic disorder in question. Drew had one type, the girl had another. In her case, in addition to severing the fibers of the ansa, it was necessary to ablate some cells in the substantia nigra that were sending out conflicting signals. The lesion you saw in the left subthalamus was from a small stroke she suffered a few days before the operation. In my judgment, the chances of recovery from that damage would be greatly improved by lesioning the ventrolateral nucleus on the same side, which I did."

Pelligrino gave Sarchi a solicitous look. "You see, everything that was done was in both patients' best interests. I do appreciate your concern, but as you can see, it was misplaced."

Attempting to salvage the disintegrating situation, Sarchi groped for an advantage. "Why is there no sign of damage to the ansa?"

"It all fades with time," Latham said. "Some areas fade quicker than others."

Damn . . . she knew that. "What about—"

"You must excuse me now, Doctor Seminoux," Pelligrino said. "But I have a meeting. By all means, take the time to collect the items you brought. I'll leave you in the care of my secretary."

He and Latham headed for the door.

"Wait. What about the girl's head wounds? If . . ."

They were gone.

"So you don't buy Latham's explanations?" Sharon McKinney asked, taking half of her assembly-produced tuna sandwich from its little plastic coffin.

Sarchi eyed her own egg salad sandwich with suspicion. "I can't believe I drove four hundred miles to a city renowned for its food and I end up eating this in the Charity

Hospital cafeteria. No, I don't buy it. My neurologist contact said there was no evidence of any track leading to the ansa on the girl's scans, and the location of the access holes in her skull was wrong for an ansa target. I should have demanded that a neurologist and radiologist be there."

"It sounds like Pelligrino didn't *want* to believe you."

"He didn't."

"Then he wouldn't have brought anyone else in even if you *had* demanded it."

"I guess not."

"What are you going to do now?"

"As usual, I don't know."

"It was a rotten thing Latham did in making sure you didn't get that chief residency."

"He's got a real vindictive streak."

"That worries me. He warned you to stay out of this, but you didn't. And now he knows it."

"What more can he do?"

"Depends on how malicious he is."

Sarchi's posture grew defiant. "I'm not afraid of him." Then she wilted. "Actually, I sort of am. But I can't let this be the end of it. There's more to Latham's clinic than appears on the surface."

"Because some anonymous person sends you an e-mail saying so?"

"Partly. But *I* can feel it, too."

"Assuming you do want to push it further, where would you start?"

Sarchi thought a moment then said, "With you."

"I don't get it."

"Didn't you tell me you knew someone here at the hospital who used to do the PCR tests Latham ordered for all his patients?"

"Yeah."

"I'd like to know what Latham was looking for."

"Why is that important?"

"I'm not sure it *is*," Sarchi replied, "but it's a direction to take. And who knows which thread will unravel the garment."

"But this guy was just following a protocol. He never really knew what the target was."

"Is there any way he could get me a sample of the primers they were using? I've got a molecular biologist friend who could sequence them."

"Even if he could get them, why would he?"

"That's where you come in. You have to give him a reason."

"You want me to screw him for them? I like it—'Will fuck for primers.'"

"I hope it won't come to that, but . . ."

Mouth open in mock indignation, Sharon picked an edge off her sandwich and threw it at Sarchi.

About the time Sarchi reached Jackson, Mississippi, on her way back to Memphis, a cabdriver in Phoenix was loading Jackie Tellico's luggage into the trunk.

"Airport?" the driver asked.

"You're a genius," Jackie replied.

The driver's hair was thin and stringy, giving him a passing resemblance to someone in Jackie's past, so as they got under way, Jackie's mind went back in time.

"I just don't understand you," his mother, Vera, said from across the table. "I thought French toast was your favorite."

Jackie picked at his food, unable to tell her what was wrong because of what might happen to him. "Do you have to go out?"

"Glen is a fine man. He opens doors for me and pulls my chair out and has a very good job making ships that cross oceans and bring people things they couldn't have otherwise. I thought you liked him."

"I do. I just . . ."

"What?"

"Can I come with you?"

"Not tonight. But I'll talk to Glen. Maybe we can have a picnic this weekend. Now eat your dinner. We don't waste food in this house."

Jackie managed to choke down all but a few pieces of crust. While Vera cleaned up the table and washed the dishes, he stayed at the table and watched, so mixed-up inside.

His mother didn't smile much, but Glen made her laugh, and that made Jackie happy, when they were all together. But when he was left home, it was different.

Although he was only four, Jackie was smart, and even at that young age he had ideas. Later, while his mother was in the bathroom getting ready to go out, Jackie pulled a chair over to the silverware drawer and climbed up to it. He got a sharp knife from the drawer, then put the chair back in its place.

He carried the knife to his room and went to the closet, where he pulled out the huge Teddy bear Glen had won for him at the carnival. Sitting on the floor with the bed between him and the door so his mother couldn't see what he was doing if she came in, Jackie slit the seam on the Teddy bear's stomach and pulled out all the stuffing.

In the bathroom, he could hear his mother's shower running. He knew that as long as the water was running, he could work without worrying about being caught. When he finished, the bear looked as though it hadn't eaten in a long time. And there was a huge pile of its insides on the floor.

The water stopped.

A few minutes later, the door opened. "Jackie?"

"Over here, Mom."

"What are you doing?"

"Playing."

"With what?"

Not yet schooled in the principles of deception, Jackie had no answer. "Nothing." He put his hands in his pockets, scrunched his neck into his shirt, and looked nervously at the toy chest, where he'd hidden the bear's guts.

"Come on, I want to wash your face before Glen gets here."

When she had Jackie clean enough for company, Vera went into her room to dress. This gave Jackie an opportunity to return the knife to its drawer.

Before Glen arrived, Vera puttered around the small apartment, straightening the doilies on the furniture and putting away all the little necessities of life that won't stay where they belong. She hummed as she worked, making a sound like a butterfly would if it could sing. It was something Jackie ordinarily loved to hear because it made him feel safe.

But not tonight.

Then, over the humming, another sound. Jackie's heart froze. They lived at the top of a long flight of stairs that creaked whenever anyone used them. And not all creaks were the same.

Uncle Mox.

The steps grew closer, the creaking louder. A knock at the door. While his mother went to answer, Jackie hid behind the bulbous leg of the dining table.

"Hello, Mox," Vera said. "Punctual as usual."

Mox wiped his shiny forehead with his handkerchief. Even in winter when the stairwell was so cold you could see your breath in it, the climb made Mox sweat.

"Jackie's my favorite nephew," Mox said. "I wouldn't want to be late. You might get somebody else to sit him. Where is he?"

"Jackie, Uncle Mox is here."

The stairs began to creak again.

Glen.

It was obvious from the look on Vera's face that she wanted to throw the door open and run to meet him. But she waited discreetly for his knock.

"Hello, Glen. You know my brother, Mox."

Jackie wanted to see Glen, too, but while his mother told Mox where they were going and when they'd be home, Jackie slid from the room.

A few minutes later, he heard his door open. "Jackie, my boy, it's Uncle Mox. You can't hide from me."

It was true. He'd tried many times but was always found. There just weren't any good hiding places in the small apartment. But today would be different.

Mox looked under Jackie's bed then turned and crept up to the toy box. "Could it be Jackie's . . . in *here*." Mox threw the lid up and stared for a moment at the fill from the Teddy bear, wondering what it was. He thrust his hands into it and felt around. No Jackie.

He went next to the closet and opened the door. On the floor of the closet, the eviscerated Teddy bear lay on its belly, Jackie inside, trying not to breathe too hard.

Mox looked at the bear briefly and shut the closet door. He'd found Jackie once behind the laundry detergent under the sink. Maybe he'd gone there again. He stepped into the hall before it hit him—that crap in the toy box . . .

Mox went back into Jackie's room, walked to the closet, and opened the door. "Such a clever young man," he said grabbing the bear's leg and pulling the animal into the bedroom. By the time he'd shucked Jackie out of the bear's skin, he already had his zipper down.

At these moments, Jackie wanted to be someone else, someone Mox didn't know.

Because you couldn't hide from Mox.

Well, fuck you, Mox, Jackie thought in the cab's backseat. *Even the FBI can't find me now.*

Jackie was not only reliable in the field, he was flexible. It had been less than three hours since the call had come in telling him of a problem that needed attention. It was one of the reasons why he was so highly paid.

To be that untraceable and still be reachable required planning. Jackie worked it by renting a room in a fleabag flophouse using a phony name. There he kept a custom-made telephone that automatically forwarded any call that came in to that number to a similar phone in another rooming house. The second phone then would relay all calls to Jackie's cell phone, which of course was billed to one of his fake identities. If anyone tried to open either of the relay phones or tap the line to determine the number they were defaulting to, the relay mechanism would disengage.

The cab pulled up at the Delta entrance to the terminal, and Jackie got out. Because the cabby reminded him of Mox, he didn't bother tipping him. A baggage handler came for Jackie's luggage.

"Just the big one."

"Yessir. Where are we going today?"

"Memphis."

15

Sarchi got home a little after 11 P.M., so exhausted she covered the last two steps to her bed already asleep. Later, in the predawn hours, when the air was still and the night so quiet time was marked by the tick of an occasional acorn falling onto the dry leaves under the neighborhood trees, a car came down the street and stopped in front of her house. It remained for no more than a minute while the driver studied the surroundings, then moved on.

The next day, feeling as though she was on some planet with twice the gravity of earth, Sarchi used the elevators even when she only had to go up one floor.

Shortly after lunch, she ran into Pierce, who agreed that Latham's explanations at the meeting with Pelligrino were nothing but self-serving distortions of reality. His support lifted her spirits a little, but did nothing for her physically. When her shift ended, she made her way to the parking garage across the street with the same lethargy that had dogged her all day.

The hospital staff didn't have assigned parking spaces, but Sarchi had found a slot on the first level, for which she was particularly grateful. Looking forward to a hot bath and hitting the sack early, she walked back to where she'd parked. When she reached the spot, she found that her car wasn't there.

Unwilling to believe it had been stolen, she examined her memory of that morning. Had she parked somewhere else? No. She and Tim Clark, another resident, had arrived at the same time, and they'd discussed his new car, which he'd parked next to hers and which was right there beside the empty slot.

Still wanting to believe that her car hadn't been stolen, she walked the length of the floor, looking for it.

Not there . . .

It just wasn't there.

"What's the matter, Sarchi?" a voice said behind her. "You look lost."

Sarchi turned and saw Alan Pinson, the chief resident. "My car's gone."

"Stolen?"

"I think so."

"Where'd you park?"

"Back here." She led him to the spot.

"You're sure?"

"I'm not mistaken about this."

"Then we'd better get hold of security. There's a call box on the lower level. Be right back."

In addition to leading the country in sales of Elvis memorabilia, Memphis is right up there for car theft. It had happened to the Lanzas and to Kate McDaniels. Hearing the story from friends, Sarchi discovered, doesn't prepare you for the experience.

Rachel Moore, the next chief resident, and another woman came onto the floor and walked toward her. Embarrassed and not wanting Rachel of all people to see her at such a disadvantage, she tried to look as though there was no problem.

It was too difficult.

"Anything wrong?" Rachel asked.

Reluctantly, Sarchi told them what had happened. They clucked over her specific misfortune and the problem in general, then, at Sarchi's urging, went on to other business, probably discussing how some people just attract bad luck.

Sarchi and Pinson waited for security in his car, neither of them able to mount much in the way of conversation. When they saw a white van with the hospital logo pull into the garage, they got out and flagged it down.

Sarchi told her story, then expressed her unshakable belief that she'd *not* parked on another level to a sturdy black woman whose uniform looked too tight to allow any strenuous movement.

"Just to be sure, let's take a quick tour of the garage," the woman said when Sarchi was finished.

"It's a waste of time. I *told* you I parked here."

"Humor me, hon. It won't take but a minute. Just climb in the van."

"I'll wait for you," Pinson volunteered.

Reluctantly, Sarchi got in the van. The garage had a floor below and one above their present location. They first cruised the lower level. Sarchi's car, of course, was not there.

They circled around to the ground floor entry and, by necessity, covered that floor again before taking the ramp to the higher level. Sarchi was deeply immersed in thoughts of insurance and rental cars when all that suddenly became gloriously unnecessary. "There it is."

Just as quickly she became acutely embarrassed. "I have no idea how it got up here."

"It's all right, hon. It happens to all of us. You probably parked next to the red one yesterday and just lost track of time."

"I wasn't *here* yesterday."

"The day before then."

"No. The red car is new. It couldn't have been then."

"Well, anyway, your problem is solved. I'll circle back and tell your friend everything's okay."

Too confused to even say thanks, Sarchi got out and stared at her car as the van pulled away. She had *not* parked here. She was sure of it. On impulse she walked around to the hood and felt it. Though it was a cool day and the sun was not shining on the metal, the hood was warm. She went to the driver's door, unlocked and opened it, and popped the hood release.

It wasn't easy raising the hood with the car so close to the wall, but she managed to do it. The engine was warm, too.

16

HMO rep Harry Bright stepped outside and wrinkled his nose at the chill in the air. The sky didn't look so great, either.

Every day for the last month the new delivery boy had unerringly thrown his paper in the azaleas. So it was a novel experience this morning to find it sitting nicely on the walk, halfway to the house.

Somebody must have finally gotten through to the lunkhead, Harry thought, leaving the porch. Probably wouldn't last, though. He walked to the paper and bent down to pick it up when something caught his eye.

Harry's yard was a magnet for trash. On windy days, he couldn't believe how much shit would end up on his property. Mostly empty potato chip bags and school papers—Christ, he'd collected more homework assignments than the teachers at the school. But today it wasn't trash that had blown in and stuck. It was a ten-dollar bill, caught in the monkey grass in such a way that only half of it showed.

The ten seemed like a sign. He glanced at his car, focusing on the black license plate embossed with a spilled stack of poker chips under the word *Gambler*. A yearning for the casinos thirty miles away in Mississippi awakened in his belly.

Found money . . . Ten bucks . . .

Ten pulls on a dollar slot. Two on a fiver.

Who knows what could happen? And found money was the best to bet with because it *came* to you through luck.

But he couldn't. Not with all he'd lost in the last six months. Hell, he wasn't even caught up on the house payments. And Beth . . . Jesus, was she pissed the last time. She almost moved out.

"Harry, what are you doing out there?"

"Nothing." Feeling guilty for even thinking about casinos, Harry snatched up the paper and walked back to the house, pocketing the ten.

An hour later, as Harry pulled up at a light on his way to work, he'd pretty much put casinos out of his mind. Better he buy lunch with the ten. But it did seem like a waste. A horn blared behind him, and Harry glanced at the light. Still red.

Looking in the mirror, he saw a guy in a white car pointing at him and then jabbing his finger toward the gas station on the right. Figuring the guy was trying to tell him he had a flat or something, Harry turned the wheel and eased off the road. The guy behind him followed.

Harry found a spot off to the side where he wouldn't be in the way of people wanting gas and got out to check his tires. The guy who'd coaxed him into the station stopped a few feet away, and Harry could now see he was a redhead with a wind rash on both cheeks. The redhead climbed out of his car and came at Harry with a big goofy smile on his face. And he had his hand out like they were old buddies. Without enthusiasm, Harry raised his mitt for docking.

The guy grabbed Harry's hand and pumped it. "Congratulations. I'm the RiverKings Rover. I guess you've heard about our promotional campaign."

The RiverKings were the city's minor-league hockey team. Harry was a fan, but he'd heard nothing about any promo. "What kind of campaign?"

"To raise interest in the team and reward our fans we're giving prizes to the first ten people I find with RiverKings bumper stickers on their cars. And that's you, brother."

"Prizes?" Harry said, his enthusiasm growing. "What kind of prizes?"

The guy reached in his jacket pocket and handed Harry an envelope. "Dinner for two at Paulette's."

Harry grinned. "How about that?"

"I hope if you haven't done it already, you'll pick up some season tickets," the guy said.

"I do every year," Harry said happily.

"That-a-boy. Enjoy the dinner."

Harry watched the guy get back in his car and leave.

A ten-dollar bill in his front yard . . . and now this.

Oh, man. Harry felt like he was emitting light. Static electricity played with his hair. All his planets must be in alignment, because this was definitely his day.

Heart thumping, he pulled over to a pump and gassed up. Then he drove to the nearest ATM.

The casinos south of Memphis rise improbably from vast fields of cotton and soybeans, a towering land of Oz that appears to be solidly rooted in Delta dirt. Actually, as required by law and according to a long tradition of riverboat gaming, all the casinos float in great ponds connected to the Mississippi River.

Aware that the stretch of Highway 61 from Memphis to the casinos had become a death trap, Harry went south on I-55 as far as Hernando, then cut over to the Delta on 305, a scenic route that wouldn't get you killed.

For twenty-five miles, Harry managed to keep his mind off his destination, but when the road dipped sharply down to the delta, his nerves went on a stage-one casino alert. Five miles later, when the Grand came into view in the distance like a great mythical palace, he went to stage two, metamorphosing into a gambling machine.

The road to the Grand from the highway was filled with twists and turns that taxed Harry's patience. He'd driven the same route a hundred times but never with Lady Luck's legs spread quite so wide.

It was still early enough that the parking lots weren't even half full. That was good because it reduced the chances of some schmo tourist sitting at a slot Harry wanted. He caught a shuttle to the casino entrance and blended with a herd of old geezers getting off a charter bus. Watch out nickel slots.

The doorman, alert for minors trying to sneak in, gave them all a benevolent look as they passed. Finally, Harry was inside.

He paused on the steps and looked at the scene: acres of slots and gaming tables lit by gaudy chandeliers, short-skirted waitresses with their boobs pushed up to their chins, the air filled with the satisfied burble of slots taking in cash mixed with the occasional coin clank of a small payout. Deep to Harry's right a slot broke into *Happy Days Are Here Again*. In the distance, he saw the beacon that signaled a hand payout. It was as though this was life and everything else with the exception of sex and RiverKings games was some kind of punishment.

Itching to get started, Harry went down the steps and headed for the five dollar slots. Knowing that the progressive slots with the million dollar jackpots didn't pay off as frequently as the others, Harry usually avoided them. But not today. No way was he going to miss the best chance at a million he'd ever had.

He stopped at a bank of machines that only had one player, and he walked the row, touching the face of every slot. Feeling a small surge of electricity passing into his arm at the fifth machine, he took the ten he'd found that morning from the special place he'd put it in his wallet, added another ten, and slid onto the stool.

He fed the bills into the machine, uttered a small prayer, and hit the maximum bet button. Heart in his mouth, he watched the drums spin . . . around and around.

The first drum stopped—three bars. Come on, baby. Two more like that and he was home.

The second drum stopped . . . again three bars. Unable to sit still, Harry jumped up and clasped the machine between both hands. The third drum stopped . . . one bar. No win. But just above the one bar was the group of three he'd needed. So close. Luck would have her little joke.

He reached in his wallet for one of the twenties he'd gotten from the ATM.

Still wearing his RiverKings Rover makeup, Jackie located Harry's car in the casino parking lot. It hadn't been possible to tail him; instead he'd relied on the information he'd been given about Harry—that he always went to the Grand.

Jackie parked a safe distance from Harry's car. Aware that he needed to work fast, Jackie then set about changing his face. Ten minutes later, assessing his work in the mirror he'd propped on the dash, he felt a surge of pride at what he'd accomplished on the fly. Now to find Bright.

Inside, it took Jackie only a few minutes to locate Bright at the five dollar slots. Not wanting him to remember later that this new face had been at the casino, he took up a position where he would be screened by a group at the roulette table. Actually, from the way Bright was concentrating on the slot in front of him, he wouldn't have noticed a jackass if it was standing beside him. Jackie had sunk two fair-sized hooks into Bright's hide but felt he should snag him one more time.

At the slots, Harry's confidence was beginning to slip. He'd withdrawn two hundred and fifty from his checking at the ATM in Memphis and had used his Master Card to get another three hundred from the casino ATM. And all he had left of that was fifty bucks. Hands sweating, he put another twenty in the machine and bet the max.

Zip . . . nada.

This was getting serious.

Across the casino by the roulette table, Jackie handed a cocktail waitress a twenty and pointed at Bright.

Harry helplessly watched his last double sawbuck head south. He looked dubiously at his remaining ten spot. The only way to win the million was to bet the max. Hit the jackpot with any less in the machine and all you get is a consolation prize. Maybe he should drop back to the nonprogressive dollar slots, build a stake, and come back.

"Can I get you a drink?" a voice said by Harry's side.

He looked in that direction and saw a cocktail waitress so

skinny that without her Wonder Bra she'd be as flat as his wallet. "Yeah, thanks. A zazarac'd be nice."

"I'm not supposed to do this," the girl said, looking around to see who was listening, "but you kind of look like my brother. This morning I overheard the manager and the guy who programs the slots say this one would hit the big payout sometime today. And so far, it hasn't."

Harry's heart began to slam in his ears. He needed more money. "Honey, here's a ten. Would you watch my seat for a minute?"

She nodded and took the money.

Over at the roulette table, Jackie turned and watched the little ball bounce on the spinning wheel. *Where will Bright stop? Jackie knows.*

How did this happen? Harry wondered, staring into the muddy water below the casino's entry ramp, where a school of bream waited motionlessly near the surface for the answer.

It wasn't a new story, not even a new wrinkle. He'd stayed too long, slipped past the hope of a big score into a hole where he didn't dare leave without recouping his losses—a sucker's mistake. And losses had led to more losses. He'd dropped back to the dollar slots and still the money had run through his hands like blood, a wound whose flow couldn't be stanched.

Three thousand dollars, as much as his MasterCard would permit. There was no way to keep this from Beth. The first five hundred was for the house payment. Now, he couldn't even borrow on his card to pay that. Where had his luck gone? He considered driving back to Memphis and jumping off the bridge into the river, but the way his luck had turned, he'd probably hit a barge, survive, and be sued for damages.

From the other entrance ramp thirty yards behind Harry, Jackie saw him give the casino the finger then turn and begin the long walk to his car.

•   •   •

Going to the HMO office after screwing up so badly at the casino was out of the question. Instead, when Harry got back to Memphis, he drove to the bluff and plopped onto a bench overlooking the Mississippi to think.

He'd been there only a few minutes when a bearded guy dressed like a college professor came down the path along the bluff. He stopped a few feet from Harry's bench and gazed out at the river.

Harry hoped the guy would have his look and move on.

"Quite a sight isn't it?" the guy said.

Harry made a noncommittal gesture that should have let the guy know he didn't want to talk. But the guy didn't take the hint.

"A few years ago I stood at the origin of this river in Minnesota," the professor said. "Would you believe it's so small there you can jump across it?" He walked in front of Harry and sat down beside him.

Harry started to get up, but the guy put his hand on Harry's arm. "Give me just a moment of your time, friend. I have a proposition that might interest you."

Harry was puzzled at the familiarity implicit in what the guy had said. "Do I know you?" Harry said, looking hard at him.

This was the real test, Jackie thought. Not standing on a stage ten yards from the nearest member of the audience, but making it work close up, passing the kind of scrutiny the mark was now giving him. "No, friend, we've never met."

Suddenly, struck by a thought, Harry jumped up. "Look, I'm not gay."

"Neither am I," Jackie said. "Now if you'd like to hear how you can make ten thousand dollars for a few minutes' work, sit down."

Helpless to resist, Harry returned to the bench. "What would I have to do?"

Jackie presented his proposal in a hushed voice.

"I could lose my job for that," Harry whispered back.

"If there was no downside, it wouldn't be worth ten Gs," Jackie pointed out. "Actually, if you're careful, I'd think the risk is very minimal."

"What's the point?"

"All you come away with is the money. You don't get any explanations."

"I need to think about this."

"Sorry, the offer expires when I walk away." This was, of course, a bluff as big as the one on which the two men were standing. If he didn't come along, Jackie would be jammed up. "Make your decision. I've got other business today."

Harry took a deep breath and looked out at the brown water roiling by on its way to the gulf. "Well . . . hell Okay, it's a deal."

Jackie outlined the plan to Harry and then walked away, thinking how wrong Harry was to believe his future in any way had hung on his decision.

17

After determining that her car had been driven without her knowledge, Sarchi suspected it might be damaged. But she found no dings or scratches, and it performed no worse than before. The only lasting effect of the incident was a slight dent in her reputation around the hospital for clear thinking illustrated with a few jokes about someone hiding her patients from her.

Over the next couple of days her life slipped back into its old routines. Her patient load and the arrival once more of her thirty-six hour shift allowed little time to marshal her thoughts about finding a job, let alone pursuing Latham. Reaching home Tuesday night after a hellishly busy day, her brain felt like cold oatmeal. She pulled the mail from the box and put her key in the lock.

Suddenly, someone was close behind her, pressing a cold round object against her neck.

"That's a gun you feel," a nasal male voice said. "Inside."

Reflexively, she began to turn her head, but was stopped by a gloved hand against her cheek. "Don't look at me. Inside." He pushed her head forward.

Sarchi's once-sodden mind was now boiling with fear. They say never get into a car under force, but what about your home? It seemed the same. She should run, but the gun was a fact she couldn't overcome. Linda . . . No. She'd be at Huey's for at least another hour.

Fear clotting in the back of her throat, Sarchi unlocked the door. The moment she had it open she was shoved forward. The mail spilled from her hand.

"Your purse," the thief said.

Robbery. He just wanted money.

But sometimes thieves kill even when they get what they want. She took her bag from her shoulder and thrust it behind her. "Take it."

The bag was ripped from her hand. "Where's the bathroom?" the guy asked.

"Why?"

He cuffed her on the back of the head. "Don't get me upset."

"Down that hall."

He shoved her again. "Move."

Sarchi thought she was as frightened as she could get, but as they entered the hall, her situation worsened. She'd realized after her first attempt to look at the thief that her chances of escaping unharmed would be far better if she couldn't describe him. Now she didn't *want* to know what he looked like. But as they stepped from the living room, she got a clear view of him in the mirror at the end of the hall.

He had a long, acne-scarred face, small eyes, and disheveled black hair that covered his ears. She stiffened and moved the door key between her fingers so it could be used as a weapon. But then, shockingly, he grinned and cocked his head as though preening.

"Which door?" he said.

Sarchi pointed to her right.

"Open it and get inside. Stay there until you've counted to a hundred. Stick your head out before that and I'll put a hole in it."

Relieved that she was going to live, Sarchi darted into the bathroom and slammed and locked the door. No longer in fear for her life, she grew uncooperative. Thinking of escape, she glanced at the bathroom window, an elongated piece of stained glass in a frame that didn't open.

If it had been easier, she'd have gone out the window. As it was, she decided to stay put. But by God, she would not count to a hundred. She'd just wait the right amount of time.

While her life had been at risk, she'd thought nothing about losing her bag. Now, the inconvenience of it began to sink in—driver's license, credit cards . . .

She stayed in the bathroom for five minutes, then opened the door. Without showing herself, she shouted, "I'm coming out." Hearing no warning, she tentatively stepped into the hall and listened for any sounds.

Nothing.

She moved carefully down the hall to the living room, paused at the corner, and listened again. Still she heard nothing.

"I'm coming into the living room," she shouted. "If you don't want that, tell me now."

The house absorbed her announcement and fell silent. Believing he was gone, she walked openly into the living room and looked toward the kitchen. No one there. Unable to do anything else until she was sure he'd left, she went through the house. Satisfied, she headed for the phone and called the police.

While waiting, she picked the mail off the floor and put it on the phone table. She then got out her credit card statements and looked for the number to report them stolen. With the thief gone and all danger past, she became angry at not being safe on the steps of her own home, at having to get a new driver's license, at the ridicule for not remembering where her car was parked, at losing the chief residency, and at having no one to turn to.

Forty minutes after she'd made the call, a patrol car with only one cop pulled up in front of the house. Forty minutes, one cop. She was outraged at being treated so lightly.

He fiddled around in the car for at least two minutes, then got out and came up the walk, a big blond guy with the build of a fitness trainer. Maybe one cop would be enough after all.

She went onto the porch to meet him.

"I'm officer Metcalf," he said. "Are you the woman who was robbed?"

"He stole my handbag."

"What's your name?"

"Sarchi Seminoux."

He took out a small notebook. "Could you spell that please?"

He put her name in his book. "I understand he had a gun."

"I didn't see it, but I felt it against my neck."

"Exactly what happened?"

They remained on the porch for a few minutes while Sarchi explained that part of her experience. They discussed the rest inside. Talking to him, Sarchi was quickly convinced that officer Metcalf alone could handle most anything that came his way.

After she'd told him everything, including a description of the thief, he asked a question about something she hadn't even considered.

"Is anything else in the house missing?"

"I haven't really looked. When he told me not to come out until I'd counted to a hundred, I figured it was just to give him an opportunity to get away. I mean, that's not enough time to search the house. If he wanted to take anything more, wouldn't he have tied me up or something?"

"Sarchi, what's happened?"

It was Linda.

"I was robbed. Someone took my handbag. Right here in the house."

She rushed to Sarchi's side. "Are you all right?"

"I'll never think of this neighborhood the same way again. Otherwise, I'm fine." Sarchi explained that Linda was her housemate.

"We were about to determine if anything other than her bag was stolen," Metcalf said. "Maybe you could help."

"Of course."

Sarchi and Linda went through the house taking inventory. As Sarchi suspected, nothing else was missing. Having reached the end of what he could accomplish there, Metcalf reminded Sarchi to cancel her credit cards.

"I've done that."

"You should also change the locks on your house."

"He didn't get my keys."

"What did this guy look like?" Linda asked. Sarchi described the thief for her. "Sounds creepy," Linda said.

"I don't believe you'll ever see him again," Metcalf said, "but I'll cruise by a couple times each night on my next few shifts and keep an eye out for him."

Linda remained at the door watching Metcalf until he'd driven off.

"If I could have ordered a cop, he's the one I'd have asked for," she said. "Wonder what he looks like under his uniform."

"Oh, thanks for all your concern," Sarchi said.

"I'm an insensitive tart. What can I say? Of course, being a cop and looking like that, he probably crushes beer cans on his head and is therefore not your type. Now, I want to hear *exactly* what happened. Come on, I'll make you some tea, and you can give me all the details."

They went into the kitchen, and Sarchi sat at the breakfast table while Linda filled the teakettle with water and put it on to heat. Her cavalier response to Sarchi's confrontation with a man who might have killed her was vintage Linda, and it made Sarchi wish she and Sharon McKinney lived in the same city or—she had a brief vision of officer Metcalf in street clothes listening to her tale of the stolen bag, his concern for her real instead of paid for with her taxes.

Linda set out two mugs, put a tea bag in each one, and walked to the table. "Come on, let's hear that story."

She pulled out the other chair and looked at the seat, her eyes wide. She turned to Sarchi. "The handbag he stole—was it that tan one you always carry?"

"Why?"

Linda reached down and came up with the missing bag. Sarchi jumped to her feet and took it from her. Knowing that her wallet would be gone, she looked inside. But there it was.

She took out the wallet and opened it.

"I don't get it," she said, looking at Linda. "Everything's here." She dumped the contents of the bag on the table and sorted through them. "*Nothing's* missing. This is crazy. Why would someone take my bag at gunpoint just to bring it in here and put it on the chair?"

Linda had an odd expression on her face.

"What?" Sarchi asked.

"Nothing. I was just wondering the same thing. What did you say this thief looked like?"

Sarchi repeated her description.

"I thought you said he had brown hair."

"I've been very clear on that. It was black. I never said brown."

"Don't take my head off."

Sarchi got the impression that Linda was wondering if she'd simply misplaced the bag and made up the thief story. "I didn't imagine this."

"I know you didn't."

"And I didn't forget where I parked my car the other day, either."

"Get a grip, girl. I'm on your side."

Side? Sarchi thought. Why are there sides? There were only the facts. There weren't *sides*. She was about to say that when the whistle of the teakettle called Linda away. With Linda's attention diverted, Sarchi thought better of pushing the issue.

Linda filled the cups with hot water and brought them to the table. "I do think, though, that you should call the police and tell them you found your bag intact."

That at least was a sensible comment, so after they drank their tea in awkward silence, Sarchi went to her room and made the call. She was lying on her bed thinking about the robbery that wasn't when Linda knocked on the door.

She came in holding a white envelope. "I guess in all the excitement, you didn't notice this in the mail."

Sarchi got up, took the envelope, and glanced at the name on the return address. Sharon McKinney. Good old Sharon. There when she needed her. But why a letter? They always communicated by phone or e-mail.

"You're welcome," Linda said.

"Yeah, thanks, really."

When Linda was gone, Sarchi took the letter to her bed and opened it. Inside were two small zip-top plastic bags, each containing a white powder. Accompanying them was a handwritten note on Charity Hospital letterhead:

Here's what you asked for. To get it, I had to agree to marry the guy. Hope your wedding gift will be commensurate with my sacrifice. Let me know what you find.
Sharon

Latham's primers.
Sarchi's recent brush with attempted larceny took a step into the past. Aware that Carl Lanza often worked late, she went to the phone and punched in his office number.

It rang five times and rolled over to the lab, where the soft voice of his Chinese graduate student, Mabel Li, answered.

"Mabel, this is Sarchi. Is Carl there?"

"I'll call him."

A few seconds later, he came on the line. "Carl, this is Sarchi. Can you talk?"

"Sure, what's up?"

"I have a favor to ask. Could you sequence some PCR primers for me?"

"What kind of molecular biologist would I be if I couldn't? I'm intrigued. What's the deal?"

"I'll fill you in tomorrow when I drop them off."

"I've got a full morning doing some transfections, so how about we make it at one-thirty."

"That's fine. How long will it take to get the results?"

"It's not difficult. There are just a lot of steps involved. I'll probably need a week. Is that too long?"

"It takes as long as it takes."

She then thought briefly about getting his opinion on a thief who takes nothing, but realizing he was likely too busy to listen, she simply said, "See you tomorrow."

Nudged now into thinking about Latham, Sarchi went to her computer and turned it on. Though she had yet to receive a second message from the anonymous source who'd given her the Stanhill's address, she wondered tonight, as she did every night when she checked her e-mail, if there'd be another. But the silence from that quarter continued.

In his motel room, Jackie winced at the smell of the acetone he was using to remove the rigid collodion he'd employed to fashion the pock marks on his face. He was glad they'd happened onto a mirror when they'd gone into that hall to put her in the bathroom. To be convincing, he'd *had* to pretend he didn't wish to be seen. Actually, he'd wanted very much for her to view his work. He mentally placed a check mark opposite step three of this most interesting assignment. Step four would be harder, and five would be a major test. But he was up to it.

18

The morning after the stolen handbag excitement, Sarchi stepped out of her room ready to mend the rift the incident had created in her relationship with Linda. She found her at the kitchen table having a cup of coffee and a toaster pastry.

"Are those things any good?" Sarchi asked.

"I just eat them for the antioxidants," Linda replied. "There's more coffee."

"Thanks. About last night. I'm sorry I acted like that."

"Forget it. I have."

Sarchi was hoping Linda would be willing to take a little of the responsibility, but obviously that wasn't going to happen. She finished her pastry and brushed the crumbs from her hands. "Well, off to the wonderful world of medicine."

If they hadn't just gotten over a tiff, Sarchi would have reminded Linda to put her cup and saucer in the dishwasher. Instead, she did it herself.

A few minutes later, as she was putting her own cup in there, the doorbell rang. Puzzled at who it could be, she went to the door and found officer Metcalf on the porch dressed in stone-washed jeans and a bomber jacket. In the driveway was a blue pickup.

"Hi. Sorry to bother you so early," he said, "but after I heard you found your bag with nothing missing, I got to wondering what that was all about."

"So you came to see if there really *was* a thief?"

He gave her a surprised look. "Not at all. I'm here to suggest that the guy might have simply wanted to get inside and unlock a window so he could come back when you're at work and clean you out at leisure."

"Guess I should check the windows then."

"I would."

"Please, come in."

He stepped inside.

Leaving him in the living room, Sarchi went through the house, looking at the window locks.

"It was a good thought," she said, coming back. "But everything's in order."

"Then I don't get it," he said.

"Lately, I seem to be a sink for odd occurrences."

"What do you mean?"

"A couple of days ago someone moved my car from where I parked it to a different spot."

"That's interesting."

Metcalf's cologne seemed to be beckoning her. "You must be a very dedicated policeman. I mean you're obviously not on duty, but you're still working." It was a leading comment, something Linda would be more likely to say than Sarchi.

Metcalf seemed to give that careful consideration. He then threw out a feeler himself. "Some cases are inherently more interesting than others."

Unaccustomed to this kind of banter, Sarchi went swimming for an answer. Happily, Metcalf rescued her. "You and the woman who lives here are doctors?"

For the first time since he'd arrived, Sarchi realized that she was dressed in scrubs. "We're residents . . . at the children's hospital." Remembering he'd seen her dressed the same way the night before, she added. "I really do have other clothes."

Up to that moment, Robert Redford's smile was the most

appealing Sarchi had ever seen. The one that came to Metcalf's face was better. He extended his hand. "John Metcalf."

They exchanged a lingering handshake. "You already know *me*."

"No, not yet," Metcalf said.

Sarchi waited to see if he'd follow up with something more concrete. When that didn't happen, he left her with no choice except to say, "If I don't get out of here, I'm going to be late for work. Thanks for the thought about the windows."

"My pleasure. Take care of yourself. If I have any more ideas, I'll let you know."

"Do that."

Sarchi went to her car and drove two blocks thinking about John Metcalf—totally male, completely self-assured, but without a hint of a swagger. It was clear he hadn't come back just to tell her about the windows. He was interested in her. So why had he left without asking to see her again? For that matter, why had she let him? The mating game . . . It was all too diffuse and fuzzy for her tastes. She much preferred activities with clear rules and boundaries, like racquetball. There's a thought. Maybe he plays.

She pulled up at a stop sign and checked the intersecting street in both directions. As she was about to make a left turn, a horn sounded lightly behind her. Looking in her mirror, she saw Metcalf's truck. He got out and came to her window, which she opened.

"I did have one other thought," he said, bending down.

Once more enveloped in his cologne, Sarchi said, "What was it?"

"That I'd like us to spend some time together."

"Unofficially, you mean?"

"I believe it's called a date."

"When?"

"When's your day off?"

"Tomorrow."

He grinned. "It just happens I'm free. How about I pick you up at 11:30. We'll have lunch at a place I know, then I want to show you something and ask your opinion."

"We aren't talking about a medical problem are we?"

"I wouldn't do that to you. It's something else."

"Now I'm curious."

"Then my work here is done. Eleven-thirty tomorrow. Dress for hiking." He winked and returned to his truck.

She made her turn and watched him in the mirror as he proceeded through the intersection and disappeared.

Reflecting on how much the prospects for her day off had improved, a word in capital letters suddenly flared in her mind. PRIMERS. She'd forgotten the primers Sharon had sent. Damn. She turned into the next driveway and headed back home.

Her two talks with Metcalf and the trip back to get the primers made her ten minutes late to work. In the spare moments when her hospital rounds did not require her full concentration, she thought about Metcalf and the primers, in that order. Then, as the morning wore on and her appointment with Lanza to give him the primers drew closer, her thoughts began to dwell on Latham and the reality that, except for the primers, she had no idea what to do next in that regard. What she needed was access to more of Latham's patients. But how could she get the names? Her anonymous e-mail contact was apparently not going to communicate again.

A little after nine o'clock she saw Harry Bright coming her way in the hall. Her first reaction was to duck into the rest room, but then she was struck by an idea. Bright's company was huge. Drew couldn't have been the only patient they'd sent to Latham. But why should Bright give her the other names?

She caught his eye about ten feet before they passed and held it until they were close enough to speak. "Hello, Harry. Could I have a word with you?"

"What about?" Bright said, his manner guarded. "The last time we talked, it seemed like you couldn't wait to get away from me."

"I was just busy. I've been thinking about your request for a racquetball game, and I've decided to accept your challenge. But there's a condition."

"What's that?"

"Let's get out of the traffic."

She led him to a corner behind a building support and in hushed tones said, "If I win, you give me the names and addresses of all the patients your company sent to a clinic in New Orleans operated by a Doctor George Latham."

"I can't do that."

"Sure you can. You wouldn't be breaking any laws. Besides, you aren't going to lose, remember. If you don't lose, you don't have to do anything."

"I can't help you. And I don't want to play anymore anyway. I have to go."

He turned and walked quickly away. Sarchi was surprised by Bright's reaction. She'd expected him to be reluctant to give her the names, but had felt sure that she could at least goad him into playing. Then, when he lost, which he surely would, she could shame him into paying off. Shows how much she knows about men.

As Harry steamed away from Sarchi, his heart was racing—she was the *last* person he wanted to run into.

A little after ten o'clock, while Sarchi was writing up her observations on a seven-year-old with a case of impetigo that had progressed to cellulitis, Kate McDaniels walked up to the nursing station.

"Did you see Melissa Arnold this morning?"

"Around nine o'clock, why?"

"Did you write up your visit?"

"I ordered her albuterol increased and made a few notes about chest sounds."

"You're sure?"

"Of what?"

"That you wrote her up."

"My entries were the first on a new page. What's going on?"

"I just saw her and there are no entries for this morning."

"Did you check with the nursing staff?"

"No one up there has it."

"When you picked the chart up was it red-flagged?"

"No."

"One of the nurses must have entered my orders in the computer and misplaced the page."

"There were no orders in the computer."

"Then I have no explanation."

"I followed up, so there's no harm done. But we can't have this kind of thing going on."

"I agree."

Kate's choice of words suggested that she blamed Sarchi for the mix-up. Before Sarchi could respond, Kate excused herself to check on some of the other patients on her service.

Unwilling to believe that her entries for Melissa Arnold were not in the book, Sarchi finished up her notes on the impetigo case and went up to six west to see Arnold's chart for herself.

She found the chart in the rack and opened it to the first page of progress reports, which were in reverse chronological order with the newest entries on top. The first page was full. At the bottom was the note she'd added yesterday. Thinking that her entry for today might have somehow been misplaced in the book, she thumbed through all the progress reports.

Not there.

She leafed through it all, page by page.

It simply wasn't there.

Sarchi questioned the floor staff about the missing page but found no one who knew anything about it. Yet another thing to distract her from her work.

At one o'clock, she grabbed a sandwich at the hospital cafeteria, then set out for Carl Lanza's lab at the university. Fifteen minutes later, she found him sitting at his inverted microscope studying the contents of a plastic tissue culture dish so intently he didn't realize she was there.

"Are they doing what you want?" she said.

He looked up. "Sarchi . . . hi. Are they ever. Have a look." He yielded his rolling chair to her. "The focus control is right here," he said, touching a ridged silver knob at the back of the instrument.

Sarchi nodded and leaned into the eyepieces.

Her eyes were different enough from Carl's that she had to touch up the focus before she saw hundreds of ghostly pancakes with branching processes spread over the bottom of the dish. She turned to Carl. "They look happy."

"You saw the processes?"

"Nerve cells, right?"

"Yes, but yesterday they weren't."

"What were they?"

"You got a few minutes to hear this?"

Considering the big favor he was doing her in agreeing to sequence Latham's primers, she couldn't very well say no. Besides, Carl was virtually an encyclopedia of interesting and potentially useful information so if he thought something was worth conveying, she was always ready to listen.

"Educate me."

"First, a little background. You know how we were taught that the brain is an immunologically privileged site, and bits of brain tissue can be freely exchanged between subjects without worrying about graft rejection?"

Sarchi nodded.

"It's not true. Grafts between unmatched subjects definitely provoke an immune response, partly because injury to the graft cells stimulates them to upregulate antigens the host doesn't recognize. I believe that's one reason why attempts to treat Parkinson's with grafts from aborted fetuses aren't more effective."

"They don't use matched donors?"

"It's not feasible. Fetal brains are so small, it takes ten abortuses to produce enough cells for one Parkinson's patient. So even if you wanted to use tissue-matched cells, you'd have a helluva time getting enough of them."

"What about antirejection drugs?"

"Some groups use them, but it doesn't seem to help the final outcome. And you've got the additional disadvantage of having an immunocompromised patient on your hands who could die any time of some opportunistic infection. Even without worrying about compatibility matching, fetal tissue is so hard to get it takes a while to accumulate enough to work with. And how do you hold the tissue you have while waiting for more?"

"Freeze it?"

"Exactly. Which I believe damages the cells and makes success even more remote. In addition, fetal cells don't have the same metabolic machinery as postnatal cells, so they don't integrate well into the host brain. But I've got the answer."

Sarchi didn't know much about this subject, but it was clear to her that if Carl really did have the answer, he'd soon be world famous. And she hoped he did, for the sake of all those faceless sufferers of Parkinson's, but mostly for little Stephanie Stanhill, who, because of Latham's incompetence, likely had the disease in her future. The thought of Stephanie put the discussion on such a personal level that Sarchi couldn't wait to hear Carl's solution.

"And that answer is . . . brain marrow."

"I never heard of that."

"No reason you should have. I only made up the name five minutes ago. All the cells you see in the dish were grown from a small number of special cells that lie in the area adjacent to the brain ventricles. The cells are special because even in adults they're still embryonic, each one a blank slate waiting to be written upon and, unlike nerve cells, they still have the capacity to divide. We grew the original small number of cells into thousands, then treated them with a mixture of growth factors that turned them into nerve cells. So those few cells we started with can be made to act like stem cells, becoming an inexhaustible supply of new neurons, the same way stem cells in bone marrow make new blood cells. And being from an adult brain, they've got the adult metabolic machinery."

"Jesus," Sarchi said. "I see where you're going with this. Take a few embryonic cells from someone's brain, grow them into thousands, turn them into neurons, then put them back into the same brain to replace any dead or damaged cells."

"That's the plan."

"And humans have these cells?"

"Those cells you looked at are human."

"Someone let you go into their brain to get them?"

"In treating epilepsy, it's sometimes necessary to remove

small regions of the patient's temporal lobe. We have an arrangement with the epilepsy center to send us the excised tissue. That's where they come from."

"Carl, if you're right, this will be big."

"I know."

"How long before something like this could be available for clinical trials?"

"Not soon—ten years maybe, if we work hard, have a lot of luck, and NIH doesn't cut our funding."

"Could these cells cure other brain diseases besides Parkinson's?"

"Quite possibly."

The thought that even if Stephanie Stanhill's ballismus and Drew's yawning tic didn't clear up by themselves, there might eventually be a treatment for such disorders—one that might even benefit human vegetables like Gilbert Klyce—helped shore up the damage these cases had inflicted on Sarchi's confidence in her profession. That her friend Carl was working on something so important raised her already-high regard for his abilities.

"Why haven't I heard that you were working on this before now?"

"Didn't know until today that we could make the cells differentiate into neurons."

The potential significance of Carl's new line of research made Sarchi feel guilty about asking him to dilute his efforts on that to sequence Latham's primers, especially since she had no real reason to believe anything important would come of it. In fact, her whole campaign against Latham suddenly seemed like a gnat attacking a 747.

What was she thinking? She didn't have the resources to take on somebody like Latham. It would be a far better use of what extra time she had to find a job.

"Now, where are those primers?" Carl asked.

"Are you sure you still want to work on them?" Sarchi asked. "Maybe with those new results, you won't have time."

"For you, we make the time."

With her resolve to bring Latham to earth teetering, Sarchi thought about just leaving and taking the primers with her.

But what about Sharon? What would she tell her? That she'd put her to all the trouble of getting the primers for nothing? That she hadn't even bothered to have them sequenced? It didn't seem right.

In the end, she reached in her bag and gave Carl the primers. Thankfully, he was so eager to get back to his work that he didn't press her for any details about their origin. She left feeling as though she'd abused their friendship.

Upon her return to the hospital, Sarchi went to the library to work on a presentation of osteomyelitis she was to give on grand rounds the following day. She was deep into an article on the subject when Kate McDaniels pulled out the chair next to her and sat down.

"Now what?" Sarchi said. "Did that chart page turn up?"

Kate looked at her without speaking.

"Apparently not," Sarchi said.

"Sarchi, I think of myself as more than your supervisor. I've always felt we were friends."

The ominous ring to this put Sarchi on edge. "This doesn't sound good."

"If you're having problems of any kind, I hope you feel you can come to me with them."

"What are we talking about?"

"It wouldn't go beyond me. We could keep it just between us. In fact, if you'd like to discuss anything, we could go to my office right now."

"Why are you telling me this?"

"First there was that incident this morning."

"Which I had nothing to do with."

"Now, I was just upstairs reviewing Kelly Miller's chart."

"The cellulitis case."

"And I found your entry for today to be extremely inadequate. And that's not like you. So what's wrong?"

"Inadequate? I don't see how."

"There's barely anything there."

"Show me."

They left the library and went up to the ward in question, where Kate pulled out Kelly Miller's records, turned to the progress reports, and handed the book to Sarchi. The top page of the chart was full, with the first two sentences of Sarchi's entry for today at the bottom.

"There should be another page," Sarchi said. "Look, my entry ends in the middle of a sentence. Why would I stop in midthought?"

"That's what I was wondering."

"There *was* another page."

"Where is it?"

"Maybe with the other one we can't find."

"This hasn't happened to anyone but you."

"So you think I'm losing my mind?"

"I didn't say that. Maybe you're just distracted by something."

"I'm not distracted."

"Then what's going on? You think someone is stealing your charts?"

"What other explanation is there?"

"Who would that be?"

"That's the big question, isn't it?"

19

Harry Bright sat at his desk picking at the corner of the manila envelope containing the two charts he'd lifted from the children's hospital the day before. Despite the impression he gave most people, he was not a complete asshole. He felt a twinge of regret knowing he'd probably made trouble for Sarchi. But Jesus, ten G's. How could he pass that up? Still, he felt like making amends to her. But how to do it without arousing her suspicions?

Then he thought of a way.

He made an entry on his keyboard and waited for his computer to load the file. When that was done, he made another entry to call up the appropriate subfile. He then printed out the data and added a note at the top. He folded the paper and put it into a white envelope on which he wrote Sarchi's name and hospital.

Suddenly, the door burst open and Bob Kazmerak, the other Memphis rep, blew in.

"Kazmerak is here," he bellowed. "Now there'll be some work done." He chuckled, amused as hell at himself.

The office was small, and when Kazmerak was in it Harry felt like he was in Pamplona or wherever the hell it is in Spain they release the bulls in the streets. And the guy farted all the time, silent little greasers that made Harry do as much of his work as he could at home or at the various hospitals he prowled. To cover his loss of hair in front, Kazmerak combed what remained forward, which fooled exactly nobody and make him look like a retard. The only thing that made the guy halfway tolerable was his affection for the RiverKings.

"Hey, you ought to see my new car," Kazmerak said. "I got this destination finder in it. Works off satellites. You put the address you want into the system and it shows you how to get there. And a nice soft female voice tells you where to turn. I'm tellin' you man, we're livin' in the future."

"We've had that feature in cars since they were invented," Harry said.

Kazmerak's face morphed into a frown. "What do you mean?"

"They're called wives."

Of course he didn't get it. He never did.

"Anyway," he said, unfazed by his incomprehension. "I got this baby for twenty-eight five. Saved at least eight thou. You still drivin' that . . . Chevy?"

Harry was sure in Kazmerak's mind he'd plugged the word "old" into the gap he'd left in his question. Not in the mood to hear any more about Kazmerak's new car, Harry tried to turn the tables.

"It may not have a destination finder in it," Harry said, "but it brought me a little luck the other day."

"What kind of luck?"

Harry reached into his desk and got out the dinner certificate the RiverKings Rover had given him. He let Kazmerak see what it was, then told him how he'd won it.

"This, I don't get," Kazmerak said. "I read every scrap of mail they send me in which they're always yakkin' about some promotion or other. If I'd known about this one, I'd have gotten a bumper sticker for my new car. I'm as loyal a fan as they got, so how come I didn't know?"

"It's a big conspiracy. Better alert your congressman."

"I'll just call the freakin' RiverKings' office."

Kazmerak looked up the number and punched it into the phone. He railed at the unfortunate staffer who answered, then paused. "Well, my friend not only saw him, but he got a dinner certificate from him. . . . You're sure about that? Okay . . . thanks."

Kazmerak hung up and looked at Harry. "That was the general manager of the franchise. There's no such person as the RiverKings Rover. Somebody was playin' a trick on you. Although I don't know why they'd go to all that trouble just to give you two dinners."

But Harry did. Seeing it all in embarrassing clarity, he snatched up the envelope containing the stolen charts and charged out of the office.

Those sons-a-bitches. He'd been played for a sucker, scammed into going to the casino so he'd be ripe for the deal they'd offered him. Accompanying the anger he felt at being manipulated was the realization that the people he was dealing with might be dangerous. And he now began to wonder if they had any intention of paying him. He looked at his watch: forty minutes before he was to meet them to turn over the charts.

He briefly considered washing his hands of the whole thing and not showing up. But dammit, he'd done his part and now they should do theirs. What he needed was a little something to make sure they'd see things his way.

When Harry got home, he was distressed to find his wife's car in the drive. His faint hope that he might slip in and reach the bedroom without her hearing him was dashed when she met him at the door.

"What are you doing here?" he asked.

"I'm glad to see you, too."

"I didn't mean it that way. I'm just surprised you're home. Aren't you supposed to be in genetics right now?"

"Class was canceled."

"How can they do that? You paid your tuition. They should give you every class meeting they agreed to provide."

"Believe me, the teacher's not that great. So I'm not missing much. Why are *you* home?"

"I left something I need in my study."

"I'm making tea. Want a cup?"

"No thanks. I need to get back."

Thankfully, the whistle of the teakettle called her to the kitchen.

Taking advantage of the moment, Harry dashed upstairs and got his .38 from the nightstand. He shoved it into his coat pocket and hurried to the study, where he grabbed a manila envelope and stuffed some scratch paper in it. Downstairs, Beth was waiting with her tea.

"Find what you needed?"

He waved the envelope.

"Harry . . ."

"What?"

"Be careful."

A chill ran down Harry's spine. "What does that mean?"

"I don't know. I just felt I needed to say it."

As Harry went to his car, the hairs on the back of his neck were still dancing at the way women seemed to know *everything*.

Harry was to pick up his money and turn over the charts in Riverside Park, a place that in the five years Harry had lived in Memphis he'd never been, partly because it wasn't contiguous with the rest of the developed riverfront and was therefore hard to find. Following the instructions he'd been given over the phone by the guy who'd recruited him, he found the entrance at the end of South Parkway where it ties into Riverfront Drive.

The road inside the park ran for a while beside an empty golf course. Then it forked. As instructed, Harry took McKellar Lake Drive, which quickly left the golf course behind and ran through what appeared to be an old-growth forest so dense that even with the leaves off the trees he couldn't see very far into it.

Eventually, the forest on his right gave way to an asphalt parking lot containing a handful of pickups with empty boat trailers attached. Fifty yards farther down the road, he came to a wide cement ramp that dipped down into a body of water that had to be McKellar Lake. The place was not the stuff of sportsmen's dreams.

On the right, the water was bordered by a long peninsula crowded with industrial buildings. In the water, barely a good cast from the bank, was a large scrubby island that made the lake look more like a river. Partway down the boat ramp, a cement apron set into the side of the bluff was littered with maritime junk. At the far end of the apron, a long set of steps led down to a T-shaped dock on the water where several dozen houseboats were moored. There, he finally saw some people: a guy fixing the railing on his houseboat, a woman sweeping her window screens.

Through the trees ahead, Harry could see a tall refinery chimney emitting a steady orange flame. In the foreground below the chimney, the road widened into a circular parking lot. At its edge was the gazebo with picnic benches under it that his recruiter had described to him.

Harry drove to the parking lot and pulled into a slot to the left of the gazebo. He'd expected to see the recruiter's car, but he was the only one there.

Behind the gazebo, running as far as Harry could see, was a treeless strip of grass about twenty yards wide. On the near edge of the grassy strip, a wide band of asphalt skirted the woods before curving and disappearing in the distance. Farther to the left, a much-narrower asphalt path went directly into the woods.

Harry picked the envelope with the charts off the passenger seat, got out of the car, and took a long look around.

Where *was* the guy?

Harry studied the narrow path into the woods. Actually, his instructions didn't say they'd meet in the parking lot. Harry was to go along the narrow path until he came to a tree that had fallen across it. That's where the exchange would be made. Thinking the guy had probably parked on the other side of the woods and come in from that direction, Harry reassured himself by touching the .38 in his pocket, then walked toward the path.

As he entered the woods, a squirrel objecting to his presence began to squeal. The only other noise was a faint hiss like the sound from the air hose at the gas station when you fill your tires. In this case, Harry figured it was the gas that fed the flame on the refinery chimney.

It didn't take him long to find the tree across the path, but there was no one there either. He checked his watch and found he was a few minutes early.

He had to agree, it was a good location for their deal to be consummated. From the fallen tree he couldn't see either end of the path, and the woods were so dense no one could observe them through it. That also made it an excellent place for treachery. His hand went again to the .38 in his pocket.

Uncomfortable standing there in the open, he walked to a large oak near the path and leaned his back against it, facing the way he'd come in. With his back protected, he felt better. The protesting squirrel had not followed him to the fallen tree, so the only sound came from the refinery chimney.

Every fifteen or twenty seconds, Harry leaned out and checked the other direction in case his recruiter might think he wasn't there. After a couple of minutes of this, he heard a woman's voice coming from the far end of the path.

"Shadow . . . Here boy . . . Come on."

Great. This was just what they didn't need. What was she going to think when she saw him just standing there? Better it look like he was taking a walk.

Harry moved from behind the oak, stepped over the fallen tree, and began to stroll in the direction of the voice. In a couple seconds an older woman wearing a long tan coat and a brown scarf over her hair came into view. She was carrying a dog leash, but there was no dog to be seen. Her head swiveled from side to side as she called into the woods.

"Shadow. Come on, boy. Let's go home."

When Harry drew close, she looked at him with an imploring expression. "Did a big black Lab pass you in the last few minutes?"

"Sorry, no."

"I never should have let him off the leash. I knew it even before I did it, but he's so happy when he can run free. I don't know what I'll do if I lose him."

"Well, I wish you luck," Harry said, silently cursing the woman's presence. Until she found her dog, she'd never leave the area.

"Wait . . . ," the woman said, straining to see into the woods behind Harry. "Is that him, do you think?"

Harry turned to look in the direction she indicated. But he didn't see any—

Jesus . . . something was around his neck—the leash—squeezing, cutting off his air. Harry swung his elbow and spun to his right, trying to knock the woman away, but she moved adeptly in the other direction. Harry's hands went to the leash, and he tried to pry it from his throat, but there was no way to get hold of it.

Air . . . he had to have . . .

Forgetting the gun in his pocket, Harry spun wildly, trying to shake the woman loose, but she matched him step for step.

Harry's head felt huge . . . the pressure . . .

He let his legs drop from under him, but she followed him to the ground, spinning him onto his belly, her grip never waning.

White light mushroomed behind Harry's eyes, his mouth stretched in silent outrage. Just before his brain shut down, he saw Beth looking into his coffin and crying. Beth . . . Beth . . .

Jackie kept the leash tightened for another two minutes after Harry stopped struggling. He then loosened it and checked Harry's pulse. Satisfied that Harry was permanently beyond springing any surprises on him, Jackie picked up the envelope with the stolen charts in it and stuffed it in his coat pocket. He then picked up Harry's body and carried it to the fallen tree, where, after pausing to catch his own breath, he continued into the woods and down a small hill to a spot where he couldn't be seen from the path.

Jackie lay Harry's body on its back. He then went to a nearby mound of leaves and retrieved the overnight case he'd left there earlier. From the case, he got out a pair of scissors and set to work on Harry's goatee.

20

Lee-Ann loved the *National Enquirer* for the way its photographers regularly captured supposedly glamorous women the way they really looked, without makeup and padding. Show her a little cottage cheese on the thighs of a major star and Lee-Ann could run for days on it. A picture showing how badly a former sex symbol was aging could lift her spirits for a week.

So even though she had something important to do, it could wait until she'd finished looking through the new issue. Her loyalty was rewarded by a spread telling how an actress who was getting twelve million dollars per film had gained so much weight that she was seeing a hypnotist for help losing it. The accompanying photographs were among the best the paper had ever published.

She spent a few minutes burning the faces off the models in a Victoria's Secret catalog with her cigarette, then turned her mind to her campaign against George Latham. She'd heard about Sarchi's visit to Pelligrino and had hoped something significant would come from it. But all it had accomplished was to make Latham angry. She'd further hoped that once Sarchi had been pointed to the Stanhills she'd be able to take it from there without further help. But nothing more

seemed to be happening. Apparently Seminoux didn't understand what she'd meant when she'd advised her not to ignore
the events surrounding the onset of Drew's condition.

The woman needed another nudge.

Lee-Ann took a last long draw on her cigarette and stubbed
it out. She then set about gathering everything she'd need to
lead Sarchi closer to the truth.

She began by going to her computer and drafting a note to
accompany the item she'd decided to send Sarchi. Because it
had to be worded precisely, it took her nearly twenty minutes
to write. After printing the note, she made a mailing label addressed to Sarchi at the hospital, then took the note and the
label into the dining room, where she put the folded note into
the item. She wrapped the item in brown paper from a cut-up
grocery sack and affixed the label, which, of course, didn't
bear a return address.

That was the easy part. The hard part was driving the
eighty miles to Biloxi, Mississippi, so the package wouldn't
have a New Orleans postmark.

Sarchi always looked forward to the one day each week
when the hospital ran without her. This week, coming as it
did the day after the two charts had disappeared, she had
mixed feelings about it. She needed to get to the bottom of
that puzzle, particularly since Kate obviously believed the
missing charts had never existed. On the other hand, she also
wanted to see John Metcalf. The weather too, which had
turned sunny and mild, weighed in on the side of taking the
day off.

John arrived with a large Irish setter in the back of his
pickup. Both the dog and the truck looked freshly washed.
The dog went delirious with joy when Sarchi rubbed his
head.

"Is this what you wanted to show me?"

"I did want you to meet him, but there's something else."

Metcalf was dressed in jeans, cowboy boots, and a denim
chambray shirt under a navy blue jacket vest.

"What's his name?"

"Guinness."

Hearing his name, the dog snapped to attention, awaiting instructions. Sarchi scratched his neck with both hands. "What a good boy."

"We'd better go," John said. "If we don't get to the restaurant before noon, it'll be packed."

"Guinness is staying in the back?"

"He loves the wind."

They got in the truck, John backed it out onto the street, and they were on their way.

"What's it like being a policeman?" Sarchi asked.

"As many domestic quarrels as I have to deal with, I should have a degree in social work instead of criminal justice. As for getting criminals off the street, sometimes when I take one in, they're back out before I can finish the paperwork. It's like I've been hired to stand in front of a trough of running water and pick out all the floating rubber ducks as they go by. I store them in a box, somebody takes the box into the next room, and puts them all back in the water."

"I know the feeling. There's a patient at the hospital who'll be practically brain dead for the rest of his life. Because of his condition he gets a lot of infections so he's in and out of the hospital three or four times a year. And the best we can do for him is never going to make him normal."

"That has to be frustrating."

"What job *isn't* at times?"

"Hey, we don't care about other jobs. This is our turn to gripe." He gave her a big grin that she returned.

"I've been wondering," he said. "The bumper sticker on your car—*Free Floyd Collins*. Who is that?"

"One of the legendary figures in caving."

"What'd he do to get locked up?"

"He wasn't in jail. He was trapped in a crawlway in Sand Cave in 1925. During the two weeks he was trapped, the attempts to rescue him were front-page news across the country. Thousands flocked to the scene to get in the way. It was bizarre. He was trapped fifty-five feet underground, and the chute that allowed people to bring him food and water had collapsed, so no one could reach him anymore. Aboveground, they sold hot dogs, apples, sandwiches, soft drinks, anything to make a buck. Even Floyd's father passed out handbills for Crystal Cave, the family business. There was a movie about it, *The Big Carnival*, with Kirk Douglas."

"Did he get out?"

"Eventually they dug a shaft to get to him, but they found him dead. The coroner figured they were three days too late. It was two months before the family got around to recovering the body."

"So you're a caver?"

Sarchi smiled self-consciously. "What gave me away? Yeah, I love caves. They can be incredibly beautiful or unforgivingly treacherous, often at the same time. There's no solitude like you find in caves and no darkness quite like it. Sometimes I turn my lamp off and just sit there enjoying the quiet."

"For me, it's scuba diving. Being underwater makes all my problems seem too far away to matter."

"I've actually solved a few of mine underground. Sounds like we both have a strong need to occasionally lose ourselves in a different world."

"It's probably our work—high stress, being around people in trouble all the time."

"Hadn't thought about it like that. Makes sense."

"And maybe, in a way, we're both loners."

"Then why are we together?"

"Even loners need somebody."

They drove to Southaven, Mississippi, a fourteen-mile shot down I-55, and John pulled into the crowded parking lot of Dale's Restaurant, a large stucco building sporting a mango colored paint job trimmed in turquoise.

"I've probably eaten here five thousand times," John said. "It'll hold two hundred people now, but it started as an ice cream stand with only a couple of picnic benches out front. I used to work here as a waiter when I was a kid."

John gave Guinness instructions to stay in the truck, and they went inside, where they had to que up behind a short line and wait for a table. In the five minutes they stood there, six of the customers who left recognized John.

"Do you know *everybody* in Southaven?" Sarchi asked.

"Most of those were from Hernando, where I went to school. People from all over north Mississippi eat here."

"Is this what you wanted to show me?"

"One of the things, but not the main thing."

Following a hearty lunch of country cooking and after Guinness ate the chicken fried steak John bought him, they drove back to I-55 and once more headed south, passing the exits for Nesbit and Hernando. Finally, on the other side of a picturesque wetland that flanked the highway for a mile, they turned off at the Coldwater exit and drove for a while through rolling countryside that reminded Sarchi a little of where she grew up. They left that road and took a country lane for perhaps a mile before John turned into the dirt driveway of a little white clapboard house on a small hill.

"Here we are," he said, getting out.

Guinness jumped from the back of the truck and ran ahead of them to a big farm gate. They went through the gate and walked toward a herd of cows, dodging piles of manure, some of which were sending up wisps of steam.

"Whose cows?" Sarchi asked.

"A neighbor who rents this part of the property. That's what pays the taxes."

Before they reached the herd, John detoured through another gate, taking them on a route that led behind the little house, through a large stand of waist-high pines, and into a hilly pasture.

"This is it," John said, turning to his left and sweeping his hand from one side to the other. "Nine Ponds . . . the Metcalf family estate."

Fifty yards away, a succession of eight ponds on a gentle slope brought the blue sky to earth. The ninth was a huge blue horseshoe that filled the valley to their right.

"There are about eighty acres here," John said. "My plan is for all this to eventually be garden and walkways. The area we came through will be pines with an underplanting of azaleas, rhododendrons, and dogwoods. I'm going to fill in the second pond to a depth of a foot and make it a marsh. Cattails, lilies, that kind of thing, with a footbridge across it so you can see what's growing and what's living in it. Over there, between the first two ponds, will be daffodils, thousands of them, growing as if they just appeared on their own. On this side, fifty beds of tulips about four feet from the edge of the ponds. And willows . . . there and there."

He went on describing his vision, his eyes obviously seeing it all, his face glowing. Finally, he turned to her. "What do you think?"

"It sounds glorious. I'd love to see it when it's finished."

"Will you be here? I mean, when you've completed your residency, where will you go?"

"I've assumed I'd be heading back to east Tennessee."

His face showed his disappointment.

"But now, I'm not so sure."

Catching her meaning, he looked into her eyes. The distance between them closed.

Suddenly, Guinness barked and bolted after a blue jay that had the gall to land nearby. Their intimate moment gone, they watched the chase until the bird landed in a tree near the road and began taunting the dog for being so slow.

Before the interruption, a kiss would have been natural. Now, both felt it would seem forced. Covering the awkwardness hanging in the air, Sarchi pointed at the little white house. "Is that where your parents live?"

"They're both dead. Most of the week Guinness and I live in Memphis. When I've got my two nights off, we spend those days here, so he can chase birds and rabbits and I can work on the garden. And there's plenty to do as you can see." He pointed at a small outbuilding behind the house. "I've got two thousand daffodil bulbs in there I need to get in the ground."

"So let's do it."

"Now?"

"Why not? It's the right time of year isn't it?"

"Sure, but . . ."

"We won't be able to get all of them in, but we can make a dent in the job. I should warn you though, plants hate me."

"It's only because they don't know you as I do. Anyway, daffodils are foolproof. Next year's flower is already locked in the bulb."

"What are we waiting for?"

They were only able to work a few hours before John had to get back to Memphis and dress for duty, but they managed to plant two hundred bulbs before leaving.

At her door, John said, "Ever since I met you, 'Brown Eyed Girl' by Van Morrison has been running through my head."

"I know the song."

"You're a fan?"

"I've got a concert T-shirt around somewhere. Bought when I was younger, of course."

"Brown eyed girl," John said reverently. He bent forward and finally kissed her. At first she merely accepted it, then she responded.

Letting herself inside after he'd left, Sarchi thought it was the most unusual date she'd ever had and definitely one of the best.

Had Sarchi spent the day at the hospital instead of with Metcalf, it's possible she would have noticed the presence of a nicely dressed gray-haired man who spent several hours talking to Kate McDaniels, Mel Pierce, Linda Grainger, and several other people who were known to be fond of Sarchi. Since Gail and Carl Lanza worked somewhere else, it's unlikely she would have seen the man also talk to them.

In all those conversations the man explained at length the importance of confidentiality regarding his inquiry. And everyone he spoke with assured him they understood. But a secret is a difficult thing for active minds to contain, so even though the man had specifically chosen not to speak to Dr. Koesler, by the end of the day, Koesler knew he'd been around and was aware of his purpose.

Afraid that once her official admitting shift started, it might be several hours before she could see if the wayward charts had reappeared, Sarchi got to the hospital a few minutes early the next morning. She checked the asthma case first and found that the boy had been sent home. His missing chart had not reappeared.

The child with cellulitis was improving but still wasn't

ready to be discharged. Like the asthma case, her missing chart was still AWOL. Sarchi added a few notes to the current page in that chart and put the book back in the rack. She left the floor with the same impression as on her previous stop, that the nursing staff was staring at her when they thought she wasn't looking.

On her way down to the emergency room to take over admitting duties from the resident who'd been on call last night, Sarchi ran into Janie Ledbetter, a third year resident from Iowa. Janie was a large woman with a disconcerting amount of dark hair shadowing her upper lip. Aware that she tended to frighten kids when they met her, she always carried a hand puppet to break the ice. Normally, Janie's moods were easy to read, but today Sarchi saw conflicting messages on her face. Her first reaction at seeing Sarchi had been open pleasure. Then something had muted that.

"Hi, Janie. What's new?"

Sarchi thought Janie wasn't going to stop, but the question seemed to change her mind.

"Have you seen the morning paper?" Janie asked.

"Didn't have time. What'd I miss?"

"Harry Bright, the HMO rep, is dead . . . murdered."

"When did *that* happen?"

"Sometime yesterday. They found his body in Riverside Park."

As a physician, Sarchi was far better acquainted with the clinical details of death than the average person, but she was as shocked as anyone would be to hear that someone she knew would never draw another breath. "God, I just saw him the day before yesterday. We talked. How was he killed?"

"The paper didn't say. Guess they're withholding those details until they catch the killer."

Sarchi felt obligated to say something nice about Bright. "I'm sure his company will miss him. He was very conscientious in his work."

"And an asshole," Janie said.

"That too, at least superficially."

"I guess superficially is the only way we ever know anybody."

Janie was searching Sarchi's eyes for something. "What do you mean?"

"Just that people often have traits and problems they don't let others see."

Janie had an expectant look on her face, as though she had more than a casual interest in the response this would elicit.

"I get the impression we're having two different conversations," Sarchi said.

"I don't know what you mean."

"I think you do. What's going on? A few minutes ago I had the feeling the nursing staff was staring at me behind my back, and now *you're* acting strange."

"Is it strange to be concerned about a friend?"

"If I'm the friend you're referring to, yes."

Before Janie could reply, her pager went off. She checked it, then looked up apologetically. "I have to go. If you want to talk some more, locate me when you're free and we'll find a quiet place . . ."

As Sarchi watched Janie lumber off down the hall, she was so full of curiosity about how she had suddenly become the focus of everyone's attention that she didn't feel she could go one more minute without knowing why.

Once she hit the emergency room, all that was forgotten. Over the course of the next hour she saw ten kids, four of whom were sick enough to be admitted. Just as things began to slack off, she got a page that displayed an extension she wasn't happy to see. She picked up the phone and entered the number.

"This is Doctor Seminoux."

"Yes, Doctor," a woman said. "Doctor Koesler would like to see you."

Sarchi felt a surge of apprehension "When?"

"Right now if you can."

The room suddenly felt icy. "I'll be right there."

When she arrived at his office, Koesler's secretary sent her in. She found him head down, reading something in a folder on his desk. Without looking up, he pecked the air in front of him with his finger, ordering her into a chair.

Hands freezing, she sat and waited for him to get around

to her. On the front of his desk sat one of those toys in which a swinging steel ball hitting a row of stationary balls produces enough clattering activity to amuse someone without much to do. She was thinking what a surprisingly frivolous object this was for him to have when suddenly he looked up. "Second in your class," he said. "Impressive."

He was, as usual, impeccably groomed. Looking directly into his face, Sarchi realized for the first time, contrary to the opinion she'd had of him up to that moment, that he was not a handsome man, had probably not been even when he was young. But he had a dignity and bearing that made you see what wasn't there. The power he wielded over the hospital's residents, though, was no illusion. The emperor may have had no clothes, but he was still the emperor.

"You have great promise as a physician," he said. "A fine intellect, keen clinical instincts, and a bedside manner that puts both frightened children and their parents at ease."

Suspecting now that he'd summoned her to explain why he'd picked someone else as chief resident, Sarchi relaxed a bit. At the same time, she wondered how he would handle the fact that Latham had influenced his decision. Surely he'd never admit he'd done it as a favor to a friend.

"But mere promise doesn't carry us far," Koesler continued, interlacing the manicured fingers of both hands and resting them on his desk. "To succeed, promise must translate into accomplishment. There are countless examples in life of promising men and women who through a certain deficiency in character have squandered that promise. Do you have any idea what I'm getting at?"

"Actually, no," Sarchi said, now confused.

Koesler squinted at her. "I'm referring to the lack of a will to succeed, an unwillingness to face hard work and long hours with nothing but backbone."

Eyebrows lifting, he leaned forward and paused to see if she got it now.

Sarchi shook her head. "Sorry."

Koesler's lips firmed, and he nodded in resignation. "I understand you reported your car stolen a few days ago."

"Someone moved it from where I parked."

"I see. And there was something about your purse being stolen, but it was actually on a chair in your kitchen?"

"How did you know about that?"

"It's my responsibility to be aware of everything that affects the way my residents function here."

"With all due respect Doctor Koesler, my bag wasn't 'actually' on that chair. It was taken forcibly from me and placed there without my knowledge by the man who took it. I don't know why he did it, but those are the facts. All that aside, I don't see how what happened to my handbag has any relevance to the operation of this hospital."

"By itself, I wouldn't either. But it appears to be part of a pattern that includes some slipshod work in your clinical duties."

"You mean those two missing charts?"

"Don't you see how absurd all this sounds? Someone moving your car, stealing your purse, stealing your charts. It's never you, it's always someone else. I want you to tell me the *real* explanation for these events."

"Those *are* the explanations."

"No, they aren't. Show some backbone and admit the truth. I'm not here to destroy you. I want to help you. But I can only do that after you admit the truth."

"Which is . . . ?"

"*You* need to say it."

"I can't say what I don't know."

"Don't fight it. Tell me now, and we can start you on the road back."

"Back to what?"

"To becoming that physician I believe is inside you."

While Koesler waited for her to answer, Sarchi went swimming for a reply, because she had no earthly idea what he was talking about. "If you'll forgive the analogy Doctor Koesler, I feel like I've just chased the white rabbit into wonderland."

Koesler's face grew hard. "Believe me, Doctor, this isn't wonderland. It's the real world, and it's time you faced up to it. Since you refuse to do so, I'll help you. Do you know who Doctor Sam Brookings is?"

"No."

"He's the investigator for the Tennessee impaired physicians program. He was here yesterday gathering information about you. It seems his office has received information that you are so strung out on uppers and downers it's finally affecting your work."

"That's absurd. Who said that?"

"The call was anonymous."

Sarchi sat straighter in her seat. Now it all made sense. The car, the handbag, the missing charts. It was Latham harassing her, trying to make it appear as though she was a drug abuser. It was so clear now, she couldn't imagine why she hadn't seen it earlier. With her mind speeding through the possibilities, she wondered if Koesler was in on it. He'd already cooperated once with Latham. Why not again?

"So you're willing to take the word of a faceless accuser over mine?" she said.

"It does explain things."

"But it's wrong."

"I don't think so."

"I'll take a drug test."

"Which only tells me you know the standard screens won't detect the ones you're abusing." He shook his head. "I gave you a chance to come clean with me, but you've chosen to squander the opportunity. I'm not prepared to suspend you at this time. But you'd better watch your step, Doctor, because you and I are on a collision course. Now get out."

21

Sarchi wanted all this to stop. She wanted to go back to the way life had been before she met Latham. She'd tried to tell Pelligrino what Latham was doing, but he'd ignored her. Fine. She had no further responsibility in this. Let someone else take up the cause.

For the rest of that day and the next, every time she filled out a chart, she wondered if she'd ever see it again. And the thought of being in Koesler's doghouse was enervating. When she left the hospital at the end of her shift, she was completely wiped out.

Arriving home she found that just as usual all of the workmen who were renovating the house next door had gone home. Before getting out of her car, she checked the surroundings for lurking figures. The Dumpster next door was a worry, but it was on the far side of the property, so anyone running toward her from behind it couldn't surprise her. Still, she waited until another car came down the street before starting for the house.

Pushing her front door open a few seconds later, she smelled gas. Now what? Was Latham trying to blow her up?

She remembered on old warning: never turn on a light switch in the presence of gas. Was it also dangerous to use the phone? She grabbed the directory and the phone and went back onto the porch. There, in the waning daylight, she looked up the number for Light, Gas, and Water, and reported the smell.

"Where are you now?" the LG&W rep asked.

"On my porch."

"We'll send an inspector right over. Wait nearby, but not in the house."

Leaving the phone outside, she went back to her car and moved it across the street. In about ten minutes, with the sun now set, a white LG&W car arrived and parked at the curb opposite her. A young man carrying a toolbox and a flashlight that looked as though it could produce a beam he could climb, stepped from the car.

"I'm the one who called you," Sarchi said, crossing the street to meet him. "The smell is very strong inside."

Moving to the sidewalk the inspector said, "Is the door unlocked?"

"Yes."

"You wait here. I'll check things out."

He was gone long enough for the evening chill to creep into Sarchi's feet. Then, through the storm door, she saw him flick on the living room lights. He came out and motioned for her.

"I found the problem," he said when she reached him. "I'll show you. Don't worry, it's safe. I opened the back door and aired the place out."

Dropping her handbag onto a chair as she passed, she followed him through the front room, into the kitchen and to the closet by the back door where the heating unit was located.

"You've got a defective part on your furnace."

"Can you tell if it was damaged intentionally?"

"What do you mean?"

"Never mind."

He looked at her quizzically for a moment, then said, "It was probably an inferior product from the start. I've made a repair that should last for several months, but you need to get someone in to replace the part. It's that valve in back."

He moved out of the way and held his flashlight high over

his head, directing the beam down into the closet. Figuring she'd better see this valve, Sarchi stepped past him and bent over for a look.

Behind her, the inspector slipped his right hand into the pocket of his coveralls. It came out gripping a white athletic sock with a string tied above a bolus of sand in the foot. Holding the sock by the free end, he whipped it in a horizontal arc hitting Sarchi on the back of the head, stunning her in a way that would leave no bruise. He then stepped forward and captured her neck in the crook of his left arm, applying just enough pressure to compress both her carotid arteries. Within seconds, feeling her knees buckle, Jackie lowered her to the floor, faceup. Shucking off his work gloves so his hands were now covered only by rubber gloves, he removed Sarchi's coat and put it on a kitchen chair.

To make it appear that there had been a gas leak, Jackie had entered the house a half hour earlier and put a rag soaked in 2-mercaptoethanol, the additive that imparts a smell to natural gas, into the furnace blower. When he'd reentered the house posing as an LG&W inspector with Sarchi waiting outside he'd retrieved the rag, put it in a sealed plastic bag, and hidden it in his toolbox. Now, he moved the bag aside and picked up the two Ace bandages he'd brought.

Careful to keep the fabric flat so it wouldn't produce any long-lasting marks on Sarchi's skin, he wrapped her wrists together with one bandage and secured it. The other he used on her ankles.

He reached again into the toolbox for a small bottle of white pills. Kneeling by Sarchi's head, he unscrewed the cap on the bottle and shook a half milligram tablet of Ativan, an easily absorbed cousin of Valium, into his palm. With some difficulty, he put the tablet under Sarchi's tongue. In this he was trusting Latham, who had said one pill should keep her unconscious during everything Jackie had to do. Just in case, he slipped a couple of pills into his pants pocket, then recapped the vial and put it back in the toolbox.

He carried Sarchi into her bedroom and put her on the bed. Even though she was well trussed, he unplugged the phone and moved it out of reach. Returning to the front room, he got her keys from her handbag and locked the front door. From there, he went to the phone line in the backyard and disengaged the trap that had directed Sarchi's call to his cell phone instead of to LG&W.

With the trap stowed in his toolbox, he returned to Sarchi's bedroom. Satisfied that she was still drugged, he went to the front door and checked the street for moving cars. When it was clear, he darted to his car, tossed the toolbox and flashlight into the trunk, and moved the car to the driveway next door, where it was hidden on one side by the Dumpster and on the other by a thick stand of bamboo.

Convinced that he wouldn't be noticed by anyone in a passing car, he got out, removed his coveralls, and put them in the trunk, trading them for a jacket. The adhesive-backed LG&W letters on the side of the car had arrived yesterday from a sign shop in Tampa. Their purpose served, he stripped them off and threw them in the trunk with everything else. He then moved the car to a side street half a block away.

Still wearing rubber gloves, which he hid by keeping his hands in his pockets, Jackie walked briskly back to Sarchi's house and returned to her bedroom, where she was doing just fine, still breathing and still unresponsive.

Now it was just a matter of waiting until the city quieted down and everyone settled into their homes. He had plenty of time. Resident assignments were posted right out in the hall at the hospital where anybody could see them and know that Sarchi's housemate would be on duty all night.

He sat on the floor next to the bedroom door with his back against the wall and crossed his legs. He was not bored as he waited because when a man has taken the lives of as many people as he had, he has much to think about.

He sat there quietly for nearly two hours. Finally, it was time.

He went into the backyard to open the wooden gates that led to the front, but the right one had sagged so much the bolt holding them shut wouldn't slide free. Eventually, he managed to inch it loose.

He moved Sarchi's car into the backyard and closed the gates. After opening the trunk, he returned to Sarchi's bedroom and put the phone back where he'd found it and plugged it in. He paused to run through his mental checklist.

Her coat and handbag.

He retrieved both and put them on the passenger seat of her car. Now, for the big bundle.

Compared to Harry Bright, carrying Sarchi was a breeze. He put her in the trunk and closed the lid. After backing her car out and securing the gates from inside, he went through the house and out the front, locking the two doors he'd used behind him.

There were many ways Jackie's goal for tonight could have been achieved. But even with the difficulty of working around a housemate, the absence of immediate neighbors had made this approach irresistible, so as he backed Sarchi's car into the street, he was confident no one in the area had noticed him.

Jackie drove to Overton Park, a forested area less than a mile away that was home to the zoo and a public golf course. He went in the main entrance, drove past the darkened art museum to the statue of the World War I doughboy thrusting his bayonet at shadows, then followed the road as it curved to the right, skirting the dappled front lawn of the art school. Apart from someone going in the side door of the school, the park was empty.

He turned left just beyond the school and proceeded slowly to the pavilion parking lot where the city had put up barricades to prevent cars from following the road into the woods.

Shit . . .

There were two cars parked side by side in the lot. In one, he saw the flare of a cigarette.

Since he'd anticipated this might happen, it was a disappointment but not a disaster. Shifting to his alternate plan, he turned the car around and headed back toward the school.

Two minutes later, Jackie was pleased to see that site B, a short road leading to the golf clubhouse driveway, was deserted. He eased the car down the road and used the clubhouse driveway as a turnaround so he could park on the road with the trunk facing the woods.

Before getting out, he grabbed Sarchi's coat and tossed the zip-top plastic bag he'd stowed in his jacket at the start of the operation onto the passenger seat. Even if the Ativan had worn off, the bandages on Sarchi's wrists and ankles would keep her from going anywhere. Even so, he didn't open the trunk from inside the car, but went around and used the key.

And there she was . . . still out and still breathing.

He was now maximally exposed, so more than ever he needed to be quick and efficient in his movements. He draped Sarchi's coat over the side of the raised trunk lid. In the dim glow of the trunk light, he untied her and stuffed the bandages into the pockets of his jacket.

There was no room to slip her coat on her in the trunk, so he first lowered her to the ground. Apart from their relative seclusion, the two potential dump sites he'd chosen were places where he wouldn't leave footprints. In this case, there was a footpath lined with crushed gravel running beside the road, so as he worked on Sarchi there, he didn't have to worry about where he stepped.

Finishing up, he put Sarchi's keys in her coat pocket and paused to review the scene.

Was the car unlocked? It had to be unlocked. He checked and found it so. Now he had to make sure she was found before the Ativan wore off.

To do that, he jogged to the Circle K convenience store across from the park's main entrance. Using their pay phone, he called 911 and reported a woman's body by the clubhouse, then called a taxi to pick him up several blocks from the park and take him back to the general area where he'd parked his car.

22

There was light above her, a way out of the black void in which she floated. She felt that if she kicked her feet and swam with her arms she could escape. But she was paralyzed—just like Drew and Stephanie.

Billows of gray smoke drifted into the void and across her face, hiding the light. Behind the smoke there was something very close . . .

Sound invaded the profound silence—someone talking, but the words were slurred as though being played too slow. The smoke thinned, and she saw a man's face . . . his lips moving.

"Ma'am, are you hurt?"

His words were distinct now but seemed to be a beat behind the movement of his lips.

"What's your name?" he asked. This time everything was in synch.

"Sarchi Seminoux," she said slowly. "What's happened?" She now realized she was lying on her back and the man asking the questions was kneeling over her. Shifting her eyes, she saw another man standing and holding a flashlight . . . a cop. A cool breeze blew over her face. *They were all outside . . .*

"Where am I?"

"Overton Park," the cop leaning over her said. "I'm Officer Varela. Can you get up?"

Overton Park. It seemed impossible. As she shifted her arm so she could use her elbow to lever herself into a sitting position, Varela moved around behind her to help.

They let her sit for a few seconds to see how she'd react.

"Think you can stand?" Varela asked.

"I guess . . ."

The cops helped her up, and Varela moved back to where she could see him. "Do you feel like discussing what happened?"

Discussing it? She was on the ground for God's sake, with no knowledge of how she got there. Dazed and confused, she didn't answer.

"No need to stay out here," Varela said.

She let him guide her to one of two patrol cars whose dithering lights hurt her eyes. As Varela put her in the backseat of the nearest car, police chatter crackled from their radios, calling the other cop away to answer it.

Varela went around to the other side of his car and got in beside her, leaving his door cracked so the overhead light would stay on. He opened a little notebook and got ready to write. "I'm sorry, could you tell me your name again?"

Preoccupied with clearing her thoughts, she ignored him until he repeated the question. Usually, when she gave her name to someone who was going to write it down, she also spelled it for them. Now, needing to concentrate on her own problems, she provided Varela with that additional information only after he asked. Then, feeling it was important somehow that he know it, she added. "I'm a doctor . . . a resident at the Children's Hospital here."

"Doctor, can you tell me how you came to be in the park?"

Trying to tune out the distracting radio messages being spit into the front seat, Sarchi searched her uncooperative mind for an answer. "I have no idea. I remember that a man from LG&W was showing me a defective part on my furnace and then . . . there you were standing over me."

"When were you with this guy?"

"Around five o'clock. What time is it now?"

The cop checked his watch. "Nearly eight."

His answer chilled Sarchi far more than lying on the cold ground had. *For nearly three hours* she'd been utterly defenseless, unable to control what happened to her, part of that time in a public park. The thought was monstrous. "It must have been him," she said. "He did something to knock me out, then brought me here."

"Is there any reason to believe he might have sexually assaulted you?"

Oh my God. . . . He could have. Did he? She tried to focus on what her body could tell her, but the lines were down. *How could you not know something like that?* The question galloped across her mind in boxcar-sized letters. Eyes wide and swimming, she looked at Varela. "I . . . don't know."

"I understand," Varela closed his notebook. "I'm going to talk to Officer Martin and be right back."

Through the side window, Sarchi watched Varela and Martin confer in voices too low for her to hear. After no more than a minute or two, Martin nodded, went to his car, and got on the radio. Varela returned to where Sarchi was waiting, opened the door, and leaned down. "Doctor, we'd like for you to be examined at the sexual assault center. Would that be all right?"

No, she thought. *It was all wrong.* In her confused state she felt that somehow going to the center would mean it *had* happened. She resisted. "I'd rather just go home."

"We really need for you to do this, and it's something you should do for yourself. If you were assaulted, there are health risks that have to be addressed."

He was right. Damn him, but he was right. Resigned that this nightmare would last awhile longer, Sarchi said, "Where is this place?"

"It's not far."

Ten minutes later, Varela came to a stop at a darkened multistory parking garage where a civilian car with its engine running flicked its lights at them.

"That's your nurse," Varela said, looking at Sarchi in the

rearview mirror. "When it's after hours like this, whoever's on call comes from home."

The nurse backed up and pulled forward so she could feed her access card into the garage gate control. The barricade arm over the entrance lifted just long enough to admit her. She used her card in another reader inside to let Varela and Sarchi in.

Varela followed the nurse through the empty garage up to the second level, where they both parked by the elevator. Varela got out and opened Sarchi's door. When Sarchi got out, the nurse, a small dark woman with sympathetic eyes, was waiting.

"I'm Eileen," she said. "I'm so sorry we had to meet under these conditions. But you were right to come. We'll be going upstairs in the elevator."

Sarchi nodded, grateful that the nurse hadn't expected her to reply.

They all rode to the eleventh floor in awkward silence. When they arrived, the nurse led them down a long hall to a locked door. Once she had unlocked it, they went into another hallway.

"You can hang your coat right there," the nurse said, pointing at three hooks on the wall beside some molded plastic chairs. "Then have a seat while I do a little paperwork before we start."

While Sarchi hung up her coat and slumped into one of the plastic chairs, Varela and the nurse went into a room to the right and shut the door, leaving her alone, so far from her normal life she couldn't have seen it with the Hubble telescope.

In a few minutes, Varela came back into the hall. Behind him, the nurse beckoned. "Would you come in please?"

The room was quite small but efficiently laid out: an examining table in one corner, a bench and cabinets along the opposite wall, good lighting.

As she shut the door, the nurse pointed at another plastic chair beside a small desk. "Please, sit down."

"Could I have a drink of water?" Sarchi asked.

"We need to talk a bit first. Officer Varela said you were

unconscious in the presence of a man unknown to you for approximately three hours. Do you think he took advantage of
you sexually during that time?"

"I realize I should know the answer to something that important, but . . ."

Seeing how upset she was, the nurse reached out and
touched her arm. "It's not your fault. But under the circumstances, we have to consider all forms of assault, so before I
can give you anything to drink, I need to take some swab
samples from your mouth. Would that be all right?"

The implications of this turned Sarchi's stomach. But she
knew why it had to be done.

"Go ahead."

The nurse got some swabs from the bench behind her and
positioned herself. "Now, if you'll just open your mouth and
lift your tongue . . ."

She ran a swab under Sarchi's tongue and probed around
her gums, invading and scraping.

"Just a bit longer . . ."

After scouring Sarchi's mouth with a second swab, the
nurse rubbed two more in tandem over the upper surface of
her tongue. "I know that was unpleasant," she said, finally.
"There's some mouthwash and paper cups in the bathroom.
I'm afraid the only water I can offer you is from the tap."

Implanted with the thought of what the kidnapper might
have done to her, Sarchi used nearly half the bottle of mouthwash, not stopping until her mouth was on fire. She rinsed
that taste away with some water and only then slacked her
thirst.

Upon her return to the examining room, she was directed
once more into the plastic chair. The nurse turned off a noisy
blower drying the swabs she'd taken, then came back and sat
at the desk.

"Now, I have some more questions for you and some
things to explain." She began by gathering the usual background information and entering it on a form she plucked
from one of the stacks on the desk.

"If we should need to contact you is it all right to call you
at home?"

"I suppose."

She pulled a different form from a pile in front of her and handed it to Sarchi. "This is a consent for the examination. Take as long as you need to read it."

The form contained a long list of things they wanted to do to her, most so obnoxious she considered leaving. But her need to know what had happened persuaded her to stay. She signed the form and handed it back.

The nurse then asked her a series of brutally personal questions about her usual sexual practices, asking her how long it had been since she'd voluntarily done things she'd *never* done. From the answers she gave, the nurse decided that no pregnancy prevention medication was required. But there was even a form to sign for *not* being treated. Then the nurse handed her a paper gown and a large manila envelope. "Go into the bathroom and slip this on. And put your panties in the envelope."

And now, they were taking her underwear. For the first time since waking in the park, she felt the stirrings of anger. She thought of asking why they didn't just hang her panties from one of the Christmas decoration brackets on Union Avenue. Instead, she did what she was told. The gown was typical hospital issue, open at the rear. When she came out of the bathroom she was instructed to sit on the examining table, which was covered with a strip of disposable white paper that crinkled when she touched it. The nurse then drew some blood. The next few minutes on the table were humiliating. With her heels in obstetric stirrups she was videotaped, swabbed inside and out, combed, patted down with an adhesive tape "lifter" and studied with a hand-held light.

Finally, after spending a few minutes at a microscope, examining the slides she'd made from some of the swab samples, the nurse came back to the table ready to talk.

"I've found no physical evidence to suggest that you were assaulted."

With her life in free fall, this gave Sarchi something to reach for. "How sure can you be?"

"There are some lab tests yet to be done . . . for seminal products, but I'd be surprised if they show anything."

"How long before you'll have the results?"

"About a week."

"So you're very confident nothing happened."

"When we *find* certain types of evidence, it's possible to be a hundred-percent sure an assault took place. But that degree of certainty is never possible when a conclusion is based on a lack of evidence."

"I need a figure from you. Would you say you're ninety-nine percent sure?"

"It's hard to reduce something like this to a number."

"Try."

"I can't."

"You *have* to."

Seeing how much this meant to Sarchi, the nurse gave in. "All right. I'm ninety-five percent sure nothing happened."

Not good enough . . . not nearly good enough. Sarchi slumped in her chair.

"Since I can't be completely confident that I'm right, we need to discuss some health issues. You're a doctor, so what I'm about to say is probably familiar to you already. But just to be sure, I'm going to be as detailed with you as I would with anyone else."

She explained the various STDs Sarchi needed to be protected against, then gave her some pills to take home, and four of a different sort to swallow right then, swallow, followed by an injection.

"Some of the blood I took from you will be sent for HIV testing. That won't reveal if you were infected with HIV tonight. It will only tell your HIV status before this happened. Assuming you were negative, it will take at least six weeks for any transmitted virus to make you HIV positive. So you'll need to be tested again later, even though it's probably going to show nothing."

Finally, except for her panties, which the nurse kept, Sarchi was allowed to get dressed. Before releasing her, the nurse showed Sarchi a printed card with a handwritten name in a blank at the top. "This is the name of the counselor assigned to you. The card will explain her role." She gave Sarchi the card. "And with that, we're done. Now, I believe there's a detective outside who'd like to speak with you while I finish up in here."

In the hall, Sarchi found officer Varela gone. In his place was a man in a dark suit.

"Doctor Seminoux, I'm Sergeant Redmond. I'd like for you to tell me what happened tonight."

Redmond had sandy hair and a blond mustache. His heavy neck spilled over the collar of his shirt. There was no question that Sarchi wanted the guy who had abducted her caught, but she was also tired of being prodded. "Couldn't we do it some other time? I want to go home."

"Actually, we couldn't."

Too tired to resist, Sarchi dropped into a chair. "Let's get it over with."

"We'll be more comfortable down here." He looked at the nurse for corroboration and she nodded. Sarchi followed him to a small room with a black metal desk and four more plastic chairs. Redmond sat behind the desk and Sarchi in front. He produced a tape recorder from his pocket.

"You don't mind if I tape this do you?"

Once he had her permission he started the tape and put the recorder on the desk. He backed up the tape with a little police notebook.

"Now, Doctor Seminoux, how'd you get in the park?"

Sarchi told her story again.

Then, from a pocket in his jacket, Redmond produced a pair of rubber gloves and put them on. Reaching into another pocket, he pulled out a plastic bag full of white pills. "Do you recognize this?"

"No."

"It was found on the front seat of your car."

"I've never seen it before."

"So you don't know what they are."

"White pills."

He put the bag on her side of the desk and shook it so a couple of pills separated from the rest. "They have a distinctive shape, flat at one end, sharp on the other."

"I see that."

"I stopped at an all-night drugstore and showed them to

the pharmacist. He said they're a drug called Ativan. It's a tranquilizer."

"I've heard of it."

"They're two-milligram tablets. According to the pharmacist, that's a high dose."

"I'm not up on that. What's the point of this?"

"A person who would take that much has probably been on it for a long time or is using it to come off a high produced by, say, amphetamines. Do you use amphetamines?"

"No. I told you they're not mine. They must belong to whoever took me to the park. My car . . . is it still there?"

"We haven't been able to find the keys. Do you have them? In your coat perhaps?"

"I wouldn't think so."

"May I look?"

"Go ahead."

He went into the hall and came back with her coat. He found the keys in the first pocket he checked.

"Not only do I not know how they got there, I don't even know how I came to be wearing the coat when they found me."

"We're going to have to process your car," he said, draping her coat over a chair.

"Process?"

"Search it for evidence."

"How long will *that* take?"

"A few days."

"You've got to be kidding. Haven't I gone through enough?"

"It's procedure, Doctor. I have to do it."

"So you'll want my car keys."

"All your keys."

Already seething at the loss of her car and the accusatory nature of his questions about the pills, this pushed her to the brink of open rebellion. "I don't have a spare house key," she said, glaring at him.

"I'll see what I can do."

It wasn't exactly a promise, but it inched her back from the precipice.

"We also found your handbag in the car. I'll get it."

He went back into the hall and returned with her canvas bag, which he opened and held in front of her. "Is that the way you left it?"

"I don't know. Everything's always a jumble in there."

He emptied the contents onto the desk. "Is anything missing?"

She reached for her wallet.

"I'll get that," he said, picking it up. He took out the contents a compartment at a time and spread them on the desk.

"Everything's there," she said when they'd been through all of it. "You're not keeping that, too, are you?"

"Just for a few days."

The precipice beckoned. "I can't be left without my driver's license and my credit card."

"We'll also see about that."

The nurse leaned into the room. "I'm ready to leave."

"So are we," Redmond said. He put everything back in Sarchi's bag and they were soon all going down to the garage. Before separating, the nurse touched Sarchi lightly on the arm. "Doctor, you take care of yourself."

Redmond put Sarchi in the backseat of an unmarked car, and they followed the nurse out of the garage.

"Now can I go home?" Sarchi asked.

"Exactly our destination."

When they got there, Redmond walked her to the door, where he gave her back her driver's license, her credit card, and all her keys but the one for her car. Eagerly, she opened the door, anticipating the moment when she could shut it in Redmond's face.

"Doctor, I hope you don't mind, but I'm gonna need to come in and take a look around."

As much as she wanted to be rid of him, Sarchi saw that he was right. This had all started here. Who knew what might be inside? But this reminder that her home was no refuge from danger made her feel as though she was standing naked on a vast tundra.

When they were both in the living room, Redmond said, "Should anyone else be here?"

"I have a housemate, but she's working tonight. So, no, the place should be empty."

"Why don't you wait here while I check."

He wasn't gone long. "We're alone."

Sarchi got off the sofa to see him to the door, but he stopped in the middle of the room. "You know, I don't think anyone coming from LG&W to check for a gas leak would drive a car. They'd use a truck with one of those built-in tool-boxes in the back."

"Don't tell me. Tell the guy who drugged me."

"Did he touch anything, like the door when he came in?"

"He was wearing work gloves."

"You said that earlier didn't you?"

"I'm sure I did."

He took a card from his jacket pocket and gave it to her. "If you'll call that number in the morning, they'll give you the name of the detective who'll be handling your case from now on. He'll answer all your questions."

He thought a moment and Sarchi prayed nothing more would occur to him.

"I guess that's all then. When you feel up to it, you should check your belongings and see if anything's missing. If there is, mention it to your case officer."

After practically pushing Redmond out of the house, she shut the door and locked it. She then ran to the back door and made sure it was locked as well. Unwilling to take Redmond's word that the house was empty, she got the biggest knife she could find from a kitchen drawer and went through it all again, searching the closets, looking under the two beds, and making sure every window latch was secured. She then took the knife back into her bedroom, which no longer felt snug and safe.

After checking again for anyone lurking under the bed or in the closet, she switched on the bedside lamp and turned off the overhead light, focusing her surroundings so that the room would seem like a cave known only to her. She climbed into bed and with the knife beside her sat with her back against the headboard, knees drawn up, hugging her pillow.

From the times she'd left the main party on caving expeditions to explore a lead on her own, she'd believed she knew what it meant to be alone. But she'd had no idea. There had always been someone nearby, out of sight and too far off to be heard, but certain to miss her and provide assistance if needed. Now, having seen how easily someone could get to her, she felt utterly alone and completely defenseless.

Though the room was warm, she began to shiver. She wanted it to stop, but like the abduction, her wishes were ignored and the shaking continued, growing until she was rattling the bed.

Determined to at least impose her will on her own body, she grabbed her legs through the pillow and squeezed. But this dampened the shaking only slightly.

She wanted to cry but couldn't even do that. So she sat there, victimized again.

Finally, the tremors ran their course, and her body lapsed into a leaden state from which she somehow managed to fall asleep.

23

Sarchi's abduction took place on a Saturday. The next morning, having forgotten to set the alarm and with no work crew to wake her, she slept until she heard the sound of the doorbell.

She was still sitting with her knees drawn up, her back against the headboard of her bed. She tried to move, but her muscles were frozen in place. The doorbell rang again. She glanced at the clock on the nightstand: nine-thirty. Lord, she was late for work.

Then, reality came flooding back . . . The park . . . sprawled on her back, her feet in obstetric stirrups . . . the swabs . . . her mouth burning . . . three hours of her life missing . . .

Jesus, she was still wearing the same clothes, except of course for her panties, which were in a manila envelope somewhere.

Whoever was at the door rang again.

She threw the pillow from her lap and forced her legs over the side of the bed, realizing that her clothes were soaked from a night sweat that must have gone on for hours. Every muscle in her body seemed unhappy with her decision to stand, and a lightning bolt practically split her skull so she wasn't sure she could make it to the front door.

But after a few steps, the clamor from her muscles subsided by half and her headache, though still one of the worst she'd ever had, no longer threatened her life. Hating the way her clammy clothing felt against her skin, she hobbled to the front room.

When she looked out the sidelight of the front door, she saw a fat man in a brown suit and a uniformed policeman on the porch. There was an unmarked car and a patrol car in her driveway. Seeing her, the fat man held up a shield.

"Detective Treadwell, Doctor. I'd like to talk to you about your trouble in the park."

Suspicious now about anyone coming to the door, she said, "Who was the detective who talked to me last night?"

"That'd be Sergeant Redmond."

Convinced he was the real thing, she opened the door.

He dismissed the cop with him and came inside.

"Sorry to bother you so early, but I was in the neighborhood and wanted to introduce myself. I'll be handling your case from now on."

His skin was the color and texture of liverwurst, and he had thin eyebrows that looked like they belonged on a woman. "Have you made any progress?" she asked.

"I just spoke with some of your neighbors, and no one remembers seeing any unusual activity around your house last night."

"Did any of them see the LG&W car?"

"No. About that car—you make a call to LG&W. They don't send anybody, but this guy you've told us about shows up instead. How do you suppose he managed that?"

Angered at the tone of his question, she said, "You're the detective."

"Redmond talked to the utility company last night, and they don't have any record of you reporting a gas leak."

"I don't know what to say."

"No, of course you wouldn't. Just thought I'd pass that along. We'll keep working on it." He gave her his card. "If you have any questions or need to contact me for any reason, don't hesitate."

"When can I have my car and handbag back?"

"Call me late tomorrow. I should have an answer for you then."

As she shut the door behind him, Sarchi was convinced that neither of the detectives she'd spoken with believed her story. She nearly called Treadwell back to tell him who was behind the kidnapping, but quickly saw the spot she was in. The entire charade had obviously been set up to further the fiction that she was a drug abuser. And the detectives had apparently bought it. With no proof that Latham was involved or even that the kidnapper really existed, Treadwell would listen to her with apparent sincerity, then probably do nothing. She also saw that even a half-hearted attempt to follow up on what she'd say would lead Treadwell to Pierce for corroboration and maybe to Kate, thereby spreading the story of her apparent drug overdose to the hospital.

Thinking about all this was making her headache worse. And she was *so* late for work.

Fortified with a couple of aspirins, she headed for the bathroom, where, still feeling unsafe in her own home, she showered without drawing the curtain and kept both eyes open. She then threw on some fresh clothes and called a cab to take her to the hospital.

Later, when Kate asked why she'd arrived so late, Sarchi mumbled something about car trouble, which, in a way, was true. For the rest of the day, between patients, she thought about the chances that she'd been sexually assaulted.

Ninety-five percent sure nothing happened—almost complete assurance. Even scientists accept such a high percentage as proof. A comfortable number. Nothing to worry about. She'd used it herself to calm worried parents.

But this was different. This involved *her* life. And she now discovered that when it was personal, five percent could fill your head.

What had he done to her? Before this, she wouldn't have believed the loss of a mere three hours could prey upon a person's mind like this, fragmenting it so she could barely function. The thought that at any moment someone might mention the park was a further distraction.

Shortly before quitting time, she called Treadwell and learned that the cops weren't ready to release her car. Unwilling to be without transportation any longer, she got Linda to drive her to the nearest place where she could rent one. As she had done with Kate, she avoided telling Linda what had actually happened.

That night, all she was holding inside clamored for release to the point that she considered calling Sharon McKinney in New Orleans and unburdening herself. But that seemed like such a dependent, selfish thing to do that she decided against it. Even though she felt a little safer with Linda in the house, sleep came reluctantly, held at bay by thoughts of what else Latham might have planned for her. By one A.M., that damned five percent lay across the bed like a suffocating shroud. Finally, worn out from worry, she slept. But even then, the battle raged, and she woke the next morning with her pajamas clinging wetly to her skin.

At the hospital, she managed to work a few hours without thinking too much about her troubles. Then, a little after ten o'clock, she was paged to Koesler's office.

Finding him as usual at his desk, she crossed the room and prepared to take a seat.

"Don't," Koesler said. "You won't be here long."

He reached toward the little device with the row of hanging steel balls at the front of his desk and pulled the first ball in the row away from the rest. "The last time you were here, I saw from the look on your face that you believed this was a childish thing for me to have."

Sarchi felt she should apologize for that thought, but couldn't think how to phrase it.

Koesler released the ball he was holding, allowing it to hit the others and kick out the one on the far end. He watched while the ballet set in motion played out. "I like this device because it demonstrates that certain actions in life lead to inevitable consequences. You, Dr. Seminoux, apparently do not believe that."

From the moment she'd received the page to see him

Sarchi had feared he knew about the incident in the park. Now she was sure of it.

"I told you we were on a collision course," he said. "But you chose to ignore me. That will not continue." He shook his head. "Unconscious in a public park. Why, you're a danger even to yourself. So now you have two choices. Admit your problem to me right now and accept counseling or be suspended."

His ultimatum was a crushing addition to the burden Sarchi was already carrying. She couldn't admit to being an addict when it was all a hoax. "It's true I *was* found drugged in the park, but it wasn't my doing. Someone— "

Koesler held up his hand. "No more of that. Just choose."

"I can't."

"Then leave."

Unable to believe her life had come to this, Sarchi didn't move.

"Would you rather I call security and have them show you to the street?"

Dazed, Sarchi got up and walked to the door.

"Doctor Seminoux . . ."

She turned and looked back.

"Come to grips with your problem," Koesler said. "It's the only way."

In a fog, Sarchi went to Kate McDaniel's office. Through the open door she watched Kate at her computer for a few seconds, unsure of what to say. She settled on a direct, unadorned statement. "Kate . . . I have to leave."

Kate turned. "Oh, hi. I didn't know you were there. What do you mean you have to leave?"

"I've been suspended."

Kate's face fell. "I was afraid that might happen. Sit down and let's talk about it."

"Not now. Maybe another time. I have to go."

With leaden steps Sarchi left the hospital and got in her car. Before pulling onto the street, she paused. Where was she going? She was in no frame of mind to be cooped up at home. Without making a conscious decision, she headed for the heart of downtown.

Oblivious to her surroundings, she took Union Avenue to Front Street and turned north, a route that took her past the statue of Ramesses the Great in front of the stainless steel–clothed pyramid sports arena sitting cold and dull under the overcast sky. At the next light she turned left and went over the Auction Street bridge to Mud Island, the bustling new residential development on the banks of the Mississippi.

Drawn to the river by the same power that had attracted Harry Bright when he was in trouble, she pulled into a parking bay that looked out over the water barely thirty yards away and shut off the engine.

What was she going to do? Being a doctor wasn't just a job. It was part of her, like her heart or her eyes. What would happen to her now? Without her work, she was nothing.

The river was high and moving fast, a broad gray sheet topped with foam near the shore where eddies twirled and played with flotsam the river had brought from St. Louis or some other point to the north. As she watched the debris moving at the mercy of the currents, she suddenly saw how her whole life had been controlled by other people: her parents when she was a kid; and all her teachers, especially those in med school, who regularly handed out more work than anyone could reasonably handle, leaving her practically no time for herself, expecting her to keep her mouth shut when they said things that were wrong or insulting.

And there was Koesler, ruling the hospital like a feudal king, wrong not to have an MRI tech on call at night, imposing his will on everyone, taking her chief residency away just because someone had asked him to do it, believing she was on drugs when she wasn't . . . Carolyn dying . . . and her mother . . . Drew, damaged . . . None of it right, all of it out of her hands.

And the night she was kidnapped, forced into a situation where she was spread-eagled on a table and objects were inserted into her. It was all too much, just too much.

Unable to think anymore, her mind closed to everything but the river rushing south to its destiny. She remained for some time lost in that water world. Then, Koesler's last words called her back.

"Come to grips with your problem. It's the only way."

Her eyes hardened. He was right. She was through being controlled. She was taking charge. With or without the help of the police, she was going to make Latham wish they had never met.

24

Sarchi began to think in practical terms. The clinic was the way to get Latham. This wasn't just about mistakes made during surgery. There was something criminal going on. And she was damned sure going to find out what. But she was not a professional investigator, and this was a dangerous situation. She'd need help. But from whom?

Certainly not Pierce. He'd wanted to put his head in the sand from the beginning. Kate? Hardly. Sharon would have been her first choice for a lot of things, but not this. She needed someone who could handle themselves in a tight spot and knew how to conduct an investigation—a private detective maybe.

Wait a minute.

She started the car, backed out of her parking bay, and whipped it into drive.

Knowing she was going so far out on a limb a squirrel couldn't hold on, Sarchi opened the phone book, hoping he was listed.

He was.

She rehearsed what she'd say, then punched in his number. It took him four rings to pick up.

"John, this is Sarchi. I realize it's early and we barely know each other, but I need help, and I don't know who else to ask."

"What kind of help?"

"It's too complicated to go into on the phone. Could you possibly come to my house to discuss it?"

"When?"

"At your convenience. But soon I hope."

"How about thirty minutes?"

For the first time since she'd awakened in the park, Sarchi felt a flicker of optimism.

She put on a pot of coffee and sat down to wait for Metcalf to arrive. Suddenly she remembered that Redmond had recommended she check the house to see if anything was missing. But there was no need for that. This wasn't about petty theft.

Metcalf pulled into the driveway twenty-eight minutes after she'd called him. He got out of his truck and came up the drive wearing his tan bomber jacket over a rust-colored cable knit sweater and tan houndstooth slacks. She had the door open before he reached the porch.

"I really appreciate you coming."

"I was actually about to call *you* and see when we could get together again."

She stepped back and let him in. "How about some coffee? It's already made."

"Sure."

He followed her to the kitchen and sat at the table. Feeling very awkward now that he was here, Sarchi put a cup and saucer in front of him and another at the opposite seat. Not thinking, she filled his cup nearly to the brim, leaving no room for any cream.

"Nuts. Did you want cream? My housemate takes it black and she likes a full cup—I must have done that out of habit."

"Black is fine."

She poured herself a cup, added a little cream, and sat down. "I don't know where to begin."

"Start anywhere."

"Are you aware of what happened to me Saturday night?"

"No."

"Did you hear any calls on your radio about a woman being found unconscious in Overton Park?"

His brow furrowed. "I was off duty. Are you saying that woman was . . ."

"I'm afraid so."

"Unconscious . . . how?"

"When you came here the second time to talk about the apparent theft of my bag, do you remember me saying that it wasn't the first odd thing that had happened to me lately?"

"The other was your car. Someone had driven it without your knowledge and left it in a different place than you parked."

"Shortly after those two incidents, the progress charts of two of my patients disappeared. Then someone told the Tennessee Medical Board I was into drugs, and the board sent out an investigator to check up on me. All this has really screwed up my reputation at the hospital. They all think the drugs I'm supposedly abusing are affecting my memory. Then, Saturday night, things really got rough."

She explained those events in as much detail as she could, finishing with "They left a bag of tranquilizers on the front seat of my car to make it look as though I'd driven to the park in a drugged stupor. And I'm pretty sure the detectives who questioned me believe that, especially since LG&W doesn't have any record of me calling them that night."

"Has anyone examined your phone line where it comes into the house?"

"For what?"

"Let's go see."

Sarchi followed John into the backyard, where he quickly located the line and bent to study it. After a few seconds, he slipped his finger behind a spot about five inches above where it entered the house and lifted it away from the siding. "Have a look."

Leaning close, she saw some tiny punctures in the line.

"That could be where a device was attached to the line in order to shunt your LG&W call to another phone."

"We should show this to those detectives."

"Without any other corroborating evidence to support your account, I don't think they'll be very impressed. Who would want to do all this to you?"

"A man named George Latham. He runs a clinic in New Orleans. It's a long story better told inside."

For the next fifteen minutes, Sarchi described to Metcalf all that had happened since Drew's operation. "And my guess is Latham is worried I'll figure out what he's up to and will try again to bring him down. By making it appear I have a drug problem he's hoping to undermine my credibility."

Sarchi paused and waited for Metcalf's reaction. He stared into his coffee cup without speaking for so long she was sure he was searching for the words to say he didn't want any part of this.

Finally, he looked at her. "You may be underestimating Latham's intent."

"Does that mean you believe me?"

"Why would you call me over here just to lie to me?"

"Maybe as a ploy so you'll convince those detectives I'm not an addict."

Metcalf leaned back in his chair and gave her a puzzled look. "That's an odd thing to say. I was under the impression you wanted my help."

"I do. I just don't want you thinking of that later and begin to wonder."

"That won't happen."

For a moment both of them were silent.

"Tell me what you meant when you said I may be under-estimating Latham," Sarchi said.

"It's possible he intends to have you killed in such a way as to make it appear it was an accidental drug overdose. That way no one would ever look at him."

Sarchi stiffened in her chair. "I never thought of that. If it's true—if he'd be willing to commit murder—then he's got to be hiding something extremely important."

"You need around-the-clock protection."

"Where would I get it, the police?"

"Probably not. How about bodyguards?"

"Are you volunteering?"

"It's not a one-man job, particularly if the one man has other obligations."

"I don't have any money for a bodyguard."

"You could borrow it."

"I'm already seventy thousand dollars in debt for my education. And anyway, I can't have my movements hindered out of fear. I've got work to do."

"I know your work is important, but . . ."

"I don't mean at the hospital. I've got to figure out Latham's secret and expose him. Isn't that really my best protection?"

"In the long run, maybe."

"So the faster I move, the better off I'll be. The problem is I don't know where to begin. That's why I called you."

"You're committed to bringing this guy down?"

"Irrevocably."

"Do you own a firearm?"

"No."

"You need one. I've got a .38 special I'll lend you. Do you know how to shoot?"

"No."

"I'll also throw in a free lesson."

25

Sarchi and John picked up the .38 and spent an hour on a firing range. Then John gave her a short course in self-defense. They stopped for lunch at Molly's, a popular Mexican restaurant in Overton Square.

After they'd ordered and shifted their chairs around so the legs no longer rocked on the rough tiled floor, John leaned across the table. "I should mention that if you're planning on carrying that gun around in your bag, you'll need a permit."

"How long will it take to get one?"

"A month if you're lucky."

"Considering the circumstances, you expect me to obey that law?"

"From this point on, I'm not gonna think about it."

The waitress brought their drinks and some tortilla chips. When she moved out of earshot, Sarchi said, "How do you think I should start my investigation of Latham?"

"First thing you should do is get some background on him. Where he was born, where he went to med school, where he did his residency . . ."

"I already have that. In fact . . ." She dug in her bag and gave him the page containing the bio of Latham that Sharon had copied from the specialty directories in New Orleans.

He tried to read it, but couldn't figure out the abbreviations. "I'm afraid I need a translator."

Sarchi moved her chair closer and interpreted for him.

"So, is there anything significant there?" she asked.

"Not by itself. But it's a start." He handed the paper back to her. "I'd also look up his publications—if he has any—to see what he's done and who he's worked with. That anonymous e-mail you mentioned sounds like a potential gold mine. Whoever sent that is very close to the heart of what's going on, but they obviously aren't willing to reveal what they know directly. They want you to work for it. But if we could figure out who this person is, we might be able to tap them for more than they want to give."

Sarchi was pleased at his use of "we." "There's a woman in the information services department at the hospital who's a computer genius. We can go over there and ask her if there's a way to use the return address on that message to track it back to the sender. Then we could stop by the UT library and get more information on Latham." Then, realizing she was assuming he was as interested in all this as she was and didn't have plans for the rest of the afternoon, she said, "Sorry . . . I'm usually not this self-absorbed. I can't expect you to give up your whole day."

"After the story you told me, you don't expect me to go home now, do you? I want to know who this guy is and what he's hiding, too."

Despite John's objections, which arose partly from Sarchi's admission earlier that she was hugely in debt, Sarchi paid for lunch. They then drove to the medical center and parked John's truck in the commercial lot at the corner of Dunlap and Madison, a location between their dual destinations.

Sarchi suspected that by now her suspension was common knowledge around the hospital. Heading that way, she prayed they wouldn't run into any of the other residents.

As it turned out, the promising possibility that they might gain some insight into the identity of the author of the anonymous e-mail could not be immediately explored because the woman they'd come to see had taken the day off. She would, however, be there tomorrow. More than a little disappointed, they set out for their second stop.

The six-story health sciences library was perched on ten tall cement piers with a disconcerting amount of space between them, as if Memphis wasn't in a major earthquake zone. Access from the street was in the back, through a foyer that also served as the library's smoking lounge, so as John and Sarchi waited for the elevator they were bathed in the effluvium from the cigarette of a thin woman reading a paperback.

When they had reached the reading room on the second floor, they went immediately to the computers, where Sarchi gave John a quick lesson on how to search the MEDLINE database. They agreed Sarchi would check everything from 1990 to the present and John would check from 1980 to 1990.

In about thirty minutes they were finished. They found that Latham had a long-standing interest in myelin, the material that insulates nerve fibers. He had also dabbled in studies of Parkinson's, Alzheimer's, and Huntington's diseases with a variety of collaborators. More recently, after joining the Department of Medicine at Vanderbilt medical school in Nashville, he'd worked with a biochemist there named Timmons. Together they had published a series of papers dealing with the molecular biology of myelin protein expression. Three years ago, Latham moved to Westbank Medical. Interestingly, although he'd published at least two papers a year for nearly two decades, there was nothing listed for the last three years. A gap that could probably have been filled with papers on his treatment of paralyzed kids had he chosen to write them.

"I don't feel any closer to what he's hiding," Sarchi said on the way to the car.

"We've just located some building blocks," John replied. "Patience is more than a virtue in a detective. It's a requirement."

"What now?"

"I'll have to think about it. I've got some errands to run be-

fore my shift starts. Maybe something will occur to me while
I'm doing that."

Parked out in front of Sarchi's house, Sarchi could tell that
John was apprehensive about parting. "The police can't protect you twenty-four hours a day, but in the future if you see
anyone around your house you don't know, call the south
precinct and have a car sent over to check things out. I'll alert
everyone there to give any call from you the highest priority
they can."

Sarchi agreed to call immediately if anything seemed suspicious. In the morning, Sarchi was to make another run at
the computer expert, and they would meet at one o'clock for
lunch at the Public Eye.

They hadn't advanced their investigation to any significant degree, but as she watched John drive off, Sarchi felt
considerably better than she had earlier. So much so that after
determining that there were no more anonymous messages
waiting in her e-mail account, she was able to put her troubles far enough out of mind to peruse several days worth of
caver's digests with real interest.

She'd been home about forty-five minutes when the phone
rang.

"This is Doctor Sam Brookings," a voice said, "from the
Tennessee Impaired Physicians program. Would it be possible for me to come to your home this afternoon and talk with
you?"

The hairs on Sarchi's neck prickled, for it seemed likely
that this guy had no relationship to the program he mentioned, but was actually part of Latham's campaign against
her. Seeing a chance to snare him and give detective Treadwell something to work with, she said, "When would you
like to come?"

"I can be there in fifteen minutes."

"I'll expect you."

As soon as she hung up, Sarchi hurried into the backyard
and checked the phone line to see if there was anything attached to it. There wasn't.

Back inside she called the south precinct, gave her name
and address to the woman who answered, and explained

what she wanted. "There's a man on his way to my house who I believe, intends to harm me."

"I just talked to officer Metcalf about you," the woman said. "But I didn't expect to hear from you so soon. I'll send a car."

Five minutes later, a cruiser pulled into her drive and a black cop graying at the temples and with a paunch worthy of a detective got out. She met him on the porch, where he introduced himself as Officer Rivers. After a brief consultation, they put the patrol car behind the gates to the backyard and Rivers came inside to wait.

Only moments later, a car slowed in front of the house and turned into the driveway.

"He's here," Sarchi said.

Rivers joined her by the door.

When the driver got out, Sarchi began to think she'd overreacted. He looked so old and thin she could have handled him by herself. Following the plan they'd agreed upon, Rivers stood out of sight behind the door when Sarchi opened it.

Brookings introduced himself through the storm door and Sarchi let him in. Rivers then took over.

"Doctor, would you show me some identification, please?"

The little bit of color in Brookings's face drained away. "What's going on here?"

"Some identification, please," Rivers said firmly.

The old man fumbled for his wallet and produced his driver's license. Rivers looked at it and said, "Would you come with me, please."

"Where?"

"To my car. It's in the back. It'll only be for a few minutes."

Rivers led the bewildered Doctor Brookings through the kitchen to the patrol car, where they stayed for a quarter of an hour, doing whatever cops do to check people out. Then Rivers came back inside.

"He's exactly who he says he is. Should I bring him in?"

"I don't want to talk to him. Tell him to leave. I'm sorry to have brought you over here for nothing."

"If one of my friends had called the precinct for help and John Metcalf was on duty, he'd have done the same for me."

Even so, Sarchi felt foolish for calling him.

That night, when Linda came home, she was upset with Sarchi. "I thought we were friends."

"What's wrong?"

"We live in the same house yet I had to hear from the grapevine about your problem in the park and your suspension."

So it *was* all over the hospital.

"Is it true?" Linda asked. "*Do* you have a drug problem?"

"It's not true. Koesler is mistaken. You *all* are."

"What about the park?"

"Is the gossip mill also conveying my explanation for that?"

"No. What is it?"

"Please don't take offense at this, but it's very complicated and not easy to tell."

"I've got time."

"It'll just sound self-serving."

"Try me."

"Look, I'm trying to dig up some corroborating evidence to support my position. Until I have it I don't want to say any more. If we *are* friends, you'll understand that."

"Well . . . sure. Of course I do."

"I knew you would."

Later that evening as she reflected on Linda's belief that failure to confide in her was a betrayal of friendship, Sarchi decided to call Sharon McKinney and bring her up to date. After that call, feeling now that she had two allies in her campaign against Latham, her spirits rose higher than the circumstances dictated.

Bob Kazmerak stopped by the office first thing Monday morning to pick up some papers before hitting the trail to see how the dipstick docs in his area had been pissing away his company's money over the weekend. Being there made him think of Harry Bright and how he'd never see old Harry sitting behind his desk again, never again hear him bait the announcer at the RiverKing's game by shouting "How much time is left?" a couple seconds before the guy made his usual announcement that there was one minute left in the period. Then Harry'd yell "Thank you." Funny guy.

It was good they'd opted for a closed casket funeral with just a picture of Harry and not the actual cold carcass for everybody to have to deal with. It was . . . thoughtful. Bad as they usually do at the box office, it was a sure bet the RiverKings'd miss him.

Kazmerak tried to picture Harry in his mind and was distressed to realize he couldn't remember how Harry wore his hair, whether he parted it or combed it back. Damn, you go down and the world just closes over your spot.

Noticing a white envelope on Harry's desk, he walked over, picked it up, and read the writing on the front:

Dr. Seminoux—Children's Hospital

Well, the least he could do for old Harry would be to stop at the hospital and drop this off.

Eager as Sarchi was to talk to Ella Dodge about locating the sender of the anonymous e-mail, she waited until all the other residents would be on duty before going to the hospital. And instead of parking in the hospital garage, she went to the commercial lot that she and John had used the day before.

Ella's office was on the second floor, with windows looking out over the hospital lobby. Glancing up as she came in from the street, Sarchi's expectations fell, for Ella's windows were dark.

Hoping Ella hadn't decided to take another day off, Sarchi went up to the second floor help desk to ask about her. The news was good. Ella had called in to say she would be about an hour late. But what to do until she arrived? Thinking of a possibility, Sarchi went downstairs and made a phone call from the information desk.

"Carl, this is Sarchi. I was wondering if you'd made any progress on sequencing those primers I gave you."

"Funny you should call. I just sent my technician to pick up the results."

"Okay if I come over?"

"Sure."

When she arrived, she found Carl in his office working inside a U-shaped enclosure formed by a desk and two long tables that gave him easy access to his computer and stacks of journal articles. "Looks like we got some good data," he said. Sarchi was relieved that he didn't seem to know about any of her problems. He handed her two sheets of paper with one line on each page accented with an orange highlighter. The accented portion on each sheet consisted of a line of twenty capital letters representing the arrangement of the four DNA building blocks, *A*denine, *T*hymine, *G*uanine, and *C*ytosine in each primer.

The sequence for primer one was:

5`-TAAGACGGCTCCGGGAAAAA-3`

The sequence for primer two was:

5`-CGCCGGGGTTCGAACAATTG-3`

By itself this meant nothing. "If someone were to use these primers in a PCR reaction what would they be looking for?" Sarchi asked.

"Come around here and we'll see," Carl replied, turning his chair so it faced the computer behind his desk.

Sarchi circled the desk and entered Carl's inner realm.

"Just push some of those things aside and sit."

Clearing a space for herself, Sarchi perched on the edge of the desk so she could see what he was doing.

He connected his computer with the National Center for Biotechnology information, chose a sequence identification program, and entered the sequence of the first primer. While the computer searched the databases, a DNA helix icon in the corner of the monitor spiraled along a progress line. When it reached the end, the results flashed onto the screen.

Carl leaned forward, scanned all the information displayed, and pointed to a line halfway down. "Primer one exactly matches a sequence in adeno-associated virus two."

"What's that?"

"A virus that can't replicate on its own, but needs help from adenoviruses."

"So the other primer will just match another region of the same virus."

"Probably."

He entered the sequence, and they waited for the results.

When they came up he muttered, "That's odd. We got a match with an engineered form of Molony mouse leukemia virus, a retrovirus that, like adeno-associated virus, can't replicate by itself."

"What does that mean?"

"If these primers ever detected anything, it'd be a hybrid stretch of nucleic acid derived from parts of both viruses."

"You said the retrovirus was engineered . . ."

"It's a form that was made by scientists to serve as a gene carrier."

"So you would never expect to find that virus in nature."

"Nor the hybrid the primers would detect. What's this all about?"

"I'm not sure, but I think what you've told me is important. I can't thank you enough for doing this."

"That's what friends are for. I hope you know Gail and I both are always available to you for *whatever* you need."

This was obviously not a generic expression of friendship, but meant something more. Perhaps he too thought she might be on drugs. Whatever his motivation, she wasn't going to engage in a discussion about it.

"You both are the best," she said, moving out of his work enclosure. "We'll all get together soon."

Walking back to the hospital, Sarchi racked her brain trying to figure out why Latham would be searching the tissues of his patients for evidence of a virus that didn't exist in nature.

26

Ella Dodge had the biggest chair in the information sys-
tems department because nothing less would accommo-
date her. Sarchi found her in that chair arranged as usual,
with her sneaker-clad left foot and phlebotic left leg resting
on a small rolling stool. Seeing Sarchi in the rearview mirror attached to her monitor, Ella said, "Doctor Seminoux,
what brings you to the nerd ward?"

Sarchi walked around and stood by Ella's elevated foot.
"How's the phlebitis?"

"Better when I don't think about it."

"Sorry."

"You meant well, so I won't hold it against you. Might
even help you with whatever you want."

As much as she liked Ella, Sarchi couldn't help thinking
that her life would be far better if she lost a couple hundred
pounds. Apparently she either hadn't heard about the suspension or had chosen to keep it to herself. "Is there a way to
track the return address on an e-mail back to the sender to get
some information on who they are or where their computer
is?"

"Did you bring a printout of the header?"

Sarchi dug in her handbag and gave her the anonymous

e-mail, which was folded in half so she couldn't see the message.

Ella looked at it briefly. "At least it's not one of those snooty providers that won't give an outsider access to their client data. So, who knows?"

She hit some keys and called up a new screen. "First let's try *Who Is*. That's mostly for military addresses, but we might get something."

Her fat fingers flicked over the keys with amazing dexterity.

"Unrecognized host," she announced. "*Finger*'s a better program anyway."

She played the keyboard like a prodigy and waited for results. "And there it is," she crowed a moment later. "Virtual Joe, your Internet home away from home. Now serving Seattle's finest. Open 11:00 A.M. till midnight seven days a week." She recited the phone number and address. "New Orleans, Louisiana." She looked at Sarchi. "Sometimes businesses set up their server so if anybody fingers them, they send a commercial back. Great name for the place, except it sounds like when you get there and order, they'll bring you a cup with nothing in it."

Sarchi was pleased to have an address, but if the business identified was what it sounded like, it wasn't going to mean much. With the printout bearing the address of Virtual Joe tucked in her bag and Ella properly thanked, Sarchi walked to the elevators.

Driving home, she rolled her morning's work around in her head, trying to assemble it into a plan of action. But even having had a little time to assimilate them, the PCR results sat like a ton of granite in the path of progress. Blocked so effectively in that direction, she allowed herself unrealistic hopes for Virtual Joe. Maybe it's not what it sounds like. Maybe if she knew exactly what the place was, what it looked like, and how it worked, there would be a way to discover the person who'd sent the message. She couldn't determine those things herself, but Sharon could.

• • •

Sarchi was welcomed by the din of hammers and power saws from next door when she arrived home. Propped in the holder below the mailbox was a thin package wrapped in brown paper, addressed to her, but with no return address. She looked at the postmark: Biloxi, Mississippi. Who did she know in Biloxi?

Grabbing the rest of the mail, which was as uninteresting as usual, she went inside, chucked everything else on the table by the door, and tore at the wrapping on the package.

It was a children's book. How odd.

She saw a folded sheet of paper protruding slightly from the pages. Believing it to be a letter of explanation, she pulled it free and opened it. It bore only three typewritten lines:

Find the friend who has a copy of this book.
and
Think about how children communicate in secret.

Virtual Joe, Sarchi thought. Another message.

Sarchi thumbed through the book, which had lots of pictures but few words. It was about a rabbit family whose two kids ignored all the advice their parents gave them about crossing the street and avoiding lawn mowers. At the end, a hidden device played a little tune sung by speeded up voices like the Christmas songs sung by the three chipmunks.

Wait a minute . . .

She'd heard this story and the song before.

Of course. Marge read it to Drew that night in the hospital. *She* had a copy. But where did she get it? And what did it have to do with all this?

Sarchi called Marge at work to talk about the book but had to settle for leaving her name with the receptionist because Marge was in a meeting. With the phone in her hand, she then called Sharon's pager in New Orleans and left her number.

Now, what did Virtual Joe mean about a child communicating in secret? How do they do that . . . pass notes . . . tin can telephone . . . whisper?

The phone interrupted her thoughts. It was Sharon.

"Hope I didn't call you away from anything important," Sarchi said.

"Just the dullest seminar in the history of the planet," Sharon replied. "What's happening?"

"Remember that anonymous e-mail I got warning me about Latham? Well, it was sent from a place called Virtual Joe there in New Orleans. I think it's some kind of coffee-house. Would you consider dropping by and taking a look at the layout, see what goes on and how it's set up with an eye toward figuring out who might have sent that message?"

"I'll do it tonight. Did you learn anything from those primers?"

"Something strange. They were constructed to detect nucleic acids from a virus engineered as a gene carrier."

"This is all making me extremely curious," Sharon said. "Anything else I can do to help, let me know. Even if there isn't, keep me informed."

Sarchi was about to mention the book that had just arrived and ask Sharon how kids communicate in secret when Sharon was paged from intensive care and had to go.

At least Sarchi didn't have the distractions of patients to deal with. But even with that advantage, she couldn't see what kids communicating secretly had to do with *anything*. She was spared further thought on that by Marge returning her call.

"Sorry to bother you at work," Sarchi said, "but do you remember that book about the rabbit family, the one with the song in the back. You read it to Drew in the hospital."

"I remember. It's also the one I was reading to him the night he got sick."

Sarchi had a crazy thought. "Did Drew touch the book?"

"No. I was holding it. Why do you ask?"

"Where did you get the book?"

"It came in the mail."

"You ordered it?"

"It simply arrived. It was a promotional gift from some new publisher of children's books."

"Do you still have it?"

"I'm sure we do, somewhere. Why are you so interested in that?"

Sarchi's mind was racing. Marge was reading that book to Drew when he got sick . . . as if . . . no. How could a book make him sick? One he wasn't even holding. If it was the book, Marge was the one who should have become ill.

"Sarchi . . . are you there?"

"It's kind of complex. Can I have a rain check on explaining?"

"Sure. We need to get together anyway. I haven't seen you in ages."

"I know. How's Drew?"

"Generally, he's great. And his tic seems to be less pronounced—not by much, probably it's something only a mother could see, but I think it's getting better."

Sarchi's love for Drew and her guilt at having allowed him to fall into Latham's hands made her want desperately to believe Drew *was* improving. "That's great news."

"Come over tonight and see for yourself if I'm right. I'll make some shrimp scampi and we'll catch up."

Sarchi didn't want to tell Marge what had been happening. Though she was unable to see how she could avoid that for a full evening, she longed to see Drew and also wanted to get a look at their copy of the book. "I'll be there."

Her questions about the book and how kids communicate secretly and what significance all this might have were still without answers at one o'clock when she walked into the Public Eye and spotted John Metcalf waiting for her at a table in the back by the barbecue buffet. Just seeing him gave her an unexpected lift.

He stood as she approached and helped with her chair. When they were both settled, he said, "I talked to the detective handling your case, and you were right. He's blowing off the part of your story about being abducted. He thinks you took too much Ativan and made it up to cover yourself. I told him about the puncture marks in your phone line, but he barely reacted. He said they weren't finished yet with your bag or your car."

"Thanks for checking. I've had quite a morning." She held

her story while their waiter put a bowl of popcorn on the table and took their drink orders. As he moved off, Sarchi told John about the PCR primer results and locating Virtual Joe.

After their waiter brought their drinks and they told him they were having the buffet, Sarchi dug in her handbag. "Then this came in the mail today." She handed John the book and the note. "I don't know what it means, but the mother of my nephew, Drew, got a copy of that book in the mail and was reading it to him when he got sick."

"Could there be a connection between his illness and the book?"

"I can't see how. His mother didn't get sick, and I suppose the book is still in their house. If it made him sick once why not again?"

"I agree. That seems an unproductive way to go."

"What about the second part of the note? How do kids communicate secretly?" She told him all the ways she'd come up with, and waited to see if he could add any.

He considered it briefly, then waved his hand. "I can't think of anything else. Maybe after I eat something."

They went through the buffet line and returned to their table. Before starting on his food, John lifted the lemon out of his iced tea with his spoon. "I should have told him to leave that out. I'm just not a lemon guy." Then he froze.

"What?"

"I've got an idea about how kids communicate, but it requires a demonstration. When we're through here we'll go back to your place and see if I'm right."

John turned the control for the heating element on the cooktop to medium-high and waited for it to get hot.

"I still don't get it," Sarchi said.

"Patience. It will all become manifest in time. Unless, of course, I'm wrong."

When the element was glowing, John held the letter close to it and moved it around to heat it evenly.

"You think there's a hidden message on there that'll be revealed by heat?"

"Invisible ink made from lemon juice. You never did that as a kid?"

"Somehow I missed that one."

John removed the letter from the heat and examined it carefully. "Nothing." He returned it to the heat and held it a little closer.

After examining the letter again, he turned it over and heated the other side.

That didn't produce anything either.

"Do it with pages of the book," Sarchi suggested.

John picked up the book, opened it, and played the first page over the heat. About the time Sarchi was sure it was seconds from igniting, he examined the results and broke into a big grin. He turned the page so she could see in the second line of printing that the heat had produced a brown ring around the letter "t."

"I'll get a pen," Sarchi said.

By the time she returned, John had another letter—an "i."

It was tedious work, but over the next few minutes they found two "m"s, an "o," and an "n." One more letter gave them "timmons." "Where have I seen that name?" Sarchi said.

"As coauthor on the last five of Latham's published papers," John said.

27

To be certain they'd found everything encrypted in the book, John kept working. By the time he finished the last page they'd added a comma and a first initial for Timmons as well as the phrase "Acta N."

"Any idea what that is?" John asked.

"Looks like an abbreviation for a scientific journal."

"Back to the library."

Upon reaching the reading room, they divided the database as they had before when searching for Latham's publications. Christopher Timmons was well published, but only two of his papers were listed in *Acta Neurologica*. The first, published in 1988, was titled "Breakdown, a New Mouse Mutation." A year later, "Studies on the Mutant Gene in the Breakdown Mouse" appeared.

Generally each paper listed was accompanied by a brief summary, but there were none for the two *Acta Neurologica* papers, possibly because they were in such an obscure journal. For that same reason, the journal was not among the library's holdings.

"I'd sure like to know what's in those papers," Sarchi said.

"The titles don't tell you anything?"

"Very little. I'm just trusting Virtual Joe that there's something to be learned from them."

"Can we get the library to borrow the journal from someone for us?"

"Interlibrary loan—it's done all the time. Usually the lending source will simply copy the articles and send those. Hard to say how long that'll take, though. But if Tulane or LSU has the journals I might be able to get my friend Sharon in New Orleans to copy them and send them quicker."

"She's the one who got the primers for you?"

"And tonight, she's agreed to check out Virtual Joe to see what sort of place it is and how it works."

John ran his hand through his hair and winced. "Hope you told her to be careful."

"Actually, I didn't. She's just going to take a look around."

"I'm concerned about the anonymous tipster. I think there's a good chance this person is mentally ill. They'd like for you to know what Latham is hiding and do something about it, but they don't want to be directly responsible. So they've convinced themselves that if they only give it away through hints and riddles, it won't be their fault if anything happens. One side hates him, the other doesn't want him hurt. And it has to be someone close to him."

"It *does* seem like schizoid behavior. I'll call Sharon and tell her to be careful. But first, let's see if those journals are in either of the New Orleans med schools."

While the librarian checked on that, Sarchi and John set about gathering some biographical information on Timmons. From his published papers, they knew he was a Ph.D. They therefore looked for him in *American Men of Science*. Despite its considerable length, his entry there illuminated nothing.

As Sarchi was putting the book back on the shelf, the librarian who was helping them came quietly up beside her. "Doctor Seminoux, neither Tulane nor LSU has that journal. But we did find it at the University of Iowa medical library. They usually respond to our requests very promptly, so I would think we could have those articles for you in three or four days."

"No sooner?"

"For a ten dollar fee in addition to the three for filing the request, they can fax them to us."

"How long will that take?"

"Rush requests must be filled within twenty-four hours."

"I'll pay the extra fee."

Sarchi and John drove back to her house to call Sharon. Following the usual wait for her to answer the page, she was on the line.

"Sorry to be such a pest," Sarchi said, "but I wanted to tell you to be careful when you visit Virtual Joe. We think there's a good chance the person we're looking for could be dangerous."

"Whose 'we'?"

"John Metcalf . . . that policeman I mentioned. He's helping me."

"How old is he?"

"Late twenties." Sarchi looked at John with an expression she hoped conveyed her embarrassment at talking about him like this.

"Is he good looking?" Sharon asked.

"Yes, but . . ."

"I'll have to think about this awhile, but right now, it sounds like he has possibilities. Anyway, thanks for the warning, but I've already been there."

"I thought you were going tonight."

"Got too curious to wait. I went there on my lunch hour. It's a funky place with sort of a Caribbean motif: multicolored pastel walls, fake palms, and lots of neon sculptures of stylized female faces."

Figuring John ought to hear this, Sarchi turned on the speakerphone.

"You walk in the door and there's a bunch of tables and chairs where you drink coffee. On risers in the back are three rows of computers, each one in a little cubicle closed on the top and the sides so no one can look over your shoulder. They're open at the front so anyone inside can look past their computer and see what's going on.

"To use a computer, you give them some form of ID, and they give you a special password that allows you to access the system. Once you get hooked up, you can play computer games, surf the net, send e-mail, or do word processing and make hard copies on a printer behind the clerk's counter. They have simple instructions posted in each cubicle for sending e-mail or surfing. You can get return e-mail only as long as you're on-line. Once your session is over, the server ignores any e-mail replies."

"So anyone in the city could have sent that e-mail from there."

"Sorry."

Sarchi and Sharon finished their conversation with the usual chatter between friends, then Sarchi turned to John. "If we had access to the coffeehouse records, we could check the credit card receipts for the day that message was sent. I know that could yield more names than we'd like, but wouldn't it be a start?"

"They'd have no reason to show us their records, and even if they did, your contact could have paid in cash. But basically that's the kind of thing we need to be considering. I know I'm not indispensable or anything, but early tomorrow I have to drive up to McKenzie to help a friend of mine raise the walls and put the roof on a timber frame house he's building. I promised him months ago that I'd be there. I'll be back before noon on Friday."

"You don't have to work?"

"After my shift tonight, I'm taking some vacation time. I'll call you when I get home. If you'll find me a pen and something to write on, I'll give you my friend's number, although we probably won't be there much."

When he left a few minutes later, Sarchi was surprised at how empty the house felt.

Reflecting on what they'd accomplished, it still didn't seem like much. There *were* those Timmons papers, but who knows what was in them, maybe some cryptic clue they'd *never* figure out. There had to be something else she could do to push the investigation while they waited for those articles.

But after pacing the house for fifteen minutes, she was still without an idea.

Perhaps if she got her mind off the problem.

She rounded up some clean athletic gear and headed for the car.

It was a little early for the racquetball crowd, so when she got to the gym a court was available. She worked out by herself for a few minutes, then accepted an offer of a game from a guy who'd been watching her from the observation deck. He needed work on his backhand, but was good enough that she had to push herself to beat him, which she did three straight games. After a stint in the weight room and a shower, she left the gym feeling warm and loose.

Five minutes later, heading down Union Avenue, she nearly hit an old white pickup as it exited the interstate right in front of her. Had the driver not been a dangerous-looking man with matted yellow hair who had indicated his love of firearms with an NRA bumper sticker, she might have signaled her annoyance by leaning on the horn. Instead, she merely followed quietly at a respectful distance. In addition to the NRA sticker, another proclaimed that he was against the proposed east Shelby County landfill.

Landfill . . .

Landfill . . .

Sounds like Stanhill . . .

She began to think of Stephanie Stanhill. Such a beautiful little girl, her life possibly changed irrevocably. She recalled the anguish on Regina's face as she recounted the onset of Stephanie's illness.

Then Sarchi remembered something she'd forgotten with all that had been happening. Regina had been *reading* to Stephanie that night.

Find a friend who has this book . . .

Suddenly needing a phone, Sarchi stepped on the gas.

Five minutes later, she was home waiting for someone at the Stanhill's to pick up. Remembering her last conversation with Stephanie's father, in which he realized she wasn't telling him the truth about Stephanie's MRI scans, she prayed for Regina to answer.

"Hello?"

It *was* Regina.

"Mrs. Stanhill, this is Sarchi Seminoux."

"I don't know if I should talk to you."

"Believe me, I'm trying to help Stephanie, but I'm faced with difficulties I can't begin to explain. If you would just speak to me for a few minutes, it could help me figure out how Stephanie got sick and maybe keep other children from having this happen to them."

Unable to resist this plea, Regina said, "Go on."

"How is Stephanie?"

"About the same."

"The night she got sick, you said you were reading to her. What was the book?"

"A cute little story about badly behaved little bunnies."

Already clipping along at a rapid pace, Sarchi's heart picked up speed. "Did it play a song at the end, with the rabbits singing?"

"That's right."

Where did you get the book?"

"It came in the mail. Why are you so interested in that?"

"I'm not sure. Has Stephanie read it since she had the operation?"

"Several times. This all seems very strange to me."

"It's making my head swim, too. So I've got some thinking to do. Thank you for talking to me."

Sarchi hung up and sat by the phone in amazement. Both Drew and Stephie had fallen ill while being read to from the *same* book.

She was now so eager to see Marge's copy that she didn't know how she could wait until seven o'clock. To help pass the time, she left the house and drove to Buster's Liquors, where she bought a bottle of wine for dinner. She then picked up a few items at Kroger's. When she got back home, she met Linda on her way out.

"Shopping," Linda said, looking at Sarchi's bags. "Always good therapy when things aren't going well. How're you doing?"

"I'm coping."

"I'm glad. There's something for you on the table. It was in your box at the hospital, so I brought it home. See you later."

Sarchi went inside and picked up the long white envelope on the phone table. No stamp and no return address. But the handwriting was vaguely familiar. She opened it and unfolded the single sheet inside.

At the top, the same hand had written, "Patients treated at the Latham Clinic."

Harry Bright. This was from him.

But he was dead.

On the list were the names and ages of ten patients, all of them children either five or six years old. Drew Harrison was fifth on the list. Stephanie Stanhill was not there, probably because the Stanhills weren't covered by Bright's company. For each patient, the list included the names of their parents, their address, and phone number.

Forgetting in her excitement the question of how the list got in her mailbox, Sarchi noticed that five of the ten patients lived in New York State. The others were scattered, one in Vermont, Pennsylvania, Maryland, California, and Tennessee.

And Stephanie Stanhill—*she* lived in New York.

Six of eleven from New York. The possibility of that occurring by chance had to be remote. But what did it mean?

A more specific question quickly rose. Did these families all own a copy of the book?

Rushing to the phone, she entered the number for Rose and Tom Lacy in Albany. After three rings, a woman answered. "Mrs. Lacy, this is Doctor Seminoux in Memphis. I'm—"

"Seminoux did you say? I'm sorry. We have nothing to talk about."

The line went dead.

The woman had recognized her name. How?

Latham.

He must have called the parents of all his patients and made up some lies about her. Well, two can play that game.

She next called Anita and Steve Kennedy in Scranton, Pennsylvania.

This time, a man answered. "Mr. Kennedy, this is Doctor Melinda Eggar. I'm a neurologist working on a book about movement disorders in children and was wondering if we could discuss your son's illness for a few minutes."

"I'll have to clear that with my son's doctor," Kennedy said. "Give me your number, and I'll get back to you."

"I don't want you to have to pay for a long-distance call. You check, and I'll call you in a day or two."

Sarchi silently cursed Latham's efficiency and his ability to generate loyalty in those who should be the most wary of him. She'd hoped to have a general discussion with each family about their child's illness. That was clearly not going to happen, which left her one option. Go for the book.

She went to get her copy and thumbed through the first few pages, looking for the publisher's name. There—Del Mar Publishing. For an address it gave a box number in Culver City, California. But it was printed in Hong Kong.

Returning to the phone, she called the third name on the list, Diane Shupe in Burlington, Vermont. After it rang ten times with no answer, she moved on to Betty and Pete Mitchell in Middleton, New York.

One ring . . . two . . .

"Hello, Mrs. Mitchell, I'm calling on behalf of Del Mar Publishing. Some time ago we sent you a copy of one of our books, and I was hoping you could give me a minute of your time to answer . . ."

The woman hung up.

Latham couldn't have warned her about someone inquiring about the book. She must have just considered it a nuisance call, which meant she should try again.

Two rings brought Alma Verbeck in Poughkeepsie to the phone.

"Ms. Verbeck . . ." Sarchi launched into the same spiel she'd used on the previous call and actually got to finish it.

"What book was it?" Verbeck said.

"The one about the rabbit family. It played a song at the end."

"I remember. A lovely little book."

Sarchi's heart lurched against her breastbone. Another book, another sick kid. She wanted to move on to the next name but felt she should play the charade out in case she needed to call back. "Did it hold your child's interest?"

"Oh, yes. I'll bet she's read it ten times. But how did you know to send it to me? I mean how did you learn I had a daughter at just the right age to enjoy a book like that?"

Good damn question, Sarchi thought. "I'm sorry, but distribution is a different department. I don't know how those decisions were made. But thanks so much for your time. We're delighted you liked our product."

How *did* they know who to send books to? Her daughter had read it ten times? If the book was making kids sick, how could she read it ten times? Sarchi needed to talk openly with these families about the book and their kids. But if she strayed to the subject of the illnesses, they'd know who she was and would clam up. She could talk openly to Marge about it, though. And it was now time to head over there.

28

Upon returning home after dinner with Marge, Sarchi took Marge's copy of the book directly to the kitchen and held the first page over the heating element on the cook-top. When it was as hot as she thought it could get without burning, she looked at the page for circled letters. There were none. She worked awhile longer on that page, then tried a few more with the same result.

Other than the lack of a hidden message in Marge's book, hers and Marge's appeared identical. No difference even in the song at the end.

That song . . .

Marge had said the night Drew got sick he was fine until the book played that song. How could a song make a child paralyzed? Like the Verbeck girl, Drew had read the book several times since coming home from the clinic, and it hadn't done anything to him. How could a song make a kid sick when it was heard the first time but have no effect after the child had been treated by Latham? It seemed crazy.

She walked into the living room, wishing John was with her. There was so much to talk about—the list of patients she'd received and the fact that at least one other family on the list had received a copy of the book. She looked at her watch. Eleven o'clock. He'd be off work at one.

She called Metcalf's number and left a message for him to get in touch with her when he got home. With nothing left to do but wait for his call, she finally fell into the grasp of the fatigue and the wine that had been pursuing her all evening. The last thought she had before nodding off was that Drew was *not* any better.

"Doctor Seminoux . . . Doctor Seminoux . . ."

Sarchi opened her eyes to see Linda's face a foot away.

"Wouldn't you be more comfortable in bed?"

"What time is it?"

"A little after one o'clock."

"I'm waiting for a phone call."

"Anyone I know?"

"Not really."

"Okay, be mysterious. It just whets my curiosity."

"Where were *you* tonight?"

"As close to heaven as you can get and still have a pulse."

"Not going to tell me?"

"I can't."

"*Now* who's being mysterious?"

Their banter was interrupted by the phone. Sarchi picked up and looked pointedly at Linda, who was still hanging around. Throwing her hands up in surrender, she headed for the kitchen.

Sarchi raised the receiver to her lips. "John?"

"Have you learned something?" Metcalf said.

"I hate to impose so late, especially when you have to get up early tomorrow, but could we meet somewhere?"

"Your place?"

"I'd rather not." She lowered her voice. "My housemate's here."

"If I didn't care what you thought of me, I'd suggest you come here. I've got a lot of good points, but I'm not very tidy. Well, *that* was smart . . . I just gave it away. How about CK's coffee shop on Madison at Evergreen in fifteen minutes?"

When the streets were cold and nearly deserted like tonight, it was hard for Sarchi to believe there were enough kids in the city to create the kind of bedlam that sometimes reigned in the hospital's emergency room. In a way, the night made the city seem like a giant cave, except here, the darkness held evil. Despite the warm air pouring from the car's heater, she shivered at the thought of what the kidnapper might have done to her.

The coffee shop came up on her right like a beacon. She joined the single car in the lot and went inside to wait for John.

The only other customer was a young black man smoking and writing in a legal pad while the one waitress swabbed the floor around him with a mop. Sarchi carefully made her way across the wet floor to the opposite end of the place and slid into a booth. It seemed risky to have only one waitress working at this hour, but she looked like she wouldn't give up the receipts without a fight.

"Be right with you," she called out.

Before she could make good on that promise, John arrived. As he came toward her, the place seemed a lot more inviting.

"How was your shift?" she asked.

"I took a few ducks out of the water, at least for a while. How are you?"

"Confused." She got the list of Latham's patients out of her bag and handed it to him.

After scanning the list he said, "Did you notice that half these families live in New York?"

"It's actually six out of eleven. The family Virtual Joe told me about was also from there. Jesus, I just realized. Drew, my nephew, was *born* in New York."

"How'd he get here?"

"Drew's mother was my sister, Carolyn. Carolyn, Marge—the woman who adopted Drew when Carolyn died—and I all went to Cornell together."

"Now, what can I get you," the waitress said, rubbing her hands on her apron.

They both ordered coffee.

"How about some pie?" the waitress said. "We got choco-late, blueberry, and apple. I can give you a good price on it."

They both passed on the pie.

When the waitress went back behind the counter, Sarchi continued her story. "Marge and Carolyn were a year ahead of me and were best friends from their sorority."

"Were you in it, too?"

"I was too busy with premed for sorority life." She paused, not caring for the way that came out. "I hope that didn't sound like a criticism of Carolyn or Marge."

"It didn't."

"They both met men they loved, both got married, and both stayed in the state. When my sister and her husband were killed in a car accident . . . I don't know why I call it an accident. It was a drunk that caused it. To me, that's murder. Anyway, Marge took Drew. Then, when she left her husband, she found a job with an ad agency here."

Sarchi expected John to ask why *she* didn't take Drew. Instead he said, "So it's seven of eleven with a New York connection."

The waitress brought their coffee and left them to continue talking.

"I wonder if the other four are also tied in some way to New York?" Sarchi said.

"We've got their phone numbers. We'll call and ask them."

"Latham has warned all his patients not to talk to me."

"How do you know that?"

"I already tried a few of them. When they heard my name, they hung up."

"So we devise a ruse to get the information without rais-ing their suspicions."

"That thought occurred to me, too. When I realized they wouldn't talk to me, I called one name on the list posing as a publisher's rep and found out she also has a copy of the book where we found the hidden message. So does the family I visited in New York whose daughter was treated by Latham. In fact, just like Drew, when the girl got sick, her mother was reading to her from the book."

John's brows drew together. "Those can't all be coincidences."

"Marge told me tonight that Drew was perfectly fine until the book played the song at the end, but I don't see how a song could have affected him."

"Of course that's your area, not mine. But just because we don't understand something doesn't mean it can't happen." He curled his hands around his coffee cup and stared into it. "We ought to have that song analyzed by somebody who knows how to break sounds down into their separate components."

"Looking for what?"

"That's for them to tell us."

"The University of Memphis has a speech and hearing center a block from the hospital. They might have someone."

"Now I *really* feel guilty about running off tomorrow."

"Don't. I can take the book over there alone."

"It's not that. There are some other big questions here that need attention. We've already discussed whether all the names on the list have some relationship to New York. Why are all the kids who got sick five or six? Why aren't any of them four years old? Or seven or any other age? And why did this happen to these particular families? What do they have in common that other families don't?"

"Not that we need another question, but how do we work on that?"

John smiled. "Maybe we don't."

"Meaning?"

"I've got a friend who's a PI in Brooklyn. Let's give him the assignment of finding out if the families who don't live in New York have some relationship with the state. We'll also ask him what else they all have in common."

"What'll that cost?"

"I'll just call in a favor he owes me. I've got his card in my wallet. Let's go over to Kinko's right now and fax him the list and a note."

Cleaning up the table after they left, their waitress wondered why people ordered coffee they weren't going to drink.

Sarchi and John sent the list off to Brooklyn, then Sarchi headed home and went straight to bed.

The next morning, Sarchi managed to control her eagerness to contact the Speech and Hearing Center until it was reasonable to believe most people would have begun their workday. Her call was passed along to several people there until she finally reached Dr. Hugh Kelsey, who agreed to take a look at the song she wanted analyzed. But he couldn't do it until nine A.M. the next day. Hugely disappointed at the delay, she politely pressed him to make time for her sooner, but his day was already solidly scheduled.

While wondering what her next move should be, the UT library called.

"Doctor Seminoux, about the papers you requested: the library we've ordered them from said those journals are checked out until Saturday."

"Can't we get them somewhere else?"

"That's the only source we've found in this country."

"Okay, thanks for letting me know. But please call me the instant they come in."

Three more days, she thought, hanging up. *Why must everything she needed be so far out of reach?*

Then she had a thought. Carl Lanza had a vast neurobiology reprint collection. He might have copies of the Timmons papers. Needing to actually do something other than make phone calls, she decided to check this possibility out in person.

Carl was bent over the benchtop in his lab, carefully pipetting a sucrose-laden DNA solution tinted with a blue indicator dye into a row of tiny slots in an agarose gel. Having done this a few times herself and knowing how much concentration was required to get the DNA into the slots and not lose it to the buffer bathing the gel, Sarchi stood quietly off to the side without announcing herself and waited for him to finish.

Carl loaded three more samples from the rack of little vials beside him, then capped the apparatus and turned on the current that would separate the pieces of DNA in the slots by size.

"Big as he is, he still works at the bench," Sarchi said.

Carl turned, grinning. "Use it or lose it. Are you on a mission or is this a social call?"

"Both."

"But more a mission?"

"I'm looking for two papers a guy named Christopher Timmons published in *Acta Neurologica* in the late eighties, and I was hoping you had copies."

"Timmons . . . yeah, I know who you mean. I've talked to him a couple times at conferences. He's at Vanderbilt, right?"

"That's him."

"Come on, let's see what I've got."

Sarchi followed him to his office, where he went behind his defensive perimeter to sit in front of his computer. He entered Timmons's name and clicked a search button. After a short delay, the titles of three papers appeared on the screen. Carl scanned them and turned to Sarchi with an apologetic expression. "No luck."

"I knew it was a long shot."

"Can't the library get them for you?"

"In three days. I need them now."

"So let's call Timmons at Vanderbilt and ask *him* to fax you copies."

Sarchi's stomach knotted at the suggestion. She didn't want Timmons, and through him, Latham, to know what she was doing. "Would you mind pretending *you're* the one who wants them and just not mention me?"

Responding to Carl's look of curiosity, she added, "I know this all seems like strange behavior, but I have good reasons for everything I'm asking. Can you believe that without questioning me? Can you simply trust me?"

"I do have one question."

Sarchi's hope that she wouldn't have to drag Carl any further into her problems dimmed.

"What are the titles of the papers I want?"

Immensely relieved, Sarchi reached in her bag for the complete citations.

After consulting the membership roster of the Neuroscience Society for Timmons's number, Carl placed the call.

"Doctor Timmons please. Really? I wasn't aware of that. . . . Do you know where he can be reached . . . ? Could you transfer me to Doctor Tony Walsh? Thanks." Carl looked at Sarchi. "Timmons resigned six months ago. This person doesn't know where he went, but Walsh might."

"Tony? Carl Lanza. . . . That's the truth. . . . How's it going? Say, I just heard Chris Timmons resigned. Any idea where he is?"

Carl put the call on speakerphone so Sarchi could hear what Walsh was saying.

"I expect he's home," Walsh said. "Apparently, he came into some money, enough to retire and raise horses like he's always wanted. He's got a small farm about thirty miles west of Nashville. I was out there a few weeks ago. Nice place. Doesn't seem to have improved his disposition, though. The day I visited he was mad as hell over an argument he'd just had with that neurosurgeon he used to work with here. The guy who moved to New Orleans, I forget his name."

Latham, Sarchi thought. Timmons had argued with Latham.

"Do you have his phone number?" Carl asked.

"Yeah, but he often doesn't answer even when he's there. Just a sec."

Impulsively, Sarchi went into the lab and got a paper towel from the pile by the sink. Returning to the office, she scribbled Carl a note: *Ask for Timmons's address and instructions on how to get there.*

When Walsh responded to Carl's questions, she took it all down on the towel. The conversation between the two men then turned to things that didn't involve her. To her relief, Carl adroitly maneuvered this phase to a quick termination. As predicted by Walsh, their call to Timmons went unanswered.

"I can try again later and let you know what he says when I get him," Carl suggested.

"That'd be a big help. What does this guy look like?"

"I think I've got a picture." Carl got up, came from behind

his furniture, and picked through the items on the top shelf of
a nearby bookcase. "Ah, here it is."

He pulled a booklet from the shelf. "These are the proceedings of a conference we both attended two years ago in
Crete. In addition to summaries of the talks that were given,
it contains photos of all the participants." He thumbed
through a few pages and held the booklet out to her. "That's
him."

Timmons was a nerdy-looking dark-haired man wearing
wire glasses with round lenses. On the side of his face turned
to the camera, the skin in front of his ear was discolored by
a port wine–colored birthmark that extended onto his neck.

"Why'd you want his address?" Carl asked. Then, catching himself, he said, "Sorry, forgot I'm allowed no questions."

"I don't know how, but someday I'll find a way to repay
you for all the help."

"I've always liked Ferraris . . ."

Going back to her car, Sarchi mulled over what she'd
learned. Timmons had recently come into enough money to
retire. Could that have anything to do with Latham? Was that
what they'd argued about—some deal they were in together?
What did the Timmons lead from Virtual Joe really mean?
Were the two papers in *Acta Neurologica* the entire story, or
was she supposed to do more?

Her thoughts turned back to the argument between Timmons and Latham. Now that they were on the outs, Timmons
might be willing to talk. She certainly had nothing else to do
today and, without even pushing it, she could be there in
three hours.

For a hundred and thirty miles east of Memphis, Interstate 40
runs through relatively flat uninspiring countryside that very
much needs the face-lift it gets in the fall when the leaves
turn. But it was several weeks past their peak, and the trees
now looked tattered and tired. But even had they been worth
a roll of film, Sarchi had so much to think about, she wouldn't
have noticed.

She stopped for a quick lunch at the Casey Jones Village

in Jackson, Tennessee, a point roughly halfway to her destination, and was back on the road by a quarter to twelve. Fifty miles later, she came to a bridge high over the Tennessee River, the one scenic view between Memphis and Nashville that couldn't be ignored. Wide and blue, the Tennessee stretches north to south in a beckoning abundance that divides around heavily wooded islands and sends meandering channels into the forest on both banks: The Tennessee River is a natural wonder that makes even the most landlocked mind wish for a boat.

A half hour later, with the river forty miles behind her, Sarchi left the interstate at the exit Walsh had indicated and turned north. Proceeding exactly three and two tenths of a mile, she turned west onto a two lane country road and drove until she came to a mailbox bearing a picture of a horse's head with a DNA helix on its neck. Behind the horse, white lettering spelled out

Base Pair Farm

C. Timmons, owner

Base Pair Farm . . . named after the base pairs that make up DNA. Cute, Sarchi thought.

The dirt driveway, which was closed by a white wooden gate, disappeared over a hill that obscured any view of a house. The entry to the drive was muddy and heavily rutted. Leaving her car far enough off the road so it wouldn't get sideswiped, she skirted the mud and let herself onto the property.

The driveway was flanked on each side by pasture enclosed with a white post and rail fence. On each shoulder, the fence was accompanied by a row of freshly planted saplings without a leaf left on them. It was colder here than in Memphis, so as she tucked her gloveless hands in her light poplin jacket and started up the hill, the effort of the climb could be read in her breath.

When she reached the top of the hill, she saw the house about seventy yards away—a beautiful building constructed out of Arkansas fieldstone with white trim and white shutters. Behind the house and off to the right sat a red barn that looked new. She had thought when she set out there was a chance she'd arrive only to find Timmons away, so she was relieved to see a car and pickup in front of the house.

Then the cloud of steam issuing from her mouth abruptly ceased.

Suppose the car belonged to Latham? She definitely didn't want him aware of her interest in Timmons, and a confrontation *could* be dangerous. She glanced down the drive and considered the three hours it had taken to get there. She couldn't turn back now on the mere possibility that Latham was here. He probably wasn't. She was just being paranoid. Still, she checked her bag for the .38 even though it couldn't have gone anywhere. Attempting to calm herself, she resumed walking.

A mare and a colt stood in the pasture to her left. Neither paid her any attention as she walked by. When she was about twenty yards from the house, a big roan stallion trotted up to the fence on her right and began walking with her. She was now close enough to see that both vehicles bore Tennessee plates. But if the car was a rental, it could still have brought Latham.

She and the stallion parted company where the driveway gave rise to a fieldstone walk which led to the house. Standing on the porch she reached for the bell. Suddenly, she noticed that the front door was slightly ajar. She rang the bell, waited a half minute for someone to answer, then rang again. She waited another moment, then pushed the door open. "Is anyone home?"

No answer.

"Doctor Timmons . . . Are you here?"

Still getting no response, she considered going inside. Then, realizing he might be in the barn, she pulled the door shut, left the porch, and crossed the yard to a gate in the white fence, where she was met by the big roan.

She hesitated a moment before entering and then asked, "Are you a good boy? Can I trust you?"

Amazingly, the horse bobbed his head and whinnied, his breath curling upward in the crisp fall air. Knowing a little about horses from her childhood, she decided this one wasn't dangerous and went in.

While she was securing the gate, the horse nudged her gently with his head, leaving a wet nose mark on the shoulder of her jacket.

"What is it, big fella? You want some attention?"

She rubbed his huge neck a bit, warming her hands on his skin, then started walking, choosing a course to one side of the heavily marked track the animals used. The horse let her get only a few steps away before following. Halfway to the barn he nudged her again, and once more she rubbed his neck.

"Now that's all."

The door to the barn was half open, and she could smell horse manure and feel warm air even before entering. Inside, six pigeons sitting on a rafter fluttered in surprise at her appearance. Attached to that rafter and to several others were the ducts that undoubtedly served as the barn's heating system. To heat a barn was in itself extravagant, but the way Timmons left doors open, he seemed to have no concern whatsoever about money. And what *was* he feeding his animals to produce such a smell?

The barn interior largely consisted of four stalls on each side of a wide, straw-littered central aisle. All the stall doors were closed except the third on the right. There was no sign of Timmons. Behind her, she could hear the horse breathing. Above, the pigeons had started a cooing fest. But there was something else. . . . She listened harder, trying to tune out the animals.

There . . . a faint high pitched beeping.

Taking a route such that she would avoid passing directly under the pigeons, she moved slowly forward, trying to locate the sound and forget the manure smell, which was growing stronger. Again, the horse nudged her.

Tired of the game, she waved him away. "Not now."

As she moved deeper into the barn, she realized the sound was coming from the open stall. At the exact moment she stepped through the open door into the stall, the horse nudged her again, this time so hard she lost her balance and fell facedown onto what was left of the rat-gnawed corpse of Christopher Timmons.

29

The pressure of her fall caused the corpse to exhale, filling her nostrils with an odor so foul it made her eyes water. On the verge of retching, she pushed herself up, her hands barely indenting the corpse's tightly stretched blue flannel shirt and the bloated flesh beneath. Though her vision was slightly blurred by tears, she saw that the head, too, was swollen and distorted by the unmistakable imprint of a horseshoe that had caved in its skull. Despite this terrible damage, the mangled wire frame glasses riding what the rats had left of the nose and the port wine–colored mark still visible through the gathering decomposition pigments on the cheek left no doubt about the dead man's identity. The beeping sound she'd heard was coming from his wristwatch, reminding him of some event that no longer mattered.

Unable to tolerate the stench any longer, she turned and headed for the door, all thoughts of avoiding the pigeons forgotten. Behind her, the horse that had probably delivered the fatal kick remained at the stall, looking at the corpse.

Beside the door, Sarchi paused just long enough to swish her hands in a galvanized watering trough and dry them on her jeans. Outside, the crisp fresh air against her face as she hurried to the gate cleared her head but chilled her damp hands so that her fingers were stiff and clumsy as they worked the gate latch. Letting herself out, she stood on the other side and gathered her thoughts.

There was no way to know when Timmons had died, but it certainly had to have been at least a few days ago. She should have realized that smell wasn't just manure. What to do now?

Tell someone—but how?

The house was unlocked . . .

She went to the porch, stepped up to the front door, and paused, feeling very ill at ease about going inside a dead man's house. But it had to be done.

She quickly found the phone and hit the key for the operator. The person who answered connected her with the county sheriff.

"I need to report a death."

The sheriff asked her to stay until he arrived. After hanging up, she looked around at the heavy masculine furnishings and thought of how close she might be to copies of the two papers she wanted, then, feeling like a ghoul for coveting a dead man's reprints, she returned to her car to wait for the sheriff.

By the time he arrived, she'd begun to wonder about the timing of Timmons's death. He has an argument with Latham and shortly thereafter is found dead. It seemed like more than a coincidence. But how do you get a horse to kick a man in the head and stage it so that it's a direct hit the first time, for there was only one mark on him. It seemed so impossible she didn't even mention her suspicions to the sheriff or tell him any more about the reason for her visit than to say she came to discuss some of Timmons's work with him. After the sheriff took a look in the barn and sniffed around the house a bit, he let her go home.

The trip back seemed much longer than the drive there, possibly because she hadn't accomplished anything for her cause. She'd still have to wait for the library to come up with those papers.

When she got home she called John Metcalf in McKenzie.

"John, it's Sarchi. I saw Christopher Timmons."

"How did you—?"

"He's dead. *I* found the body."

"Whoa. You're gonna have to back up a *mile* for me to get on."

She recounted how she came to be in Timmons's barn.

"I'm not sure this passes the stink test," John said. "And I don't mean the smell in the barn."

"My thoughts, too, at first. But how could something like that be staged? The body only had one mark on it."

There was a brief silence, then John said, "I suppose it *could* have been sheer bad luck."

"For Timmons *and* me."

"More for him, I'd say."

"No argument there. But I sure didn't accomplish anything for my efforts."

"You kept the man from lying neglected one more night in that barn. What's on your agenda for tomorrow?"

"I've got an appointment at the Speech and Hearing Center to have that song analyzed."

"Good luck. Let me know what you find."

That night the faces of Timmons and the man who'd kidnapped her took turns infesting Sarchi's dreams. She was awakened the next morning as usual by the carpenters next door. Her first thoughts were of Timmons's crushed head and the sound of his watch futilely trying to get his attention. She was rescued from these images by the realization that in just a few hours she was to take the book with the song in it to the Speech and Hearing Center.

As she stood in the bathroom brushing her hair, her eyes fell on the vial of pills the nurse at the sexual assault center had given her.

The pills.

As long as she had to take them, she couldn't forget that damn five percent. Blotting out the worries that threatened to immobilize her, she swallowed the pills with some water and went back into the bedroom to catch up on her e-mail.

The subject of the first message to come in was *Carolyn's senior prom,* obviously an inquiry from her father about some detail of that event he was trying to remember. The next, *Shop at Home and Save* could only be a damn advertisement.

The third got her attention: *We've got to talk.*

That being the last message her connection to the server was then terminated. She eagerly opened the message of interest. What she saw was riveting:

If you want to discuss the Latham Clinic, meet me at seven o'clock Memphis time on the undernet on the IRC channel, ZZ3. If this channel doesn't exist when you sign on, wait a few minutes and try again. Use the nickname Dr. S. and whatever real name you wish. My nickname will be Helper, real name, Cyberguide. If you don't have the software for IRC you can find it on the Internet.

She didn't know quite what all this meant, but it appeared that her anonymous contact wanted to communicate more directly. This was such a bombshell that she printed the message and called John Metcalf in McKenzie, hoping he hadn't left yet for wherever he was working. But there was no answer.

She turned back to her computer.

IRC . . .

What the hell was that?

She connected to the Internet and used the Lycos search engine to find IRC. One of the entries retrieved was something called *An IRC Primer*. Opening it, she learned that IRC was an abbreviation for Internet Relay Chat. This was a way to "talk" in real time with people all over the world via your computer without long distance phone charges. You meet people on one of the thousands of existing channels or you can create a channel just for you and a friend.

That's what the message meant. Helper was going to create a channel called ZZ3 just for the two of them.

Searching further, she found that the best IRC software program for her Mac was something called Ircle, which she could download from the Internet and try free for thirty days.

She managed to get the program onto her hard disk but couldn't figure out how to "expand" and "unstuff" it as was apparently required before it would work. Tired of fooling with Ircle and seeing it was now nearly time for her appointment with Hugh Kelsey, the man who'd agreed to take a look at the song she wanted analyzed, she shut off the computer. Kelsey had cautioned her that it might be nearly impossible to determine if the song contained anything "unusual." She set out for the medical center figuring that even if he didn't come up with anything, she could drop by the hospital and ask Ella Dodge how to get Ircle running.

The Speech and Hearing Center was of modern design, a low and boxy building of institutional red brick. Sarchi told the receptionist behind a glassed-in cubicle her name and that she had an appointment with Doctor Kelsey.

He appeared a few minutes later in dark slacks, a crisp white shirt, and a tie bearing splashes of blue and red. He was no older than forty, with broad shoulders and a trim waist. He had an olive complexion and slightly hollow cheeks that gave him a hostile and dangerous look. She suspected that no one would vote against him in a promotion and tenure meeting.

"Doctor Seminoux." He offered his hand and Sarchi took it, finding his grip warm and confident.

"Let's go upstairs and take a look at this song," he said.

She followed him up a short flight of stairs and down a red-brick-lined hallway to a room that looked a lot less like a scientific laboratory than she'd expected. He led her to a computer with two chairs in front of it.

"Why don't you sit right there so you can see what I'm doing," he said. "Not that I'm expecting to produce anything dazzling."

Sarchi wished he'd show a little more optimism but wouldn't have said so even if he hadn't looked like a hit man.

"This song—it's in one of those books?"

Sarchi gave him Marge's copy. "It plays when you open the last page."

Kelsey turned to the final page and listened to the song for a few seconds, then put the book facedown on the table. "If it was just voices, it'd be better," he said. "The instrumental background will introduce a lot of complexity. Tell me again what I'm looking for."

"I don't know. Anything that shouldn't be there."

"Like something that's been added to the mix?"

"Exactly."

"That would be easier if we had the before and after. With only the final product, I don't know . . ."

Sarchi felt like saying, "Just look at the damn thing," but she merely nodded.

Kelsey flicked a switch on some equipment that sat on a shelf above the computer, then picked up a microphone. He opened the back cover of the book and let the song play into the mike, filling the computer screen with vertical black lines.

He let the song go through one cycle, then closed the book and put the mike away. He hit a button on the keyboard and used the mouse to pull down a menu. Rapidly, he displayed the sounds in several different ways, so intent on his analysis that he seemed to forget Sarchi was there.

Finally, he stopped at an image that consisted of ghostly dark smears. He studied this version with great interest for a while, working his way from screen to screen. Then he turned to Sarchi and said, "You see these repeating squares?"

She followed his finger to a clear part of the screen above all the smears.

"This is not from a voice or a musical instrument."

"Then what is it?"

"Digital pulses of sound at a frequency not commonly encountered in daily life."

"So you're saying it shouldn't be there."

"Definitely not."

30

Before leaving the Speech and Hearing Center, Sarchi had Kelsey check the song for the same anomaly in the book she'd been sent. It was there, too. And she'd bet it was in every other copy that existed. But what did it mean? Kelsey seemed satisfied just to have her out of his hair and didn't bother asking her for an explanation. But she was sure planning on asking Helper for one if she ever got Ircle to function.

Forty minutes after leaving Kelsey, she arrived home with enough knowledge from Ella to join her first IRC channel on the undernet. On a whim, she picked one called KKK and watched a lot of nasty sentiments against various minorities scroll by from a large number of participants. Unable to resist and wanting to practice, she typed *Jewish merchant bankers rule* and sent it. She was promptly kicked off the channel.

She then joined a benign group discussing whether tattoos were works of art or disfigurements. Feeling strongly that they were the latter, she contributed freely. During this practice run, she tried the *Who Is* command several times on the nicknames scrolling by and discovered that in addition to learning the "real name" the person in question signed on with, it also gave the city they lived in. Since she hadn't entered any such information for herself, she concluded that the software used for IRC automatically knew the city each participant's computer signal was coming from.

Deciding she'd had enough of tattoo talk, she changed channels. By some mistake, she found herself on two channels at the same time.

Two at the same time . . .

The germ of an idea with hazy possibilities popped into her head.

She signed off IRC and turned her attention to nurturing this thought. Under her care it grew into a wondrous thing.

Longing to share the idea with John, she called the number of his friend in McKenzie.

She let it ring fifteen times, then hung up with a poor opinion of his friend for not having an answering machine.

So she'd carry on alone.

She reopened the Ircle program and practiced setting up her own channel. When she could do that, she closed Ircle, logged off her Internet connection, and called Sharon's pager in New Orleans.

She answered as promptly as always, and Sarchi presented the plan she'd devised. Sharon readily agreed to her part, and the trap was set.

Unable to wait any longer for her boyfriend, Steve Oakley, Sharon McKinney threw on her coat and took the elevator down to the apartment house lobby, intending to go by herself. But as she went out the front door, Steve came hustling toward her.

"Sorry, I got out of surgery late and then my research tech was having a problem." He turned and hurried to keep up with Sharon.

"I told you I have to be there at 6:45 . . ."

"I just lost track of time."

"Can you get us there in ten minutes?"

"If I know what's good for me I will." He looked for a smile, but Sharon wasn't ready to forgive him.

They piled into Steve's car, and he got them moving. "What is it you're supposed to do at this place anyway?"

"A favor for a friend."

"And I'm there to . . ."

"Make all the other women jealous."

Steve smiled with relief. "I'm baaaack."

"Don't gloat. It's only because I'm easy."

"That's what attracts me."

Sharon tapped the clock on the dash. "Eight minutes, Oakley."

He shot through a light that turned red even before he entered the intersection.

"I hear thirty isn't such a bad age," Sharon said. "I'd like to be alive to find out."

"Not me. I want to go out with my student loans still unpaid, make some people genuinely unhappy at my demise."

"Don't say that even jokingly."

"I talked to my mother last night," Steve said. "She's expecting us for Thanksgiving."

"I told you I didn't want to go there this year."

"I know, but she looks forward to it so much."

"The whole time I'm there I feel like I'm standing on her tongue."

"She likes you."

"Then why did I overhear her last year telling you about an article describing the psychological trauma being abnormally short inflicts on kids?"

"Okay, so on that one point she's concerned."

"I don't want to go there."

"I already told her we'd come."

"Then untell her."

"C'mon, it's just for a day and a night."

Sharon didn't speak again until they arrived at Virtual Joe.

"Just let me out by the front door," she said coldly.

"Okay. I'll find a place to park."

"Don't bother. I'll take a cab home."

"Sharon—"

"Go find your mother a woman who'll give her normal-sized grandkids."

She got out and went inside without looking back. As Oakley pulled away, he believed the worst thing about a woman's body was that sometimes it came with a mind attached.

Sarchi opened Ircle, logged onto the undernet, and tried to go to channel ZZ3, but it didn't exist yet. This was good, because it meant their target hadn't arrived at Virtual Joe. She set up a channel named T1 and waited for Sharon, checking every thirty seconds or so for the existence of ZZ3. After a couple of minutes, Sharon joined her on T1. Sarchi typed "Everything okay?" in the message box and sent it.

"Where do they keep the men who haven't talked to their mothers in twenty years? I'd like to order one." Sharon sent back.

"Pay attention now," Sarchi typed. "And watch who comes in. I'll let you know when the target arrives."

"Target," Sharon said. "I feel so *clandestine.*"

"Just keep your eyes open."

"Man or woman?"

"Don't know."

In the cubicle next to Sharon, Lee-Ann decided it was time. She closed the game of solitaire she was playing and opened the IRC program Virtual Joe provided. She then created a channel named ZZ3.

In Memphis, Sarchi tried again to connect with ZZ3. This time it was there.

She selected T1 and typed "Target has arrived. Who came in?"

That would be the last she'd communicate with Sharon for a while. Now, her attention had to be on ZZ3, where Helper had already sent her a message. "Did you get the book I mailed to you?"

Sarchi typed, "Yes."

"Did you find the friend who also has a copy?"

"Yes. Who sent it to her? Was it you?"

"It wasn't me. Do you understand the book's significance?"

"Not entirely. I think the song in the back somehow makes kids sick. Is that right?"

In her cubicle at Virtual Joe, Lee-Ann was surprised at how much Sarchi knew. She was doing very well but had apparently not found the clue Lee-Ann had hidden in the book. "Do you know how kids communicate in secret?"

"By invisible ink," Sarchi wrote. "I found the message and looked up the Timmons papers in *Acta Neurologica*. But I can't get copies of them for several days. Are they important?"

"Yes."

"What will I find in them?"

"Part of the answer."

"Why can't you just tell me? Why are you making things so difficult?"

"Don't push. I'll tell you what I want you to know."

Not wanting to anger this person to where they would sign off prematurely, Sarchi typed, "Sorry."

"The answer is in two parts. If you understand everything we've discussed so far, there would still be much hidden from you."

"How do I learn about the other half?"

"Be at the main entrance to the Westbank Medical Center in New Orleans at one o'clock tomorrow. Watch for a thin bald man carrying a red and white insulated container. Follow him to his destination."

"That doesn't give me much time."

"Don't miss this chance."

Suddenly, the screen displayed the message, *Helper has left ZZ3*.

Switching to Sharon's channel, Sarchi typed, "Target signed off. Whose leaving?" She expected a small delay while Sharon figured out who the target was. But then a message said, *Sharon has left T1*.

31

The only person who had left the computer area was a plump blonde with short hair and a round face. Feeling that her assigned role in this operation greatly underutilized her abilities, Sharon decided she'd give Sarchi more than just a description of the woman.

Sharon hurried to the counter and stood by Lee-Ann while the clerk in the turquoise Virtual Joe T-shirt checked Lee-Ann's charges. Lee-Ann paid with cash, and the clerk returned her driver's license. But there was no way for Sharon to read the name on it. As Lee-Ann headed for the door and the clerk turned his attention to Sharon, Sharon said quietly, "Who was that woman?"

But Sharon's voice was not made for whispering. Giving no indication she'd heard Sharon's inquiry, Lee-Ann left the shop, walked a few steps along the front window, then paused and looked back at the counter inside.

The clerk told Sharon that Lee-Ann's name was Angela something, conveying the name Lee-Ann had chosen for the phony driver's license she'd been using there. Thrilled that she'd learned Lee-Ann's first name, Sharon wanted more— like the license plate number of her car.

On the sidewalk, Lee-Ann was upset. She'd always been

nervous about communicating with Sarchi through Virtual Joe, fearing that Sarchi would somehow use the cyber cafe to figure out her identity. And that would be a disaster, because it wouldn't take much thought for a detective to connect the dots from Seminoux to her, to Latham, to Greta Dunn, the woman Lee-Ann had killed in the hospital. And now someone had asked the clerk her name. *Oh-oh, she was coming out.* Lee-Ann resumed walking.

Seeing Angela through the window, Sharon moved slowly to the door to give the woman time to get a little distance from the shop. When Sharon stepped onto the sidewalk, Angela was about half a block away and walking briskly. Sharon turned in that direction.

Panicking over Sharon's whereabouts and having no idea where she'd put the phone number for Virtual Joe, Sarchi logged off her Internet connection and called information. For a half dollar, she let the phone company make the call.

"Virtual Joe, your Internet home away from home."

"Is there a young red-headed woman there, small and attractive with a deep voice?"

"She just left."

"Was anyone with her?"

"No, but she seemed to know another woman who was here—a chubby blonde named Angela."

"What do you mean she seemed to know her?"

"Well, maybe that's not exactly right. She asked me the other woman's name like she recognized her."

"This other woman, do you know her last name?"

"It was on her driver's license, but we don't need it for anything so I didn't bother to look. Say, we're kinda busy right now so I gotta go."

He hung up, but Sarchi stood with the receiver frozen to her hand. Why was Sharon there alone? Why hadn't she sent back information on who she'd seen? And this Angela— would Sharon allow herself to be distracted by on old friend just at the most important moment in their plan? Highly unlikely. Which meant Angela was Helper and Sharon had . . . damn.

Sarchi called information again and had them connect her with the New Orleans police.

"This is Doctor Sarchi Seminoux in Memphis. A few minutes ago a friend of mine, Doctor Sharon McKinney, left a place there called Virtual Joe, a cyber cafe on Magazine Street, and I'm afraid she may be in trouble."

"What kind of trouble?" the man on the other end said.

Sarchi's mind scrambled for a simple answer that would get results. She decided to lie. "When she left, a woman named Angela followed her. Angela has been threatening her for weeks, and I'm afraid of what she might do."

"If you're in Memphis, how do you know all this?"

"I was talking to a clerk at Virtual Joe on the phone, and he told me."

"Okay, I'll send a car over there. But first . . ."

Sarchi gave him her name, address, and phone number, then did the same for Sharon. She described Sharon and told him what kind of car she drove. She also told him as much as she knew about Angela's appearance.

"Will you call me back and let me know what you find?"

"I can't promise anything. Try to relax. Your friend's probably fine. Goodnight."

"Wait . . . what's your . . ."

She wanted to get his name, but he was gone.

At the corner, Lee-Ann caught the light and crossed to the other side, a favorable angle that allowed her to see that the nosy redhead was following.

By the time Sharon reached the corner, the light had changed to *Don't Walk*. Ignoring it, Sharon dodged the traffic and made it safely to the other side. But Angela had disappeared. She'd seen her enter the street straight ahead. *So where was she?*

Halfway down the block, an illuminated sign marked a small parking lot where Angela had most likely left her car. The street was one way going toward the sign, which meant that when Angela came out of the lot, Sharon would be able to get her license number, *if* she wasn't already gone. Sharon began to walk faster. Just another minute was all it would take to be in position.

When the thick bottom of the Mad Dog 20-20 wine bottle crashed into Sharon's skull, fragments of shattered bone tore through the thick covering of her brain, rupturing a large venous sinus. One particularly sharp piece of bone penetrated an inch and a half into her frontal cortex. Mercifully, Sharon felt nothing as she crumpled to the sidewalk and was pulled by the ankles into the alley.

In the alley's dark recesses, Lee-Ann knelt by the body and pinched Sharon's nostrils closed while shoving hard on Sharon's lower jaw to make sure she couldn't breathe through her mouth. This time, there would be no replay of the Greta Dunn fiasco.

Two minutes into Lee-Ann's attempt to finish Sharon off, a rat crept from between two garbage cans and watched her, the one dim light in the alley making its eyes look electrically powered. Finally, finding the murder of Sharon McKinney of no more interest, it waddled off into the darkness.

When there could be no question that Sharon was dead, Lee-Ann released her. Now she began to think about fingerprints. Could you take them from skin? Better to be safe.

She took off her scarf and carefully wiped Sharon's nose and chin. She did the same with her ankles. Except for the bottom, which she'd never touched and which had some blood on it, Lee-Ann wiped the wine bottle clean and set it aside.

Money . . . She should take whatever money the woman was carrying to make it look like a mugging. But to get it, she'd leave prints all over her purse. Maybe it'd be better to take the whole bag.

Behind Lee-Ann another light came on. She heard a key in a lock.

Dewey Breaux, the seventy-eight-year-old owner of the Lafayette Cafe came out lugging a big black plastic bag. A flash of movement at the mouth of the alley drew his attention. But if there had been someone there, they were gone now. So concerned about how his overhead was eating up his profits that he didn't notice the body in the shadows, Breaux dropped the bag beside his already overflowing garbage cans and went back inside to make sure the help wasn't stealing food.

As Lee-Ann walked back toward Magazine Street, where she'd parked, she realized she must never go to Virtual Joe again. And she likewise would never again contact Seminoux. She had nothing more to tell her, anyway. It was all in Seminoux's hands now. If she didn't get it, she was too dumb to be a doctor. The question now was whether Lee-Ann could get out of this unscathed.

Lee-Ann abruptly stopped walking. Ahead of her, a motorcycle cop was putting a ticket on her windshield. Her first thought was how ludicrous this was. She'd just killed someone and the police response was to give her a parking ticket. Forgetting her rule to never smile, she grinned.

But a chilling thought erased the smile. If she ever came under suspicion for the redhead's murder and they figured out when it took place, the parking ticket would prove she was here. Feeling very conspicuous now, she stepped into a darkened doorway.

Two blocks down Magazine Street on the other side of Virtual Joe, Eddie "Buck" Rogers eased his patrol car toward the cyber cafe, looking for a short redhead and a plump blonde, hoping he'd find them prone on the sidewalk, having a catfight. There was just something so erotic about women fighting, especially redheads. But he saw no fight, didn't even see many pedestrians.

Was that a Honda? Christ, why does every car look alike? Deciding it *was* a Honda, he ran the plates, but it didn't come back belonging to Sharon McKinney, one of the two he was looking for.

Lee-Ann remained in the doorway until the cop who'd given her a ticket got on his motorcycle and drove off. Then she bolted for her car, grabbed the ticket, and slid behind the wheel. In seconds she was in pursuit of the cop.

Eddie Rogers saw Lee-Ann pull away from the curb so

fast she drifted over the center line. He considered giving chase, but decided he'd rather look for the redhead.

Keeping two or three cars between them, Lee-Ann followed the motorcycle cop for a quarter of a mile, until he stopped to write another ticket. Unable to stop in the middle of the street without drawing attention to herself, she went past him and turned right at the corner. Pacing herself so he'd have time to finish the ticket, she went around the block, reappearing on Magazine just as he climbed back on his cycle and resumed cruising.

Even in her desperation, she knew she couldn't just run him down. But what *could* she do? She uttered a little prayer promising God if he'd just get her out of this, she'd never kill again. The plea was barely past her lips when the cop pulled into the parking lot of a McDonalds, got off his cycle, and put something in the saddlebag before going inside.

Lee-Ann pulled in beside the cycle and got out of her car. Crouching so she couldn't be seen from inside, she made her way to the motorcycle saddlebag and opened it. Reaching inside, she grabbed two ticket books and duckwalked back to her car.

From the McDonalds, she drove to a K and B drugstore, pulled into the lot, and looked at what she'd taken. One ticket book was unused. The other contained the carbons of a dozen tickets. Number eleven was hers.

Up to that moment, she'd had her doubts about the existence of God, but now, seeing how he'd assisted her tonight, she decided she might have to give the matter a little more thought.

Eddie Rogers had checked Magazine Street for three blocks on either side of Virtual Joe without spotting either of the women he was looking for or the redhead's car. Going around again, he turned right onto the side street where Sharon had followed Lee-Ann. At the alley he stopped and raked the shadows with his spotlight. Just before the beam would have picked up Sharon's body, he got a call young cops yearn for and veterans dread. "Shots fired. Officer needs assistance." He waited for the address, then flicked on his lights and siren and sped off.

It wasn't enough that a patrol car was on its way to Virtual Joe. Sarchi needed to do something herself. Though it wasn't likely Sharon was carrying it outside the hospital, she called Sharon's pager and left her number. After that didn't produce anything, she called Sharon's home and left a message to contact her the *moment* she got in.

To keep her mind occupied while waiting to hear something, Sarchi turned to her computer and played a dozen games of video solitaire, missing some obvious moves in every game. Then she called Sharon again, once more without success. The cops in New Orleans should know something by now.

She hadn't written the number down earlier, so she had to use information again. This time she jotted the number on a piece of scratch paper and made the call herself.

The woman who answered didn't know anything about her previous call. "Isn't there someone you can ask?" Sarchi said. "I talked to a man before."

Getting nowhere, she hung up. John—maybe he could help.

She called him in McKenzie and this time someone answered. "John Metcalf, please."

In a few seconds he came on the line, and she poured out her story to him.

"Let me make some calls," he said. "I'll get back to you in a few minutes."

Seven minutes later he did. "The uniform they sent over there didn't find anything."

"Not even her car?"

"That's what they said."

"Then where is she?"

"How long has it been since she left the cafe?"

"About an hour."

"That's not much time. I'm not saying you're wrong to be concerned, but it's too soon to conclude she's in trouble."

"I never should have involved her."

"Let's just have good thoughts about this."

Sarchi wished she was in New Orleans so she could look for Sharon herself. *New Orleans . . . West Bank Medical Center, one o'clock.* "John, I have to go to New Orleans. Will you come with me?"

"To look for your friend?"

"And for something else." She told him about the bald man with the insulated container.

"How were you planning on getting there?"

"By plane, if there's a flight tonight. Car if I have to."

"Certainly I'll go with you, but it's going to take me two hours to get back to Memphis. Even if we could get a commercial flight tonight, which isn't likely, the earliest we could get there would be around 2 A.M.. That's six hours. If we drive, including my trip back to Memphis, it'll be ten hours. Those aren't time frames in which you could do much for Sharon if she *is* in trouble. Assuming she needs help, it'd be better to alert someone there who cares for her, like a boyfriend."

Of course, why hadn't that occurred to *her*, Sarchi thought. "Steve Oakley—they've been going together off and on for two years."

"Do you have his number?"

"I can probably get it. What about the guy we're supposed to follow tomorrow? To get there in time, we need to make some travel plans fast."

"I've got an idea about that. You call Oakley, and I'll see what I can arrange."

A few minutes later Sarchi eagerly waited for the only Stephen Oakley in the New Orleans listings to pick up. *Please be him and please be home.*

Someone answered. "Steve, this is Sarchi Seminoux, Sharon's friend in Memphis. Is she there with you?"

"No. I took her to a place called Virtual Joe tonight. Far as I know, she's still there."

She told him what had happened.

"Dammit," he said. "I shouldn't have left her."

Feeling that the fault was hers if anything had happened,

Sarchi said, "Sharon has a strong will. If she told you to leave, she wouldn't have *let* you stay."

"I'm going over there and see what I can find out."

"You'll call me and let me know?"

"Absolutely."

Shortly after she'd talked to Oakley, John called back. "I've arranged for a friend to fly us to New Orleans tomorrow morning on his private plane. I'll pick you up at seven-thirty."

32

"Did you sleep at all last night?" Linda asked, putting her coffee down. "I heard you rattling around at midnight and again at 2 A.M."

"I'm worried about a friend," Sarchi said.

"So am I. Everybody at the hospital misses you."

"That's nice."

"Kid, I'd love to chat, but I have to leave. I've got the admitting rotation, so I won't be home tonight. Maybe we could have dinner tomorrow night."

"You'll be too tired."

"I'm not suggesting we stay up all night, but if you don't want to . . ."

"We'll see."

A few minutes after Linda left for the hospital, John arrived.

"Heard anything about your friend?" he asked as she got in the truck.

"She's simply disappeared."

"Did you get in touch with her boyfriend?"

"He couldn't find her. I called her again this morning and she's still not home."

"That's not good."

"He tried to get the cops to help, but they won't even list her as missing until tonight."

"When we get there, maybe I can convince them to bend the rules a little."

"I never should have involved her in this."

"Don't beat yourself up over it. You took precautions. Things just went wrong."

As he backed the truck out of the drive and headed for the airport, his words brought Sarchi no comfort.

"When I got home this morning I had a message from my PI friend in Brooklyn," John said. "He found something interesting about the kids on that list we sent him. Even the ones who didn't live in New York were born there. And in every case, the parents let the New York Cord Blood Repository have their umbilical cords."

"I know about that place," Sarchi said. "Umbilical cords contain stem cells, the mother cells that form all the different cells in blood. If a kid gets leukemia and needs to have his bone marrow replaced, they can give him back his own stem cells to repopulate the marrow. Or sometimes if there's a tissue match, they can give a different kid those stem cells. This is important."

"What does it mean?"

"I don't know yet, but I have the feeling that when I figure it out, it's all over for Latham."

It soon became apparent that they were not headed for Memphis International.

"Where are we going?"

"Olive Branch, Mississippi. My friend keeps his plane at the small airport there."

At eight-ten they pulled into a parking place adjacent to the Olive Branch airport, a minimal operation consisting of a few metal buildings and a smattering of small planes tied to the pavement. When they got out of the truck, the only sounds were from the distant hiss of an air-operated tool and a flock of chattering birds picking at half a doughnut. They were met at the front door of the nearest building by their pilot, Danny LaPlante, a guy with a ruddy face and teeth that looked like the rubble in a jackhammered sidewalk. When

John had said private plane, Sarchi had not imagined he was talking about a craft as flimsy looking as the purple and white Cessna LaPlante led them to. Seeing the look of apprehension on her face, LaPlante said, "First time in a single engine plane?"

She nodded.

"Don't worry. You were at greater risk of bein' hurt in the truck comin' over than you will be on this flight."

"But one engine . . . There's no safety margin."

"If anything is gonna happen to the engine, which it ain't, it'd be in the ignition system, and we have two of 'em. Every cylinder has two spark plugs, and we need only one. But say we lose power, like in some weird world I don't live in. For every mile of altitude we're flyin' we can cover twelve miles of ground lookin' for a place to land. And we don't need much. Any farmer's field, or maybe a mall parkin' lot. Last year at the Oshkosh air show I saw this guy cut his engine, do a loop, an eight point roll, a hundred and eighty degree turn, land, and roll up to his parkin' place, all with no power." He hooked his thumbs in his belt and adopted an exaggerated sneer. In a Mexican accent he said, "So we don't need no stinkin' engine."

"No parachutes then?" Sarchi said.

"I wouldn't even know how to put one on."

Though the weather had been on a binge of benevolence and there were only a few scattered herringbone clouds in the sky, she had to ask, "Are you instrument rated?"

LaPlante looked at John. "Why's she so worried? You tell her about the time we took out a barn and a silo in a fog?"

Then he looked back at Sarchi. "Just kiddin'. Yeah, I'm rated. It's too inconvenient not to be. For the first five years, when I wasn't, I can't tell you how many times I flew somewhere and had to leave the plane there for a few days until the weather cleared so I could fly it back. For those five years my wife thought private aviation meant flyin' somewhere and takin' a bus home. We ready to go?"

"Guess I'm satisfied."

Sarchi climbed into the backseat of the Cessna, leaving the copilot's seat for John. LaPlante got in and put on a set of headphones. He fiddled with the controls for a few minutes, then yelled "clear" out the open window even though no one was around. The engine coughed once and came to life. Heartened by its prompt response, Sarchi felt better about the whole trip.

They taxied down a paved strip parallel to the runway. Where the taxiway connected with the runway they turned and paused while LaPlante gunned the engine. Abruptly, he cut the throttle back and shook his head.

"What's wrong?" John shouted over the sound of the engine.

"Don't like the way the instruments are operatin'. We might have a vacuum pump problem."

He got the plane in motion again, turned it around, and taxied back to the maintenance hanger, where he shut off the engine and looked at Sarchi. "This is going to take at least an hour. You two might as well wait in the office." He gestured toward one of the buildings. "They got snacks in there and coffee. I'll come and get you when we're airworthy."

On the way to the office, John said, "Sorry about this."

"Once we get in the air, how long will the trip take?"

"About three hours. How far is the hospital from the airport?"

"I've driven it in forty minutes."

"If Danny is right about the repair taking an hour, we're going to be cutting it close."

Sarchi spent the next sixty minutes nursing a Coke and trying to find something to take her mind off Sharon and the possibility that they weren't going to reach Westbank Medical in time. Unable to find even the sports section of a newspaper or any portion of a magazine, she passed some of the time in front of a big bulletin board looking at sixty Polaroid photos of people who'd ceremoniously had the tail of their shirt cut off after completing their first solo flight.

Finally, LaPlante came for them. "We're fixed."

Hoping they weren't going to find out in the air that he was wrong about that, Sarchi walked quickly with the others back to the plane.

When they were all seated, John said to LaPlante, "Our

one o'clock appointment is at a hospital forty minutes by car from the airport."

LaPlante looked at his watch. "It's gonna be tight. When we get close, we'll call ahead and have somebody standin' by to take you over to the car rental."

This time there were no problems, and they were soon heading down the runway at full throttle, the engine sounding strong and reliable. Then they were off the ground.

For the next minute, it felt as though they were suspended in air, the engine and gravity at an impasse, the plane neither progressing nor falling. Sarchi was worried that if the engine failed now, there'd be no time for LaPlante to make any kind of corrective maneuver. They'd just plummet to the ground. But the engine kept stroking, and slowly it carried them upward.

Although they were still so low that Sarchi could see the tails flicking on a herd of cows, LaPlante leveled the plane. For the next few minutes it was like riding in an elevator simulator as the Cessna was buffeted by air currents. But then LaPlante put it into another climb, eventually reaching an altitude where Sarchi no longer felt as though she might throw up.

Five-year-old Karen Owens was wheeled back into operating room three at Westbank Medical Center, where the anesthesiologist quickly reconnected her to his equipment. The reassuring repetitive beep of the pulse oximeter registered every beat of the child's heart, and its pitch indicated that she was well oxygenated. Preparations for invasion of her brain were moving into the final stages. Behind the anesthesiologist, George Latham fed the RAS coordinates he'd obtained from the MRI scan they'd just done into the OR's briefcase computer.

In two minutes he had the data he needed. He hung the printed calculations on the wall next to the X-ray viewer and went to the patient's head, which was surrounded by the stereotaxic frame, a titanium ring screwed to her skull in four places. Attached to the ring so it enclosed the child's head was the titanium cage they'd used to obtain the RAS coordinates.

"Okay Lee-Ann, let's move her up so we can get her position fixed."

They moved the patient so her head lay at the table's edge. While Latham held the cage steady, Lee-Ann crawled under the table and secured the ring to it. With Lee-Ann's help, he removed the orientation cage and replaced it with the arc, the attachment that would guide the biopsy probe. Latham then shaved the child's head in two places, each the size of a silver dollar.

Lee-Ann donned a fresh pair of sterile gloves and spent the next five minutes scrubbing the two areas of scalp with Betadine soap, working it into a lather. Looking at the rusty froth she'd created, her mind went back to the redhead she'd killed the previous night. If only she'd been able to think of another answer. But things had moved so fast. It wasn't as if she'd had time to consider all the possibilities. What exactly the redhead was doing at Virtual Joe and how she'd spotted Lee-Ann weren't clear. In any event, time should be running out for the old whoremonger Doctor Latham, unless Seminoux doesn't get here in time. She should have given the woman more warning. She glanced at Latham being helped into his surgical gown by the scrub tech. He really was *such* a bastard.

Finished with the soap, Lee-Ann wiped the two areas with a sterile towel and painted them with Betadine prep.

"Ready for me?" Latham said from behind her.

Lee-Ann moved aside and Latham replaced her. In less than two minutes, he had sterile blue toweling sewn to the child's scalp all around the perimeter of the shaved areas. He next applied Ioban film to each site, sticking it firmly to the exposed scalp.

The field was then isolated with sterile blue drapes until the only portions of the patient visible were the two naked circles in her hair. Latham lined up the probe in the right circle using the coordinates he'd obtained from the computer. He then moved the probe to the side and held out his hand.

Lee-Ann gave him a syringe loaded with a mixture of li-

docaine to dull any pain reflexes and epinephrine to contract
blood vessels. Through the Ioban film, Latham injected a
small amount of this liquid into the child's scalp. He then
made a one-inch scalpel cut through the Ioban into the tissue
beneath.

Lee-Ann handed him a mastoid retractor, which he used to
spread the wound. He deepened the incision with a Bovie, a
scalpel that cauterizes blood vessels as it cuts, producing a
dry field with clear visibility. With the acrid smell of cauter-
ized tissue still hanging in the air, he repositioned the retractor and went to work again with the Bovie.

As much as Lee-Ann despised Latham, she could not dis-
miss his skills. He might have the morals of an animal, but
he was a great surgeon.

"Midas."

Lee-Ann gave him the Midas Rex, the skull drill, which he
quickly used to create a dime-sized burr hole filled with wet
bone oatmeal in the child's skull.

"Saline."

With the transfer pipette Lee-Ann handed him, he washed
the oatmeal from the hole and resumed drilling. Finally, he
reached a pulsating white membrane—the dura—the tough
fibrous covering of the brain.

He opened the dura with two deft scalpel cuts in the shape
of a cross, then touched the incision with the bipolar cautery,
a tweezer-like instrument that sealed any nearby blood vessels and caused the edges of the dural wound to contract.

Able now to see the rolling white contours of the brain, he
touched the bipolar cautery to its delicate blood-vessel-filled
covering. He moved the biopsy probe into position.

The probe was a tube within a tube. At the bottom of both
tubes was a small rectangular window. With the core tube
turned so its window did not coincide with the window in the
sleeve, he inserted the probe into the child's brain to the desired depth. He then turned the core so its window and the
outer window were superimposed.

Using a syringe attached by a plastic connector to the core,
he created enough suction to draw a small plug of the child's
brain through the two windows into the core. With the cap-

ture complete, Latham turned the core so its window was closed, severing any remaining tissue connections between the child's brain and the plug.

He withdrew the probe from the brain, removed the core from the sleeve, and handed it to Lee-Ann, who discharged the plug of tissue into a test tube of culture medium fortified with all the factors that would make the next steps possible.

Lee-Ann glanced contemptuously at the gas passer they always worked with. His lack of intellectual curiosity was disgusting. It was almost incomprehensible that Latham had done this under his nose so many times without him understanding what he was witnessing. In his defense, though, it hadn't exactly been easy to figure out. It had taken a long time, but she'd done it. Latham still wasn't aware of all she knew.

She handed the core back to him, and he reassembled the probe for another sample from the same site. They would repeat the entire procedure on the other side, and one more child would go back to her parents "cured." But if Seminoux was where she needed to be, this might be the last one.

Even with LaPlante pushing the Cessna to its maximum airspeed, it didn't roll to a stop at Moisant Field in New Orleans until ten after twelve. Sarchi was immensely relieved when LaPlante cut off the engine, giving her back her hearing.

"We can't stop to check on Sharon," John said, throwing his door open. "We've got to get that rental car and go." He hopped to the pavement, turned, and offered his hand to Sarchi.

"I'll try to call her later," Sarchi said, accepting his help out of the plane.

"Mind if I come along?" LaPlante said, joining them.

"By all means," John said. "We have no idea where we'll be going after the hospital, so we should stick together."

From the moment they left the Cessna, it felt to Sarchi as though some malevolent force was speeding up time and holding them back. From where they'd landed, they could see the rental car lot beyond a distant chain-link fence. But it took their driver nine minutes to get them to it.

Inside, there were two people ahead of them and only one
clerk, a dark-haired woman with her head bent over a map,
helping an old woman who looked like she shouldn't be out
by herself.

"The best way to go is to take Airport Drive to I-10, then
pick up 610 first chance you get," the clerk said. "That'll take
you to the other leg of I-10 avoiding this loop."

"Will it be easy to see the signs to 510?" the old woman
said.

"Not 510, it's 610, like it shows right here," the clerk said
patiently. "And all the signs are huge."

"What if I should have car trouble?"

"I'm sure you won't."

"But what if I do?"

As the precious minutes slipped away and the old lady
kept coming up with questions, Sarchi's anxiety could barely
be contained. Finally, just as she was considering removing
the old lady by force, the woman left on her own.

She was replaced by an efficient looking man dressed in a
blue suit and carrying an attaché case. He gave the clerk his
name and waited for her to check his reservation. After
dithering at her computer awhile, the clerk looked at the guy
with an expression that made Sarchi close her eyes and pray
she wasn't going to say—

"I'm sorry sir, but I don't have any record of your reserv-
ing a car."

"I don't see how that's possible," the guy said.

Sarchi felt like getting the gun from her bag and demanding a car—*now*. At twelve thirty-five, with Sarchi in despair
over the time lost, they finally left the lot with her behind the
wheel of a four-door Toyota Camry. Even LaPlante, who was
by nature an optimist, believed the short cut the rental agent
had shown them on the map wouldn't get them to the hospital by one o'clock.

33

At 12:50, ten minutes before the courier was to arrive, Lee-Ann set aside a small sample of the tissue Latham had removed from Karen Owen's brain. She put the tube containing the rest into an insulated container filled with ice. She then took the set-aside down to the lab for the usual PCR analysis.

That test would take approximately three hours. The lab would then call Latham with the results, and he would relay them to the courier's destination, which was another thing Latham wasn't aware that Lee-Ann knew. If the inactivation reaction had taken place as expected, the final procedures would be set in motion. If something had gone wrong and the gene insert was still functional, a great deal of time and money would have been wasted. But this presumption of success was the best way to provide the group on the other end with the freshest possible cells.

With the samples safely delivered to the lab, Lee-Ann hurried back upstairs to meet the courier. As usual, he walked through the door precisely on time, wearing the same gray suit as always.

Lee-Ann was most relaxed around those as homely as she pictured herself. The courier fit that criterion. Even if he had not lost most of his hair, his low ears and soaring forehead would have made him an anatomical curiosity.

"Hello, Charles," she said. "It's good to see you again." Along with all the other things she'd learned, she knew his name was not Charles. But she was always careful not to reveal that.

"You're looking well," Charles said. "Is that mine?"

She picked up the red-and-white insulated container beside her and gave it to him. "See you next time."

Charles nodded and left.

Lee-Ann gave him a few seconds, then stepped into the hall and hurried in the opposite direction. At the first window she reached in the east wing, she looked down at the hospital's main entrance, where the courier's cab was waiting. She saw no one who resembled Sarchi Seminoux. Maybe she was waiting for him in the lobby, or in one of the hundreds of cars in the parking lot.

Two miles away, Sarchi was trapped behind a tractor trailer rig loaded with new Fords. In the outside lane, she was pinned by a flatbed truck carrying a huge yellow pipe fitting.

Charles rode the elevator down to the first floor and headed for the front entrance. Near the information desk, he paused at a water fountain, then, deciding that a hospital was no place to drink from a public facility, he resumed walking.

Sarchi let up on the gas, immediately drawing an angry horn blast from the car behind. As soon as there was a car's worth of daylight between her and the rear of the truck carrying the big pipe fitting, she checked the mirror and made a hard left, swerved across two lanes, and pushed the accelerator to the floor.

She shot past the rig with the Fords and was then in the clear. Where *was* that exit for the hospital?

Charles entered the waiting cab and settled in his seat, the insulated container nestled beside him. On the way over, he'd told the driver where they'd be going after the hospital, so there was no verbal exchange between them before the cab pulled away. The cabbie made a big loop around the first row of cars in the parking lot and headed back to the divided drive that led out.

Tires sliding sideways, the Camry turned into the hospital entry at 1:05. Afraid they'd missed him, Sarchi's eyes searched the hospital's front entrance for their target. On the other side of the line of crape myrtles that separated the two lanes of the entry, the cab with Charles in the back passed them.

"Hey," John said. "There's a bald guy in that cab."

What to do now? There were lots of bald men in the world. Was this the right one? Maybe the man they were supposed to follow was late. They might run after the wrong man and miss the right one. In the mirror, Sarchi saw the cab turn onto the frontage road.

What to do?

From the window in the East Wing, Lee-Ann was very disappointed. Charles's cab had left and no one had followed. The tip she'd given Seminoux had been wasted.

But then, the car that had come in as the cab left suddenly speeded up. It quickly made the same loop the cab had, then went back to the frontage road and gave chase.

God was still on her side.

Sarchi followed the cab onto the Westbank Expressway heading back the way they'd come. "I hope this isn't a big mistake."

"We'll know when he gets out," John replied.

Sarchi glanced at him. "What if he *is* the right guy and he's supposed to leave the insulated container in the cab? We'd never know then if we're right."

"You supposed to follow the container or the man?" La-Plante said.

"The man, I guess," Sarchi replied.

"Then you follow him when he gets out whether he has the container or not."

They tailed the cab across the Huey P. Long Bridge and onto Airline Highway, where it turned toward the airport.

"What if he doesn't have the container and he gets on a plane? How committed are we to this guy?"

"If either of you are thinkin' we could beat him to his destination in the Cessna and pick him up as he gets off his flight, forget it," LaPlante said. "Our top speed is 130 miles an hour. A commercial jet cruises at 600."

"Maybe he isn't even going to the airport," Sarchi said.

Fifteen minutes later, the cab turned into the airport.

"It's possible he won't get on a plane," John said. "Who or what we're supposed to see could be in the terminal. So either way, with or without the container, we're going to follow him inside. Danny, you park the car, then come inside and wait for us at the Delta counter."

Hanging back so there were a few cars between them, Sarchi tailed the cab to the Northwest Airline entrance. When the cab stopped and the back door opened, she and John leapt from the car.

At first it wasn't visible, but when the bald man turned to go inside, Sarchi and John saw a red-and-white insulated container in his left hand.

They followed him inside and stayed well behind while he studied the Northwest arrival and departure information on a bank of overhead monitors. He then moved off, heading toward concourse A.

As they passed the monitors, Sarchi looked up, hoping the one he'd looked at was for arrivals.

It wasn't.

"He's taking a plane out of here," Sarchi hissed. "What are we going to do?"

"I'm working on it," John said.

As they approached the security checkpoint and the bald man queued up to pass through the metal detector, John pulled Sarchi aside.

"You still carrying that .38 I gave you?"

"Yeah."

"You'll never get it past security. I could probably get *my* gun through by showing them my police ID, but I don't want to risk being delayed or draw attention to myself." He pulled her around so they faced the wall, and he handed her his 9mm automatic. "Hold this for me while I see where he's going."

As soon as his gun was out of view in Sarchi's bag, which was beginning to feel as though she was carrying a bowling ball, John hurried to the shortest line at the security check, craning his neck around the metal detector to keep their quarry in sight.

In less than a minute, both men disappeared into the crowd choking the concourse.

With her adrenaline pumping from the chase, it was nearly impossible for Sarchi to simply stand by and do nothing. There were so many people coming and going, she wasn't even able to pace. When she thought she couldn't stand it another second, she saw John coming back fast.

"He's going to Chicago," he said, reaching her and pulling her along with him as he headed back to the terminal. "There's only one seat left on the flight, and they're already boarding, so we don't have time to discuss this."

"You're going to get a ticket for that seat?"

"I'll follow *him*. You stay here and check on Sharon." He took out his key ring and removed the key for the truck. "Whenever you get back, take the truck to your house. I'll call you as soon as I learn anything."

They bought the last ticket for the flight to Chicago, and John asked for his gun back.

"What if they won't let you past the checkpoint with it?"

"Then we'll adjust."

John went through the metal detector with his badge and his ID out. He conferred briefly with the security contingent, and they let him pass. He waved to Sarchi and sprinted for the plane.

Wanting very much to believe that Sharon would now be home, Sarchi found a bank of pay phones and fished in her bag for a quarter.

After just two rings, the phone in Sharon's apartment was answered without the accompanying hiss of the tape on her answering machine.

She was home. "Sharon, are you—"

"Who's speaking please?" a man's voice asked.

"Sarchi Seminoux. I'm a friend of Sharon McKinney. Is something wrong? Who are you?"

"Detective Veret, homicide. I'm afraid your friend is dead."

Hearing her worst fears confirmed, Sarchi grew so limp with despair the phone nearly slipped from her hand.

"Sorry to have been so blunt," Veret said. "But if I had phrased it more delicately, it would only have misled you into believing there was still hope."

Sarchi's mind was an abyss that didn't hear a word of Veret's apology.

"Doctor Seminoux. Are you there? Doctor Seminoux . . ."

Realizing that the only way she could help Sharon now was through Veret, Sarchi choked out an answer. "I'm here."

"Steve Oakley said you sent Sharon to a place called Virtual Joe last night and you called him saying you thought she was in trouble. I'd like to discuss that."

"I've certainly got a lot to tell you, but I'm on a pay phone at the airport, and it's too noisy for all I want to say."

"What airport?"

"Moisant."

"When did you get here?"

"This morning. In a private plane."

"How long are you staying?"

Hating the city for all the trouble it had brought her, Sarchi suddenly wanted to be as far from it as she could get. "Only long enough to help you."

"Have you got a car?"

"Yes."

"How about we meet in twenty minutes at the Holiday Inn at Causeway Boulevard and I-10?"

"I'll need some directions."

"Take Airline to Causeway, hang a left, and keep your eyes open. Whoever gets there first will get us a quiet table in the restaurant where we can talk. How will I recognize you?"

Sarchi felt like saying she'd be the one who looked like shit because I killed my friend. Instead, she said, "I'm five-seven with short black hair, and I'm wearing a black turtle-neck sweater and jeans."

"On my way."

Sarchi hung up and went to find LaPlante, who was watching a shapely blonde check her bags at the Delta counter.

"I was about to have you paged," he said. "Where's John?"

"On his way to Chicago with the guy we were following."

"Are we through here then?"

"Not quite." She wasn't in the mood for a lot of supposedly comforting platitudes regarding Sharon's death, so she decided not to mention it. "I'm supposed to meet a detective in twenty minutes at a Holiday Inn nearby."

"You sure live a more interesting life than I do."

"Right now, I'd trade you even. Anyway, when I finish with this guy, we can go home."

Sarchi had neglected to ask Veret what he looked like, so when they walked into the Holiday Inn restaurant, she had no way of knowing if he was already there. But no one even looked at her.

"Guess we got here first," she said to LaPlante.

"Why don't I get a table by myself," he suggested. "That way you two can have some privacy."

"I appreciate that."

The hostess wanted to put both of them at tables near those already occupied, but Sarchi insisted on one in the center of the room, where she took the seat facing the entrance.

Three minutes later, a man with prematurely gray hair walked in, saw her, and came to her table.

"I'm Claude Veret."

They exchanged a handshake, and he sat in the chair beside her.

Veret's hair was gray, but his mustache and eyebrows were brown. Unlike the two detectives she'd dealt with in Memphis, Veret was beautifully dressed in a charcoal pinstriped suit, a pale blue shirt, and a patterned yellow tie that picked up his suit stripe. She hoped his attention to detail in clothing carried over into his work.

"Seminoux," he said. "Any Cajuns in your family?"

"Not that I know of."

"Pity." Small talk over, he took out a pen and a little note-book. "Now, why did you ask Sharon McKinney to go to Virtual Joe last night?"

Over the next twenty minutes, interrupted only by the waitress bringing coffee for Veret and a cup of hot tea for herself, Sarchi bravely laid the story before him without breaking down. But when she reached the end, her courage wavered. Brushing back tears that threatened to embarrass her, she said, "Whoever killed Sharon must be very close to Latham, most likely someone who works with him."

It was a conclusion Veret had reached long before she voiced it.

34

Claude Veret didn't like Yankees adding to his troubles even if they did have a French name. He also believed you shouldn't be able to smell a woman when she walks into a room. He was therefore relieved when he finished questioning Latham's nurse, Julia, whose lavender perfume reminded him of bathroom deodorizer.

"Thank you Ms. Price. Would you ask—" he looked at the notes he'd made when he'd asked Latham for a list of everyone who worked for him—"Lee-Ann Hipp to come in please."

When Julia was out of the room, Veret waved the air in front of him to disperse her smell. The door opened and a plump blonde came in.

A plump blonde . . .

Veret's interest in these interviews, already keen, instantly sharpened. Angela, the person Sharon McKinney had asked about at Virtual Joe, was such a woman.

"Ms. Hipp, please have a seat."

Lee-Ann saw that Veret was sitting in the chair she used when she did the billing. That just wasn't right. She should have had her regular chair and *he* should sit in the one for visitors. Well aware of the risks he posed, she was careful not to let her feelings about this show.

"I'm Detective Veret. I'd like to ask you a few questions."

Though Lee-Ann had no doubts about the reason for his visit, she furrowed her brow and said, "What's this about?"

"A murder that occurred last night."

"What does that have to do with the people in this office?"

"Probably nothing. But I'd like to talk to you a bit anyway. Do you mind?"

"I'm not a very good conversationalist. I always say exactly what's on my mind, and sometimes that makes people uncomfortable."

"I happen to like it. How long have you worked for Doctor Latham?"

"Three years."

"That's a long time."

"It doesn't seem so to me."

"You must enjoy your work."

"It's always gratifying to see sick children get better."

"I understand you assist Doctor Latham in surgery and handle the billing. That's kind of an odd combination."

"I've been doing it so long it seems natural to me."

Veret smiled. "I guess it would. Do you know a Doctor Sarchi Seminoux?"

Lee-Ann pretended to search her mind. "I think I've seen that name on the medical records for one of our patients."

"So it's part of your job to look through those records?"

"On occasion."

"For what purpose?"

"Before they come to us, our patients have all spent several days in another hospital. Doctor Latham likes to know what medications they've been given before they arrive." This was actually Julia's job, but it was all Lee-Ann could think to say.

"Is this a task you alone perform?"

He knew it was Julia's job. She was sure of it. "Generally, that's something Julia does. But if Doctor Latham needs the information on her day off or if she's ill, then I do it."

"Have you ever contacted Doctor Seminoux for any reason?"

Lee-Ann considered the question briefly then said, "Not that I can recall."

"Why did you hesitate before answering?"

"I was trying to remember if I might have called her for Doctor Latham. But I'm sure I never have."

Veret couldn't put into words how he knew it, he just had well-honed instincts for deceit. In the short time they'd been talking, he'd become convinced that Lee-Ann was a skilled liar. "Does the name Virtual Joe mean anything to you?"

Trying to keep her pupils from dilating at this direct hit, Lee-Ann said, "No. Is that a person?"

"It's a place, a coffeehouse where you can surf the net—is that the expression?"

Lee-Ann saw through the question. He was trying to determine if she was Internet literate. She almost played dumb, but then she saw the hidden barb. Everybody knows that phrase. If she said she didn't, he'd know she was lying. Better to simply avoid it. "I didn't know we had a place like that here."

"So you've never been there?"

"If I had, I wouldn't have been surprised there was one in the city, would I?"

"That's true."

Lee-Ann now saw just how dangerous Veret was. All that was necessary to prove she was lying was for him to take the picture from her driver's license to Virtual Joe and ask the clerks if they'd ever seen her there. And since the redhead had asked her name, if Veret found the clerk who was on duty last night, he would surely remember her. She looked at Veret and briefly wondered if it would be possible to kill him. But even if she could manage that before he filed a report, they'd just send a replacement. She thought about killing the clerk who posed the greatest threat, but there was no time. And there were certainly other clerks who'd seen her there on different nights.

Veret flipped his notebook closed. "I think I have all I need. Thanks for being so helpful."

Veret left the hospital and headed for the office to pick up some driver's license photographs, hoping the clerks who'd worked last night at Virtual Joe would be on duty when he got there and he wouldn't have to track them down.

Lee-Ann was frightened. She knew Veret would be back. And next time, he would probably have a warrant for her arrest. Well, she wasn't going to make it easy for him. If he wanted her, he'd have to work for it. As much as she hated Latham, she felt that after three years, she should at least say good-bye. Her biggest regret was that she wouldn't be around to see Seminoux bring him down.

She found him checking on Karen Owens, the child they'd operated on that morning.

"How's she doing?" she asked.

"Very nicely."

"I have to tell you something."

He looked at her with a puzzled expression.

"I have a family situation that requires me to leave New Orleans."

"For how long?"

"I don't know."

"Weeks? Months?"

"Maybe for good."

To Lee-Ann's surprise, Latham looked devastated. "This is very bad news for me. Because, frankly, you're the best surgical nurse I ever worked with." He reached out and took her hand. "I don't know what I'll do without you."

Lee-Ann's hand tingled from his touch, and its warmth traveled up her arm and spread through her body, making her knees tremble.

"So if you ever need anything, particularly your job back, just let me know." He leaned over and kissed her on the cheek, setting her nerves ablaze. "When will you leave?"

"Today . . . right now. I'm sorry I couldn't give you advance notice about this."

"Don't be. At some time in our lives we're all acted upon by forces we can't control."

There was no doubt in Latham's mind that Lee-Ann's sudden wish to get out of the city was related to the visit of

Claude Veret. He didn't know what she'd gotten herself into, but couldn't have been more pleased that she was hitting the road and taking her troubles with the police away from *him*. And there *was* another bright spot in this development. She was a great surgical nurse, but she'd been around too long to be completely unaware of certain things in his clinic that didn't add up. He'd been considering arranging a fatal accident for her, but the Seminoux problem had made that too risky at the moment. Luckily, now she no longer worked for him and wouldn't even be living in New Orleans.

Latham remained at Karen Owens's bedside a bit longer, wondering if Veret's visit meant he should call off his field man in Memphis. Instead, he decided that things there should proceed as planned.

Lee-Ann cleared out her checking and savings accounts, taking it all in cash, and threw as much of her clothing as she could get into the two suitcases she owned. Everything else was left behind in her haste to get moving.

She'd been driving only a half hour or so when she saw a woman with an overnight bag hitchhiking. Had the woman been the least bit attractive, Lee-Ann would have delighted in passing her by. But seeing she was on the homely side and plump, Lee-Ann stopped the car and waited for her.

When the woman reached the car, she opened the door and appraised Lee-Ann for a moment before getting in.

"Hey, thanks for stopping."

"I could use some company and you need a ride," Lee-Ann said, checking behind her before pulling back onto the highway. "It's a fair exchange. Where you headed?"

"St. Louis," the woman said, arranging her bag on her lap. "I got relatives there who'll take care of me until I get back on my feet."

Now that she was in the car, Lee-Ann realized the woman wasn't as young as she'd looked. Actually, they were both about the same age.

"They don't know I'm coming, but that shouldn't be a problem, do you think? I mean, I'm family."

"Why don't they know you're coming?"

"I'm running out on my old man. Didn't exactly plan it, but I just suddenly had enough of his abuse. Never thought I'd have the nerve, but here I am. He hit me, see . . ."

She pulled her lower lip out and bent closer. Just to be polite, Lee-Ann turned to look at her but couldn't take her eyes off the road long enough to see anything.

"He hit me and then went in the can. Know what I did? I nailed the damn door shut with him inside, packed a few clothes, and took off. He may be locked in there yet. So you see how I didn't have time to call nobody."

Where most people might have found this woman's tale boring, hearing about *her* troubles sort of made Lee-Ann feel better about her own.

35

The Memphis city lights splayed across the land like a terrestrial galaxy as Sarchi and LaPlante arrived back at the Olive Branch airport, where LaPlante put the plane down as softly as hitting a pillow.

It had been about four hours since John had left for Chicago, enough time, Sarchi thought, for him to have discovered the bald man's destination. She was so eager to hear what he'd found that after she thanked LaPlante and he left for home, she called her phone from the airport office to see if John had left her a message.

The answering machine came on after only two rings, meaning that at least one message was waiting. At the end of the tone, she entered the remote access code and waited breathlessly for his voice.

But it was a woman. "Doctor Seminoux, those articles you ordered on interlibrary loan are here. They'll be waiting for you at the circulation desk."

The Timmons papers. With all that had been happening, she'd forgotten about that lead.

As much as she wanted to know why Helper had directed her to those articles, she needed even more to hear John's voice so she could know he was okay. But there was no other message.

Damn.

Her thoughts began to turn on her. It was just like Sharon. He was hundreds of miles away, maybe in trouble, and she couldn't do a thing about it. She was a menace, drawing everyone she cared about into her problems. And they were the ones who suffered for it. Disgusted and angry at herself, she headed for John's truck.

Underdressed for the evening chill in the air, she climbed into the truck, wondering how Guinness, John's Irish Setter, had managed alone all day.

Guinness . . . Of course John was okay, but suppose he couldn't get a plane back to Memphis until tomorrow? How would Guinness get along until then? Would he need food or water? She didn't even know where John lived or if the dog was there. No. She shouldn't worry. If the dog needs anything, John would contact her and tell her what to do. *If he could*.

Damn.

She wished Guinness was there now so they could wait for John together. This way she had to handle it alone.

She sat staring at the windshield, thinking about what John had said. "Even loners need somebody." Sharon was gone. They'd never talk again. And now she didn't know what might be happening to John.

Feeling utterly miserable, she started the truck and headed for the UT library. On the way, her body reminded her she hadn't eaten anything all day. Disgusted at the thought that she should be hungry mere hours after learning Sharon had been murdered, she drove on, refusing to indulge herself.

At the library, she was handed a tan envelope with her name written across the front. Too curious about the contents to wait until she got home, she took the envelope to one of the long tables by the book stacks and removed the two papers inside.

Whoever had copied the articles hadn't pressed the bound center of the journals tightly enough against the copier. Consequently, a couple of letters were missing from each line. Though distracting, this didn't make them unreadable.

She started with the earlier of the two: *Breakdown, A New Mouse Mutation.* Hurriedly scanning the abstract, she discovered that the mutation in question led to a sudden paralysis of most of the voluntary muscles.

The same thing that had happened to Drew and Stephanie Stanhill and who knows how many other children.

She felt as though she'd just emerged from a long, muddy crawlway into virgin walking cave. This was big.

With her heart threatening to blow a rod, she plunged further into the article, which was written in an almost anecdotal style that included information not generally seen in scientific papers. The mutation had been discovered by accident, when several important animals in an experiment were found one morning unable to move their legs, a phenomenon that couldn't be explained by the treatment they'd been given.

Over the next few weeks, this happened to two more sets of animals. Intrigued and puzzled as to the cause, Timmons had poured over all the lab records of the paralyzed mice as well as those that were unaffected. Two facts emerged. The condition appeared only in litters from the matings of one particular pair of animals and only when susceptible animals were put in the smaller of the two mouse rooms in the vivarium.

After considerable study, Timmons discovered that the inducing stimulus for the paralysis was a high-pitched sound emitted by the room's air-conditioning vent.

Sarchi began to breathe faster as the horrible truth took shape. The inducing stimulus was a sound. And there was a hidden sound in the books someone had sent to all the children who subsequently became Latham's patients. These facts *had* to be related. But how?

Convinced that she held the answer in her hand, she read on. But the rest of the paper merely described a lot of physiological testing of the affected animals, documenting the nature of the paralysis, which appeared to originate in the brain.

She turned to the other paper, *Studies on the Mutant Gene*

in the Breakdown Mouse. From her physiology course in med school, Sarchi knew that the normal functioning of nerve cells requires the regulated movement of charged particles known as ions into and out of the cell through tiny pores, the ion channels, in the cell membrane. This knowledge wasn't much help in understanding details of the various experiments Timmons described in the first part of the second paper, but she was able to grasp the significance of his conclusion: the breakdown mutation had its effect through production of an abnormal ion channel in nerve cells. He had determined that when the defective channel was activated and opened for the first time, it remained open, disrupting normal neuron function. The inciting stimulus for the channel to open came from auditory pathways originating in the part of the inner ear mediating high frequency sounds. Even though the affected cells replaced the channel subunits every few hours, the channels remained open.

The rest of the paper contained proof that he had indeed isolated the mutant gene. This is commonly done by putting the gene into cells that don't have it and determining if those cells then behave like cells from the mutant animals. To get the gene into a host cell in a functional form, viruses incapable of reproducing on their own are usually used as the transporting agent. Though much of the terminology and nearly all the techniques Timmons used in this part of the paper were also over Sarchi's head, one fact leapt from the page: the transporting agent into which he had put the gene was a virus consisting of parts of adeno-associated virus two and the mouse Molony leukemia virus—*the same hybrid virus Latham's PCR primers were designed to detect.* There was no question now in her mind. *Latham was making kids sick by infecting them with a virus carrying the breakdown gene.*

36

In the last part of the second paper, Timmons described experiments in which he was able to selectively turn off the breakdown gene in the virally infected animals. Within hours, as the short-lived mutant ion channels began to disappear, the paralyzed mice recovered. That was obviously how Latham had been curing all the kids he'd made sick.

In the beginning, Latham had probably cured his first few victims for free to show the HMOs he was the best chance for anyone with that kind of illness. Whatever his fee, the HMOs would find it cheaper than paying for a lifetime of care for someone like Gilbert Klyce.

With her head spinning from all she'd learned, Sarchi left the library and returned to her car. As she headed for home and the heat of her discoveries cooled, all the still-unanswered questions swam before her.

If Latham could cure the disease by an injection, why was he boring holes in his patient's heads and damaging their brains—to make the cure look more difficult? He could have accomplished that without doing damage: Bore a hole, slip a probe into a silent area of the brain, and quit. Why didn't he go into the same part of the brain on every child? And why choose only kids whose umbilical cords were given to the

New York Cord Blood Repository? And the bald guy? Where did he fit in?

She thought of what Helper had said during their Internet Relay Chat. "The answer is in two parts."

Virtual Joe . . .

Sharon . . .

Oh, God.

During the time Sarchi had been in the library, her interest in Timmons's papers had shunted Sharon's death from the main track of her thoughts to a siding. How could she have allowed that? What kind of person was she?

As upset as she was at what she believed was a callous disregard for the loss of her best friend, her thoughts turned to John Metcalf, who was somewhere in Chicago, alone and maybe in trouble.

With the thrill of discovery, the misery of loss, and fear for Metcalf's safety flashing through of her mind like different colored sheets in a clothes dryer, she arrived home, where she was welcomed by the sound of the phone.

She snatched up the receiver just in time to hear her own voice on the answering machine. Over the recording, she announced her presence. "Hello . . . I'm here. Hello."

But no one responded.

John Metcalf hung up the pay phone in the Memphis International lobby, wondering if Sarchi was still in New Orleans. He had stepped off a flight from Chicago five minutes earlier, eager to discuss with her what he'd learned about the bald man's destination. What to do now? If she wasn't back yet, there was no point in going to her house.

Sarchi let the machine rewind, then stared at it, hoping there was a message from Metcalf waiting. But the only activity it had recorded was her own voice answering. Plagued by the potential importance of that call, she locked the front door and started for her room.

She'd barely taken two steps when the doorbell rang. Wanting it to be John, but also alert to the possibility of trouble, she took the .38 from her bag.

Returning to the door, she looked out through the left side-light to see who it was.

No . . . that was impossible.

Standing on her front porch, looking at her from under a porkpie hat, as alive as she was, stood Harry Bright.

37

B right produced a scrawled note and held it to the glass.
*We have to talk. I know everything that's been going
on at the Latham Clinic. My death was faked to throw them
off.*

Astounded at this development, Sarchi opened the door,
the .38 trailing out of sight behind her leg. She unlatched the
storm door and stepped back.

Stooped like an old man, Bright opened the storm door
and awkwardly came inside, relying heavily on a cane. Although they'd never been friends, Sarchi felt a twinge of pity
for whatever had happened to him.

Suddenly, quicker than any man should be able to move,
he was on her, his left hand snaking around to grab the .38,
the V formed by the thumb and index finger of his right
under her chin, driving her back so they weren't standing in
the doorway.

Behind the death mask of Harry Bright's face he'd made
by applying quick-drying liquid latex to the inside of a plas-
ter cast, Jackie had suspected Sarchi might be armed. Feeling
that it was a revolver, he clamped his fingers firmly around
the cylinder, rendering it impossible to fire. There wasn't a
woman in the world he couldn't subdue by force even if she

was armed. But this assignment had the constraint that he had to prevail without leaving any bruises on her and without producing any signs in the room that there'd been a struggle, otherwise when she was found with a lethal drug overdose in her blood, there might be questions about how it got there. He therefore, had to be careful that his fingers didn't exert *too* much pressure on her neck.

He moved quickly to Sarchi's right, intending to circle behind her, bend her gun hand up to her shoulder blade, and get her neck in the crook of his elbow so he could drop her by carotid compression as he had the last time. But Sarchi turned toward him and stepped forward so they remained face to face. Then, shit . . . despite his best effort to keep the gun pushed away from him, he felt it lifting, coming up. And he couldn't stop it.

Christ, this woman was strong. For the first time since he'd arrived in the city, he felt a twinge of doubt about the outcome of his plan. With control of her weapon the focus of his concern, his hand left Sarchi's throat and went to the gun, which was now pointing at him. He still had hold of the cylinder, but it was not good to have the barrel in his chest.

As Jackie's right hand joined the struggle for the revolver, Sarchi took advantage of the open route to his face and clawed at it with her free hand. Feeling her nails tear into the latex of the death mask, she grabbed it and yanked, peeling the appliance free. For half a heartbeat they stared into each other's eyes, then Sarchi put her foot behind Jackie's leg and pushed. He lost his balance and fell backward, but he still held tightly to the gun and her wrist, pulling her down with him. When he hit the floor, the impact caused his fingers to loosen on the revolver's cylinder and the gun discharged into his chest.

In the confusion, Sarchi ripped herself free from Jackie's grasp, but the hammer of the gun caught on the fabric of his jacket, pulling the weapon from her hand and leaving it in his possession. Afraid he'd been shot, but without checking to see, she ran for the kitchen.

• • •

Jackie lay there stunned, a blazing trail of pain on the inside of his right forearm, gunsmoke burning his eyes. The bullet had plowed a furrow along the skin of his forearm, then hit him just to the right of his sternum between his second and third ribs.

Though he never would have believed something like this could happen, he was also a careful man, which is why the round had been stopped by his Kevlar vest. He checked to see if he was bleeding onto the carpet, but all the blood was pooling inside his jacket, held there by the tight elastic at his wrist. He heard the back door open as Sarchi ran from the house.

This was a mess. There was no way now to kill her in the controlled way he'd planned. He could handle the failure, the fact that all the work leading up to tonight had been wasted. He could deal with being bested by a woman, could even ignore the pain from the gunshot, that was all just a matter of willpower. He needed now to get off the floor and leave, to finish the contract in some other way at another time. But she'd seen his face, the first person to do so in twenty-three years. She'd violated him. And tomorrow, she'd be describing him to a police sketch artist. The thought of being so *exposed* turned his stomach. Despite the risk, he had to end it tonight, any way he could.

Keenly aware that the man in the house was the one who'd abducted her and had probably also killed Harry Bright, Sarchi darted out the back door and ran to the front gates. In the dim light from the half moon, her fingers, clumsy with urgency, clawed at the bolt that held them shut. It gave ground slowly, squealing in protest as she worked it back and forth. Then, over the gates, she saw Jackie come around the front corner of the house.

There was no time for thought, only action. Flashing on the two fence boards some kids had loosened in the back of the yard, she ran for the spot, lifted them, and slid through the opening. She quickly learned what a bad idea this was. Beyond the two rows of pines screening her house was a huge field of prickly bushes that crowded against the pines so she couldn't go left or right. But straight ahead the bushes seemed smaller.

Ignoring his throbbing arm, Jackie scaled the gates and dropped into the backyard just as Sarchi disappeared through the two-board gap in the back fence. He, too, realized her mistake, for he had scouted the area when he'd first arrived in town and knew that the field of wild blackberry bushes behind the house would hinder her flight.

"Danny? This is John."
   "Where are you?"
   "Memphis airport. When'd you get back?"
   "About six o'clock."
   "Do you know where Sarchi went?"
   "Home, I guess."
   "I just called her there, but she didn't answer."
   "Want me to come and get you?"
   "No thanks, I'll catch a cab. Thanks for everything you did today."
   "What'd you find out? Where'd that bald guy go?"
   "I'll talk to you later about it."
   John hung up, went outside, and hailed a cab.
   "Where to?" the cabby asked.
   Home was where he should go. Guinness was probably hungry and there was no telling when Sarchi would return. But he was so anxious to see her, he decided to take a chance. He gave the cabby her address and settled back for the fifteen-minute ride.

The bushes snagged Sarchi's thin jeans and tore at her flesh, thousands of tiny claws trying to hold her until she was overtaken. But slowly, she pushed forward, high stepping, so as each foot came down, it pinned and crushed a few of the wild blackberries' looping branches. But she was still being sliced into stew meat.

   She glanced behind her and saw Jackie duck through the gap in the fence.

• • •

Jackie plunged into the bushes, wondering if he was leaving a trail of blood that could be used against him later.

This was so out of control.

He'd snatched up the death mask before running out but had left the cane. And his prints were still on the handle of the storm door. Worse, he was out here undisguised. At the least, he *had* to get back to the house after he'd finished her, get the cane and wipe the door handle. Then he must get to his car. His prints were all over that, too. And with all he'd had to do in the last few days, the four-by-four with the horseshoe nailed to it he'd used to kill Timmons was still in the trunk. The sound of the gun firing had been muffled by his jacket, so he was fairly certain it wasn't heard outside the house. Big deal—a small handhold above a raging sea of shit.

Sarchi looked again and saw that Jackie was slowly closing the distance between them and was now no more than twenty yards away. Her course was taking her directly to the drum reclamation plant, a sprawling building that lay darkly across her route for fifty yards in each direction. She prayed for a path between the building and the bushes.

A minute later, when she reached the building, there was, indeed, a small area devoid of bushes close to the wall. With no knowledge of the place and no time to reconnoiter, she lurched to the left.

Most of the plant was constructed of cement blocks, but in places the block was replaced by corrugated metal sheets. As she ran past such a place, her foot caught on a metal corner that had curled outward, cutting her ankle and pitching her to the ground.

She struggled to her feet and looked back.

Close. He was so close. She'd managed to surprise him in their first encounter, but she knew it would be a different story this time. Run . . .

She flew along the wall for another ten yards, then ran into a tangle of bushes taller and more impenetrable than any she'd seen. Jackie had already shown he could move faster

through the shorter bushes than she could, so if she went
back and set off again through them, he would change course
and intercept her. But maybe . . .

She dashed back to the metal flap that had tripped her,
grabbed it, and peeled it back. Yes. It was a way into the
building. She dropped to her knees, ducked, and slithered
through the opening.

Inside, the plant was a cavernous space dimly lit by occasional bulbs fixed to the high ceiling. In the poor light, Sarchi
saw thousands of empty buckets stacked inside each other,
forming hundreds of white plastic stalagmites that towered
over her. Behind her, she heard Jackie pulling at the metal
flap.

Sarchi darted into the maze of buckets to hide herself.

Jackie came through the hole, stood up, and took Sarchi's .38
from his jacket. Holding his breath, he surveyed the area, listening carefully. In the darkness, he heard the telltale hiss of
Sarchi's labored breathing.

From where she cowered, Sarchi could hear him moving toward her. Suddenly, there was a tremendous racket as Jackie
began kicking over stacks of buckets that fell into neighbor-
ing stacks, toppling them.

With her source of concealment rapidly vanishing, Sarchi
ran, heading for a collection of chrome lattice boxes, each
containing an empty plastic container as big as a car.

Seeing his quarry flushed from hiding, Jackie spun to his left
and fired the .38.

Sarchi felt the bullet nip the arm of her sweater. Before he
could fire again, she ducked behind the lattice boxes.

Jackie sprinted to his left and circled the lattice boxes, approaching Sarchi's new hiding place from the opposite way
she'd come to it. Prepared to fire the instant he saw her, he
popped around the corner and saw nothing.

Jackie moved as quietly as he could along the container

wall where she'd been. He flashed around the next corner and again failed to see her. Where the hell was she?

There . . . He whirled to his right and snapped off a round at the fleeing figure that had come from the opposite side of the boxes.

The last round sliced past Sarchi's head and buried itself with a hollow thunk into one of the blue plastic barrels stacked along the other side of the wide aisle down the middle of the building. Why had she come in here? It was a death trap.

The blue barrels were stacked high enough that once she rounded the corner and got behind them, she rose out of her bearwalk and ran upright, toward the far end of the building, where she prayed she would find a way out.

The blue barrels stretched along the aisle for about twenty yards, stacked so closely that Jackie couldn't see behind them. Unaware of what Sarchi was doing, he skirted the lattice boxes back the way he'd come, charged across the aisle, and muscled the blue barrels aside. He burst through the wall just in time to see Sarchi disappear into a huge doorway on the left.

He reached the spot a few seconds later and ran into a large room in which hundreds of short chains capped with metal hooks dangled from a maze of tracks overhead. Except for that, the room was bare. At its far end it opened into another massive chamber filled with thousands of fifty-five-gallon steel drums. Dismayed at all the hiding places they offered, Jackie sprinted toward them.

Against the wall opposite where Jackie had come in, Sarchi watched him from behind a screened alcove where reclaimed steel drums were spray painted. With his attention taken by the far room, she moved quickly to the opposite end of the alcove and ran back the way she'd entered.

Her heart beating so hard she could feel the blood surging behind her eyes, Sarchi burst through the doorway back into the room with the big center aisle. Though Jackie hadn't seen her, he'd heard the echo of her footsteps behind him. Now

she heard *his*, coming for her. If there had been time, she
would have gone back to the entrance hole and tried to out-
run him through the bushes back to the house. But he was too
close.

To her left she saw the same room full of steel drums
they'd both seen a moment ago through a different doorway.
Believing it offered her only hope, she fled that way.

Five seconds later, Jackie reached the aisle and saw her. He
was a marksman with any kind of firearm, but Sarchi's dark
clothing and hair made her tough to see in the gloom. She
was also quick. Neither of these facts comforted him. He'd
missed *twice*, and that was inexcusable. This time, instead of
just snapping off a round, he took time to get into a decent
stance.

Sarchi heard the sound of the gun and felt the hot skewer in
her side at practically the same instant. She *had* to find cover.

To her right was a two-tiered cache of steel drums with
metal rings around them at the top and middle that kept adjacent drums from touching. This produced at their closest
point, approximately an eight inch space between them.
From years of experience gauging the accessibility of tight
spots in subterranean passages, Sarchi believed she could
navigate those spaces. Throwing herself to the ground, she
turned on her good side and thrust herself into the cleft between two drums.

38

By the time Jackie got there, Sarchi was fully out of sight. He thought he knew exactly where she'd gone, but he couldn't look down from above to check because the drums on the upper tier were offset so that they sat over the spaces between those on the bottom. Pocketing the gun, Jackie tried to pull an obscuring barrel off the upper tier, but it was too heavy. He tried another. They were all immovable.

He looked around for something he could use to get at her. Spotting a forklift over by a stack of wooden pallets, he ran to it and checked the ignition. No key.

Frustrated and without another idea, he circled the drums where Sarchi was hiding to make sure she wasn't coming out the other side. Returning to where he started, he knelt, thrust the .38 into the hole where he believed she'd gone in, and fired the two remaining rounds in the gun.

In the maze of drums, Sarchi's nose scraped against cold steel as she negotiated an impossible turn into a side passage. But her legs were still in the cleft where she'd started. The first round from the .38 hit the cement floor an inch from her shoe and ricocheted upward, punching through the bottom of a drum on the second tier. From the hole, used engine oil dribbled onto her. The following slug clanged off the side of a drum at a spot a quarter of an inch from her hip, pinballed into two more drums in a potentially deadly fusillade, and exited the maze through a rear opening. As the echo of the ricocheting bullets died away, Sarchi's heart leapt at the sound of the revolver's hammer falling on an empty chamber. He was out of ammunition.

Then she heard a sound that brought all the terror she'd felt a moment earlier flooding back, a sound she'd heard next to her at the firing range with John—a round being chambered into an automatic.

The maze became a war zone as Jackie ran from cleft to cleft, firing blindly into its dark recesses, sending slugs whining and clanging on a search for Sarchi's hide.

Inside the maze it was impossible to tell exactly where Jackie was at any given moment. Along with the unpredictable course of every round he fired, there was no place in there that seemed better than another. So all Sarchi could do was lie helplessly and curse the decisions that had led her to this.

Suddenly, the echoes of gunfire and ricochets faded and there was only the sound of her heart hammering against her eardrums. Was he reloading?

She listened hard for the snap of a clip being removed from his automatic and another slamming home. But it didn't come. What was he *doing*?

Jackie stopped firing when he had two rounds left. Was she hit, wounded, or dead? It was like poisoning a rat and having it die in your walls. The only way you could tell if you got him was when he started to smell. And he couldn't wait for *that*.

"I hope you understand I don't dislike you," he said. "In fact, I admire you. You're smart, resourceful, and incredibly strong. What do you think of me?"

He waited to see if his ploy would work. He knew she was too intelligent to respond, but he was after an emotional reaction, an epithet perhaps, anything to tell him if she was still alive and approximately where she was.

• • •

In the maze, Sarchi wanted to curse him in defiance, but she kept quiet, hoping he'd think she was dead. Though she needed to concentrate on a way out of this, her focus shifted to the fiery notch the .38 slug had clipped from her side. Then, in her left calf, the start of a cramp, growing. Jesus, *not now*.

She flexed her foot to stretch the muscle, but the cramp pulled it back, knotting her calf into a fleshy rock that made pain seem like something you could see. To her horror, an almost inaudible cry of agony slipped from her lips.

It wasn't loud enough or of sufficient duration to allow Jackie to pinpoint her location, but he now knew he had more work to do. He never carried an extra clip for his gun. If he couldn't resolve a situation with thirteen rounds it was so out of control that thirteen more wouldn't do him any good. But he'd never anticipated a deal like this.

Unless there was a dramatic change in the situation, it wasn't likely the two rounds he had left would accomplish any more than the others had. He needed to flush her out of there. But how?

He surveyed the area.

Between the two entrances to the room, an asphalt berm about six inches high ringed an area where greasy puddles glistened in the dim light. Hanging on the wall inside the berm was a coiled hose tipped by an insulated metal wand.

Slipping his automatic back into his shoulder holster, Jackie ran to the hose, hefted the coils onto the floor, and triggered the wand. As billows of steam poured from the tip, he grinned.

The game was now over.

The coiled hose was more than long enough for him to carry the wand back to where Sarchi hid. At the cleft where she'd disappeared, he poked the wand deeply into the darkness and pulled the trigger.

Sarchi heard the scrape of the hose on the floor, but had no idea what it was. Suddenly, the maze was filled with an explosive hiss that could only mean a new kind of trouble. She was out of range of the initial attack, but a wave of wet heat surged around the corner of her niche and washed over her.

She was three drums deep, lying in a side passage, her body parallel to the first row of drums. Her legs, upper chest, and head were protected from a frontal steam assault, but her midriff lay in a crawlway directly accessible to a wand thrust from where Jackie was working. So if his next stop was one drum to his right, she'd be broiled. She needed to get deeper into the maze. But with her back to the desired direction, a turn that way was physically impossible. Despite that it would put her weight on the side where she'd been shot, she had to turn over.

Still in agony from the cramp in her calf, she pushed against the floor with that foot and humped her shoulder forward, trying to get her hips to the widest region of the passageway. This brought her head into a space that led directly to the front, meaning that if Jackie skipped two drums to his right and steamed that crawlway, she'd take it in the face.

If Jackie had thought about the way Sarchi had been facing when she went into the hole, he'd have realized how unlikely it was she'd gone to his left in the maze of drums. But it didn't occur to him. As a result, he adopted a systematic but poorly conceived approach that sent him down the front line of drums in the wrong direction.

Hearing the hiss of steam growing more remote, Sarchi stopped moving and tried to think how she might take advantage of this.

Jackie worked his way to the left, sterilizing each crawlway he encountered. When he reached the last drum on the front row, he turned the corner and began working the openings down that side.

Soon after the steam hiss moved away, Sarchi heard it directly behind her, but not very close to where she lay. Following a short interval, a dissipated wave of wet heat rolled over her from that direction. If he kept to this pattern, she could use that predictability.

Jackie moved steadily along the side of the drum cache until he reached the end. Believing that if Sarchi was still mobile she'd probably be crawling toward the back or the other side, he dropped the wand and crept as quietly as he could, gun drawn, along the back of the cache, ready to fire the instant he saw her.

As soon as she felt the latest steam head disperse, Sarchi humped and shoved herself backward so her midriff lay across a crawlway Jackie had already steamed. Then she waited, worrying that if he abandoned any pattern in his attempts to broil her, there'd be no way to evade him. With the sudden cessation of the steam, she worried even more.

Jackie crept quickly along the entire back row of drums, turned the corner, and came rapidly forward, disappointed that he hadn't been able to make a verified kill. But she could simply be too hurt to move. This in turn meant that if she wasn't already dead or dying, a methodical approach with the steam that covered all the areas he'd missed so far and revisited those where he'd already been, followed by a thorough but unpredictable sweep in which he'd come in from above, would surely finish her. Eager to get out of this place, he returned to where he'd dropped the steam wand and resumed work.

By sound alone, it was hard for Sarchi to tell exactly where Jackie was working. But she also had heat to help her. Shortly after the hissing had resumed, her feet grew warm, then her back, followed a few seconds later by her head. Knowing now that he was working along the back row, which was too far away to hurt her, she decided that her best hope for survival, if she could manage it, would be to sneak out of the maze unseen, hide somewhere else, and hope he'd believe the steam had killed her.

Helped by the heat, the knotted muscle in her calf had relaxed. So at least she wouldn't be hampered by that. The quickest and best place for her to emerge was the side Jackie had just left. But this meant she'd be coming out blind, feet first. With no other choice available, she began inching backward.

She soon discovered that the used oil leaking from the overhead drum punctured by Jackie's first shot had turned the floor so slippery it was almost impossible to get any traction. With a little experimentation, she found that by pushing against the drums with her hands she could move through a combination of sliding and squirming. As she passed under the leaking drum, used oil filled her ear.

Thirty-two seconds after she'd made the decision to leave the drums, and at the precise moment Jackie reached the last crawlway on the back row, her feet emerged. Slicked down like a duck caught in a tanker spill, the rest of her quickly followed.

With oil draining from her ear, she got into a bearwalking stance and looked for another hiding place. Nearby, she saw the ancient machine the plant used to clean rust from the inside of steel drums. Shaped like a cylinder with the top cut off, it stretched about thirty feet away from her. On its near end it was equipped with a lot of big gears turned by a couple of monster bicycle chains. When it was in use, a dozen barrels filled with chains were lashed into the bed. Powered up, the rollers rotated the barrels on their long axis, and the bed rocked like a cradle. Needing to find cover fast, Sarchi scurried for the far end of the machine.

The way things had been going, what happened next shouldn't have surprised her. Halfway to her goal, she kicked a metal bung stop and sent it skidding across the floor, directly toward another stand of drums. Just before it hit, Jackie shut off the steam and started for the next crawlway. The bung stop wasn't moving very fast, but when it hit the drum, the sound echoed through the building.

Jackie dropped the wand and pulled out his automatic. With the echo distorting the sound, he couldn't tell where it had originated, but its meaning was clear.

"Very good, Doctor Seminoux. You're a worthy adversary. All you're doing though is prolonging things. But I understand. It's perfectly natural. I don't hold it against you in the least." Listening hard, Jackie moved down the back row of drums, turned the corner, and stopped at the end of the drum cleaning machine.

"Have you ever wondered why people who say they believe in an afterlife better than this one fight so hard for survival? I can understand an atheist doing that, but the other has always puzzled me. Are you a religious woman?"

From Jackie's monologue, Sarchi realized where he was standing. For the first time in the chase, he was between her and an escape route. She was finished.

Then, she got an idea—not a great idea, one she wouldn't even have considered if she could have thought of anything else. Because if it failed, he'd know where she was. This made her hesitate. But if he moved, she wouldn't even have that chance.

She decided to go for it. But she needed something to throw. Groping around the floor, she could find nothing. She looked longingly across the room at the bung stop she'd kicked. She thought of using her shoe, but didn't want to be rendered that handicapped.

Her belt.

She stripped off her belt, coiled it, and pivoted toward the machine. As she didn't dare stand, this would all have to be done by intuition. There were six sheathed cables snaking from the machine to an electrical box with a switch lever mounted on a two-foot-tall steel bar to her left. After a quick run-through in her mind, she lobbed her belt into the bed of the big machine.

Hearing the belt hit, Jackie whirled to his right, leaned over, and peered into the drum cleaner's dark interior, his automatic lifted high.

As Jackie leaned forward, Sarchi pushed up the switch that operated the machine. With a gnashing groan, its big gears engaged, starting the rollers that found no drums to turn. At the same moment, the bed of the machine scooped forward and lifted, beginning its rocking motion.

At the first sound, Jackie jumped back, or at least that was his intent. But his jacket was caught in the chain that drove the roller gears. Dropping his gun, he tore at the zipper, but the chain was pulling him down, feeding his jacket into the gears, which slowly drew his face toward them.

Jackie believed only in this life, and he wasn't ready to give it up. He fought the fabric tethering him to the gears, demanding that it tear and free him. But he always insisted on quality goods. This time those high standards betrayed him.

As his nose and lips were mangled by the gears and their teeth crunched through the bones of his face, his last thought was what an incredibly stupid way this was to die.

39

Filthy and exhausted, Sarchi made her way back through the blackberry bushes, her momentary elation at having survived now muted by the cold realization that she had engineered the death of another human being.

Jackie had torn the loose boards completely free from the fence, so going through the gap this time was easier. As she slid through, the back door of her house opened and John came onto the porch. Seeing her, he shouted her name and came running.

Ignoring the oil and grime on her clothing, he took her in his arms. "What happened?"

Sarchi briefly gave herself fully into his embrace, washing her mind of everything but the comfort and safety of his touch. Then she looked up at him. "Latham sent a man to kill me. He's back there in that building—dead."

This was hardly a sufficient explanation for what had taken place, but John didn't press her. "Come on. Let's go inside."

He helped her into the kitchen and put her in a chair at the breakfast table. It was then that he noticed the blood on her sweater. "You're hurt."

"A bullet grazed me. It's no big deal. It still stings, but the bleeding's stopped. I can treat it myself."

"I'll get something to clean you up."

He returned with a couple of wet washcloths and some towels, which he used to wash and dry her face and hands.

"We have to call the police," Sarchi said.

"We'll do that, but when they get here, we're not going to have a chance to talk alone for a while. If I knew the details of what happened, I might be able to guide things a bit."

Sarchi nodded. John pulled the nearest chair closer and sat down.

She began her story with Harry Bright's appearance at the front door. When she finished with the description of how she'd saved herself, John said, "This is clearly a case of self-defense. I can't see anyone questioning that."

"But I *killed* someone."

John reached out and took her hands. "The law imposes no penalty in these circumstances because self-preservation is the most fundamental right there is. Actually, he caused his *own* death. A thug like that was bad enough when he was able to hurt people directly. To let him continue to affect you now is just giving him more power over you. He's gone, and the world is a better place. That's the end of it. We're not going to ever be concerned about this again, agreed?"

He'd said nothing Sarchi didn't already know, but she still needed to hear it. "You're right. It's just too bad it wasn't the one who sent him. I figured out what Latham's been doing, at least part of it. It was all in Timmons's papers, which were waiting for me at the library when I got back. All the kids he's treated—*he's* the one who made them sick."

"How?"

"I don't know the details, but he somehow infected them with a virus carrying a gene that makes nerve cells defective. He was causing the disease he alone knew how to cure. The embedded sound in the book he sent each kid was the stimulus that set the gene off."

John's mouth gaped. "I think I know the rest."

"What?"

"The bald guy with the insulated container. He took it to a

clinic specializing in experimental treatment for Parkinson's, Alzheimer's, and Huntington's disease."

Seeing where he could be going with this, Sarchi's insides shriveled in horror. No. It was too unspeakable. No one could be that immoral.

"They claim their treatments involve the grafting of brain cells from aborted fetuses," John said. "But I'm betting the cells came from the kids Latham operated on."

"The New York Cord Blood Repository," Sarchi cried. "He must have accessed their database. He was tissue matching the kids to the recipients who were to get their cells."

40

The authorities acted quickly on the information Sarchi and John provided. Within forty-eight hours, Latham's clinic and the one in Chicago were closed and their records confiscated. Latham and Dr. Gerald Couch, the head of the Chicago end of the operation, were both arrested. That same day Sarchi learned that the lab tests for seminal products on the swabs from her examination at the sexual assault center had come back negative. The next afternoon, she was informed that the AIDS test she'd requested on Jackie Tellico's blood showed no evidence of HIV. Armed with this knowledge, Sarchi was finally free of him.

Wishing to set things right with the Stanhills, Sarchi called their home and talked to Stephanie's mother for nearly twenty minutes, during which Regina asked many questions. She also cursed Latham at length and thanked Sarchi effusively for stopping him. Despite the role she'd played in Latham's downfall, Sarchi found little satisfaction in it, in part because the harm he'd inflicted on Drew and Stephanie persisted unchanged. But John Metcalf was right. It *was* too early to tell how those stories would end.

Sharon's parents took her body back to Lexington, Kentucky, where she'd grown up and where they still lived. Before Sarchi could learn when the funeral would be held, it had already taken place. Coming on top of the responsibility she felt for causing Sharon's death, Sarchi was extremely disturbed that she hadn't been there. She also felt that she had unfinished business with Latham, that she not only had to actually see him in jail but also needed to confront him. She was, therefore, in no frame of mind to resume her work at the hospital even though Koesler had conveyed through Kate McDaniels that she was welcome.

Learning of her wish to see Latham, John set up a visit and got Danny LaPlante to fly them back to New Orleans. Figuring that this was between Sarchi and Latham, John let her enter the visitor's area alone, where, sitting in front of the glass partition waiting for the guards to bring him in, her palms began to sweat.

Finally, the door opened and there he was, in an orange prison jumpsuit. When he saw her, a look of such animosity appeared on his face that she thought he might try to break through the partition. Instead of being frightened, she reveled in this.

He stared at her without moving for at least half a minute, then the guard said something to him. He came forward and sat down. Jaw clenched, the muscle under his right eye twitching, he reached for the phone. Finding him smaller and less powerfully built than she remembered, Sarchi did the same.

"What do *you* want," he said through clenched teeth.

"To see you in your new habitat. I hope everything is satisfactory."

"You think you're so damned clever . . ."

"You're a disgrace, not only to medicine, but to the entire human race. I just had to tell you that."

A dozen emotions flashed through his eyes. Settling again on hatred, he said, "What exactly was so wrong about what I did? All the people we treated with donor cells were accomplished men and women, proven contributors to society. Kids are unknown quantities. Many turn out to be liabilities instead of assets. Some even become dangerous. We were merely preserving our known resources. And where's the harm? The brains of children are adaptable. In time, all the anomalies they may now be exhibiting will probably disappear."

"You're pathetic. You still don't see it."

"What's to see? We were producing results unheard of anywhere else in the world, giving people their lives back."

"At the expense of *children*."

"The great Doctor Seminoux. Who are you to judge me? What have *you* ever done that makes any difference—bandage a few cuts, cure a couple cases of head lice. What will you *ever* do that means anything?"

Sarchi gave him her prettiest smile. "I put you here."

Satisfying as her visit with Latham was, Sharon's death still sat heavily in the path of Sarchi's return to a normal life. Wanting to help her over this and remembering how much she'd enjoyed the day they'd spent at Nine Ponds, John suggested that if the wound in her side and the cut on her ankle permitted, she return there and help him finish putting in the daffodils. The idea was so appealing and her wounds were healing so well that Sarchi accepted without hesitation.

With time out for playing Frisbee with Guinness and lunch at Dale's, the job took three days. On the third day, as Sarchi covered the last bulb and pressed the earth firmly over it, she looked at John.

"We're finished."

He took her hand and helped her to her feet. "In the spring, when they're all in bloom, we'll have a picnic on the hill."

"I'd like that."

They looked deeply into each other's eyes, then melted together in a long kiss. "Thanks for the last three days," she said against his chest. "It was just what I needed. But now, it's time I got back to my kids at the hospital."

John dropped her off at home a little after four o'clock. The first thing she did was call Kate McDaniels's pager. Within a minute, her call was returned.

"Kate, I'm coming back to work tomorrow."

"That's wonderful. Do you feel up to an admitting shift? We need someone to cover for Jim Hartley."

"Same old place, I see. Ask for a drink and they hand you a fire hose. Sure, I can do that."

The next morning, when Sarchi appeared in the kitchen in scrubs, Linda looked up from the paper in surprise. "You're going back to work? Good for you. Say, there's something in the paper this morning about that Latham character. He made a couple of statements to a reporter . . ." She riffled through the paper and folded it at the spot. "Get this . . ."

She began to read aloud the same baloney Latham had pedaled to Sarchi in jail. When she finished, Linda looked up from the paper. "I'll bet his lawyer is thrilled with this. He's admitted everything."

"We had him pretty well wrapped up anyway," Sarchi replied. "As for that crap about the kids he damaged eventually getting better, my nephew hasn't shown any improvement."

"I don't want to be siding with Latham, but there is something to what he says. The brains of kids *are* adaptable. There's still a chance for Drew."

"I hope so."

"You did a good thing, stopping this guy. To be honest, I didn't think you had that kind of grit."

"I didn't before I met Latham."

"Then something worthwhile came out of it."

"Not nearly enough to cover the cost."

"Your friend, Sharon?"

Her eyes suddenly wet, Sarchi nodded.

Linda got up and put her arm around Sarchi's shoulder. "Sure, bad things happened. But it's over, and you have to move on." She tightened her grip briefly, then let go. "I'll see you at the hospital."

But it *wasn't* completely over. When Sarchi had called Detective Veret a few days ago, he'd said there was no doubt that Sharon's killer was Lee-Ann Hipp, Latham's surgical nurse. But the woman had fled and so far hadn't been found. Veret was sure she'd be located, but, until that happened, it certainly wasn't over.

•   •   •

It seemed that everyone in the hospital knew about Sarchi's role in exposing Latham, so her return led to an endless round of congratulatory handshakes and pats on the back. When she had a few free minutes, she dropped by Mel Pierce's office to say hello. Arriving at his open door, she saw him hard at work, his desk surrounded by cardboard boxes of file folders and notebooks.

"You look busy."

He glanced up from the folder in front of him. "Well, it's the woman of the hour. I heard you were back. How you feeling?"

"Like I'm getting far too much attention."

"It's your fifteen minutes. Soak it up. You deserve it."

"What's in the boxes?"

"Copies of all the material confiscated from Latham."

"How'd *you* get it?"

"Someone with a medical background has to go through it before his trial. I volunteered and was accepted. There's a hell of a lot of stuff here, but it's the only way I'll ever find out the details of what he was doing."

"Some of it is in two papers by a man named Timmons published in the late eighties in *Acta Neurologica*."

"I've read them. There were copies in the second box I opened."

"Have you found anything that explains exactly how he was infecting the kids with the virus carrying the breakdown gene?"

"I've had to piece it together from several documents and from conversations with detectives in New Orleans, but yeah, I believe I do know that. When they had a patient who needed a transplant, they checked the tissue typing records they'd hijacked from the cord blood repository and picked a child who was an exact match for their patient. Then they sent a midget dressed as a kid to that child's school to deliver the viral vector into the target's eyes with a water pistol. I hear the midget and a woman he worked with are also in custody."

"Not that I care about their welfare, but that method of delivery sounds risky. A little wind blowing in the wrong direction and the one holding the water gun could become infected."

"Before approaching each child, they injected themselves with an antiviral agent. I also found this." He picked up a notebook to his right and thumbed through it, then turned it around and laid it on the desk so she could see the page he'd selected. "That's the formula for the gene inactivating solution they used to cure the kids once Latham was finished with them. It's a little different from what Timmons used on mice."

Sarchi leaned over and scanned the list of components, only a few of which she recognized. "So you'll probably be testifying at the trial."

"Wouldn't be surprised." His amiable expression changed to one of discomfort. "I hope you're not upset at me for refusing to back you when you visited Latham's hospital to lodge your complaints about him."

"You supplied me with the scans I needed."

"But I wouldn't let you use my name."

"Everybody involved could have done things differently," Sarchi said, thinking of Sharon. "I can't afford to dwell on that."

After a pause in which she struggled to get Sharon out of her thoughts, Sarchi looked intently at Pierce. "You seem to have all the answers today, so tell me this—what makes someone who set out to help people end up harming them and believing it's okay?"

"That's a tough one. I've talked to a fellow who was in the same residency program with Latham and another who was on staff at Vandy when he was there. Both say he was extremely ambitious and had extraordinary ability. That's apparently a dangerous combination. When you seem to have no peers, I'd guess it's difficult for some people not to get carried away with themselves to where they believe their wishes and judgment are all that matter."

"It's still hard for me to see how he could have made the choices he did."

Pierce smiled. "Good. That means we don't have to worry about *you*."

She was about to plead not guilty to possessing either of the attributes that had destroyed Latham when she felt her pager vibrate. The number displayed was Koesler's office.

Now what?

She excused herself and returned the call on a hall phone. "This is Doctor Seminoux."

"Doctor Koesler would like to see you if you're free."

After all she'd been through, Sarchi found, as she made her way to Koesler's office, that the prospect of another confrontation with the man had hardly any affect on her. She found him immaculate and pristine as ever behind his desk.

"Ah, Doctor Seminoux, please have a seat."

She put herself in a chair and waited to hear what he wanted. But he looked at her for an awkwardly long time without speaking, his fingers working the desktop like a calculator keypad. Finally, he tapped the desk hard with stiffened fingers and leaned back in his chair.

"I was wrong about you," he said. "About the drug issue. But in my defense, I was merely acting in good faith on information that had come to me. I could hardly be expected to know the data in question were unreliable."

"Is this an apology?"

"It's an explanation. However, there is another issue, the matter of the chief residency. I do owe you an apology for that. As a favor to George Latham, I gave the position to Rachel Moore instead of you. But I didn't know then what kind of man he was."

"That doesn't matter. You shouldn't deny anyone something they deserve as a favor to a third person."

"I'm not prepared to discuss my ethics with you. But I do want to make things right."

"You're not thinking of taking the chief residency away from Rachel . . ."

"I can't do that. But my private practice pediatric group is losing a member. So, if you'd like his slot, it's yours."

Much as Sarchi now wished to stay in Memphis, she didn't want a handout. "Thanks for the offer, but I'll pass."

Koesler's face clouded. "You're not even going to ask

about the details? I assure you, you won't find a better position anywhere in the country."

"Knowing the offer was made merely to appease your conscience is enough."

"That wasn't the primary reason. We live in a soft country where things come easily and people can get along fine without a backbone if they're bright enough. *You* were once that way. I'd rather not have that kind of person in this residency program, but the committee never considers anything but academics and medical skills. So I'm surrounded by weakness, except in my private practice. There, *I* make the call. You don't work with me there unless you're a fine doctor and have the fiber to stand straight under fire. After what you've done in the last few weeks, you, Doctor Seminoux, are such a person. And it would be an honor to work with you. So what do you say? Come to dinner with the group, talk to them, see what you think. Then we'll discuss details and you can make your decision."

"If I should eventually decide to accept your offer, would you be meddling in my cases?"

"Probably. But I'd expect you to defend yourself."

"Do you get the last word?"

"Not if you're strong enough."

Sarchi thought a moment and said, "Set up the dinner."

From Koesler's office, Sarchi returned to the ER to see a little boy who'd been hit under the chin with a seesaw and had bitten his tongue less severely than all the blood suggested. Shortly after she'd finished with that case, her pager displayed John Metcalf's number. He picked up in the middle of the first ring.

"Sarchi, did you hear?"

"Hear what?"

"It was just on the news. Latham is dead. He was stabbed with a sharpened spoon by another inmate. I thought something like this might happen when I read his comments in the paper. Cons hate child molesters, and, in a way, that's what he was."

"I can't say I'm sorry. With the screwed-up judicial system

in this country I was afraid he might get off with a much
lighter punishment than he deserved."

"How about we have a commemorative dinner Thursday
night to observe the occasion?"

"Isn't that kind of goulish?"

"We won't toast his death or anything. We'll just sit quietly and reflect on how beautiful life can be sometimes."

"You're on."

"How you comin' on findin' Lee-Ann Hipp?"

Claude Veret looked up at his captain. " I just learned her
family moved to Covington from Lucien, Mississippi. I'm
about to call the county sheriff over there and see if she has
any relatives in the area who might be harboring her."

"Good. Keep on it."

Veret looked at the Post-it bearing the number of the sheriff's office and made the call.

It took well over two minutes for the person who answered
to get the sheriff on the line. Veret then explained his reason
for calling.

"Detective," the sheriff said, "you want Lee-Ann Hipp,
we're gonna have to exhume her."

"What happened?"

"Died in a house fire. She had an aunt lived alone in Lucien for years back in the woods—tough old gal. *She* died
about a year ago and left the house to Lee-Ann. Far as I
know, Lee-Ann never come to claim it. Just had it boarded
up. Five days ago the place burned to the ground. Bein' so far
off the road, it was near gone before anybody could get to it.
And damned if we didn't find Lee-Ann's car there and her
body inside what was left of the house. Had no idea she was
a wanted woman or I would have contacted you."

"Who identified the body?"

"I'm from that area and I'd seen her some over the years,
so I had an idea what she looked like, but I got a copy of her
Louisiana driver's license to refresh my memory. What with
the fire and all, the body wasn't in the best shape. But you
could tell it was her. And she was wearin' her high school
class ring with her initials on it."

"How'd the fire start?"

"Probably from a tipped-over kerosene lamp. The place was wired for electricity, but I guess Lee-Ann figured if she had it turned back on, we'd know she was there."

"How do you figure a kerosene lamp tipped itself over?"

"I don't follow you."

"If you knocked a kerosene lamp over and it caused a fire that got out of control, would you stay in the house?"

"I'd get out."

"Exactly. Most people who expire in a house fire die in their sleep from inhaling carbon monoxide and other toxic gases."

"You sayin' this was no accident?"

"Maybe not."

"Any idea who'd want her dead?"

Unaware that Latham had been killed, Veret said, "One good one, but he's already in jail."

"I don't have the resources to do anything about this."

"Then don't. I wasn't there, so I can't say what happened. Leave it as is."

Veret hung up, leaned back in his chair, and closed his eyes to organize his thoughts.

A little after ten o'clock Sarchi was paged to the information desk in the hospital lobby where someone was asking for her. She arrived to find a woman she didn't know waiting.

"I'm Doctor Seminoux. What can I do for you?"

"I'm Evelyn Klyce," the woman said. " Gilbert's mother."

Gilbert Klyce—the paralyzed boy from the Brunswick Developmental Center.

"I've been reading about this man, George Latham, in the paper," she said. "And I think Gilbert may be one of his victims."

41

Shocked at Evelyn Klyce's statement, Sarchi took her to a table in the sparsely populated cafeteria where they could talk.

When Drew had come into the ER paralyzed, his muscles were flaccid, and he had no reflexes. In time, had his condition persisted, that would have changed as the nerve cells supplying his muscles became hyperexcitable, and all his joints would have become flexed as Gilbert's were. So that aspect of Gilbert's condition was not inconsistent with his mother's suspicions. But Gilbert was blind and deaf as well. And if his illness was caused by Latham, why was he still in that state? These problems made Sarchi believe, as Evelyn shed her coat and draped it on a chair, that the woman was simply grasping at hope.

Evelyn was probably in her mid-thirties, and her face clearly showed the stress of having a permanently paralyzed child. She was dressed in a white blouse and dark skirt, components that could easily be mixed and matched. That and her simple cloth coat suggested she was making do on a limited income.

"Now," Sarchi said when they were both settled. "Why do you think Latham was involved in Gilbert's illness?"

"When it happened, four years ago, Gilbert was five, the same age as those other children," Evelyn began. "And we were living in Nashville. The paper said that four years ago Latham was working in Nashville, at Vanderbilt."

"The parents of all the kids Latham made sick gave their child's umbilical cord to the New York Repository for cord blood," Sarchi said. "Did you do that?"

"No."

"Where was Gilbert born?"

"In Nashville."

This lack of a connection with the cord blood repository seemed to prove pretty clearly that Evelyn was way off the track in her suspicions. Still feeling badly about how little she'd been able to do for Gilbert, Sarchi figured she could at least appear interested in what his mother had to say. "I interrupted. Please go on."

"My husband—Gilbert's father—was a Christian Scientist. You know, the group that doesn't believe in doctors. So when Gilbert became ill, he wouldn't let me take him to the hospital. Said God would heal him. He was a very stupid man. He and his friends prayed and prayed for Gilbert, but he didn't get better."

"That explains why his records say the precipitating illness was *presumed* to be viral encephalitis," Sarchi said. "I've always wondered why the diagnosis was so equivocal. Do you remember the sequence of events when he got sick? Did it happen quickly?"

"What do you mean quickly?"

"Without warning."

"He'd had a cough and slight fever for a few days before it happened."

Another fact that didn't fit.

"The night he became paralyzed he was in his room playing. I walked in and there he was, lying on the floor. And he hasn't moved since."

"Was he reading when it happened?"

"There were some books near him, but I don't know what he was doing."

"Around the time he got sick, do you remember someone sending you a book that played a little song at the end?"

"No, but my husband always brought in the mail."

"And you don't recall a book like that lying about."

"It's been four years."

"I understand. Mrs. Klyce, I have to say that nothing you've told me fits the pattern of the way Latham worked."

"I'm not finished. I couldn't stand by and do nothing for my son. I had to get him some proper medical attention, so I put him in a facility in Nashville. My husband and I split up over the issue."

"I'm sorry."

"Don't be. He was an inconsiderate stupid ass. Anyway, about a year after we'd divorced I decided to move Gilbert here to the Brunswick Center. Of course, I had to live nearby to give him his physical therapy. You know, to keep his tendons from shortening so when he's better he'll be able to walk.

"The day the movers came I found a letter that must have slipped behind the desk my ex used during our marriage. It probably fell out the back of one of the drawers. It was from a doctor at Vanderbilt offering to treat Gilbert free with some experimental therapy he'd developed. The date on it was a year old. My husband had known about it for a year, and the bastard never said anything.

"With all the confusion of moving, I didn't have time to follow up on the letter that day. Besides, it was a Saturday. So the doctor wouldn't have been in his office anyway. I planned to call him on Monday, but somehow I lost the letter. I was sure I put it in my bag, but when I looked for it, it wasn't there. And I couldn't remember the name of the doctor. I called Vanderbilt, but without his name they couldn't help me. To this day I haven't found that letter. But when I saw Latham's name in the paper, I remembered. *That's* who it was."

"You're sure."

"Absolutely."

Evelyn's story explained why Gilbert had never been treated by Latham. With that issue resolved, Sarchi began to see how the other discordant aspects of Gilbert's situation could be reconciled. In the beginning, when Latham was infecting kids and treating them free to gain a reputation with the HMOs, there didn't have to be any New York connection with the kids he'd chosen because no one was waiting for their cells. And Gilbert's fever before he'd become paralyzed could have been a coincidence. Pick a group of kids at random and inevitably you'll get one with a cold.

Deep down, Sarchi knew all this was probably just wishful thinking on her part, but if she could give Gilbert one chance in a thousand—or even one in a million at some level of recovery—why not try it?

Sarchi filled the syringe with half a cc of the gene inactivating solution and inserted the needle into the injection port of Gilbert's IV. Everything to this point had gone incredibly well. Though most everyone involved believed for one reason or another that this was going to be a waste of time, they'd agreed to help. Even Koesler had given his permission, provided that Gilbert's mother signed the proper forms, which she did without hesitation.

Pierce had faxed the formula to Carl Lanza, who had all the ingredients in his lab. He'd made and tested the solution on a dozen rats without producing any ill effects even when he used ten times the dosage indicated on the sheet bearing the formula. She'd started putting all this together around ten o'clock. It was now a little past two. Four hours from inception to delivery—truly a remarkable achievement.

But would it work?

The room was crowded with people; Gilbert's mother, Kate McDaniels, Mel Pierce, Carl Lanza, interns and residents, two nurses, and a cardiac team. Apart from Evelyn Klyce, there wasn't much optimism in the room. So most of those present were there either to provide moral support or to lend assistance if anything went sour.

Her heart in her throat, Sarchi pushed the plunger and sent the solution into Gilbert's blood. Except for the beep of his pulse oximeter, the room was silent. But the collective anxiety of the group was almost palpable.

One second . . . two seconds . . . three . . .

Gilbert lay there, still in fetal flexion, still pitiful. But his heartbeat remained steady and his breathing normal.

Ten seconds . . .

The elapsed time stretched to a minute, then two. As the interval lengthened, the tension in the room began to dissipate. At five minutes after injection, everyone looked visibly relaxed.

"What's the earliest we could expect any result?" one of the interns asked Sarchi. Gilbert's mother, too, waited for her answer.

The question was a tough one. In his second paper, Timmons had written that the inactivation solution restored function in mice several hours after injection. But people aren't mice. Moreover, the charts of the kids Latham had treated mentioned nothing about any of this. So he must have recorded that information separately on sheets Pierce had yet to find.

"The half life of the defective ion channels is very short—a matter of hours. But we don't know how long it'll take for the affected cells to resume their normal functions after the channels are gone." Had Evelyn not been present, Sarchi might have added that even if Gilbert's condition *had* been caused by Latham, the length of time Gilbert had been paralyzed could mean his cells would never be normal again.

Seeing that Gilbert had tolerated the injection with no ill effects, the group in his room dispersed. Though Sarchi wanted to remain, she was paged to the ER. "Mrs. Klyce, I've got to go. But I'll be back when I can. You're free to stay as long as you like."

For the rest of the afternoon, Gilbert dominated Sarchi's thoughts. Each time she returned to Gilbert's room, she examined him carefully, looking for the slightest sign of improvement. But she saw nothing. And each time that she had to acknowledge his mother's hopeful look with a shake of the head, it hurt so badly she began to feel reluctant to return.

Around eight P.M. she entered Gilbert's room to find the intern and the junior resident on call at Gilbert's side.

"Any change?" she asked.

"I'm not sure," Allison Jeter, the junior resident, said. "But I believe his elbow flexion is starting to relax. See what you think."

Sarchi went to Gilbert, took hold of his right arm, and tried to straighten it at the elbow. She'd almost decided she saw no improvement when something happened she'd never forget.

Gilbert slowly turned his head toward his mother standing on the other side of the bed and made a croaking noise that sounded for all the world like "momma."

Sarchi was transfixed.

It was the first voluntary movement he'd ever made in her presence. And he could also apparently *see*. Whether he was never blind or had somehow regained his sight wasn't clear, but whatever was going on was miraculous.

Recognizing this milestone for what it was, tears began to run down his mother's cheeks. Equally overwhelmed with emotion, Sarchi's eyes also filled with tears. Evelyn bent down and began smothering Gilbert's face with kisses.

There was no way to know how far Gilbert was going to be able to travel the road back to health, and it was surely going to be a slow journey with many hours of physical therapy, but there was now reason for hope.

The nurse put her hand on Sarchi's shoulder. "Good work, Doctor. This is the best thing I've seen since I've been here."

Evelyn looked up from Gilbert, her face quivering. "Thank you. Thank you." She left Gilbert's side, ran to Sarchi, and hugged her. "I'll never forget you for this . . . never."

Feeling her pager vibrating, Sarchi gently pulled free from Evelyn's embrace and checked the number.

"I've got a patient in the ER," she said. "But I'll be back as soon as I can."

Not wanting to arrive at the ER teary eyed, Sarchi wiped at her eyes with the back of her hand. But as fast as she cleared the tears away, more came.

Waiting for the elevator, she finally got control of herself. But the feeling of elation remained. Never had she felt so much like a healer. She wanted to tell someone what had happened . . . anyone . . . a janitor . . . somebody. But it was after hours and there was no one in the elevator when it arrived and no one in the hall when she stepped from it.

At times like this the hospital reminded her of Woods Hole, where, during her undergraduate days, she'd spent six weeks taking a course at the Marine Biology Institute. Sometimes at night the fog would roll in so heavily you could walk blocks without seeing anyone. Then you'd open the door to the Captain Kidd, the most happening place in town, and there the world was. The ER, the hospital's Captain Kidd, was down the hall and around the corner, past the plastic sheeting marking the soon-to-be remodeled X-ray suite.

As she walked, she pictured once more that fantastic moment—Gilbert turning his head and actually speaking. "Momma" —she was sure that's what he'd said. This is what it means to be a doctor.

Suddenly she felt something around her neck . . . pulled tight . . . choking her.

"You arrogant, meddling bitch," a voice hissed behind her. "It's all *your* fault."

Sarchi was pulled backward into the construction area, which, except for the light from the hall, was dark.

"If it wasn't for you, George would still be alive."

George . . . Latham . . . Through her fear and the pressure building in her head, Sarchi realized this had to be the woman Veret was looking for. She tried to claw backward at the woman's face, but found nothing.

"And you just *had* to send that redhead to Virtual Joe to see who I was—*that* was your fault, too."

Though her own survival was at stake, Sarchi's brain howled in fury at this stark confession that this was Sharon's killer. With her head feeling as though it was going to burst, she pushed backward, driving the two of them across the room until they hit a wall of metal studs that buckled. Her assailant went to the floor, pulling Sarchi down on top of her.

"Just give up and die," the woman strangling her said.

With her brain now screaming for air, Sarchi reached back, got the fingers of both hands in the woman's hair and pulled hard.

"More," the woman said. "I love it."

Sarchi found an ear and twisted it. She then beat on the sides of the woman's head with both fists, but the ligature around her neck remained tight.

With only a few seconds of life left to her and a light show beginning behind her eyes, Sarchi's hands swept the darkness around her looking for an object she could use as a weapon. Her hand hit something, but it was merely a piece of pipe insulation. Then her fingers encountered a tool—a drill.

Barely conscious, she got hold of the drill and with the last bit of strength left in her, aimed the butt at her assailant's head, hoping she wouldn't hit herself. There was an impact, then she lost consciousness.

"That's Doctor Seminoux," one of the security guards investigating the noise in the construction area said. "I don't know who the other one is."

"Are they dead?" the other guard asked.

Sarchi woke to the beam of a flashlight in her face. With effort, she rose to a sitting position and looked behind her at the still-unconscious woman in purple scrubs who'd tried to strangle her. Lee-Ann had been described as blond, but this woman was a brunette. It took Sarchi a few seconds to figure out that she'd dyed her hair so she wouldn't be recognized.

Sarchi's head throbbed and her neck ached, but these were mere physical complaints that would pass. Of much greater significance was the phone call she would make to Claude Veret, telling him Sharon's killer had been caught.

Sachi would always carry emotional scars from her encounters with Latham, Jackie, and Lee-Ann, but the one comfort she could take into the future was that those three would never harm anyone again.

Now it was over.